KALOOKI NIGHTS

Howard Jacobson is the author of eight previous
novels and four works of non-fiction.

HOWARD JACOBSON

Kalooki Nights

VINTAGE BOOKS
London

Published by Vintage 2007

2 4 6 8 10 9 7 5 3 1

First published in Great Britain in 2006 by
Jonathan Cape

Vintage
Random House, 20 Vauxhall Bridge Road,
London SW1V 2SA

www.vintage-books.co.uk

Addresses for companies within The Random House Group Limited
can be found at: www.randomhouse.co.uk/offices.htm

The Random House Group Limited Reg. No. 954009

A CIP catalogue record for this book
is available from the British Library

ISBN 9780099501367

The Random House Group Limited makes every effort to
ensure that the papers used in its books are made from trees that
have been legally sourced from well-managed and credibly
certified forests. Our paper procurement policy can be found at:
www.randomhouse.co.uk/paper.htm

Printed in the UK by CPI Bookmarque, Croydon, CR0 4TD

To Ian MacKillop
1939 — 2004
Incomparable Teacher and Friend

I knew a fellow named Otto Kahn, who was a very rich man, and he gave a lot of money to the Metropolitan Opera House at one time. His close friend was Marshall P. Wilder, who was a hunchback. And they were walking down Fifth Avenue, and they came to a synagogue, and Kahn turned to Wilder and said, 'You know I used to be a Jew.' 'Really?' said Wilder. 'I used to be a hunchback.'

Groucho Marx

BOOK ONE

FIVE THOUSAND YEARS
OF BITTERNESS

ONE

Instead of the cross, the Albatross
About my neck was hung.

Coleridge, 'The Rime of the Ancient Mariner'

1

Once when no one was buying my cartoons I took a job ripping off the Tom of Finland books for an unscrupulous pirate publisher of gay eroticism. Deltoidal, no-necked, peach-bottomed sadists and cock-suckers wearing leather caps and curiously benign expressions, romping in a spunky never-never sodomitic kindergarten unimpeded by the needs or interdictions of wives and mothers. For a straight man who couldn't see what Tom of Finland had to offer, other than the clean lines of the illustrations and the absence, beyond twenty-four-hour on-tap buggery and fellatio, of any supererogatory fantasy or fuss, I reckon I made a reasonable fist of copying his creations. It was good for me too, I thought, inhabiting this alien demi-Eden for a while. It relieved some of the stress I was under. The stress of a failed marriage and a failing career – the usual – but also the stress of coming from an ethno-religious minority, or whatever you call us, whose genius doesn't extend to irresponsible recreation. Jews don't do Paradise Regained. Once you're out you're out with my people. The gates swing shut behind you, the cherubim flash their flaming swords, and that's that. This is what it means to be Old Testament. You're always conscious of having blown your chance of a good time. Now here I was enjoying a proxy frolic in the Garden again.

Where I messed up professionally was in the straining bulge all Tom of Finland's characters carried in their trousers. To begin with I failed to notice there was a bulge there at all. But even when the bulge was brought to my attention I couldn't copy it with conviction. I couldn't capture the anticipatory strain. Couldn't render the explosive tension between the glans penis and the denim. In the end I had to admit that this was because I had never worn denim or leather myself, and didn't understand the physics of the pressure from the inside. Jewish men wear loose, comfortable trousers with a double pleat. And maybe, in chilly weather, a cardigan on top. It is considered inappropriate by Jews to show strangers of either sex the outline of your glans penis.

No commandment against it that I know of. Just not what you do.

And for this, as an uncle of mine used to say, apropos anything Jewish, the Nazis tried to exterminate us.

My father's response, if he happened to be around, reminded me of someone swatting a fly. 'Since when did any Nazi try to exterminate *you*, Ike? You personally? Had I thought the Nazis were after you I'd have told them where to find you years ago.'

Upon which my uncle, who had lived with us for as long as I could remember, would turn white, accuse my father of being no better than Hitler himself, and flee to his room to hide.

Were they playing? Did they go on repeating this exchange because they thought it was amusing? Hard to decide when you're small whether people twice your size are joking or not. Sometimes everything they do looks like one big joke. But Hitler didn't sound a funny name. And 'exterminate', as I discovered from the little dictionary which my mother kept in her display cabinet, as though it were as precious as her china or my father's boxing cups, meant to destroy utterly, to put an end to (persons or animals), to drive out, to put to flight, to get rid of (species, races, populations, opinions). From which I inferred that no, my father and my uncle could not have been playing, but must have intended their jousting as a sort of magic, to ward off evil. To keep us from being driven out, got rid of, and the rest of it.

4

Thus did I grow up in Crumpsall Park in the 1950s, somewhere between the ghettos and the greenery of North Manchester, with 'extermination' in my vocabulary and the Nazis in my living room.

So when Manny Washinsky swapped me his copy of Lord Russell of Liverpool's *The Scourge of the Swastika: A Short History of Nazi War Crimes* for a bundle of comics, I was already softened up, though I couldn't have been much more than eleven at the time, to receive its contents. 'The murder by Germans of over five million European Jews,' Lord Russell of Liverpool wrote, 'constitutes the greatest crime in world history.' A conclusion which electrified me, not because it was news exactly, but because I had never before seen it written down. Over *five million*! So that was what being put an end to meant! The figures conferred a solemn destiny upon me. For it is not nothing to be one of the victims of the greatest crime in world history.

By any of the usual definitions of the word victim, of course, I wasn't one. I had been born safely, at a lucky time and in an unthreatening part of the world, to parents who loved and protected me. I was a child of peace and refuge. Manny too. But there was no refuge from the dead. For just as sinners pass on their accountability to generations not yet born, so do the sinned against. 'Remember me,' says Hamlet's father's ghost, and that's Hamlet fucked.

Manny wasn't the only boy in the street who knew *The Scourge of the Swastika*. Errol Tobias, a year or two older than us, was also a reader. Not that we were any sort of study group or book club. Because I felt ashamed of being Manny's friend when I was with Errol, and ashamed of being Errol's friend when I was with Manny, I was careful not to bring them together or otherwise to intimate our shared experience. Left to their own devices, neither existed for the other. Manny too devout, Errol too profane. They weren't simply chalk and cheese, they were the devil and the deep blue sea. Not a fanciful comparison: in Manny there were unfathomable depths, in Errol a diabolism that was frightening to be near. When he went into one of his lewd playground rages, Errol's eyes boiled in his head like volcanoes; you could smell his anger, like a serpent turning on a spit; a translucency upon his skin, as though God were trying to see through him. Yet it wasn't the devilish one of the two who ultimately did the devilish thing. Unfair, but there you are. It would seem that it isn't necessarily your nature that determines your fate. Incidentals such as spending too much time listening to your fathers' fathers' ghosts can do it just as well. But in that case all three of us should have grown up to be murderers, not just Manny Washinsky.

As for Jews not showing strangers the outline of their glans penis, Errol Tobias was either a changeling or the exception that proved the rule. A genitally besotted boy, he grew into a genitally besotted man. Manny and I were more in character. For which demureness I have not the slightest doubt that the Nazis – to borrow my uncle's favourite locution – would have tried to exterminate us. As a cartoonist I am given to travesty and overstatement, but this is not an example of either. There are serious causal connections to be traced between the Jew's relation to his body – modesty, purity, the dread solemnity of the circumcision covenant – and the Jew-baiting practised by the Germans. For reasons that will bear deep scrutiny, the world hates and fears a man who makes a palaver of his private parts. I think that's the issue: not the foreskin, the palaver. Whenever anti-Semitism is mobilised from an itch into a movement it takes flight into some ideal Sparta – a Finlandia of square-jawed analisers skylarking in the gymnasia or the baths, at ease with both their own and others' genitalia. And what is that but nostalgia for a time before the Jews imposed seriousness upon the body?

No going back into the Garden, we say. And no return to nature. Life – now that we have been expelled from Paradise –

life, as an activity of the mind and not the sexual organs, begins in earnest.

For which devotion to intellect and conscience they cannot forgive us.

That was that as far as Tom of Finland went, explain it how you like. Max of Muswell Hill in accommodating flannel pants looked a nice enough guy but he wasn't going to make a killing in the sex shops of Soho.

It wouldn't surprise me to learn I was the first and last Jew — the first and last *English* Jew, at any rate — to be employed in the homoerotic copycat business.

Jew, Jew, Jew. Why, why, why, as my father asked until the asking killed him, does everything always have to come back to Jew, Jew, Jew?

2

He was a boxer whose nose bled easily, an atheist who railed at God, and a communist who liked to buy his wife expensive shoes. In appearance he resembled Einstein without the hair. He had that globe-eyed, hangdog, otherwise preoccupied Jewish look. Einstein, presumably, is thinking $E = mc^2$ when he stares into the camera. My father was thinking up ways to make Jewishness less of a burden to the Jews. $J \div J = j$.

Had he seen me with my head buried in *The Scourge of the Swastika* he'd have confiscated it without pausing to find out whether it was mine or someone else's. Let the dead bury the dead, was his position. The way to show them the reverence they were owed was to live the life that they had not.

'When I die,' he said, unaware how soon that was going to be, 'I expect you to embrace life with both hands. Then I'll know I've perished in a good cause.'

'When you're dead you won't know anything,' I cheeked him.

'Exactly. And neither do the dead of Belsen.'

This wasn't callousness. Quite the opposite. It was our deliverance he sought – from morbid superstition, from the hellish malarial swamp shtetls of Eastern Europe which some of us still mentally inhabited, and from the death-in-life grip those slaughtered five or more million had on our imaginations.

He didn't live to see me sell my first cartoon, which was probably a blessing. It showed Gamal Abdel Nasser and other Arab leaders looking out over an annihilated Israel on the eve of what would become known as the Six Day War. 'Some of our best friends were Jewish,' they are saying.

The *Manchester Guardian* wouldn't take it but the *Crumpsall Jewish Herald* did, publishing it alongside a leader article warning of another Jewish Holocaust.

Jew, Jew, Jew.

Like many atheists and communists, my father never quite got the joking thing. He couldn't understand why, if I was joking, I didn't look more cheerful. And if I couldn't look more cheerful, what I found to joke about.

It's a mistake commonly made with cartoonists. People confuse the matter with the man. Since you draw the preposterous it is assumed that you *are* the preposterous. Everyone thinks you must be joking all the time, and in the end, if you are not careful, you come to believe you must be joking all the time yourself.

Jew, Jew, Jew. Joke, joke, joke. Why, why, why?

You can have too many of all three, as Chloë, my first flaxen *Übermadchen* Gentile wife, told me in explanation of her wanting a divorce.

'Why's that?' I asked her.

'There you go again,' she said.

She thought I was trying to get under her skin deliberately. In fact it was just bad luck. With Chloë every word I said came out differently from how I meant it. She rattled me. Made me speak at the wrong time, and in the wrong tone of voice. I felt that she was interrogating me and in fear of her interrogation I blurted out whatever I thought she wanted me to say, which was always the opposite to what she wanted me to say, that's if she wanted me to say anything.

'Do I frighten you?' she asked me once.

'Of course you frighten me,' I told her. 'That very question frightens me.'

'And why is that, do you think?' But before I could answer she held her hand up in front of my mouth. 'Don't,' she said. 'I know what's coming. Because you're Jewish. And you can't ask a Jew a question without him thinking you're Gestapo.'

Since I wasn't permitted to speak, I turned my face into a question mark. So *wasn't* she Gestapo?

Hence her wanting a divorce.

We'd just been to a St Cecilia's Day performance of Bach's *St Matthew Passion* in St Paul's Cathedral – Chloë, to spite me, cramming in as many saints as she could muster. If she could have sat me next to someone with St Vitus's Dance – say St Theresa – she would have.

'I'd call that the last straw,' she said as we were coming out.

'What are you telling me, Chloë, that our marriage is dashed on the rocks of Christ's immolation?'

'There you have it,' she said, still holding my arm, which I thought was odd given the finality of the conversation. But then again, the steps were icy. 'You call it an immolation, everyone else calls it the Passion.'

'That's just me trying to keep it anthropological,' I said.

'Trying to keep it at arm's length, you mean. What are you afraid of, Max? Salvation?'

I turned to face her. 'I don't think what we've seen offers much salvation for the Jews, Chloë.'

'Oh, Jews, Jews, Jews!'

'Well, they do figure in the story.'

'They figure in *your* story!'

'I'm afraid my story *is* this story, Chloë. Would that it were otherwise.'

'You see! We can't even go to a concert without your bleeding heart coming with us.'

'Then you should be more careful which concert you choose for us to go to.'

'Max, there isn't one that's safe. They all come back to the Nazis in the end.'

'Have I said anything about the Nazis?'

'You don't need to say anything. I know you. You've thought of nothing else all evening.'

Not quite true – I loved and had thought about the music – but near enough. I had wept – as I always weep – at the desolation of Christ's cry to a God who wasn't answering. *Eli, Eli, lama sabachthani?* My God, my God, why hast thou forsaken me? But I'd also joked sotto voce (that's to say, so that only Chloë could hear) – as I always joke sotto voce at this moment in this greatest of all liturgical works – that it was something else having the question put in German. *Mein Gott, mein Gott, warum hast du mich verlassen?*! A bit rich, a plummy German baritone 'why', when the God who last forsook the Jews did so, as one might put it – no, as one is duty bound to put it – under German auspices.

Warum? You are not, *mein kleines Brüderlein*, the ones to ask that question. Just you go about the business of building Holocaust memorials and making reparation to your victims and leave the whys to us.

Jew, Jew, Jew. Joke, joke, joke. *Warum, warum, warum?*

For which Chloë, weary with all three, was leaving me.

But it behoves a man with a story of perplexities to tell to put his whys on the table early.

Such as:

Why *did* God, having once chosen us, forsake us?

Why did my friend Emanuel Washinsky – from whose lips I

first heard God accused of dereliction (in our house we accused God of nothing except not existing) – forsake his family and beliefs and commit the most unspeakable of crimes against them?

Why, if I call Emanuel Washinsky my friend, did I keep my friendship with him separate from all my other friendships – a thing religiously apart – and why did I wash my hands of him when it was reasonable to surmise that he needed friendship most?

Why did I marry Chloë?

Why, after being divorced so comprehensively by Chloë – divorced from my own reason, I sometimes felt – did I marry Zoë? And why, after being left by Zoë, did I marry . . . but I must not give the wrong impression. This is more a tale of separation than of marriage.

Why – speaking of disloyalties, forsakings and acts that seemingly cannot be explained – did I forsake *myself* to draw cartoons, when I am averse by nature to caricature, ribaldry and violence?

Why do I wake each day as though I am in mourning?

Who or what am I in mourning for?

3

Why Elohim forsook us, or why Manny Washinsky raised his hand against those he was meant to honour, or why I married who I married, are questions which cannot be answered in a short space of time. But I can explain – which is at least a start – why I took up crayons. Because I liked the oily smell of them. Because I liked it that they streamed colours. Because I enjoyed watching a picture emerge that I hadn't intended to make. Because I discovered I could do a likeness. Because I felt there was some emotion locked away inside me that I couldn't get at until I drew it on a piece of paper. And because I wanted people to admire and adore me. Show that you can draw when you're four or five years old and everyone is awestruck. It's the same with words, only words don't win you the affection pictures do. They lack the charm.

There is something, it would seem, uncanny about sentences issuing fully formed from a cherub's mouth, as though Beelzebub must be in there somewhere, hammering phrases out on his infernal anvil. Whereas a wavy purple path leading to a little orange house with plumes of smoke spiralling from its tipsy chimney – that's the work of God, our protector, ever with us, Elohim who modelled man out of clay and put him in a garden.

But those who were enchanted by my precocious pictorial genius should have looked harder at the blackness of that plume of smoke and wondered what was burning.

I drew so the world might love me, and subsequently drew ironically, against myself, because I couldn't love the world.

The plainer explanation for why I drew at all – an explanation favoured by my mother, who blamed herself, and who thought I might have had a happier, less fractious life had I gone into commerce or the law (and I agree with her) – is that I was born into a noisy house and couldn't get a word in edgeways. Both my parents had loud voices, earnests of good lungs and therefore, you would have thought, long lives; my mother's a lovely honeyed contralto, wasted, I used to think, marvelling how beautiful my older sister Shani looked in whatever she was wearing, prior to marvelling how much more beautiful she would look if she were wearing something different; and wasted even more on shouting out 'Kalooki!' with her friends every other weekday evening. Kalooki, for those who don't know it, is a version of rummy much favoured by Jews – Jews, Jews, Jews – on account (though not all Jews would agree) of its innate argumentativeness. My mother's trumpeting 'Kalooki!' at the moment of laying out her cards, for example, was not incontestably the right thing to do. But that, as I gathered, was the joy of it: not just the game but the bickering over how and in what spirit it should be played. Some kalooki evenings were great social successes though not a hand was dealt. 'A fast game's a good game,' someone would say, and agreeing how fast was fast would take up the rest of the night.

My father stayed out of this, employing his bass-baritone in a higher cause (though not always in another room), preaching the religion of non-religion, a species of Judaism emptied of everything except its disputatiousness and liberality – a sort of secular universalism I suppose you'd have to call it, comprising socialism, syndicalism, Bundism, trade unionism, international brotherhoodism, atheism, not to mention pugilism – which he imagined would one day be the saving of the Jews. And didn't just imagine it either, but discussed it vociferously and voluminously with the communists and syndicalists and atheists and pugilists who took advantage of his open-door policy, turning up whenever they felt like it, as much to watch my mother leap from her seat and shout 'Kalooki!', I always fancied, as to change the world and the Jew's place in it. Add to their chorus the racket my sister made, slamming doors, crying over her hair and throwing shoes around her bedroom – never the right ones, no matter how many pairs they bought for her, never the right ones to go with the clothes she wanted to wear, which were never the right ones either – and you will have some understanding of the clanking foundry in which my reticence was forged.

But there was more noise still in my young life in the form of an uncle, and in the continuous voicing of my father's objections to that uncle – that's if he really was an uncle – Tsedraiter Ike. The same uncle who was always saying that for this the Nazis wanted to exterminate us, though it was my father's contention that it was actually for *him*, Tsedraiter Ike, that the Nazis wanted to exterminate us.

We had five Uncle Ikes in our family, taking family to include every Jew who shared our name, married into our name, or offered to be friendly, ours being a sort of Battersea Dogs' Home for stray Jews. Big Ike, Little Ike, Liverpool Ike, Dodgy Ike and Tsedraiter Ike – called Tsedraiter Ike because he was the tsedraitest, that's to say the most imbecile, of the five. Also called Tsedraiter mischievously, I fancied, because he could not himself,

13

with a single tooth, negotiate the word. Tsedraiter: the *Tse* to be pronounced sibilantly, with a sort of lisping hiss: *Tsss, Tsss*; the vowel sound somewhere between a *sir* and a *sid*: Tsssirdraiter/Tsssidraiter; the second and third syllables to rhyme with hater.

Why Tsedraiter Ike lived with us, I never knew. Precisely what relation to us he bore, I never knew either and suspect I wasn't meant to know. As with other family embarrassments, you just accepted and asked no questions. I think I assumed he was my mother's brother because it was she who always defended him from my father's scorn. In appearance, though, they could not have been more unalike. My mother – born Leonora Axelroth – as euphonious as her name, tall and tapering, legs and ankles if anything too thin, like an Ethiopian's, her hair almost bronze in colour, her skin, the minute it was exposed to sun, the same. A burnish on her, which made her look expensive, of the highest quality. Whereas Tsedraiter Ike (who received letters addressed to Isaac Finster, not Axelroth) was flabby, one-toothed, wet about the mouth, discoloured, as though he'd been dipped in ink at birth. I don't think I ever knew what he did for a living, but it couldn't have been much because he was almost never out of the house, at least in my early years, and, from what I gathered from the arguments about him, made no contribution whatsoever to his keep. 'Keep?' I recall my mother saying in his defence. 'He isn't an animal, he doesn't have to be *kept*. But if we're talking keeping, at least he keeps himself smart' – 'smart' being a big accolade with my mother, a word she used almost as often as 'Kalooki!' To which my father – who was never smart – replied always with the same words: 'Correction: at least *I* keep him smart.'

In fact Tsedraiter Ike wasn't smart either, merely fallen-formal in the manner of some minor shtetl functionary, one of those embittered, jeering, half-demented clerks you read about in nineteenth-century Russian novels, halfway to being rabbinical, in Tsedraiter Ike's case, in a black, far too shiny gaberdine suit and a sort of morning, or do I mean mourning, tie. It's my sense that wealthy Russian and Polish families once retained such people talismanically, partly as jesters, partly to assuage their consciences, as though they could thereby pay their dues to learning or religion or the twisted life of the mind. My father tolerated Tsedraiter Ike, though he could ill-afford him, in a spirit that was the very obverse of this. 'Look what we have left behind us,' that's what he was saying. 'Behold our ignominious past. Learn from this human wreckage what we dare never allow ourselves to sink into again.' In response to which unspoken motive, Tsedraiter Ike hummed loudly around the house, making sounds that were more a parody of Hebrew prayer, as far as I could tell, than prayer itself, rocking, rustling, moaning, wailing, whistling, choking, humming – humming Hebraically, yes, it's possible – and, whenever he caught my eye, winking at me and interrupting his devotions or whatever they were to chuck me affectionately under the chin and call me, in reference to heaven knows what, his 'old palomino'. Palomino being, by my calculation, one of the hardest words a person with only one tooth in his head could ever try to pronounce. Which could be why he never left off trying to pronounce it.

There was a song he sang, too, my Uncle Ike, whenever he felt himself to be under pressure from my father, made to feel unwelcome, or otherwise humiliated. 'It's only me from over the sea, said Barnacle Bill the sailor.' An apology for his existence which was clearly an expression of the sense of worthlessness my father instilled in him, though why the nautical reference I had no idea. But it all added to the domestic cacophony, whatever it meant.

So yes, had there been anything I badly needed to get off my chest in those early years I might well have taken the option of sketching it on paper.

Whatever the reasons, I was a mournful, withdrawn, apparently biblical-looking baby – Mendel, Tsedraiter Ike called me when my father wasn't listening, Mendel which he tried to persuade me was biblical Hebrew for Max, and which he went on using secretly in preference to 'my old palomino' when the Jewishry in which he sought to enmesh me darkened – and I remained biblical and withdrawn throughout the chrysalidal stage after that, until one afternoon, sitting on my mother's lap in a train bringing us back from an afternoon on a cold New Brighton beach with Liverpool Ike's family, my nasal cousins Lou and Joshua twice removed, I said Jew Jew, Jew Jew, Jew Jew . . .

'Sounds to me that he was imitating the train,' my father guessed when my mother excitedly told everybody about it later. 'Am I right, Maxie? Was that the sound the engine made? Choo choo, choo choo?'

'Jew Jew,' I said, clamping my teeth around the Js. 'Jew Jew, Jew Jew . . .'

'What about the whistle, then? 'Whoo whoo! Whoo whoo!'

I shook my head. 'Jew Jew,' I said. 'Jew Jew, Jew Jew.'

He gave me a cold stare. As though I'd informed him I wanted to be a rabbi when I grew up. Or that it was my ambition to return to the Russia we never talked about. Novoropissik, as he called it, a Nowhere place of piss and sick. Near where the Danube spilled its shit into the Black Sea. Spiritual if not actual home of Tsedraiter Ike.

'Your doing,' he told my mother.

'My doing?'

'Kalooki this, kalooki that. Kalooki's the only word the kid ever hears.'

'What's kalooki got to do with anything?'

'How do you expect him to grow up in a world free of all that shtetl rubbish if you won't stop reminding him of it? Kalooki, kalooki, night and day kalooki! We live in Crumpsall in the twentieth century, not Kalooki in the Middle Ages.'

'Jack, kalooki isn't the name of a shtetl.'

'Isn't it? Well, that's what you say.' Whereupon he stormed out of the house.

Years later I looked up Kalooki in an atlas, to see whether there was such a place within spitting or sicking distance of Novoropissik. I couldn't find one. But there was a Kalocsa in Hungary, and a Kaluga one hundred miles to the south-west of Moscow on the left bank of the Oka, and a Kalush in the Ukraine where Jews had lived and been submitted to the usual indignities, so maybe he was confusing kalooki collectively with those – the marshlands of our hellish past.

It's possible I imagined it, but after the Jew Jew, Jew Jew incident I thought my father shrank from me a little, as a man will shrink in fear and loathing from the ghost of someone he thought he'd murdered and disposed of long ago. And it's not impossible that his socialist friends shrank from me as well, the little cancer in the body of their hope for change.

They needn't have worried. I have not become a rabbi. Nor have I been back to Novoropissik. Or gone the way of Tsedraiter Ike. Unless hearing Jew Jew, Jew Jew, Jew Jew, whenever a train goes through a tunnel, amounts to the same as any or all of those.

To that hypersensitivity, at least, I plead guilty. I am one for whom a train can never again be just a train. First I have to enquire whom the train, please, is carrying. Then who commissioned it. Then where its ultimate destination is.

Jew Jew, Jew Jew . . .

The Auschwitz Express.

I could not of course have known anything about Auschwitz at the time I sat like a precocious Hebrew prophet on my mother's lap and blew the horror whistle. But footfalls echo in the memory, and who's to say what footfalls, past or future, a child's memory contains?

For what it's worth, I believe we would be able to hear Adam's tread if we knew which part of our memories to access. And Abraham coming out of his tent to receive the Covenant. And Moses the lawgiver, in all his years, climbing to the top of Pisgah. And the Jews of Belsen and Buchenwald crying out to be remembered.

Jew Jew, Jew Jew.

What my father tried to do was ditch the J-word as a denomination of suffering altogether. Not to forsake all those who'd travelled on that train, but to reinvent the future for them. A kind of muscular Zionism of the mind, without the necessity of actually establishing a Zionist state and going, as he put it, 'berserk in someone else's country'. Without, indeed, the necessity of going anywhere at all. Or at least, now that he was out of the puke of Novoropissik and safe in the North of England, not going anywhere *else*. But you never know what's waiting to spite you in your genes. My father wanted a new start, and had me.

It could have been worse. He could have had Manny Washinsky.

He could have had Manny Washinsky and been murdered in his bed.

Only had my father been his father, who knows? Manny might never have turned into a murderer at all.

TWO

Draw, you bastard!

R. Crumb, *The R. Crumb Handbook*

1

When we weren't refusing to divulge our names or religion to SS men, or choking to death on Zyklon B, Manny and I met in the Second World War air-raid shelter which had become our play space and discussed God.

'You don't ask Elohim to explain Himself,' Manny, not yet a teenager, not really ever a teenager, told me, fingering the squiggly ear-locks which made his new-moon face appear as though someone had scribbled on it.

I'm cartooning him. He didn't have ear-locks to finger. Sideburns turned to fluff were what he had, hardly even sideburns, little curls of unsportive fuzz run wild, which, in the event of trouble – the trouble we all half feared was only round the corner, the Crumpsall Park Pogrom which would one day come out of a clear blue sky – he would be able to conceal quickly under his school cap. These were the golden days of Jewish secularity, before the Orthodox found the effrontery to blaze their fanatic retrogression on their faces. What there was of medieval Jewishry was confined to a couple of streets of teeming five-storey houses in Lower Broughton on the Manchester/Salford borders where, for a while, Sir Oswald Mosley ran a provocative office, and through which my father occasionally walked me, holding me firmly by the hand, so that I should see, but not be inveigled into, what the long march to emancipation was emancipating us from. Frummers was how we referred to these out-of-time Talmudic literalisers among ourselves, from frum meaning devout. Not a pejorative exactly, but not approving either. I could never decide whether my father's interpolations – from frummers to frummies, and then from frummies to frumkies – were designed to diminutise them or diminutise their offence. But frumkies was the term we settled on finally. The Washinskys, to be fair to them, were not like those we saw in Lower Broughton. They did not wear long black coats or high black hats which seemed to float on a current of spirituality above their heads. They were not in the same hurry when they were out of doors, as though late for an appointment with the Almighty. And their house was not a gypsy caravan of trumperies and trinkets to protect it from the evil eye. No, the Washinskys were not living in the Middle Ages, but to us they were the halfway house on the journey back.

And they were still frumkies.

'I'm not asking Elohim,' I'd say, usually while gouging out the mortar between the bricks of our air-raid shelter – a peculiarly wanton impulse, to pull apart what sheltered us – 'I'm asking *you*.'

To tell the truth, I wasn't asking Manny anything. I was needling him. As though to pay him back for my own shortcomings as a friend, for making me ashamed to acknowledge him in such polite company as Errol Tobias's, I pestered him to distraction. Why this, Manny? Why that? When Manny or either of his parents went through their front door they put a finger to their lips and then to the mezuzah on the door frame. I knew about mezuzahs; we had one at our front door, put there by the Jewish family who had lived in the house before us, but now painted over and ignored. I knew what a mezuzah contained: words, words from the Torah, including the Shema, the holiest words of all – 'Shema Yisrael, Hear, O Israel, the Lord is one . . .' But precisely because the Lord *was* one we did not tolerate idols. In which case why did we kiss words? A word too could be an idol, couldn't it?

Why, Manny? Why the food hysteria? Why all the salting that went on in his house, salting the flavour out of everything? Why,

20

when they bought kosher meat from a kosher butcher did they have to kosher it again when they got it home? Had the Christian street unkoshered it? And why the obsessive keeping this from that? So a crumb of cheese the size of mouse bait fell on to a thrice salted, petrified slice of chicken breast from which the flavour had already been extracted to make soup, was that so terrible? Did Elohim have nothing else to do, was he so small-minded that he would notice and punish a transgression as negligible as that? And why the obsession with Saturday? How can a day be holy?

'It's a commandment,' Manny told me. 'Remember the Sabbath day to—'

'I know all that. But next to "Thou shalt not kill", remembering the Sabbath day is a bit unimportant, isn't it? We don't say "Remember not to kill". Because forgetting wouldn't be any excuse. "Remember the Sabbath day" is more like a nudge than a commandment.'

'The Ten Commandments are all equally important,' he replied. 'The rabbis say that if you break one you might as well break them all.'

I had reason to recall that in later years. But at the time all I wanted to do was break *him*. All right, all right, so his family chose to do as they were told and remember the Sabbath day, but why did that stop them from making their own fire on it? Why, though they had no money, did they employ a Gentile — a Shabbes-goy, or as we called her in our neck of the woods, a fire-yekelte — to make it for them? Why didn't they light it themselves the day before and leave it smouldering behind a fire guard? Or, if that was out of the question, if Elohim thundered 'No!' to prior preparation and a further 'No!' to a surreptitious blow into the embers on Shabbes itself, why didn't they just go without a fire for one day out of seven altogether? They could always come and warm themselves in front of ours if it was really cold, unless ours was unacceptable having been lit on the Sabbath by Jews who didn't cover their heads, didn't keep a kosher house and didn't otherwise give a shit.

Not true that. We did give a shit about treating Gentiles as skivvies. Particularly we gave a shit – or at least my father did – about calling someone a fire-yekelte, a yekelte being a coarse non-Jewish woman of the lower orders, in other words a person with whom we, having been worse than beasts of burden in Novoropissik, should have felt some affiliation. That the fire-yekelte in question didn't mind making the fires, and considered herself fairly remunerated for it – just as Elvis Presley was said to have performed a similar service for Rabbi Fruchter and his wife in Alabama Avenue, Memphis, refusing to take a penny in recompense, just so long as no spark from the fire landed on his blue suede shoes – was neither here nor there. What did it do to *us* to demean in the name of our religion – that was the issue. 'Social relations come first, remember that,' my father used to lecture me. 'Man and man will always be a more sacred connection than man and God.' So what kind of God, Manny, would hand us out a code of conduct which of necessity entailed condescension to people of another faith, neighbours who had carved crucifixes on the bricks of this very shelter when the bombs were falling, even as our parents, who shared their terror, were carving Stars of David? A God of Love, a God of Contempt, or a God who didn't give a shit?

He had a way of closing down his face – Manny, I mean, not God – as though he could make himself deaf by sheer force of will. He ought to have repudiated the condescension charge with a flick of his fingers. 'What's demeaning to either party in a favour asked for and delivered? Show me the injured Gentile. Did Elvis mind? No. The King was only too pleased to be of service. All you have to show on your side of the argument is yourself – a Jew injured by all things Jewish. It's not we who are guilty of fanaticism, it's you, the fanatics of disavowal and self-revulsion.'

But that, for Manny (leaving aside what could reasonably be expected of a twelve-year-old boy), would have been to enter the lists on behalf of a God who needed no defending. Not for him to interrogate, or to hear another interrogate, the laws of Elohim. He was not called Emanuel – meaning 'God is our protector, God is ever with us' – for nothing. Emanuel Eli Washinsky, Eli also meaning God, as in *Eli, Eli, lama sabachthani?* So I should have known something was wrong when, three or four years later he suddenly began to worry at that very question. *Eli, Eli, lama sabachthani?* Where were you, Elohim, in our hour of calamity?

An unmistakable cry for help, that, wouldn't you say, from someone with two Gods in his name?

But a cartoonist isn't there to help. Not in the conventional sense, at any rate. A cartoonist is there to make the complacent quake and the uncomfortable more uncomfortable still. So to Manny, who had been the one and was now the other, I said, 'You don't ask Elohim to explain Himself.' And was mightily pleased with the echo. I felt it was a blow struck for my poor father whose memory I feared that I traduced whenever I talked God with Manny.

It also pleased me, in some disreputably aesthetic way, to see my friend's certainties under pressure. The refuser of all questions returned to questioning. It was shapely.

But then of the two of us, I was the artist.

And I was forever looking for an excuse not to be his friend.

2

'Why do you have to look so Jewish all the time?'

Zoë talking. Zoë, catching me with my people's woes on my shoulders. Zoë, my flaxen *Übermadchen* Gentile second wife in our itchy seventh year of marriage.

Zoë, Chloë, Björk, Märike, Alÿs, and Kätchen, little Kate . . . what does it say about me that the only people with whom I am able to enjoy intimacy must have diaereses or umlauts in their names?

That I'm a Shmoë – that's what Zoë said it says.

Good job I never met Der Führer at an impressionable age.

With Zoë I wasn't ever unimpressionable. I bore the impress, visibly, of her harrying. And because I lowered my head and shouldered it, there was no inducement for her to stop. Grow a moustache, shave your moustache; wear a tie, don't wear a tie; try being sweeter to people, try having the courage of your own belligerence; come live with me in the country, why can't we have a flat in town; get a mistress, how dare you even look at another woman; fuck me hard, fuck me gently, and finally don't fuck me afuckingtall.

But it was about Jews that she harried me the most. She had been badly treated in her life by Jews. Only the once, not counting her treatment by me, but once can be enough. She had grown up next to a family of them on one of those high-blown scraps of wood and coppice you find between cemeteries and golf clubs in North London, taking 'growing up' to mean from the age of nine or thereabouts, that crucial hormonal period when, as Zoë herself fancifully explained it, she was poised to 'change from a plant into a person', a period not to be confused with that she spent in my company, during which she changed, again in her own words, 'back into a plant'. The horticulture was more than a figure of speech. Jews interfered with the natural growing process, were not themselves natural – that was what she intended by it. When Zoë was depressed she sat under a tree. When we fought she gardened. In soil she found the antithesis to me. And presumably, also, to the Krystals, the family who had stunted her. I knew the drama of their treachery by heart, she told it me so often. They came and she adored them, in her innocence drawing no distinction between the love she bore the senior Krystals, Leslie and Leila, and the love she bore the two boys, Selwyn and Seymour. Important I understood that: she loved them *all*, and loved them without design – played with them, ate with them, learned with them, progressed from late infancy to adolescence with them, then out of an unclouded powder-blue sky received her marching orders from them. When Zoë turned fifteen – 'the very next day, she couldn't even wait a week' – Leila Krystal took her to one side and told her that with her looks and figure she'd make a fine living as a whore in the cafés of Berlin. Wanted her out of the way, you see. Wanted her far from where she could light any fires (some fire-yekeltes we want, some we don't) in the hearts of either Selwyn or Seymour or both. At fifteen – so Zoë sobbed to me in my bed – she overnight became an anathema. 'They looked at me as though they'd never seen me before. The minute I became a woman, in their eyes I became filth. A prostitute. Nothing else. That's why,' she explained, 'I am in love with you.'

'Because you have reason to hate Jews?'

'Because they deprived me of my right to love Jews.'

It seemed a fair enough deal to me. Thank you, Leila Krystal. I'd get Zoë and in return be the Jew whom Zoë could love.

But it seemed I'd overdone it. Now Zoë was wondering why I had to look quite so Jewish quite so much of the time.

'Because I *am* fucking Jewish,' I reminded her.

'All the time?'

'Every fucking minute.'

'Stop swearing,' she said.

'I'll stop fucking swearing when you stop asking me why I look so fucking Jewish.'

'Why is everything a negotiation with you? Why can't you stop swearing *and* stop looking Jewish?'

'What do you want me to do, have a fucking nose job?'

She thought about it. Showed me her impertinently undemonstrative Gentile profile, every feature segregated from the other. My features, whatever else you thought about them, were on good terms, enjoyed a warm confabulation, each with each. Zoë's face was a species of apartheid.

'Good idea,' she said at last. 'Have it off.'

'You used to like my nose.'

'I used to like you.'

'Then why do you want me to stop at the nose? Why don't I have everything off?'

She pushed her mouth at me approvingly, one lip at a time, making little stars of fucking Bethlehem (nothing I could or can do about the swearing when proximate to Zoë) dance in her frosty fucking eyes. Always Christmas, always the birth of her saviour when she looked at me. Never a minute when a theological squabble two thousand years old was not present between us. Just as my mother and Tsedraiter Ike – though separately and of course unbeknown to my father while he was living – had predicted. 'She'll call you dirty Jew,' Tsedraiter Ike had warned me, whistling the prognostication around his single tooth. 'She'll accuse you of killing Christ,' my mother said. 'They always do in the end.' They didn't get that last part right. Zoë never did accuse me of killing Christ. Only of behaving as though I *were* Christ, which is a subtly different charge. But 'dirty Jew', yes, or at least 'Jew' with the dirty – meaning heated, meaning tumultuous, meaning unrefreshed and unrefreshable – implied. And now she wanted me to have my nose cropped.

Why did I so far entertain the idea as to get in touch with a plastic surgeon – who, incidentally, wouldn't touch my nose, but tried to make me a Christian by the theological route, pushing smudgy pamphlets onto me about Christ's mission to the Jews? Why didn't I gather myself to my full height, push out my profile, and leave the marriage?

The sex partly. One-time fuck me fuck me women who lie there straight as toy soldiers when their ardour cools, eyes squeezed, mouths puckered like dried figs, wondering How long O Lord, How long, exercise a fatal fascination on men of my sort. You go on labouring in the hope that one day, like a princess in a fairy story, they will become reanimated in your arms. In the fairy stories which Jewish men tell themselves, the princesses are always Gentile. So that's your task when your mother releases you into the world: to warm back into life the chilly universe of shiksehs.

Beyond that, I was sorry for her. Partly because of the Krystals who had treated her so contemptuously. But also because I'd been brought up to be sorry for any woman (this is, of course, the shadow-image of the previous fairy story) who was married to me: a Jew with the stinking waters of Novoropissik in his veins. And this regardless of whether she accused me of killing or appropriating Christ.

The other reason I didn't walk out on her when she suggested plastic surgery was that the idea answered to some extremity of exasperation in myself. You can get sick of looking like a Jew. And you can get sick of being looked at like a Jew as well. It would be interesting to see how it felt not to be forever earmarked for something or other. They regard you oddly, the Gentiles, whether they mean you harm or not. You give rise to some expectancy in them. As though, for good or ill, you've got the answer about your person to a question they can't quite find. It would be nice not to be the cause of that any longer. And – because whatever the question, you don't ever have the answer – nice not to be regarded as a disappointment. What would it be like, I wondered, not to feel I'd raised a curiosity I couldn't satisfy? Maybe I'd wake up happy instead of fucked off. Maybe I'd find a wider market for my cartoons. Maybe I'd get on better with my lozenge-stiff Hitlerian wife. With a smaller nose they say you give better cunnilingus. In fact Jews give the best cunnilingus in the world precisely because they have the nasal cartilage to give it with; though I grant you that in that case what they're giving isn't strictly cunnilingus. So maybe, pedantry aside, I'd give worse cunnilingus. That too was a consideration. Cut off my nose to spite the bitch.

3

The truth is, not everybody needs a white supremacist superwoman, or a missionary plastic surgeon, come to that, to do the prompting. You can wish away being Jewish, looking Jewish, thinking Jewish, talking Jewish, all on your ownio, to borrow one of Zoë's mother's, no, Chloë's mother's, cute locutions.

(As in 'Well, *there*, I have to say, you're on your ownio, Sonny Jim' – whenever she disagreed with something someone said to her. Which was most of the time. *All* of the time, if the someone happened to be me.)

But we each bail out according to our characters and circumstances. Some just let it discreetly lapse for professional reasons, claiming never to have noticed it was there much anyway. Some drop the subject after a long engagement with it, and think of themselves as enjoying a well-earned retirement. Others can't be goyim soon enough. In the case of Manny Washinsky, it was a matter of needing to keep his head down. The first thing he did when they let him back out into the world was change his name to Stroganoff. Hardly going to get him a job in the Vatican golf club, but then he wasn't so much not wanting to be Jewish any more, as not wanting to be the Jew he'd been. I could relate to that, as Chloë's mother also said (Chloë's mother who could relate to nothing). He had suffered great notoriety in Manchester in the early 1970s. Whatever the anti-Semites tell you, Jewish murderers are few and far between. At least they were in Crumpsall Park. And even by the standards of your average Jewish murderer, were such a personage imaginable, Emanuel Eli Washinsky – Talmud scholar and yeshiva boy – was exceptional. He'd been locked away a long time, but there were still people around, like me, who could remember him and what an unnatural thing he'd done.

I'd lost contact with Manny by the time he was incarcerated, let alone released, and probably wouldn't have seen him again or even learned that he'd come out and changed his name to Stroganoff, had not a pink-eyed, pug-nosed writer of no distinction or imagination – one Christopher Christmas, for Christ's sake – interested a small production company in a possible drama, something for television, something for twopence, based on

Manny's life, the only Jewish double homicide in the history of Crumpsall Park.

In the course of his vulturous researches into someone else he thought he could interest a producer in making a film about for twopence – based on real life, that was the line he threw out: these things actually *happened*! – Christmas had come across Manny Washinsky, and in the course of his researches into Manny, he had come across me. Grist to his mill, whatever he unearthed. A shilling here, a shilling there. It no doubt helped that my name was rustily familiar. Maxie Glickman, isn't he—?

I say no more than *helped*. They weren't offering gold dust, they were quick to make that clear. And Christmas himself was already on another project. Grub, grub. But there was a little something in it for me if indeed I was the same Maxie Glickman who'd been Manny Washinsky's friend, and if I was prepared to meet up with him again and get him to talk.

'Get him to talk about what exactly?' I asked over lunch in a rabbit-hutch restaurant in Soho, somewhere you could only get to via Berwick Street market, halfway down a passage which even a dog wouldn't piss in, elbowed between a tattooist's and a novelty shop for perverts.

My hosts were Lipsync Productions UK, otherwise the sisters Francine and Marina Bryson-Smith. Not my world, film and television. The moving picture left me cold, whatever its size. Too naturalistic. Never funny or despairing enough. Never both at the same time, anyway, which is how I like it. But for all my indifference to the medium I always seemed to know who was powering it. 'Don't watch, then,' is what they tell you when you complain of television. But it's not the watching that's the problem – it's the being made aware of those of whom, all things considered, you would rather not have heard. Francine and Marina Bryson-Smith, for example. Somehow or other, though I did no light reading, I knew of them as media socialites and, for all that I couldn't have told you the name of anything they'd made, had even heard of Lipsync Productions. A witty and rather sexy name for a production company, I thought, despite myself. Beyond the technical reference, I heard something lippy in it – an ironic, syncopated allusion, perhaps, to Francine Bryson-Smith's one-time reputation (vehemently denied) as a society lipstick lesbian, and maybe a pun on sink, as in Kitchensync – an assertion, however you read it, of the glamorously contrary. Hence, I assumed, the location of the hellhole restaurant.

That I would therefore be expected to begin our meeting on a sexual note I never doubted. 'Don't you think it's funny,' I'd remarked, even as we were shaking hands, 'that all you can ever buy in "adult" shops are toys?'

They didn't, as it happened. In retrospect I see I could have put it better, or at least not made it sound as though buying toys in adult shops was all I ever did. But they smiled at me politely enough, or rather Marina smiled. What Francine did was glimmer. She was what I remember my father calling a fascin-ator. 'It's just short-sightedness,' my mother used to tell him, reducing her own vision to show him. In Francine Bryson-Smith's case, however, it didn't look like an impairment; it looked more like wariness posing as intense curiosity. *Who are you, Maxie Glickman?* she seemed to be asking me. *Who is the real Maxie Glickman? What, if I am not careful, is he going to do to me?* And when a beautiful woman in the flower of her middle age asks you those questions through a short-sighted, green-eyed mist, you have to be an exceptional man not to feel intense curiosity in return. She had three university degrees, I believed I'd read somewhere. Not the nugatory stuff, not media studies or journalism, but Middle English, philosophy, history, possibly even divinity – real subjects. Yet before that, aged eighteen, she had won a beauty contest. Miss Whitstable, or Miss Herne Bay. Somewhere there. Because she wore her hair long and blonded, in glamour-girl flounces, and didn't skimp with the lipstick, you could still see the beauty queen in her. Miss East Grinstead,

DPhil. She was hard to say no to if you like your women vexed.

Marina hadn't made so good a job of keeping her figure, or her face. She had grey bags under her eyes, somewhat desperately flecked with silver glitter, and wore make-up more to hide than adorn. She did the shmoozing and the PR, filling me in on what else Lipsync was up to at the moment – a docudrama, still in development, about Mordechai Vanunu, the Israeli who blew the whistle on Israel's nuclear arsenal; a costume extravaganza, also still in development, about the philosopher Spinoza; and one or two other things in pre-development, but all at the serious end of the market, as I could see, programmes you made for love not money. She did the snuggling up to me, too, calling me darling and telling me how excited they were, etc, before recognising people at other tables who excited her more, and eventually, with a squeeze of my upper arm, leaving me to Francine, who all the time surveyed me, even when she wasn't looking in my direction, through sensors situated snake-like in the sides of her head.

'Get him to talk about himself. How he feels about what he did. What his life has been like since then, etc . . .' was how she countered my initial wariness.

'We were never all that close, you know,' I warned her.

'But you did know him, that's the thing. You were neighbours. You played together. Am I right in thinking you went to the same school?'

'Yes, but only briefly. He went his way, I went mine.'

'I understand that. Your paths diverged. But they diverged from the same starting place. You grew up together. You shared interests and beliefs.'

'Not exactly. In many ways our upbringings were diametrically opposed.'

She subjected me to her unnerving peer. Who *are* you, Maxie Glickman? Why are you making these distinctions? To trap me? 'That I understand,' she said, 'but you knew that world.'

That world.

So there it was. They wanted me to Jew it up for them, put some Yiddler angst and colour on the page for Christopher Christmas to draw around when he was next free. A writer whose own knowledge of Jews, needless to say, extended not a bowshot beyond Anne Frank's diary.

Uncanny, but she seemed to know what I was thinking. Who *are* you, Francine Bryson-Smith? 'Chris might or not stay with this,' she said. 'He's very busy. And he might not be the person for it anyway. There are no egos here. We can discuss all that as we get further in.' Meaning: play your cards right and the job, the whole project, could end up being yours, Max. One of the unspoken advantages of which, I took it, was any number of lunches being peered at by Francine Bryson-Smith.

We shook on it. I only knew Manny a bit, and couldn't swear that he'd admit to knowing me. But I'd give it a go. Here's to Lipsync.

And here's to you, Max.

Here's to Manny, no one thought of saying.

Before I left, Francine did a strange thing. She came to my side of the table, stood behind me, produced a camera from her bag, and got the waiter to take our picture.

4

But I had done a strange thing too. I had lied about how well I knew Manny. Though he had changed his name to Stroganoff and was almost certainly an entirely different person from the one I had known, and known well, I had disowned him again before people I didn't know at all.

Why did I do that?

Where was the necessity for it, *now*?

And why, if I'd convinced myself we hadn't been close friends, was I so troubled to hear of him again, and so rattled – no, not rattled, so *pierced* – to learn he'd changed his name to Stroganoff?

Why, why, why?

Some things you think are dead and buried, as the shitty shtetls of Mother Russia were meant to be for my father. Stroganoff was the absurd nom de plume, or in my case *nom de caricaturiste*, which Manny and I came up with after we'd grown out of playing concentration camps. The Brothers Stroganoff we thought we'd call ourselves, under which pseudonym we were going to publish works that would change the world. *Five Thousand Years of Bitterness* was our first, a comic-book history of the sufferings of the Jewish people over the last five millennia. We had argued over the title. Manny believed it should be *Two Thousand Years of Bitterness*, the sufferings of our people dating from the destruction of the second Temple in 70 CE. As an Orthodox Jew he didn't, of course, acknowledge the Christian calendar. Even 70 CE was a concession to me. Between themselves, Orthodox Jews put the date of the destruction of the Second Temple as 3829. My own view was that our afflictions began from the minute we showed we couldn't be natural in nature. We did a Jewish thing, we ate of the tree of knowledge, and didn't know a day's happiness thereafter. *Five Thousand Years of Bitterness* was already concession enough to creationists – *Five Thousand Million Years of Bitterness* more like – but if we believed that God made the world only five thousand years ago, then that was how long we'd been bitter. And I got my way. I was the one with the coloured pencils.

Manny provided the research and what you might call the background information, I did the comic illustrations. If drawing is what you turn to when the words won't come, then drawing of the comico-savage sort is what you turn to when the first word that does come is the J-word. That or shmaltz, but shmaltz was not an option in our house. Any chicken-fat sentimentality attaching to our Novoropissik origins had long been burnt off by the white fires of my father's secularity. We were a team, Manny and I, anyway. The better, we both thought, for our ill-assortedness.

33

And in no time we had produced fifty pages. We got as far as paying to have them cyclostyled and showing them to our parents. But in their view they weren't going to change the world. Not for the better, anyway.

'Get yourself another subject,' my father told me.

'Like what?'

'Boxing.'

Boxing was his subject. He'd been a champion boxer himself before I was born. Jack 'The Jew' Glickman. Not a soubriquet he chose for himself. Jack 'Drop the Jew' Glickman would have suited him the better, but his opponents knew the J-word riled him into lowering his guard. Only amateur, though by all accounts he could have made it big as a professional had it not been for a predisposition to nosebleeds. Epistaxis as I now know it's called. My father's nasal membranes dried quicker than other people's. As do mine. Quick to dry, quick to rupture. Though in my case it doesn't matter quite so much. I don't have to go twelve rounds with anybody, unless you count Zoë and Chloë and the rest. And in those circumstances a nosebleed can be a blessing in disguise. There's always the faint chance it will upset them and cause them to repent. But it never upset or planted the idea of repentance in any of my father's opponents. Once the secret of his weakness was out, they went straight for the nose, and it was all over. 'It's just blood,' he used to complain to the referee standing in front of him with his arms flailing, counting him out although he hadn't so much as touched the canvas, 'you've seen blood before, haven't you?' Indeed he had. Just never as much as spilled from my father's nose.

As it happened, this debility was a blessing in disguise for him. It meant that he was never sent to fight the Nazis on their territory. No point having a soldier who would bleed all over the regiment before a single shot was fired. So they kept him in a barracks in South Wales for the duration of the war, and let him run the gym.

34

Though he was no longer boxing himself by the time I was old enough to know anything about it, he retained his passionate devotion to the sport. He organised the boxing club at the local lads' brigade, acted as a sort of personal trainer before there was such a thing to boys with pugilistic promise, kept his gloves in my mother's display cabinet along with his cups, subscribed to every conceivable boxing magazine, drove up to Belle Vue every Friday night to see a bout, and could recite the past and present holders of every title at every weight. British Jewish boxers like Jackie 'Kid' Berg, otherwise known as 'The Whitechapel Whirlwind', and Ted 'Kid' Lewis, born Gershon Mendeloff, and Jack Bloomfield, he revered, and hung pictures of them above the stairs — one per step — where otherwise my mother would have hung photographs of Shani as a bridesmaid, or portraits of great kalooki players of the past, if such exist. But it was the American Jewish boxers who really fired my father up. I have never known why. Maybe they were more brutal in their despatch of opponents, or maybe it was just his idealising of America, American Jews having made their escape from humility and trepidation more finally than my father believed we had, or ever would. Barney Ross, for example, he admired as much for his rejection of his origins as for becoming lightweight champion of the world. Born Barnet Rasofsky, he had planned to be a rabbi like his father until thieves broke into the family grocery store and shot his father dead. Vowing revenge — a phrase my father relished — Barnet Rasofsky renounced the faith, changed his name, became a numbers runner and street-fighter, and eventually took up boxing. My father's idea of making good. But even more of a favourite was Benny Leonard, originally Benjamin Leiner, the greatest lightweight, he assured me, who ever lived. Myself, I think the real reason he admired Benny Leonard was that he too had been a bit of a nosebleeder, actually losing his first fight that way, after being stopped in the third round by the sort of squeamish referee who ruined my father's career. Thereafter he developed a defence so impregnable that between 1912 and 1932 he shed not a single drop of blood, losing only one bout, and that by disqualification.

'Think of that,' I remember my father saying. 'Twenty years without being beaten, twice the time you've been alive.'

Impressive, I agreed, but not so impressive that I wanted to do the same. Already my fingers were too important to me to risk them boxing. Break your fingers in the ring and where does that leave you as an artist? And I was a particularly fingery artist, a maker of fine satiric lines which sometimes worried me, so like needlecraft were they, so like little daggers of derision and self-hurt.

The only boxer in my father's pantheon to capture my imagination was Maxie 'Slapsie' Rosenbloom, partly because he was what was known as a hit-and-run fighter, that's to say he no sooner landed a punch than he back-pedalled round the ring so that he couldn't be punched back (a tactic I could see the point of); partly because he wasn't much of a puncher anyway and resorted in the end to slapping his opponents (hence his nickname); but chiefly because I was named after him. Whether I have my mother to thank for it, I don't know, but to this day I count myself lucky that I didn't end up being called Slapsie.

In fact no one would have been more surprised than my father had I developed an active interest in boxing. Or, I suspect, more dismayed. He would not have wanted to see me knocked around. There was a sense in which he felt he'd done that for the pair of us. In so far as the Jewish boxers whose pictures lined our stairs were intended as an example to me, they did not go beyond showing what we could do when we tried, that's to say when we gave up believing that we drank physical cowardice in with our mothers' milk. They were the obverse of those streets of medieval Jewishry through which, holding on tightly to my hand, he made a point of escorting me. They proved that we could live in the world without fear, go toe to toe with it, embrace what the daylight showed us in strong clear outlines instead of shrinking into the shadows, praying to what was unseen and unseeable. Fists were of the essence. He made fists of his own hands while he told me this – 'Grab at life, Maxie! Grab what you can see!' That lesson punched into me, he was happy for me to go to school and become a solicitor. Anything so long as I stayed away from Judaism, which he considered, somewhat illogically, to be a curse on the Jews. Farshimelt was one of his favourite words for the Orthodox. Farshimelt, meaning mouldy, mildewed. The consequence of being hidden from the air and light. What happened to you – to your skin and to your mind – when you refused the visible world.

Farshimelt. You can hear the maggots at work.

Significant, I always thought, that he, the great progressive secularist and fist-fighter, the most Aryan Jew in Manchester, needed a Yiddish word to express his contempt.

Perhaps I was looking for some equivocation in his heart to match the equivocation in mine. Yes, when it came to despising the farshimelt I was my father's son; on paper – and I worked on paper – no one could have despised them more; but there were hours when I found myself rebelling against my father's teaching. Despite myself, a lonely sensation sometimes overcame me, a longing for some of the family intimacy that Manny seemed to enjoy. Intimacy might not even be the word for it. Our family was intimate enough, God knows, shouting at one another, interfering in one another's business, our house thrown open to anyone who wanted to talk boxing, atheism, kalooki, or anything else for that matter. But the Washinskys, though more formal and reserved, were somehow hotter, darker, a consequence, perhaps, of being as a family concentrated upon a purpose from which, until the first of their family tragedies befell them, there was no divergence of view. The few times Manny invited me home I felt a peculiar privilege, as though a wild animal had let me into his lair, so packed and dense was it among the Washinskys, so bound were they by the watchful rituals of survival. Seeing Manny out with his father on their way to the synagogue, both of them spruced up darkly to attend on God, urgent on their errand, two men engaged in what never for a moment occurred to them was *not* the proper business of men, joined as I was never joined with *my* father, bonded in abstraction, but also bonded in the activity of being purposefully out and about, traversing the community, going from home to the house of worship, as though devotion wore a civic aspect – on such occasions, though it was an act of treachery to my father to be feeling such a thing, I wished my life were more like Manny's. I would then secretly envy Manny his mother, too, Channa Washinsky on the doorstep looking out for their return, halo'd in cooking fumes, her head covered by a scarf, weaving spells from under it, or so it seemed to me the one Shabbes dinner they asked me to share with them, making those welcoming motions with her hands, as though to call on the angel of light to bless their bread and ignite their candles, before covering her eyes and delivering the blessing. True, my mother wove spells over her playing cards, but when she blew on her fingers and shuffled the decks my mother was commemorating the unbroken sameness of things, another night of kalooki in a life given over to kalooki.

Whereas Channa Washinsky was not only marking the Shabbes from what was not the Shabbes, she was honouring the concept of separateness itself, the beauty of one time not occurring simultaneously with another, ourselves not existing forever and unchangingly as ourselves. What the woman ushers in on the eve of the Sabbath, the man bids farewell to at its close, pouring out a glass of wine, lighting a single candle, perhaps shaking a spice box whose aromas symbolise the additional soul to which the Sabbath has given him access, and reciting the Habdalah benediction – a thank you to the Almighty for drawing a distinction between the holy and the profane, between light and darkness, between the six days of creation and the seventh day of rest. For that, simply, is what Habdalah means: separation. And whether you light the candle and shake the spices or you don't, you cannot call yourself a Jew unless the concept is written on your heart.

In its way, Habdalah is a justification for the idea of art. Here is the daily world of fact, there is the other-worldly domain of the imagination. Here is the tongue we are obliged as responsible citizens to mind, and there is the outlandish language we speak when we are otherwise possessed. So you would think the Orthodox, who thank Elohim for dividing this from that, would be hot on the separation which is art. But you'd be wrong.

5

Manny blamed the failure of *Five Thousand Years of Bitterness* to get beyond our respective houses on me. 'You and your cartoons,' he said.

'It's the cartoons that make it,' I told him.

'Yeah, that make it blasphemous.'

That was his father talking. Blasphemy, impurity, uncleanness. Everything a sin against the Law. Everything an infringement. Leave aside the content, which Selick Washinsky was not the first and no doubt will not be the last to be repelled by, the mere fact that I drew a likeness at all offended him. Who was it – Feuerbach, Hegel, or simply every German philosopher there has ever been – who accused the Jews of being aniconic to their soul, eschewing the concrete because they would not envision God other than abstractly? Well, though I take no pleasure in their being right about anything, they were right about Manny's father. In his eyes I was an idolater. I pause before that thought, because in my eyes I was an idolater too. The difference being that idolatry frightened Selick Washinsky whereas, primarily I suppose because

I confused the word with iconoclast – and you can't really be the second until you've been the first – it energised me.

On his ownio, without the word of God at his shoulder, Manny himself liked my cartoons. They made him laugh. A pretty sickly laugh, but still a laugh. Our studio was the disused air-raid shelter in which we had talked of God and choked on poison gases. I thought of it as *my* air-raid shelter because you could only get to it by hacking your way through the hedge at the bottom of *my* garden or other gardens on *my* side of the street, but Manny considered it his by spiritual right – a dank, disused, overgrown underground space to which one fled to escape the irreverent light of day. Here, working with the help of those Second World War torches which everyone had lying around in those days, we would sit for hours on end, he rattling his chest asthmatically (there was a chemicals factory close to the shelter, which didn't help), chewing his pencil and trying to think up adjectives to match the wickedness of one oppressor of the Jewish people after another; oppressors, I have to say, who didn't only trip off his tongue but sprang from his ears and eyes, grew out of his hair and finger-nails – Pharaoh, Amalek, Haman, Torquemada, Goebbels, Goering, Oswald Mosley – mamzers, bastards, the lot of them – I clicking my tongue and making Donald Duck noises as I sought for features grotesque enough to suggest their inner ugliness. Not easy when you can't employ big noses, those having to be reserved, of course, for our own people, the eternally oppressed. In life, a button nose becomes a tyrant well enough, as witness Zoë, but it looks a lot less menacing in a cartoon. Big nose bad, small nose good – that's just the way of it, in caricature as in race relations. Something, according to Horkheimer and Adorno, to do with the sense of smell and its embodying archetypal long-ings for the lower forms of existence. The nose a disgrace because the sense of smell a disgrace, a hankering after lowly origins, a refusal to embrace the liberating separateness of civilisation. Hence, presumably, Zoë's wanting me to rid myself of mine. My solution as far as cartooning went, anyway, was the ruse of giving all the anti-Semites through the ages a Hitler moustache. Manny laughed like a drain at that. A field of Philistines with Hitler moustaches and their right hands in the air. The Pharaoh with a Hitler moustache. The Romans with Hitler moustaches. Ditto the Spanish Inquisition and the Roman Catholic Church and the Cossacks. Only Hitler himself – which seemed to me a novel concept – without. But then, as Manny observed – laughing like the dead, laughing as though his laughter were the ghost of laughter passed – how would anyone know it was Hitler if he didn't have a Hitler moustache?

Good point. So in the end I drew him just as a moustache. Which also made Manny do his drain thing. A disembodied moustache screaming 'Heil!' and banging on about the Final Solution.

Had I painted rather than cartooned, I'd have been a surrealist. Which is peculiar because I've never liked surrealism. Another argument I might have had with myself.

While I had grown up with knowledge of Hitler and extermination from an early age, thanks largely to Tsedraiter Ike, it was Manny who introduced me to the phrase 'Final Solution'. We had just moved in to the opposite side of the street (part of my family's downward social spiral), and as he was the only kid in the immediate vicinity my age – immediate vicinity meaning within my mother's melodic shouting range – I was persuaded to make a friend of him. I wasn't keen. He looked too historically Jewish for my liking. Too persecuted and unhealthy, his skin yellow and waxy, the colour of old candles. Farshimelt. I wasn't exactly an athlete in the Benny Leonard mould myself, but I didn't have that Asiatic blight on me that goes with being Orthodox. Or that fluffy moustache, which there was no explaining because Manny was otherwise physically immature, not to say underdeveloped. Was there a moustache you could go grow at that age which denoted the opposite of precocity? His chronology was all wrong, whatever the physiology. You

41

couldn't locate him satisfactorily in time; he was old too soon, and younger than he should have been.

Whether it was his anachronistic moustache I was unknowingly alluding to every time I drew Hitler's, is a question I have gone back and pondered – fruitlessly, I must say – many times since. But maybe I am just looking, in retrospect, for signs. He made my flesh creep, let's leave it at that. He made me embarrassed for Jews, and therefore for myself. Which is probably the way it worked for my father too. 'Where do they get the idea from,' I remember him expostulating, with a gesture designed to take in not just Manny, and not just Manny's family, but every household which allowed the noxious weed of Orthodoxy to take root, 'that to be frum you have to look as though you've been lying in your own coffin all day? If the God they believe in had wanted us to look like death, why did He blow life into our nostrils in the first place?'

But my mother thought it was a good idea for me to have a friend.

'Swap comics with him,' was her suggestion.

I hung back. 'He doesn't look like a boy who reads comics,' I said.

But then I didn't look like a boy who read comics either, and read them at first only to conform to my parents' idea of what a normal boy ought to have been doing. There was something about the *Dandy* and the *Beano*, the mishaps of Dennis the Menace or Roger the Dodger, that depressed me. It was the look of them, partly: the skanky paper, the low-mirth smudginess of their production; but also the dismalness of the schoolyard world they portrayed: discipline versus cheekiness, small victories, practical jokes, jeering, every teacher undernourished, every kid drawn as though he had rickets. And then one day, Dodgy Ike, who was always dropping in on us with gifts of doubtful propriety and provenance – genaivisheh was my father's word for them: knocked off, but somehow innocently, knavishly,

42

*ge*knavishly knocked off – turned up with a cigar in his mouth and a stash of contraband American comics under his arm. Superman, Batman, Captain Marvel, Dick Tracy: a brave new Technicolor world of momentous, universe-changing action and teeming metropolises, even the ejaculations, SHAZAM! and BLAMM! and ZOKK! a thousand times more heroic than the small-time COO!s and CROAK!s of the meagrely illustrated, miserly minded *Beano*. I fell in love with them at first sight, not just because they were from somewhere else and shouldn't have been in my possession at all, but also because of the architecture of their design – the sculpted bodies, the masses of colour, the dynamic sense of movement, boldly futuristic and yet as classical in their density as any of the Renaissance paintings of annunciations and miraculous births whose reproductions hung in our art room at school. How did their artists achieve that? How were they able to appropriate everything, apparently so effortlessly? What was the secret of their pictorial plunder? Although I wouldn't have put it to myself in quite this way, I recognised (correctly, as it turned out) something Jewish in them – Dodgy Ike Jewish, a bit genaivisheh in the knavish sense, full of spirited immigrant johnny-come-lately razzamatazz, and thus the antithesis to what the English expected of an illustrator of comics.

Did that explain the anti-American sentiment of the careful Gentile world in which I grew up? Was that why our teachers were always warning us off American movies and music and bubblegum, and would have confiscated my Superman comics had I brought them to school – because what they really didn't like about America was its Jewishness?

Without doubt, some of this anti-Americanism rubbed off on me. Even though I was so smitten by Lois Lane I would draw her in the arms of someone bearing a striking resemblance to me just before I went to sleep, and so envied Superman his X-ray vision that for a while all my heroes had two yellow cones of

43

light pouring from their eyes, I little by little rebelled from the extravagantly optimistic fantasy of it all. English culture called. If not the English comic book, then the English cartoon. Moralistic. Suspicious. Dour. Savage. Reductively ribald. Everything that I was not.

That I became a cartoonist rather than that more verdant creature, a comic-book illustrator, let alone an accountant or a dentist, only goes to show that you don't always follow your own best impulses, or even know what your impulses are. I recall my mother telling me with horror about a friend of hers who had suddenly fallen victim to a sort of science-fiction sickness known to doctors – in so far as it was known to them at all – as Anarchic (otherwise Alien) Hand syndrome. The poor woman had had a stroke, as a consequence of which the right part of her brain had become disconnected electrically from the left, leaving her right hand in a state of enmity with the rest of her. Sometimes the wayward hand merely wanted to grab on to something which she didn't – a door, a handle, an object in a supermarket – but at others it sought postively to hinder and embarrass her, and once she woke up choking in the night, on the point of being strangled by it. We are psychologically at war with ourselves, that's what it comes to. One half of us would destroy the other half if it could, and only the impartial intercession of the body, when it's well ordered, saves us from self-murder. Let the body become unstrung, however, and we are once again at the mercy of our feuding psyches. So it was with my illustrator's hand. Although it hasn't yet attempted to throttle me or put my eyes out – and there is no saying it still won't – it did, by wanting to draw satirically at all, act independently of me, in mischievous defiance of my nature, which was always melancholy and withdrawn, resistant to laughter and exaggeration, and not at all given to the crude and often cruel hilarity of caricature. To say that one part of me drew cartoons in order to spite the other half which abominated them, might be going too far; but I don't doubt there was

44

subversion in it, as though my drawing was impelled by hobgoblins or other spritely things of darkness I did not want to acknowledge mine.

'All boys read comics,' my mother said.

But I was right and she was wrong. Manny Washinsky had never read a comic in his life. But he, too, wanted someone to play with. So for a dozen *Beanos* and one *Tarzan* he swapped me *The Scourge of the Swastika*. 'Only I'll be wanting it back,' he told me.

'Then I'll be wanting my *Beanos* back.'

'You can have them back now. I won't look at them anyway. I'm not allowed.'

'So why are you giving me this?'

'I'm not. I'm just lending it you.'

'What's it about?' I asked.

'The Final Solution.'

'Is it any good?' It looked good, if the cover was anything to go by. Blood-red lettering on a cowardy cowardy custard-yellow background. A figure in jackboots, seen from behind and below, as a trodden worm might see him; in his belt a revolver, the jackboots themselves astride the globe, like the very portals of the earth. And between his legs, viewed from a distance, cowering and hopeless, with nowhere to hide, the trodden-worm masses of the Jewish people.

More than that, it appeared well thumbed.

'There are supposed to be photographs in it,' Manny told me, 'but my parents ripped them out.'

I wondered why that was.

Manny pulled a face. 'They said I could see them when I was older.'

The book itself, though I can recite half of it to this day, I have no memory of actually sitting down and reading. So I must have imbibed its contents some other way. And eventually, courtesy of

Errol Tobias who had his own copy – the street, it turned out, was awash with *The Scourge of the Swastika* – I got to see the missing photographs as well.

On consideration I think Manny's parents were right to have kept them from him. The pity was that he got to see them in the end.

The pity was that any of us did.

6

Emanuel Eli Washinsky was found guilty of manslaughter on the basis of diminished responsibility in 1973. The year of my first divorce. And the year Syria and Egypt coordinated a surprise attack against Israel on Yom Kippur, also on the basis of diminished responsibility. So a big year for Jews. In fact the Yom Kippur War was a bit of a godsend for Manny, in that the consternation and anger it generated distracted attention from his trial. That's assuming he cared one way or another by that time.

The crime itself had been committed the year before. I was gone from the neighbourhood when it happened. I was plying my trade. Living modestly in London and selling my cartoons – this was well before my Tom of Finland phase – to whoever would buy them: *Punch*, *Private Eye*, the *Spectator*, I wasn't particular. I doubt I had yet developed an individual style. Baleful I suppose was the word for what I did – incongruities, absurdities and falsities eyed splenetically and in the English manner: Gillray, Rowlandson et al, but more fingery in the line, more pernickety, and without the current affairs. Not yet on an epic scale, you might say. But then the epic scale I was reserving for what really mattered to me – *Five Thousand Years of Bitterness*. Yes, it had been *our* book, a Stroganoff Brothers production, but Manny had washed his hands of it, both spiritually and intellectually, years before. Blasphemous. Unclean. Unfunny. So I felt that the moral rights to it had reverted to me. Besides, I wasn't using any of his words. Beyond a few necessary AARGH!s and SPLAT!s and SKREEAAAK!s there were no words. Just pictures. Illustrations, in the grotesque mode and with lots of colour – think Dr Doom as drawn by Goya – of what successive generations of bastards had done to us in every corner of the globe. Graphic novels hadn't even happened yet, so I was at the vanguard of comic history. Not that I was drawing fiction. This was graphic history. And not just any graphic history. *The* graphic history.

I wasn't rushing. No one was breathing down my neck. When I finished it I finished it, and when I finished it the world would notice. That wasn't arrogance, merely the certainty without which you cannot do the work. The only people I couldn't imagine reading it with pleasure were the Germans, though I have since learned that collective guilt, if you know how to work it, can sell books in piles as high as bones. In the meantime I could just about earn enough to keep me in cigarettes, Bell's whisky, and the sort of Gentile women – awe-inspiring and essentially ill-disposed to me – who made me go weak at the knees. Being squeezed through the divorce courts by Chloë, post *St Matthew Passion*, had depressed my spirits and strained my finances, but I felt that when I needed more I could always draw more. As for running out of ideas, the proposition would have struck me as laughable. I was the fruit of Five Thousand Years of Bitterness which meant that I was heir to Five Thousand Years of Jokes.

It was from my mother that I first heard about the Washinskys' tragedy. A phone call at an odd hour. The call you know, from the time and from the ringtone, bodes only ill.

'Sit down,' she said. 'I have something very terrible to tell you.'

'Is it Shani?'

'No, it isn't anybody in the family. We're all all right. It's the Washinskys. Something unbearably awful has happened. Oh, Max, I don't know how to start to tell you.'

Although she had moved out of Crumpsall Park soon after Shani left, installing herself and Tsedraiter Ike into a maisonette in more salubrious Prestwich, with the intention of renting out our old house for extra income, she was back in it again for reasons of economy, neither she nor Tsedraiter Ike being capable of administering a property, or of earning a penny any other way come to that. A family feature – our hopelessness with money. Always some retrenchment in the offing, though never when it came to shoes, or indeed to any other aspect of my mother's appearance which had altered after my father died only in that sadness rendered it the more exquisite and, by Crumpsall standards, expensive. It was from our old house, anyway, in our old street and on our old phone, that she was ringing me. Though I rarely visited Crumpsall any more I could see it all as if I'd been there only the day before. Dread can do this. My skin turned cold and I saw the street, saw Manny whom I hadn't seen in years, saw his father sewing at the front window, saw the neglected garden, the forlorn weeds growing through the cracks in the paving stones, the paint long peeled from every door and window frame, giving the house not so much a derelict as a blanched, bled-white appearance, saw Manny's mother peering out of an upstairs window to look for him, frightened for him and frightened for herself, not wanting to show her face, not trusting her neighbours or the light of day, no longer welcoming home the men of the family as she used to do before her family was made a laughing stock, and saw Manny swinging from a rope in his bedroom, his eyes bulging, his body hanging like an empty sack. Then I heard the wailing, centuries old.

I doubt anybody who knew the Washinskys would have pictured any other scene had they been told only what my mother had so far told me. *Sit down. Something unbearably awful has happened* . . .

Manny. What else could you think? Manny had taken his life. The likelihood had always been that he would kill himself, he had talked about killing himself, had even practised killing himself, and now he'd done it.

'Who found him?' I asked. The hanging part was so to be expected, the only drama was in the discovery.

'Manny? Nobody's found him. Nobody knows where he is.'

My skin turned a little colder.

'Ma,' I said, 'what's happened?'

'Well, it's unclear. There are still police in the street. The house is cordoned off, Maxie. It's too terrible.'

'Ma, just tell me what's happened.'

'Channa and Selick have been found dead.'

'Christ!'

'In their beds, Max. They think gassed.'

'Gassed!'

'I know.'

You don't say 'gassed' to Jews if you can help it. One of those words. They should be struck out of the human vocabulary for a while, while we regroup, not for ever, just for a thousand years or so – gassed, camp, extermination, concentration, experiment, march, train, rally, German. Words made unholy just as ground is made unholy.

Side by side, holding hands, was how I imagined them. Like a devout Christian couple engraved in cathedral brass. Staring up at the dome from which Lord Jesus in a night sky of stars and angels looks down in celestial majesty. I had never seen inside their bedroom, but supposed it must have been like the rest of their house – unaired, unloved, not exactly unclean but uncared for, clothes and linen thrown about the floor, bare bulbs hanging from the ceilings, the furniture gaping stuffing, everything broken, the world of here and now a tribulation to them, and yet nothing suggestive of the spiritual life either, unless the flotsam of Judaic tat, cheap household objects adorned with Hebrew lettering, torn prayer books, fringed vestments thrown over the backs of chairs, and yes, yes, the odd angelically ignited candle, could be said to constitute spirituality. But the gassing of them somehow cleaned up around them. Gassed, they had joined the sacred millions, photographs of whose piled-up bodies I had first seen in Lord Russell of Liverpool's *The Scourge of the Swastika*, the righteous by virtue of victimisation, and no one stood judgement on *their* domestic surroundings.

Into the spaces my mother was granting me to digest the news, a stray thought flew.

'What about Asher?'

Asher was Manny's older brother. Somehow farshimelt and dashing in the past tense – dashed – all at once. Hollowed out, was how he had looked to me, great black volcanic gouges for eyes, and a sunken, tubercular chest. There was a touch of that about Manny too, but in his case you imagined that he had simply never inhaled enough fresh air, that his were coward's lungs, whereas in Asher you saw someone made ill by late nights, if not alcohol then coffee, and if not debauch then at least the imagination of debauch. All guesswork on my part. I hardly knew him. He appeared a handful of times to keep Jewish assembly at our school – that's to say to look after the Jewish kids while the Gentiles were hymning their saviour in the hall. He was meant to be teaching us Hebrew, or at least occupying us Hebraically, but all we did was chant a few letters of the Hebrew alphabet and throw chalk at him. He made no attempt to keep us in order. When a piece of chalk hit him he would smile and put it in his pocket. He was unnerving. He was somewhere else in his head.

Because he was six or seven years older than Manny he had never figured in our conversation, never came out to offer us his opinion on *The Scourge of the Swastika*, never followed us into the air-raid shelter to make suggestions for *Five Thousand Years of Bitterness*, and for all I knew was unaware that he even had a brother, let alone that his brother had a friend. But although he wasn't much in evidence in person, rumours about him had circulated freely, stories so wild and contradictory it was hard to believe they referred to the same person. Now he was a teacher at a Talmud Torah somewhere in the Midlands, and such was his popularity that children cried to be allowed to go to his lessons. A businessman in New York who happened to be in the Midlands at the time was so impressed by Asher's methods that he was funding him to set up a string of chederim – Sunday schools for Jews – all over the United States. But the next week he was out of work, penniless, keeping bad company, haunting low dives, in such deep trouble morally that his parents had disowned him, and not only disowned him but actually recited the prayers for the dead over him. And there's only one reason why devout Jewish families ever do that. A shikseh!

Asher and a shikseh! The whole of Crumpsall was abuzz with it.

Could Asher – training to be a rabbi – really have been found in bed with the fire-yekelte who was three times his age, a sooty-fingered woman in an apron who only ever visited the house on Saturday, and who therefore must have seduced or been seduced by him on the Sabbath? Count the sins against Leviticus, count the number of abominations the Washinskys would have enumerated in that! Once the most reserved family in the street, the Washinskys were suddenly waking us all up in our beds with their cursing. So violently did they turn on one another that Selick Washinsky had to be carried out on a stretcher, collapsing after trying to tear his son's heart out. If the father didn't kill the son, the son would kill the father. 'Help!' Channa Washinsky ran out into the street to cry. 'They are murdering each other!' My own father was dying at the time. I recall our concern that the last weeks of his sublunary sleep should not be disturbed by the war that had broken out between the Washinskys. But what could we do? A family had a right to rip itself apart if it wanted to. My father even found a sort of consolation in it. With luck these were the death throes of the Orthodox. They would tear themselves to shreds and that would be the end of this strange passage of ahistoricity and fancy dress which Jewish history had entered. Then all things stopped together: my father's breathing and the

Washinskys' shouting. Asher, like my father, was spirited away. To a yeshiva in the North-East, it was said, Gateshead no doubt, where Manny, too, went years later, and then to some convalescent camp in Lymm in Cheshire. I might have the order of those exiles wrong. Both were terrifying destinations; places of oblivion to my sense, like those schools in Dickens to which parents sent children they did not love in the hope of never hearing from them again. Gateshead, closer to Scandinavia than to Manchester, where the boys sat on hard benches and studied the head-hurting subtleties of Jewish law all day. Draitheboys Hall. Lymm no better. Always a stigma attaching to Lymm, as though the bad-chested boys who went there had brought their badness on themselves.

Manny talked to me about Asher only on a couple of occasions. An out-of-bounds confidence never to be repeated or alluded to. As if the extremity that spoke through him drew a magic circle around us. Otherwise, the subject of his brother and his departing from the straight and narrow path of Judaism was closed. *Verboten.* In later years, Asher Washinsky, now assumed to be a ruined man, was reported to be working as a shammes, a janitor, in a small synagogue in South America, or was it South Africa, or was it South Australia, but he could just as easily have been out drinking himself to death. Or sobbing in some alley. That was what he looked – a wild, hollow, melancholic rake who read the Talmud.

I envied him. I would have liked to look the way he looked, at least before the affair with the fire-yekelte ruined his life. Marked black, like Cain.

So had I been the detective in charge of the investigation, I'd have known where to look. And where were you, Mr Asher Washinsky, between the hours of . . .

But that was to jump the gun. Who'd said anything about a police investigation? What reason did I have to believe there was a suspect?

Asher? Well, in fact it was my mother's understanding that for all the rumours of his having gone to ground in the furthest corners of the earth, he had in fact returned recently to Manchester. The police found him living round the corner, woke him in the middle of the night and told him the appalling news. 'Maxie, it's so upsetting. They say he doubled over when he heard, as though someone had shot him. He's been spitting blood and howling like an animal.'

I took that with a pinch of salt. How did anybody know how Asher had behaved in the presence of the midnight policeman? And as for spitting blood, it was what Jewish sons were said to do when their parents died. It was a manner of speaking, a metaphor for the enormity of their grief. I hadn't so far spat blood myself, but I had howled right enough. Howled and howled.

'And does anybody know what exactly happened?' I asked.

'No. The Greens next door smelled a leak. It was they who called the police. We're lucky there wasn't an explosion. The whole street could have gone up.'

I knew what my late father would have said. They shouldn't be allowed gas when they're in that condition. People as primitive as the Washinskys oughtn't to be trusted with modern inventions. They crashed their cars. They turned their stoves and ovens into ancient altars which needed the breath of Yahweh or failing that a disrespected member of the Gentile working classes to light them on the Shabbes. And now they're gassing themselves.

'So is that what they're thinking? Just a leak?'

'*Just*? Maxie, you sound disappointed.'

I sighed. Did I? Would I have wanted it to be something else? Robbery with violence? Hard to imagine any robber with his head screwed on supposing the Washinskys had anything to steal, other than mezuzahs and menorahs and tefillin bags. And a few scrag ends of whatever fur it was that Selick Washinsky sewed into whatever garment it was he sewed. Not mink, not Persian lamb, not ocelot – nothing precious was surely ever allowed into that decaying house. As for an assault by Jew-haters, we would have heard, my mother would have known by now, the whole of Jewish Crumpsall would have been in uproar. The desecration, the swastikas, the burning crosses nailed to the garden gate. You can't keep those quiet. Leak it was then. Ho-hum. Having laid them down side by side in my imagination, blanched of their sins by whoever had gassed them, I was ready, since no one had gassed them, to leave them to their eternal rest. I hadn't really known them when I'd known them, and hadn't seen or thought about them for years. Their going made no material difference to me. And I had never been able or allowed to penetrate Manny's affective system. Did he care about them? Love them? Would he spit blood and howl when he found out? God knows.

So even for him I couldn't feel their loss.

Done and dusted. A gas leak. Very sad. Very sad indeed. End of perturbation. Back to my cartoons.

I had an inadequate sense of them as human beings. A terrible confession, I acknowledge. But I am, despite occasional departures from his teaching, my father's son. Something makes me except the devout from the human family, no matter that the heat of their lair had beguiled me once. They step out by virtue of their other-worldliness, so I leave them there. Had the decently secularised parents of some far more distant friend than Manny been found gassed in their beds I'd have lain awake for weeks picturing their torment. But because of the odour of mouldering prohibition in their house, because of the stained black trilby that Selick Washinsky wore for synagogue every Shabbes morning, because of the poverty of Channa Washinsky's wardrobe (nothing that would have done for even the most modest of my mother's kalooki friends to wipe her nose on), because of the holy books that occupied their bookshelves instead of encyclopaedia and romances, the torn siddurim they took out to read from on Friday nights, the holy writ or mumbo-jumbo as my father used to call it, because of all the junk there was to touch and kiss and start in superstitious trepidation from, I couldn't feel for Manny anything of what I should have felt. I couldn't anticipate his horror. Beyond a passing sadness for him, such as the death of someone's animal might bring, God help me, I couldn't participate in his grief. Is this the explanation of the Five Thousand Years of Persecution, of the pogroms, of the Shoah even, is this the answer to the age-old question – How Could They Do It? – that the perpetrators of these crimes were able to do what they did because those on whom they visited inhumanity did not themselves seem to be *of* humanity? No excuse. You should not visit inhumanity on a dog. But people do and it is important we understand how and why. Or maybe I am merely seeking to forgive myself.

There it is, anyway. Two people with whom I hadn't exactly grown up, but who had been intimate figures in my landscape, no matter that they were mostly figures of distaste, the parents of a boy I had at one time been as close to as I have to anybody – two elderly, God-revering, God-startled people with whom my life, like it or not, had been accidentally entwined, two Jews, two *more* Jews, lay gassed in their beds and other than a brief essay into the picturesque I could neither envision the scene with any pity worth speaking of, nor lament their passing.

So that when Manny was reported the next day as having handed himself over to the police, very quietly and with no histrionics confessing that he had crept into his parents' bedroom while they slept, turned on the taps of their little gas fire, made a mound of sheets outside their door to stop up ventilation, and slipped out of the house, I felt that it was my guilt he had owned up to.

THREE

Superman grew out of our feelings about life . . . this tremendous feeling of compassion that Joe and I had for the downtrodden.

Jerry Siegel, co-creator of Superman

1

I didn't go to Manny's trial. Why should I have? I wasn't his friend. I was in America at the time, getting over Chloë and trying to interest the *New Yorker* in my cartoons. Absurd. I should have been in San Francisco talking to the publishers of *Zap*. I had known about the underground comic revolution since my student days, and had even ripped off some early Robert Crumb for a rag-week publication. Whatever contradictions fuelled, or at this time failed to fuel my cartooning, I would have been better throwing in my lot with overt rudery and dysfunction, rather than trying to gain acceptance from the effete mob that ran the *New Yorker*. But I was an English Jew – that was my dysfunction – and somehow English Jews have had all the rudery squeezed out of them.

My only contact with the *New Yorker* was Yolanda Eitinger, a fact-checker with no sense of the ridiculous who had once been married to someone I'd palled out with at art college. A bigamist. Not Yolanda, the man she thought she'd married. When Yolanda found out the truth she returned to New York, combed her hair down in front of her face, doubled the thickness of her lenses, and fact-checked the life out of every piece that landed on her desk. 'I've got a portfolio of funnies with me,' I told her over the phone, 'but I'm not bringing them in if you're going to set about checking their veracity.'

'Cartoons aren't my department,' she told me, meaning she would if she could.

Yolanda was what we call a farkrimteh. A sourpuss. Try any sort of play in the company of Yolanda and she turned so nervous – sometimes going as far as to shield her face with her arm – she made you feel you'd opened a window and let a bat in. Even over the phone you could hear her covering her head.

But at least she honoured our old connection by fixing me an introduction to a junior editor who, like so many New Yorkers in the arts, got his dress sense from the novels of Ivy Compton-Burnett. Irving, he was called. Mellifluously spoken, over-shaved, and in the custody of his polka-dot bow tie. Where it led, Irving followed. Like Yolanda, Irving also looked anxious when someone released a joke into the room. But being a man, he didn't hide his face.

Over a faux English sandwich at a faux English club he tried explaining to me what made Thurber humorous.

'Desperation,' I interrupted him.

'I beg yours?'

'What made Thurber humorous was desperation. Only I don't think the word for it is humor exactly. It's not humor when you're at the end of a rope. What makes Thurber funny is that you smell death in every sentence he wrote and despair in every line he drew.'

Since Irving didn't think anything made me funny I reckoned I was lucky to get the sandwich out of him. But for everyone being jittery about flying anywhere in the aftermath of the Yom Kippur War, I'd have caught a plane back to London that night. Instead I went to a peep show on 42nd Street, paid a girl five dollars a second to let me fondle her through a couple of holes in the wall, and asked her to guess what I did with my hands. 'You fondle broads,' she guessed. 'Wrong,' I told her, 'I draw cartoons.' 'Like Disney?' 'No, like Thurber.' 'Who's Thurber?' 'A great and very desperate man.' 'Did he like fondling broads?' 'I suspect he never tried.' 'His loss.'

My point exactly.

Before she'd relieved me of every dollar in my wallet, she wondered if I ever did cartoons for *Playboy*. 'Little Annie Fanny – something tells me you'd be good at that.'

The minx!

Uncannily prescient of her, though. In a desperate hour I'd tried sending some of my work to Hefner, only to be told by one of his editors that they had their team and that I was too English for it anyway. A man should count his blessings. Little Annie Fanny broke the balls of Harvey Kurtzman, the great American illustrator who founded *Mad*. Kurtzman, I happened to know, had cut his teeth as an assistant on the *Classics Illustrated Moby-Dick*, a picture book I had especially loved as a boy. Boys get the symbolism of that maddened pursuit, the White Whale's infernal aforethought of ferocity, and all that spumescence. So it was painful, however low my opinion of *Mad*, to think of Kurtzman selling his soul to Mammon and not even being happy in the process. A fastidiousness around money I must have picked up from my father and his trade union pals. And maybe a fastidiousness around American Jewish cartoonists as well. I cared for them without knowing them. Probably because I knew I had denied them in my English Jewish heart, and wished – for my own sake as much as theirs – I hadn't.

That I had gone to New York in order to deny Manny in my heart is a charge I would have repudiated at the time, but I am not so certain now. The line I spun myself was that he had been the friend of that period of my life from which few friendships survive. No one remembers the kids they collected stamps or exchanged cigarette cards with, why should I remember Manny? But in fact I did remember Manny, even if the memory was an embarrassment to me. And there, I guess, lay the dishonesty. I did not want to have been the friend of a nutter. Criminal I could have coped with, religious nutter, no. So I closed my ears to the conduct and the outcome of his trial. I chose not to know. In that, I was no different from the rest of our community. He was for all of us – the Orthodox no less than the secular – the Jew we didn't want to acknowledge as our own. He was a throwback, and we were moving on. As time itself was moving on. The crime had been committed more than a year before. Sensational when it first broke, it was stale news now, and had been superseded by more interesting events. Enough. 'Enough,' as Tsedraiter Ike put it, 'with giving satisfaction to the anti-Semites. Just lock the meshuggener away.' And it wasn't as though there was any uncertainty as to the trial's outcome. By his own confession, Manny had done what he had done and would go to prison or a lunatic asylum for it. He had told the police he was following the example of the Austrian-born euthanasiast and flautist Georg Renno, deputy director of the SS gassing institution at Hartheim. On his belated arrest in 1961, Renno, wondering what all the fuss was about, had made a statement for which his name would always be remembered. 'Turning the tap on,' he said, 'was no big deal.' It was in order to verify this claim that Manny had turned the tap on while his parents were asleep. Renno was wrong, he said in his statement. Turning the tap on *was* a big deal. These were the grounds on which Manny's lawyers successfully argued that his mind must have been impaired by abnormality. No normal person, however engrossed in the history of the Holocaust, would have taken research to quite such lengths.

In secular Crumpsall we had our own layman's understanding of what was wrong with Manny. I am not talking about the specific circumstances, or what we assumed in a gossipy sort of way to be the specific circumstances, leading up to the murder: the unhappiness which Asher had unloosed on his family when he took up with the fire-yekelte all those years ago; the rows so violent they could have raised the dead; the ignominy that seemed to stain the Washinskys for ever after, even though Asher himself vanished from the neighbourhood and not a word of the fire-yekelte was heard again; the shame that emanated from their very house, as though it too hung its head and shrank from any form of discourse with the world; the sense we had of their morale rotting away from the inside, so that the final catastrophe felt like the operation of inevitability, fate or nature exacting its price, a tragedy which, when it happened, we all could say had been waiting to happen. These were the incidentals, or even, if you like, the trigger for Manny's monumental act. But they didn't explain what was wrong with Manny — what ailed his soul — only why what was wrong with him happened to take the form it did. And what was wrong with Manny was that he was Manny. His abnormalities were intrinsic to his religious observance. To believe as the Washinskys believed was itself a derangement. They had visited this derangement on both their sons who visited it back on them. One ran for it, the other stayed. No other enquiry into cause or motivation was necessary. The mystery wasn't why Manny had done what he had done but why all Orthodox Jewish boys positioned as he was — Jewish boys who hadn't run away — weren't doing the same.

In all my Crumpsall years I never once met a Jew, however sceptical, who didn't — as it were for special occasions — believe a *bit*. Even Big Ike, who was rumoured to have flirted with satanism, became a believer for his daughter Irene's wedding, wearing a yarmulke inside the house and taking Hebrew lessons so that he could read grace-after-meals (the long version) at the ceremony. By the time Irene came back from her honeymoon in Rimini he was — to everyone's relief — rumoured to be dancing round a goat on Pendle Hill again. We looked indulgently on such flirtations with the faith, so long as they were fleeting. It made perfect sense that when it came to the big events — birth, marriage, death — everyone should believe a little. But believing a lot — only madmen did that.

Thus the conviction of religion's inherent lunacy in which I was cradled.

Behold then, as we beheld him, the late Selick Washinsky, humped at his sewing machine in the front window of his house, mole blind, white as a worm, sewing furs. Indulge my genius for racial stereotypy. See him bent, airless, avid, not a light shining behind or above him, saving money – better to ruin his eyes than pay an electricity bill – his body wrapped in shawls, his lips moving silently to intone the God in fear of whom he lays himself down to sleep each night beside his mostly ritually unclean wife (twice a month, is it, that she's permissible? twice a month, and the rest of the time a river of polluted blood), a stunted growth of perturbations not a man, the ruination of his sons to whom he bequeathed not a single grace, a blot on the clean sheet my father imagined for us, a stumbling block on the route of our great march westwards, a shame – a shande – to our people.

Piffle, all of it, but that's how I was brought up to see him and continue to remember him.

He was pale, no more. Pale and poor. As for the greedy blindness of him, a sewing machine does that. It makes you pinched of sight, it makes you peer and stoop and count. Put any man behind a sewing machine and he will resemble an old myopic Jew stitching furs for profit. The mistake was to stitch them in his window. But it could have been that he was lonely and wanted to see the world.

Wouldn't that be sad, if all along old man Washinsky had wanted nothing more than to look out upon the varied life he had taught his family to go in fear of?

I don't believe I invented the furs. Nor the big car with tinted windows, blacker than a hearse, which slunk into our street to collect them each morning, a needlessly surreptitious exchange, as though there was no relish in the activity unless it appeared illicit – so many lined pelts smuggled out like human remains in unmarked Rexine travelling bags, so many waiting to be lined smuggled in through Selick Washinsky's back door. As for the other stereoJew behind the wheel, evil-looking, extortionate, puffing at his cigar, I never saw him. But our socialist visitors must have. Or at least they deduced him from his hush-hush Wotan's chariot motor vehicle. 'Sweated labour' they called the transaction, shaking the words from their fingers as though they were the poisoned perspiration beads of Capital itself.

What dandies they were, these commie cronies of my father, in their long coats and white scarves, their wavy hair combed back from their foreheads, their handsome faces shown boldly to the world, their moustaches bristling with universalist ambition, boulevardiers (never mind that there were no boulevards in Manchester) and brigadiers (for some had actually fought with the International Brigade against Franco's fascists before they signed up again to polish off Hitler's), men of intellect and bohemianism in the week, who on Saturdays and Sundays turned up to collect my father, and incidentally eye up my mother, sporting knee-length shorts and knapsacks, the living proof that Jews too could hike and ramble and love the country. What lungs they had, these all-talking, all-walking, un-Asianised, de-Bibled Jews. There was scarcely air left for me to breathe when five or more of them were gathered in our house, so much of it did they inhale. The new Jew, straight of back and undevious of principle, with pollen in his hair.

Of these, the straightest-backed and most weather-beaten of them all was 'Long John' Silverman, ex-infantryman and now upholsterer, unexceptional in having left school when he was fourteen and breathing in his politics on the shop floor, a functionary of the Young Communist League whose Cheetham Hill headquarters were just around the corner from us, as was his workshop, which made it handy for him to pop in whenever he felt that too much of the flock with which he stuffed his cushions had gone into his chest and he needed tea to break it down. 'Thank you, Comrade,' he would say to my mother from his great height, taking the teacup from her as though they were both giants playing house, dunking a biscuit into it, then slowly unfurling himself on to our leather couch, or better still into one of the deckchairs in our backyard no matter that snow lay all about – at six feet four-and-a-half inches an irrefutable demonstration of how tall a Jew could grow if only allowed the space. No sooner settled, 'Long John' Silverman would read aloud from the diaries he'd been keeping since his fourteenth year, diaries which he would sometimes subpoena me to illustrate – now with a humpbacked rabbi, now with a paunchy plutocrat or snarling blackshirt – the whole point of his jottings being that it was the former who softened up the Jewish people for the latter, a nexus between religion, finance, appeasement, fascism and exploitation which was as clear to me as day so long as Silverman spoke, but which unwound like the speaker himself the minute he was gone.

Silverman had two brothers, one older, one younger. A third – 'Long John''s identical twin – had died at Normandy. Too big a target. Not my joke, 'Long John' Silverman's. It was either joke or put your eyes out. Bunny, the younger, had his own band, The Silver Lining Trio, which had once played at every Jewish wedding in Manchester, from the lowest to the highest, until one Sunday evening in the ballroom of the Midland Hotel, hired to provide musical accompaniment to the engagement of the daughter of the backward-looking Director-General of the Board of Deputies to the son of a hyphenated Jewish Tory MP who rode to hounds with the South Herefordshire hunt, Bunny followed the loyal toast with the 'Red Flag' played to ragtime.

They all worked on the same principle, the Silverman men. It was either joke or put your eyes out. In this case it was both. But the Trio still operated, and gave pleasure, at the more modest end of the market.

Bunny Silverman visited us less often than his oldest brother Rodney, who, as a librarian, was the nearest to a scholar of all my father's friends. He had boxed a little in his time, which was partly what endeared him to my father, but his chief claim to everybody's respect was that the *Manchester Guardian* published his letters. He wore spectacles like Trotsky's and one day took me into a corner to show me that they served no magnifying purpose whatsoever.

'So they're just plain glass?'

'Correct, Comrade.'

'Why?'

He was a staccato man with a machine-gun laugh. When he took hold of your arm, which he did often, he rattled you to your soul.

'Why do you think, Max?'

'Effect?'

'Exactly. You've got to scare the bastards, it's the only way.'

'Do they work?'

'You tell me. When were you last beaten up by fascists, crypto-Nazis, choirboys, girls from the convent down the road, or other roving bands of anti-Semitic thugs?'

I pretended to think about it. 'Not for a very long time,' I said.

'Well, there you are then – they work!'

Another time, after he'd been in America on union work, he warned me against taking up comic-book illustrating as a career. 'I've seen what it's like over there,' he said. 'You might as well be on a conveyor belt sewing buttons. The bastards work you all hours, they pay you what they want to pay you, and you don't even hold the copyright of your own drawings.'

'I don't want to do comics, I want to do cartoons,' I said.

He put his glasses on my nose. 'What do you see?' he asked me.

'I see you.'

He took them off me and returned them to his own nose. 'I'll tell you what I see,' he said. 'I see penury, starvation and loneliness.'

Then he gave me sixpence from his pocket.

I worshipped the Silvermans but I can't pretend it wasn't confusing, having to remember from one minute to the next who the bastards were, the anti-Semites who were hell-bent on beating up every Jew they could lay their hands on, or ourselves for being so Jewish that the anti-Semites noticed.

It was the Silvermans who introduced Elmore Finkel, mountaineer and Christmas decoration manufacturer (mainly crêpe paper), to my father, thereby adding something elfin to an otherwise largely muscular and broad-shouldered group. Elmore Finkel was dainty, light on his feet — much lighter than my mother with whom he liked to dance in the living room to the radio, regardless of the direction of the conversation. He sang semi-professionally in the first half of the year, when the crêpe paper and Christmas decoration business was slow, usually with The Silver Lining Trio, a sweet Al Bowlly tenor which, in the days before sophisticated amplification, you could barely hear. This made him especially popular at Jewish events where, though people wanted music, they didn't care to have it interfering with their food. As a youngster, Elmore Finkel had accompanied the legendary Benny Rothman on his famous Kinder Scout mass trespass, sharing the beliefs of many Manchester Jewish communists that the issue of access to moorland and mountains was crucial to their fight against the ruling classes. In the course of his assault on Kinder Scout, Elmore Finkel received a blow on the head from a gamekeeper's stick, twisted his ankle in a fall, was arrested by a member of the Derbyshire constabulary, and only didn't face trial because of his age. 'And a good job too,' he told me countless times, though the trespass predated me by a decade at least, 'given that the jury comprised three captains, three colonels, two majors, two brigadier generals, and a partridge in a pear tree had they been able to find one who owned land. Be pleased your father wasn't there, I'm telling you – he'd have flattened the lot of them.'

He smiled all the time, Elmore Finkel, which was one of the reasons I liked him. Everything amused him, including his own boy-soprano features – something of the cup-bearer to Jove about him – which he exploited shamelessly, flashing his baby teeth and forever tossing a lock of chrome-coloured hair from his face. Since the Kinder Scout trespass, he had confined his climbing (and his leg-breaking, he joked) to Switzerland from which he always seemed to return with splinters of glacier in his eyes, and where – as I understood it from him at least – he sat on the top of mountains and read Wordsworth and Lenin aloud to extravagantly beautiful shikseh waitresses with golden pigtails down to their tocheses (no one ever said arse in this gathering, it was always toches) who repaid him with free Glühwein and he wasn't prepared to tell me what else.

'You want to to take the Jewishness out of a Jew – stick him on a cold mountain,' was Elmore's philosophy. 'There ain't no Yahweh when you get to the top of Mont Blanc.'

'Ain't no Yahweh, ain't no Yahweh,' I remember Bunny singing to the tune of 'Hold that Tiger', beating the rhythm out on my mother's cello-shaped walnut display cabinet.

'Yes, but just don't stick him with other Jews,' my resolutely argumentative father said. 'You know what happens when you get ten Jews together . . . they form a minyan and start davening.'

(Like here, I thought.)

'Not on Mont Blanc, Jack.'

'Even on Mont Blanc. *Especially* on Mont Blanc. Break them up, that's the only way.' Rodney, the librarian, had recently lent him the memoirs of some Jewish army chaplain serving in the First World War in France and he was full of the chaplain's observations about Jews quickly losing their Jewishness in the company of non-Jewish soldiers. 'Do you know what they missed when they got back to their families? Not danger. Not excitement. Not

66

even camaraderie. What they missed was bacon sandwiches.'

'It's what we all miss when we come here,' 'Long John' Silverman laughed. 'Excellent cup of tea, but not a bacon sandwich in sight.'

'Nor will there be,' my mother said, her voice ringing like little bells. Little burnished bronze bells was how I imagined them, the colour of her skin. She loved these afternoons of men as much as I did, a party that neither of us ever wanted to end. 'We draw the line at pig,' she went on. 'Outside the house is one thing. Inside is another. Don't tell me it's illogical. I know it's illogical. But that's just how it is.'

At which 'Long John' Silverman would have inclined his courtly head. No contradicting my mother, for one smile from whom he'd have hiked a thousand miles.

My father, as always, grew impatient. 'Forget the bacon sandwich. Take my point. What does the fact that those Jewish soldiers became less Jewish in a goyisher regiment prove – less Jewish even though they were facing death, think of that – what does it prove if it isn't that Jewishness is tenacious only as a consequence of isolation and confinement? So if we aren't from the egg Jewish and nothing else . . .'

'Is that the egg that goes with the bacon we don't get, Jack?' Bunny again.

'Be serious a minute. If Jewishness is in us only so long as we huddle together, and we huddle together only out of fear of persecution, then we are Jewish only by virtue of that persecution. That's the glue. We're Jews because Jewishness is what's been done to us. It's a religion of victimhood.'

'That's a lot of logic, Jack,' Elmore laughed, 'to arrive at where I put you at the beginning of this conversation, sitting on Mont Blanc.'

'Yes, but to get us to Mont Blanc you have first to open the gates of the ghetto.'

'So why are you here, Jack, surrounded by the Jews who

confirm you in your unredeemed Jewishness?' It doesn't matter who asked that. It was a rhetorical question which they all regularly asked of one another. What were they doing in Cheetham Hill and Crumpsall Park? How come, given everything they believed, they all still lived within wailing distance of synagogues and delicatessens and one another? Why weren't they gone their separate ways, settling into the genteel undulations of Cheshire, or breathing the bracing air of the Peaks, among the white folk?

'Because it's too late for me. It's the future I'm looking to. Shani's future. Maxie's future. Though a fat lot of thanks they'll give me.'

It was always around about this point that someone or other would look at a watch and suggest that we go for a walk while there was still future left. But for all the hiking boots and rucksacks and moorland expectation, people rarely left. It was too comfortable where they were, opening the gates of the ghetto, imagining Jews without Jewishness, dunking biscuits into tea, and looking at my mother.

3

Not true that I wouldn't in the future give thanks to my father for hurrying me out into the Gentile light.

I thought of him and thanked him frequently when I was older, going to art school in South London, dressing like a goyisher housepainter, throwing warm beer down my throat and wooing the likes of Chloë Anderson, the college beauty with the Slavic cheekbones who, on our first date, confused me with an Aaron Blaiwais in the print department, and on our second with an Arnie Rosenfield who sculpted.

'Do you think we are all one person?' I asked her on our third. 'Do we all look the same to you, or do you just like Jews generically?'

Chloë Anderson's finely etched brows arched further from her eyes than most people's, which gave her a look of perpetual disapproval. Her nose, too, was constructed on a disdainful tilt. Everything on her face wanting to be somewhere else, or with someone else. 'To be honest with you,' she said, 'I don't like Jews at all.'

'So what are you doing with me?'

For a moment I thought her brows might come away from her face altogether. 'Penance,' she said.

Was she joking? When I ask myself why I took her to wife, given her hostility to me as a representative of my people (and excluding the obvious: that it was *because* of her hostility to me as a representative of my people), that's the only answer I can come up with – to discover once and for all whether she was joking. And of course (because in my heart I knew she *wasn't* joking) to see if she would remember on the day which of the Jews she didn't like she was marrying.

I thought of my father on my wedding night, when Chloë told me that though she wasn't Catholic she had spent some time at a Catholic school where they had taught her to pray for all the Jews they knew as they were earmarked for eternal damnation. 'Do you mind if I pray for you tonight, darling?' she asked me.

Darling! Was that darling Aaron, darling Arnie, or darling me? And did it matter?

As for the praying, well, yes, that I did mind, actually. She was already on her knees by the bed, her hands folded together like a small child's, her hair tied in a ribbon, naked but for the ring I had bought her and the startlingly explicit silver crucifix with which her mother had presented her to mark our nuptials. It was a shame to interrupt her in her quiveringly voluptuous orisons – her white flesh cathedraled in solemnity, even her breath stilled so as not to offend the silence – but yes, yes I most decidedly did mind.

'Couldn't you leave it until tomorrow night?' I wondered.

'Please yourself,' she said, getting up and blowing out the great white cathedral candles she had bought (presumably from some Catholic book and expiation emporium) especially for the occasion. 'I was only trying to be nice. You'll burn in hell whether I pray for you or not.'

Thank you, Dad, I would say to myself on these and similar occasions. Thank you for the Jew-free start you gave me.

4

Not his fault. And not the fault of the Silvermans and Finkels either. They did what needed doing. They threw open the windows of our closed world, brought Europe into our homes, Europe with its chest out, the grand parades and parks and coffee houses, not the sweatshops of ancient superstition and obedience which my poor friend Manny had been born into, or the airless hovels which it was Tsedraiter Ike's function to remind us of until his dying day.

They were the children, most of them, of venerable anarchist or trade unionist families, heirs to the Jewish strikes of 1880s London, inheritors of the high hopes of revolution that had engulfed Poland, Lithuania, Russia, in the 1880s and 90s, reaching at last even as far as Novoropissik. Some of the older ones, including Rodney Silverman, remembered being carried on the shoulders of strikers – marching the length of the country they would have me believe – their baby voices raised in the cause of higher wages, better working hours, more considerate and less divisive practices, a fairer deal altogether for just such sweatees in the tailoring and cap-making industries as Selick Washinsky. My father's father had been present as a Manchester delegate or observer – spying, stirring, who can say? – at the Great Boot Strike which had broken out in the East End in 1889, ten thousand Jewish journeymen coming out of their cellars and garrets 'like the rats of Hamelin', as he had famously reported it, to protest the sweating system as a crime against 'the ineffable name of Elohim'. A crime also (and to my grandfather a far more serious one) against the indigenous British workers whose jobs were daily being put in jeopardy by alien outworking Jews who wouldn't think twice before undercutting and overtoiling their fellow Hebrews, to say nothing of Gentiles to whom they acknowledged no bond of amity or solidarity. The words of Beatrice Potter, one day to be Beatrice Webb the illustrious Fabian, were embroidered on a pillowcase, like a sampler, by my father's mother and mounted in a flimsy walnut frame which frequently fell apart but which my father always repaired and replaced where we could read it on a wall above the bath – a monument more to Beatrice Potter's research into late-nineteenth-century Jewish immigration than my grandmother's skill with the needle.

We need not seek far for the origin of the
antagonistic feelings with which the Gentile inhabitants
of East London
regard Jewish labour and Jewish trade.
For the Immigrant Jew, though possessed of many
first-class virtues,
is deficient in that highest and latest development of –
SOCIAL MORALITY

Those last two telling words, the badge of our ethnic deficiency, had been picked out by my grandmother in what at the time must have been the reddest of red threads; now, in the humidity of our bathroom, they looped limply in faded pink, like pressed roses found in a spinster's book of commonplaces.

So why over the bath? I never asked him. I think I didn't want to hear the answer. Didn't want to hear him say that it wasn't just the body's daily toll of grime we were to wash away, but something in our natures too.

My family had mixed feelings about this embroidery. That the

71

frame fell apart as often as it did I put down to my mother's hatred of it. It's only a pity that she never had the courage to destroy it altogether, or to form the words that would make my father understand what her hatred of it was about. 'I don't think that's very nice, Jack, I don't think that's a very nice thing to have said about us, not at this particular time in our history anyway,' was the best she could do, and that wasn't good enough to shake my father's resolution.

Tsedraiter Ike despised it too, but he knew better than to express an opinion. Who was he to complain about what hung above the bath? He was lucky to be allowed a bath! What my sister Shani thought I never knew. As an object that wasn't a mirror or a wardrobe, it can hardly ever have fallen within her purview. And as for me, well, I came home from school one afternoon not that long before my father died, found him repairing the frame for the hundredth time, and told him what I thought. 'You know Hitler said something pretty similar, Dad. Why don't we get Shani to embroider a selection from *Mein Kampf*?'

I did well to escape a backhander. I am unable to remember whether he drew the distinction for me between the measured thoughts of a benevolent socialist who kept company with people (my grandfather, for example) who wanted to emancipate the Jews, and the rantings of a psychopathic little bastard who wanted only to annihilate them, but the distinction blazed in his unwell eyes. Wrong son for him, I was. Shame – I'd have liked to be the one he wanted before he died. But the truth of it is that although I loved the socialists and Fabians and Bundists and the rest of them who came to do their exercises in our garden at weekends (and to listen to my mother shout 'Kalooki!' midweek), in my soul I was never much smitten by their philosophies. There was always too much of the excitement of apostasy about them for my taste. Their boldness was the boldness of public self-abuse. I am not saying I can come up with anything better, but then as a cartoonist I don't have to. Ask me, though, as the author of *Five*

Thousand Years of Bitterness, who are the greatest enemies of the Jewish people today, as bad as the Nazis in their hearts, as indurated in their detestation of us, however short they fall in practice – ask me whom I fear the most and I will whisper to you, looking up and down the street, 'socialists, Fabians, Bundists and the rest of them'. A Jewish socialist or Fabian the worst of the lot.

The day after my father died my mother threw Beatrice Potter's words into the dustbin. Beating when she took up kalooki again by more than a week.

The point about 'social morality' anyway is that it hadn't only been in order to protect the Selick Washinskys of the world from unscrupulous sweaters that agitators like my father's father had encouraged Jewish tradesmen to go on strike; it had been to protect all Jews from themselves, to save them from an imput-ation which, true or not, threatened – as witness what eventuated in Germany – their very existence. For our failure to make connections we would pay a heavy price. But that was then. Who, other than a few of my father's firebrand pals, cared about 'social morality' now? Let Selick Washinsky labour all the hours God sent if that was what he chose to do. His lookout if he sold himself cheap. His eyes to ruin. He wasn't putting anyone else out of work. Dark little men in other socially amoral parts of the world were now doing that. You had, though, to call a spade a spade, and the spectacle of him bent over his sewing machine turned all our stomachs.

Why he was such a vexation to us, the kids of the street – not a one of whom was a communist or trade unionist – or such a trouble to our games which he never bothered to observe or threatened to disrupt, I don't know. But so long as he was at his window he bugged us. When we dragged a bin into the road to be a wicket and took guard or ran up to bowl, there he was in the corner of our eye, not an incidental obstacle but the very thing we had to hit, the end and object of our game. Four runs if we smashed the ball into the main road, six if we drove at Washinsky's window, and eight (though that was normally the conclusion of the innings, tantamount to a declaration) if we managed to break it. Similarly with tennis. Traffic was light enough then for us to throw a line across the street and have to take it down only in the early evening, at rush hour when we could expect about three cars to want to come through. Almost peaceful but for disagreements as to whether a ball had gone over the net or under it, and Washinsky concentrating on his needle, ever-present like an umpire with his mind elsewhere. Fifteen-love if your first serve was an ace; thirty-love if you aced it into Washinsky's garden. Game if you got him to look up.

Jew-baiting was what it was. And we were all Jews who were doing it.

And I, who was in a manner of speaking – as someone close to Manny – a friend of the family? I was worse than anybody. I would have goaded him to death had it been in my power to do so. But then I had an excuse. I was close to Manny.

I was the first, anyway, to hit an eight. I'd clattered his window a few times when I'd been at the crease and got him to glare and wave his hands at us, but that summer we'd graduated from a soft to a hard cricket ball – the fearsome corkie which stung your fingers just to look at it – and when you hit a corkie at someone's window there was only one outcome. We heard the glass shatter, clean like a rifle shot at first, and then a sound like a whole city coming apart, whereupon we exchanged looks of triumph mixed with terror, cheered, then ran in different directions, all for none and none for all, leaving the bin in the middle of the road. I don't know how Washinsky knew it was I who struck the ball, maybe he just guessed, maybe he understood the perverse logic that made me, as his son's best friend, his worst enemy, but whatever his reasoning it was me he gave chase to, finally cornering me – no one locking their doors in those days – in the parlour of my own house.

I calculate that it was early summer, one of the long hot evenings of a northern June, because there were not many days in the year when we could have been playing cricket in the street at the same time as my mother was playing kalooki in the parlour. It was one of her quieter schools, no more than half a dozen of her friends plus my sister who had obviously been dragged in to make up the numbers. Shani was sitting at the card table when I made my unmannerly entrance, one leg up, taking advantage of a pause in the proceedings to effect running repairs to the paint on her toenails. She had my mother's lovely narrow legs and ankles, fine as a giraffe's. And the same burnished, aristocratic bearing, even when she was jackknifed in this manner, looking as though she was meaning to suck her own toes. Something of one of Degas's self-absorbed dancers about her. Until the moment she opened her mouth, you would have picked Shani for an Abyssinian princess.

'What's he want?' she said, the first to register me in a sweat and Selick Washinsky in hot pursuit, all the other women being engrossed in totting up their points.

'Shani!' my mother reprimanded her, looking up, 'that's no way to talk.'

Not expecting to have wound up at one of my mother's kalooki nights, Selick Washinsky held up the palms of his hands, as though to stave off whatever irreligious thoughts crowd in on a pious man pursuant to a game of cards and a roomful of women with uncovered heads, all sucking on the little gold pencils my mother never omitted to provide.

'My apologies, Mrs Glickman,' he said, straightening his braces and worrying at the tails of his shirt which had come out of his trousers. 'This is neither the time nor the place. Your boy Max has just deliberately broken my window – after several months of trying, I might add – but I will discuss it with your husband another time.'

Somehow foreign, he sounded. Though he was born in England

and had almost certainly lived here every day of his life, a strange intercontinental Jewishry of inflection, such as the most English of rabbis will employ when on Jewish business – a burring or doubling of an *r* here, a lisping of an *s* there – appeared to take possession of him. Romanian, was it? South African? County Cork with a hint of the Bronsk washed down with Novoropissik?

'At least have some tea,' my mother said, a touch intercontinentally herself, I thought, the condition being infectious. Then, presumably remembering that the Orthodox love kummel – 'a Russian peasant concoction the colour of goat's piss' was how my father liked to describe it – she offered him a peach brandy.

'Do we have peach brandy?' Shani said.

From the other kalooki players, too, expressions of curiosity. Peach brandy? Now you're talking.

But Washinsky was not staying. He touched his hat . . .

More cartoonery. He wore no hat. I cannot make myself see him with his head bare, but bare I believe it was. No hat, no skullcap either. So what did he touch? His ears, I think. He touched his ears as though he had a migraine. Terrible for me now to think I brought a migraine on. A broken window is one thing, but terrible to think I hurt the mind of a man who would one day be murdered by his own son.

He hadn't coloured, I noticed. Though acutely embarrassed, he didn't have the blood to change colour, unless he turned a little yellower. 'Let's say we let it go this time, with a warning,' he said, burring and lisping, backing out, almost bowing, the way he had come. I now realise that the spectacle of my mother's kalooki companions, all made up for the occasion, their hair flagrantly abundant, their eyes afire with the excitement of cards, their faces turned towards him in ironically ladylike surprise, an expectancy of peach brandy moistening their lips, must have been very daunting to him, he a man who I must guess had only ever had intimate knowledge of one woman, she being the unfortunate Mrs Washinsky, a woman of no shape, presence or vitality, though not of course deserving of dying before her time for that.

'Who's *he* warning?' Shani asked, but by then my mother had shown him, with her exaggerated courtesy, out of the house.

The following day my father repaired Washinsky's window then came home and handed me a good hiding.

'We don't do persecution, Max,' he told me.

After which our street games went on as before, with this exception: I felt sheepish about lobbing balls into Washinsky's garden or hitting eights through his window while he was sewing lining into a stole, and managed to avoid doing either – I think without being rumbled by the others – for what remained of the summer.

Manny Washinsky was not, of course, party to these games. Mainly we didn't play together, mainly we talked God, the death camps, and *Five Thousand Years of Bitterness*; but when games were called for and it was just him and me, we'd throw a tennis ball at a penny, trying to get it to flip over, or flick cigarette cards against the wall. The moment anything more communal was afoot he hung back and I did not encourage him to join in. He was weird, I wasn't. He wouldn't stand on lines in the pavement. He never left the house without ringing his own door bell to be sure it still worked, and then ringing it again to be sure he hadn't broken it the last time. Then he would have to try the door, pushing at it with all his might in case he had left it open in his anxiety about the bell. He even did the same with our air-raid shelter though it had no door; he would have to go back every time we left it, once, twice, three times sometimes, to make certain everything was where he'd meant to leave it, the torches pointing in the right direction, our pencils lying as he believed they should lie: his where he sat, mine where I did. Weird! And I didn't want to be thought of as weird by association. Especially by Errol Tobias who bossed the street, who had taken a particular fancy to me as a smart but still naive kid whom he could educate in the ways of the world, and who treated Manny as someone so beneath him he was invisible.

It was Errol Tobias who had first shown me the photographs

that were missing from Manny's copy of *The Scourge of the Swastika*, turning the pages one by one, all the while staring at me and not saying a word, as though he did not want to miss a flicker of my facial reactions or the faintest tremor of my soul.

5

Errol Tobias was the street gardener. He had no skills, he simply ripped stuff out. Weeds, if weeds were specifically what troubled you, but anything and everything was his speciality. Few people did much with their gardens in our street. No feeling for it. Occasionally someone laid off from work essayed a bumpy lawn bordered with lupins; now and then a few geraniums in primary colours appeared; otherwise all our gardens were tangles of privet hedge and ivy which twice a year, during school holidays, Errol Tobias would pull out by the roots for you. He had his own shears, his own barrow, and his own staff. The year he initiated me into *The Scourge of the Swastika* illustrated I was his staff.

As for my salary, it was never discussed. Tacitly, I settled for *The Scourge of the Swastika*, unexpurgated.

Did I say Errol Tobias 'showed' me the missing photographs? Too feeble a verb, 'showed'. He divulged them to me, rather. Like Moses coming down from Sinai with the tablets, he made them manifest to me, inducting me in them, one revelation succeeding another, as though the photographs weren't merely in his possession but had somehow been divinely vouchsafed him, and were now his by metaphysical right.

We were in the long grass of somebody or other's garden. Mrs Margalit's. Mrs Getzler's. They were all the same. The overgrown gardens of people forever on the run. You garden when you can be sure you're staying and the Margalits and Getzlers had not been here long enough to know whether they were staying or not. This was why each generation of Jewish immigrants was scornful of the next, why the German-born Jews who had been here since 1820 looked down their noses at those of us who came from Novoropissik a half-century later, and why we looked down on those who came from places even worse a half-century after that. Every influx reminded us of our antecedents and threatened the fantasy of permanence we'd erected around ourselves like a stockade. In the new arrivals the Gentiles would see who we really were.

Fools, the fools we've been, to suppose they have ever needed reminding.

How long the Tobiases had been here I didn't know. They were hard to pick. By virtue of something in their pigmentation, they could have passed for non-Jews of a lower, somewhat rural station. Not quite pig farmers, more a pig farmer's chauffeur and maid-of-all-work. In fact, Mrs Tobias ran a hairdressing salon in the back room of her house, and other than sneer at her clients in their curlers, Mr Tobias did nothing. Errol, too, had the lewd, obscenely confidential air of a gentleman's gentleman. That moral fastidiousness which is itself indecent. But in the long grass I didn't scruple to be inducted by him into the illustrated *Scourge of the Swastika*. He must have made a good job of it, because not only am I able to remember in considerable detail all the photographs I saw, I am able to remember the order in which I saw them . . .

The charred bodies found in the church at Oradour.

The slaughter at Autun.

The village of Lidice, quiet in the snow, like a Brueghel winter-scape.

Then Lidice after the massacre, the buildings ripped apart, the bodies lined up on their backs for all the world as though they are schoolkids on the gym floor, waiting for permission to get up again.

The photograph of a mass execution found on a German prisoner.

Birkenau before the crematorium was built, the naked bodies smoking in pits.

Patriots hanged at Tulle, the German officers smiling.

Arbeit Macht Frei – the gateway to Auschwitz.

A crematorium oven at Buchenwald, with a charred skull inside.

The disfigured limbs of human guinea pigs at Auschwitz.

The pile of discarded artificial limbs taken from victims of the gas chambers.

Ilse Koch. Ilse Koch, wife of the commandant of Buchenwald, not looking as enticing after her capture (this a judgement made with the benefit of hindsight) as she did before it.

Below, a couple of the shrunken heads said to have been commissioned by her for her collection.

Josef Kramer's driving licence.

The confession of Rudolf Hess – 'I personally arranged on orders received from Himmler in May 1941 the gassing of two million persons . . .'

A mass grave at Belsen – the bodies almost beautiful in their abstraction, that's if you dare let your eye abstract in such a place.

The British soldier with a kerchief over his nose, bulldozing those abstractions to clear the camp.

Corpses by the wagonload at Buchenwald – boots, feet, faces, the inspiration for Philip Guston's distracted cartoons of ignominy and death (there is, you see, a place for great cartoonery, even here).

And finally and most famously and shamelessly, the one we looked at longest, the naked Jewish women being paraded for medical inspection, running across the prison yard while the German guards, some with their hands in the pockets of their uniforms, look on. My first sighting, God forgive me, of pubic hair in print.

If I am not mistaken this last photograph is among those which Orthodox Jews in Israel, following the earlier example of Manny Washinsky's parents, have petitioned to be removed from public display. Not to be shown anywhere, not for whatever educative purpose, not even in Yad Vashem. It affronts, they say, the modesty of the women, thereby implying that modesty is something that might live after you. A woman's immortal modesty. I agree with them. The photograph should not be shown. It certainly should not have been shown to me or to any other boy my age. I would rather not have been aroused by it. Yes, even in the most careful household, a boy is always in with a chance of seeing more of flesh and bone and hair than is good for him to see, but an actual sighting, at speed and in confusion, is not the same as a photograph on which one can rest one's eyes for all eternity. It was unwelcomely arousing, too, without a doubt, to share the experience with Errol in the long grass. Whatever else we knew, we knew we should not have been looking. Because what might just have been most arousing of all was our knowledge that the women were petrified, perhaps about to be subjected to all the degradations a boy's imagination can invent, death being among the kinder of them.

And if you think that denotes derangement you should have heard what Errol had to tell me about Buchenwald in the days of Ilse Koch, the cock-shrinker.

Don't I mean the head-shrinker?

Yes, that too.

6

Ach Buchenwald ich kann dich nicht vergessen
Weil du mein Schicksal bist.

O Buchenwald, I can't forget you,
Because you are my fate.

'Buchenwaldlied'

They sang songs in Buchenwald. Figure that.

A mystery to me, who found it hard enough to sing in Crumpsall Park. True, they were ironic songs about *Schicksal*, but a song's still a song.

Schicksal – meaning fate or destiny.

Shikse – meaning floozie. From which shikseh – meaning Gentile girl. Otherwise, wife to Maxie Glickman.

They used to say that character was destiny, but now they know that language is.

So shiksehs were my destiny.

'I am not,' Chloë said, the day she left me, 'your floozie.'

'My daughter is not—' Chloë's mother said.

'I know what she is not,' I interrupted, 'she is not my floozie.'

'That she certainly is not.'

'Say goodbye, then,' I said.

'Goodbye.'

I was sorry to part from her. Leaving women's mothers was always harder for me than leaving the women themselves. Somehow more final when you leave the mothers. And I'd grown attached to Chloë's mother, Helène, in an equilibrium-of-detestation sort of way. I hated the way she would say, when we were staying with her, or she was staying with us, 'I will be saying goodnight now – goodnight.' And she hated everything about me.

After she had said she would be saying goodnight, and saying it, she would add that she was going 'up the little wooden hill to Bedfordshire'. Should that have annoyed me to the extent it did? She came from Cheshire, naturally from Cheshire I mean, not as a newly moneyed import. People just talked like that there. Genteel Southern-Northern cute. It was what you signed up for when you fell in love with cutesie genteel Gentile girls from the Southern North – their cutesie genteel Gentile mums. Part of the appeal of the daughter, a mother who wore knitted frocks to show off her 'figure', white or knitted stockings, sometimes white *and* knitted stockings, nipped-in waist, little perky acorn tits in padded bras, the smell of the racecourse in her hair, and a cutesie country turn of phrase. Exactly what a shikseh-loving Yiddler from the inner city should have thanked the Almighty for giving him as a ma-in-law, you'd have thought. 'Gott tsu danken. Now equip me with the male equivalent of cutesie country Gentile tits and I will think that I am an English person born.' But I didn't have it in me to accept my good fortune and make peace with it. I couldn't rest – night after night I got no sleep – until I was able to match my mother-in-law's little wooden hill to Bedfordshire with some odious genteel Gentile punning cosiness of my own. I ransacked the English counties. Sussex, Essex, Cornwall, Devon, Leicestershire, Cheshire itself. Nothing. What I needed was a county called Hell. 'Why don't you be off down the little wooden hill to Hellshire, Helène?' Or a town called Blazes. 'Hey, Helène, how about going to Blazes for the weekend?' Though neither of those, I grant you, would have been a patch on the inspired inanity of Bedfordshire.

Then, at the sleepy-byes end of one particularly irksome evening *à trois*, to employ another Helènism – I was doomed in this marriage either to be *à trois* or on my ownio – I believed I'd hit the jackpot. We'd been playing fish, the card game where you have to remember the whereabouts of downturned cards, and then match them with upturned cards, a game at which I happen to excel, something Helène and Chloë put down to Semitic deviance of the brain.

'So clever in all the small things of life, your husband, Chlo.'

'It's in the genes, Mama. Terminal triviality to genius level. It's why they make such good accountants.'

'Too true, I wouldn't trust my stockings and shares to anyone else. Ho-hum, well, I'll be saying goodnight now, goodnight.'

At which moment, espying her heading in the direction of retirement with a volume of G. K. Chesterton in her hand (if it wasn't Chesterton it was Belloc, and don't ask me what stopped her taking the annotated English countrywoman's *Letters of Heinrich Himmler* up to Bedfordshire), something induced me to call out, 'Off up the little wooden hill to Buchenwald, are we?'

Chloë was outraged. 'Max!'

'What?'

'How dare you talk to my mother like that!'

'Like what?'

'How dare you wish my mother in a concentration camp!'

'Book,' I said. '*Book*enwald, for fuck's sake.'

'Leave it,' Helène shouted down. 'He spent his formative years in Dewsbury, remember.'

'Jewsbury!' I shouted back. 'Did you just say Jewsbury?'

But she'd won again. I knew that. She was mistress of the gazetteer of the British Isles, to whatever end of phobia and whimsy, and that was that. A man must know when he is beaten. A man must accept his *Schicksal*.

And I accepted mine.

7

We like a thread in my business. We like a leitmotif. Strip cartoonists more than one-offers of the sort I am, but then *Five Thousand Years of Bitterness*, when you come to think of it, was a strip cartoon of sorts.

So let's run with maps and gazetteers, a recurrent theme in my life, anyway, considering that I met Björk (who later introduced me to Kätchen) in a map shop in Covent Garden, and wouldn't have got to know Zoë had Kätchen not walked out on me after a row about her navigation skills.

And then there was Shitworth Whitworth MA, senior geography master at Bishops Blackburn Grammar School . . .

For one year Manny and I were at Bishops Blackburn together. After which his parents took him away. He did well, I reckon, to last a year, given how ill they accommodated even a Jew of my milk-and-water sort, let alone one who held to Manny's rigid and irrational system of beliefs. I am not accusing the staff at Bishops Blackburn of being anti-Semitic. They simply had us on the brain. When they beheld us, and in fairness there were quite a lot of us to behold for a school with strong Church of England associa-

84

tions, they could see nothing but the Jew in us. I am the same. But then I'm a caricaturist: I am meant to concentrate only on what's salient. Whereas our teachers were meant to see us all round. They tried. I sincerely believe they had the best intentions. But when they looked at us all round they saw even more Jew than when they looked at us on one plane.

'Can someone tell me how come a Jew can't draw a map?' was the question that precipitated the row that finally precipitated Manny Washinsky from the school. The question issuing from Shitworth Whitworth MA, a sarcastic man who appeared to have been overwound, whose skin vibrated like a percussion instrument when he was upset, and who owned the biggest collection of detachable stiff white collars, always worn with blue and pink striped shirts, and always half a size too tight, any of us had ever seen.

Geography. Most ethnic troubles in most schools originate in geography or PE. They do for Jews, anyway, who can neither draw a map nor hang upside down from a wall bar. The two deficiencies are not entirely unrelated. Jews cannot draw a map nor negotiate a wall bar because they have seldom had any use for either.

To that degree, Shitworth had said nothing that wasn't just. True, he should not have held up Manny's suppurating map of Canada by one corner as though it were something one of us had brought in on his shoe. Nor should he have declared that a spider with a pen in each leg could have drawn it better, nor rolled it into an inky ball and thrown it into Manny's distorted face. Nor should he have eared Manny out of his seat and demanded what he was grinning about, boy, when it ought to have been obvious to a teacher of his years and competence that Manny grinned out of some strange reflexive instinct, the alternative being a total collapse of his facial musculature, followed by annihilation of his personality and maybe even cessation of his or someone else's heartbeat. Teacherly ineptitudes, those. You are meant to know when you have a homicidal maniac in your class. But fair's fair – it was the case that none of us who were Jewish could draw a map. Even I couldn't draw a map and I had already been picked out as the school's star drawer. It's possible that we'd have fared better had the maps Shitworth asked us to draw contained matter more germane to our interests and experience. Of the atlases I presently own, a good 90 per cent of them are atlases of Jewish migrations, expulsions, marches, pogroms, ghettos, shtetls with names like Kalooki and Kalush, ruined synagogues, graveyards, inquisitions, executions, massacres, gas chambers, concentration camps. We know whereby we are engaged. 'Do me a map showing the most recent liquidation of your people, Glickman,' might have elicited a positive response. The corn belts of Manitoba on the other hand . . .

Fair or not fair, Shitworth Whitworth was the recipient by 9 a.m. the following morning of a letter from the parents of every Jewish boy in the school, even mine – something I admired in my father; his utter inconsistency in all matters relating to criticism of Jews – the sum content of which was as follows:

Mr Shitworth sir dear sticks in the gullet insensitive not to say offensive not to say ignorant of catastrophic Jewish history otherwise would understand inability to draw map tragic consequence of being homeless people without choice as to domicile for almost as long as you you anti-Semitic bastard have been teaching geography proof of Jewish genius otherwise in arts Chagall Sigmund Freud Sammy Davis Jr [not to forget, in my parents' letter, Maxie Glickman] whose shoes you not fit to lick you telling me Chagall couldn't have drawn Canada had he been so minded yours faithfully.

Why Shitworth couldn't have let it go at that, since no one was asking more of him than a grovelling apology, I will never understand. Instead, the next time an ill-executed Jewish map of maize fields in the Americas provided him with the opportunity, he held it up by one corner, screwed it into a ball again, threw it at me, because it was mine, but missed and hit Manny Washinsky again, for which he also did not apologise, and said, 'It has recently been brought to my attention that the Twelve Tribes of Israel have not sat still long enough to find the time to consult an atlas or otherwise acquaint themselves with the lineaments of the physical world. Wouldn't you have thought, boys, that the opposite would be true, and that our Hebrew brethren's love of foreign travel would have encouraged curiosity in them as to the contours of every country they have visited?'

'Not exactly "visited" sir,' I found the courage to pipe up, since my map was the cause of this.

Watching Shitworth Whitworth trying to swallow under the constriction of his collars was one of the few consolations our twice-weekly hour of geography afforded. Would his stud fly off, or would his Adam's apple burst? This time it looked as though his whole chest was about to explode, like the Incredible Hulk's coming out of his shirt.

He had advanced upon me, isolating me from the class. The whole of him compressed into the two fists he placed with great deliberation upon my desk, first one, and then the other, like grenades.

'Not *exactly visiting*, weren't you, Glickman? So what *exactly* were you doing?'

'Running away, sir.'

'Ah, running away. And now, here? Struggling against persecution, are you?'

'No, sir.'

'Are you saying you are a prisoner here, Glickman? Are you here under duress?'

I didn't have the language – you never have the language when you need it – to talk spatiality to him, to tell him that I thought it unreasonable of Gentiles to complain that Jews were always in constant motion, incapable of the arts of repose, when it was they, the Gentiles, who were forever moving Jews on. 'No, sir,' was all I could find to say, instead.

He closed his eyes, as though praying to God (his, not ours) to give him strength. Then he opened them and sniffed.

'You're a cartoonist, aren't you, Glickman?'

'I hope to be one, sir, yes.'

A cartoonist, you see, not a landscape painter or gardener or cartographer. Agitation, satire, distortion, not the beauty of the visible world humming exquisitely on its axis.

'You hope to be one? Good. I hope you to be one too. And no doubt as part of your education to that end you will be studying other examples of the art. I assume you are familiar, Glickman, with the Katzenjammer Kids?'

I was. Though not exactly an enthusiast. Brilliantly drawn though they were, they made me feel queasy. Something to do with the undigested immigrant nature of the knockabout. Hans and Fritz the kids were called, and something about those names made me feel queasy too.

I nodded.

'Zen in ze immortal vords of ze Katzenjammers, Glickman, let me put zis proposition to you. Could it be zat ze reason you and your fellow Chews feel so unvelcome in country after country is zat you do not do your hosts ze courtesy of noticing vere you are? As for example, Glickman – and you, Vashinsky – by consulting a map?'

I knew a rhetorical question when I heard one. As did Shitworth Whitworth. 'And now I suppose you will all go home and get your parents to write me another letter?' he said, rather sadly suddenly, like a man reading out his resignation speech.

8

He was gone by the end of the week. Put over someone's knee and thrashed, it was fun to think, like the Katzenjammer Kids receiving their leitmotif beating from Mama Katzenjammer. Manny and I drew a map of hell and posted it to him care of the school. But whether he received it or not we were never to discover.

A term later Manny was gone too, removed to a Jewish school at the other side of town, where it didn't matter how bad you were at cartography so long as you put your tefillin on every morning. So there are deficiencies in all systems of education.

I can't pretend I was sorry to see Manny leave. Having him as a friend in our air-raid shelter was one thing. He was my private life. But as such he no more belonged in my class than my mother did. Besides, I felt that my association with him was doing me no good. He was too odd. Four, five, six times a day he put his hand up and asked to be excused. No boy at Bishops Blackburn – maybe no boy in the *history* of Bishops Blackburn – needed to go to the lavatory as often as Manny Washinsky. And once he was there he wouldn't return. Mainly we would all forget about him, but occasionally his absence would rile a teacher who would then send one of us, occasionally even a party of us, to search for him and bring him back. Reports of Manny-sightings in the lavatories varied. Some told of Manny sitting in a cubicle with his trousers fastened, reciting Jewish prayers. Others heard him swearing, though I never did. Fuck, fuck, fuck, fuck, fuck, fuck, fuck . . . just that, over and over. One person said he'd watched from a distance while for fifteen minutes Manny washed and rewashed his hands, sometimes no sooner drying them than going back and washing them again, pulling back the skin at the tip of his fingers so that the scalding water could get under his nails. Another said he saw Manny winding toilet paper from a roll and stuffing his pockets with it. Thieving toilet paper, could you believe that? Jewing it. The one time I was sent to get him I found him sitting on the toilet with his jacket covering his head – this, as he explained to me later, to stop anyone who was standing on a seat in another cubicle from looking down and recognising him. 'But who'd bother to do that?' I asked him. 'Well, you just have,' he reminded me.

To be absolutely candid, I didn't consider Manny's behaviour around his ablutions to be anything like as bizarre as others did. Far more peculiar, in my view, was the casual attitude the Gentile pupils of Bishops Blackburn adopted to the inconveniences of the body, their carelessness as to privacy and hygiene, the small circumstantial, not to say spiritual difference pissing and shitting seemed to make to them. That they didn't understand why a person might take precautions as regards taps and switches, etc, I also attributed to the absence in them of any imagination of disaster. As for praying or cursing in the lavatory, while I would not have been able to explain *why* Manny did it, *that* he did it surprised me not at all. I cursed or otherwise called on God whenever I visited the lavatory myself. The relief of finding sanctuary? The fear of loneliness? Sheer existential astonishment? Who knows. But it was second nature to me to say 'Jesus fucking Christ!' the moment I undid my trousers, or, when I had finished and was looking at my reflection in the mirror, 'God fucking help me!' Half the time I did not not even know I was saying anything, and only confronted the phenomenon years later when Zoë overheard me and made me promise on my life never to swear or call on God in the toilet so long as we shared one. It was also her belief that I should accompany her to a clinical psychologist that minute.

For her sake, because of the love I bore her, I refused the psychologist, but forswore the swearing. Only on the night she left me did I revert, looking long at my reflection in the mirror, little by little recognising someone I thought I had seen the last of, and hearing him cry out 'God fucking help me!'

At school, though, and in the glare of classroom publicity, I found Manny as weird as everybody did and disowned him. I wanted to be with the more normal kids, like Errol Tobias, who famously Chinese-burned the neck of the school bully –

Broderick 'The Bull' Chisnall – leaving him with orange-coloured striations visible above the collar of his shirt for the rest of his days at Bishops Blackburn. It was Broderick 'The Bull' Chisnall who used to order any stray Jew he found in the playground at the end of break to stand with his hands on his head for forty minutes, and not move until Broderick released him hypnotically with the words, 'Jew, Jew, run away, till Broderick gets you another day.' It is mortifying to recall how many of us did what Broderick told us to do, standing in the rain and freezing cold, trying to count the 2,400 seconds in forty minutes in case we missed the hypnotic release. Because for us to be found by Broderick still standing there *after* the expiry of the forty minutes was no less serious an offence than to be caught trying to escape *before* it. Broderick would probably have tyrannised us without detection, or without anyone much caring even had he been detected – for ours was a school which believed in the manly virtues of bullying and being bullied – had he not tried it on with Errol Tobias. Though he was half Broderick 'The Bull' Chisnall in height and weight, Errol had the beating of him in the beserk department. It was over in seconds, like one of those filmed encounters between an anaconda and a field mouse. Broderick made as though to touch Errol's arm and the next thing he was lying on the playground the colour of jam roly-poly with Errol twisting his head off. I later drew the encounter to please Errol, with Broderick 'The Bull' Chisnall walking in one direction and his head facing in the other. A bit Disney for me, and probably for Broderick, but Errol liked it.

The other advantage Errol enjoyed over Manny as a friend was his sexual precocity. By our third year at Bishops Blackburn Errol was the organiser of a ring of onanists who, on his instructions, kept diaries in which they listed times, whereabouts, details of ministering images or narratives, duration, outcome, etc, which they exchanged at the far end of the football field every lunch time to ejaculations of merriment or disgust. Though I counted it an honour to be friendly with the boss, I stayed aloof from the organisation. Some things I felt better about doing on my own. This was a disappointment to Errol who wanted me to be the official artist not only of what conduced to my arousal but to everybody else's. He chased me for a whole term, even offering to waive the joining fee of one and six. Not wanting to appear stuck up, I agreed, but backed out again after about a fortnight. When I told him it wasn't working, that none of it was working, that the minute I shared a fantasy it became public and therefore no longer a fantasy, he said, 'What about Ilse Koch?'

FOUR

Each time Herman read such news, it awakened in
him fantasies of vengeance in which . . . he managed
to bring to trial all those who had been involved in
the annihilation of the Jews.

Isaac Bashevis Singer, *Enemies: A Love Story*

1

Strange to tell, there was an Ilse in my mother's kalooki group,
but a Cohen not a Koch. Ilse Cohen, an intense woman with tragic
brown eyes, whom I took on that account to be intelligent. No
umlaut or diaeresis in her name, so I was never in any danger of
falling in love with her, but she had a fleshy face which I liked,
and short agitated fingers with blood-red nails which it was impossible not to imagine taking gouges out of your back. In retrospect,
I now realise that for erotic purposes I divided women, and had
from a very early age, into vegetarians and meat-eaters. Ilse was
a meat-eater. Vegetarians I took no interest in.

Though I seldom played kalooki myself, agreeing with my
father that of all card games it was the most womanly, a form
of sedentary shopping or hoarding, I looked on sometimes, not
least because of the opportunity it gave me to study hands.
Fascinating, the human hand, both as a piece of engineering in
itself (of particular expressive value to a cartoonist) and on
account of its wilfulness, the independence it enjoys from the
rest of the body. And from the rest of the personality, come to
that. You never know – I defy anyone to predict – what sort of
hands a person is going to have. Where you would expect
tapering artistic fingers, you find five amputated stumps, barely

93

more than carpals, like broken bits of chalk. Where you imagine you are going to encounter a gorilla's fist, you come instead upon a little rolled-up ball of pads and creases, as heartbreaking as a newborn baby's. Zoë, for example, though more delicate than a Byzantine madonna, had hands that would not have shamed a wrestler. Björk, who *was* a wrestler, from her wrists up could have made it as a Cambodian temple dancer. Only Chloë, of the women I lost my heart to, was manually consistent: she was an anti-Semite in her soul and she had anti-Semitic hands. The phalanges preternaturally straight, the knuckles pale and taut, the lunulae fastidiously cleared of cuticle, as perfect in their crescents as any moon over Arabia. Get her to turn her hands over and show you her palms and there was nothing to see – no warm accommodating pouches of skin, no comfortable adjustment of one finger to another, no life or love lines, just a vexed crisscross of Judaephobia like the railway tracks going in and out of Auschwitz, and (though you will have to take my word for this, since it was never put to the test – Chloë, unlike Ilse Koch, never being tried for war crimes) no fingerprints.

Whatever the surprises of the human hand, the one thing you could be sure of on kalooki nights was that every one of my mother's friends would arrive with freshly painted fingernails. In later years, when the technology of nail painting had grown more advanced, they would turn up in silvers and magentas, tangerines and blacks, sometimes a different colour on each nail, and more latterly with the extremities painted the colour of white emulsion. Many years after these of which I speak, when I was in Manchester for Tsedraiter Ike's funeral – an august enough event, but one which did not call a halt to kalooki – I saw that Ilse, a great-grandmother by then, maybe even a great-great-grandmother, sported nails which had the suits painted on them, a heart, a spade, a diamond, a club, and a joker on the thumbnail. But then it was Ilse who had gone further than the others in the early days, sometimes leaving the crescents of her nails unpainted, as

94

though to grant whoever cared to look a shockingly precise sliver of nudity. Otherwise, a velvet rich incarnadine prevailed on every hand. Which satisfied me. Little pools of blood bejewelling the pastoral green of the card tables.

That poor woman, by the by, who had a stroke and then fell victim to Alien Hand syndrome, that friend of my mother's who had to fight with her own hand to stop it strangling her, was Ilse Cohen. That she still continued to lavish attention on the hand that hated her, rubbing cream into its joints, putting jewels upon its fingers, showing no favouritism whatsoever to the other hand, as far as I could tell, in the matter of buffing and decorating the nails, is evidence of a remarkable capacity for forgiveness.

Now if I could feel that way about those Jews – servants of a syndrome no less unnatural or anarchic – who by silence or connivance have gone for the throats of fellow Jews, meaning to strangle them themselves, or permit them to be strangled by others, the apostates, the name-changers, the crawlers to the cross, the *Taufjuden* (who sound like DevilJews, but that would be *Teufel*, whereas *taufen* means merely 'to baptise' – as though between *taufen* and the *Teufel* in this context there might be said to be a difference) . . .

But then if I were able to show the *Taufjuden* anything like the compassion Ilse Cohen lavished on her renegade hand, I would be out of a job, wouldn't I? Or at least out of half a job since that too is what I'm paid for – excoriating my people when I'm not shielding them from harm.

2

Charming, silky names women had in those day. Ilse, Irma . . . The Irma who played kalooki at my mother's table was not a regular as Ilse was, and not a meat-eater either, but she was handsome enough if you had a taste for women who piled their hair like German sausages and looked as though they were on the point of coming apart. Not loose-limbed or loose-jointed so much as loose-nerved. Explicable in Irma's case on account of her parents having sent her to Manchester from Munich at the first sniff of National Socialism. She was a slip of a girl at the time, but old enough not to mistake the uncle and aunt who looked after her in Cheetham Hill for the mother and father she had left behind. She exchanged letters with them every week until, early in 1940, they fell silent. She went on writing, hoping for a reply, for a further five years. Some 250 letters, all of them unanswered. And even ten years after that, I recall my mother telling me, she had not given up hoping to hear from them.

Was that why she piled her hair away from her face, so that she could keep her ears clear for news? That's how I like to draw my victim-Jews in *Five Thousand Years of Bitterness* anyway, always with an ear cocked, always listening for something – a hoofbeat, a train approaching (Jew Jew, Jew Jew), a word from home.

An Ilse and an Irma, turning up together to play kalooki in my house – what's the chance of that? Ilse and Irma, both lovely women, mirroring that other Ilse and Irma, Ilse Koch and Irma Grese, two of the least lovely women (speaking ethically now) who ever lived. Maybe it wasn't such a coincidence as I thought. Maybe Ilse and Irma were common enough names in those days, at least if you happened to be the children of parents who had once loved the sound of German. And maybe they fell out of favour because of Ilse Koch and Irma Grese.

There is no photograph of Irma Grese in *The Scourge of the Swastika*, and only the briefest mention of her as the person who tutored Dorothea Binz in depravity during the time they were at Belsen together, Binz later graduating to Ravensbrück, the women's camp, while Grese stayed on at Belsen, liking it where she was. I owe what I know about these women to Manny Washinsky, though not the photograph of Irma Grese which I happened upon, all on my ownio, a little later. Striking, you would have to say – eyes wide apart like a Tartar's, an incongruous woolly cardigan tucked into an equally incongruous tartan skirt which she wore over boots, but too high on the waist, foreshortening her torso in a way that Chloë for some reason favoured too. Probably the same photograph which Myra Hindley was said to have carried around in her handbag.

An extravagantly beautiful woman, Irma Grese, yes, in the tragic Slavic-Chloë mode. Of a sort of beauty whose influence one can never calculate.

You could argue that they ought to ban photographs of monsters likely to be seen as role models by monsters-in-waiting; but then Ian Brady was an avid reader of Dostoevsky, and you can't start banning Russian classics as well. It's all grist to the deranged, that's what it comes to. There is no such thing as an innocuous image. Or idea.

If you're going to ban anything it should be the person likely to be susceptible. As they did with Myra Hindley and Ian Brady, and as they subsequently did with Manny Washinsky. Too late, of course.

But then isn't it always too late?

Impossible to say whether Manny's new school intensified his interest in the leading lights, in particular the leading ladies, of the Third Reich, or whether he was making progress simply by dint of lonely scholarship. It was handy for me all right, the numbers of new enemies of the Jews he was unearthing. Good for our project, *Five Thousand Years of Bitterness*, whether or not he still saw himself as part of it. But you could argue that it wasn't particularly good for *him*.

Couldn't have been healthy, a school just for Jews, all calling on God in the lavatory. Not that he ever told me what it was like, or talked about the other Jewish boys he met there, any more, I suspected, than he talked to them about me. We were both each other's secret. I liked to believe that I was his sole confidant, but of course it's possible he spent every spare second between classes telling other kids called Emanuel and Eli about Irma Grese and Ilse Koch, unless it was they who were telling him. I have a lurid conception of what happens in a Jewish school – for which I suppose I must thank my father who as an atheist thought religious education was the devil's work. Maybe the headmaster addressed them on the subject of Irma and Ilse at every school assembly. Fringes out, tefillin on, and now, boys, let's dilate upon these most recent torturers of the Jewish people. Not all that different from my mornings if you leave out the tzitzis and tefillin.

He was my education, that much has to be said, no matter how he came by what he educated me in. Errol Tobias would rather that privilege had fallen to him. But Errol was merely the snake in the garden, whispering of fruit. Manny was the tree.

On my own I wouldn't have remembered all their names or ever have been able to tell them apart – Vera Salvequart the poisoner, Dorothea Binz the dog-woman, Carmen Mory otherwise known as 'The Monster', let alone Ilse Koch and Irma Grese.

I catch myself out in a disingenuousness there. Ilse Koch I was always able to tell apart. Ilse Koch came to me via Errol Tobias as well as Manny, though I didn't let on to Manny that I supped from a second fountain of Koch corruption, or that hers was a name which bound Errol and me in a knowingness of a sort of which Manny surely had no comprehension. Ilse Koch was a secret I shared with each of them separately.

'You'll have to remind me,' was the usual way one of our induction sessions would begin – I inviting it, I the empty vessel, I offering myself to Manny like a flower opening up its countenance to the sun – 'which is Dorothea Binz again?'

'May her name be wiped out . . .'

That was what I had to say before he'd tell me about any of them. He was my tree of knowledge but he was also my angel of oblivion. Not an easy task for him to be both at once –

illuminator and expunger. But I suppose that's what we're all doing, making people remember what we would wish them to forget.

In our air-raid shelter it felt queerly ritualistic, as though the voices of the old rabbis were inhabiting the brickwork. 'Dorothea Binz, may her name be wiped out,' I'd say, 'what did she do again?'

God knows what my father would have said had he caught me chanting one of those ancient curses. A boy, however, must get his education whichever way he can, and my father hadn't interested himself in Dorothea Binz.

Once, when I was asking about her for what must have been the hundredth time, Manny answered by biting me. Not a feral leap at my throat, but not exactly what you could call a playful nip either. Without any warning, without even any show of temper, he dipped his head and sunk his teeth into my wrist. An uncanny action by virtue of its silence, as much as anything else.

I cried out. Not from the pain but from the shock. And also out of fear. A terror amounting to phobia attached to bites in Jewish Crumpsall. There had been an alarming incident in the neighbourhood, not many years before, when someone's pet bulldog turned savage for no reason – as though a bulldog needs a reason – and chewed off a baby's ear. An event which it was impossible to forget on account of that terrible twist of flesh, like an end of burnt vegetable, which the child was doomed to carry on the side of his face for all time. So we were all more than routinely conscious of mad dogs, especially Tsedraiter Ike who froze and lost his inky colour whenever a dog of any sort approached. 'Look confident,' he would warn me, flattening himself against a wall if he could find one, or failing that, flattening himself against me, 'they can smell fear.' But even Tsedraiter Ike never warned me about Manny Washinsky.

'If it's making you so angry I'll stop asking,' I said, looking at the marks at the base of my thumb. 'Christ!'

How the Gentile world felt about the thumb, or to be more

99

specific the skin between the thumb and forefinger, I had no idea, but in Jewish Crumpsall we were almost as phobic about the thumb as we were about mad dogs. In some households bread knifes were kept under lock and key and kids my age were not allowed to use them without at least two adults being present. My mother was less strict but she still filled my head with the terrible things that could happen to you if you took a cut anywhere near the thumb. Lockjaw for one. Bread knife, not looking what you were doing, slip, break skin, blood – lockjaw. Simple as that. Face set in rictus of horror. Dead in an hour. And that wasn't the worst of it. The worst of it was when our two phobias came together and a mad dog bit us between our thumb and forefinger. Then it was lockjaw followed by foaming at the mouth. Rabies. With rabies you had a chance, medically, of living longer than an hour, but they had to shoot you in case you went on to bite someone else.

I was relieved, after Manny's bite, to discover that my jaw still moved, and that my lips, when I wiped them, were free of foam. But I still snarled at him.

'Now you won't forget who Dorothea Binz is,' he said. The lunatic that he was.

'So what are you going to do to make me remember Vera Salvequart . . .'

'. . . may her name be wiped out . . .'

'. . . may her name be wiped out . . . Chop my head off?'

'No. To be consistent I'd have to poison you. What I just did to you, Dorothea Binz did to her prisoners. Only she did it harder.'

'She bit them?'

'Not personally, as far as I know. But her dogs did. They tore Jewish women's arms off. She was taught to do it when she was at Belsen.'

'They had a school at Belsen?'

'I don't know if they had a school, but they had a teacher. Irma Grese, may her name be wiped out. While they were in Belsen together she showed Dorothea Binz what you could do with a dog.'

(May its name be wiped out, I thought.)

This was the hard part – not the names so much as the family connections, this one knowing that one, that one receiving tuition from the other. Listen to Manny Washinsky and you could never believe there'd been a German who hadn't known what was happening. Not only did they know what was being done, they personally knew or were related to every person who was doing it. Manny's genealogy of guilt. It didn't surprise me to learn that when he was in prison he compiled lists and tables. No good at maps, but if ever anyone could have drawn the tree that showed the interconnectedness of German responsibility, from Martin Luther to the trump of time, Manny was that person. As it happened he was drawing lists of a very different sort.

'Irma Grese,' I said, wanting to be sure I had this right, 'may her name be wiped out, being the one who poisoned her patients . . .'

'I've just told you – Vera Salvequart, may her name be wiped out, was the poisoner. The one who'd been imprisoned herself at Theresienstadt, for being in love with a Jew. Then they moved her to Ravensbrück and put her in "The Tent for Pigs". After that she took up poisoning fellow prisoners.'

'What, as a hobby?'

'No one knows why. Maybe the Jew she was in love with had left her.'

I nodded. Dangerous for a Jew to leave a woman. There could be grave consequences. The women lost their wits. I'd heard many stories to that effect. Lose a Jew and you lose your mind. That was what a prize we were. 'So Irma Grese was . . .'

'Senior SS Supervisor at Auschwitz and Belsen. They called her "The Grey Mouse".'

'Doesn't sound very frightening.'

'Might not sound very frightening to you, but at Auschwitz she killed on average thirty people a day.'

'And at Belsen?'

'The same.'

'By the dog method?'

'Some. Others she shot. She carried a revolver that was always cocked. She was also a bisexual.'

Did I know what a bisexual was at that age? Did Manny? I doubt it. But if it happened in Auschwitz or Belsen I assumed it wasn't a good thing.

'So she taught Dorothea Binz, may her name be wiped out, that as well.'

'What?'

'To be a bisexual.'

He thought about it. He had turned very red in the face. There was an experiment he was conducting, which he only partially allowed conversation to disrupt, to see how long he could go without breathing. First he was trying it in the open air. Later he would continue the experiment underwater. He was anxious to discover how much privation he could suffer. You never knew when it would come in handy, being able to stay alive without the benefit of oxygen. Over a number of years I saw him put all manner of objects over his head – paper bags, tallis bags, the tallis itself, pillowcases, his mother's tablecloths, his satchel, my satchel, the cushion covers from a three-piece suite. On one occasion he invited me to tighten his school tie round his throat like a noose, making me promise not to loosen it until he told me to. In the event, I stopped long before he was ready. 'Hanging's too good for me,' he once said, apropos of absolutely nothing. When I asked him what he meant he told me he just liked the sound of the sentence.

His thoughts, in between choking, must have been following the same direction as mine. 'Hanging would have been too good for her,' he said, rather dodging, I thought, the question of bisexuality.

'So what did they do to her?' I wondered.

'They hanged her.'

'And what would you have preferred?'

From what appeared to be a number of suggestions he could have made, he chose 'Pickaxing?'

'Is that a question?'

He thought about it. His mind seemingly somewhere else. 'No, I don't think so.'

It occurred to me that I had now lost track of who we were talking about. 'Is that Irma Grese or Dorothea Binz, may both their names be wiped out?'

'Binz. Gas chamber for Grese. Pickaxe for Binz because she pickaxed Jewish women to death. She also rode her bicycle into them. And got them to stand to attention all day long while she slapped their faces.'

How did he remember these details? How was he able to go on attaching atrocities to names?

'They had to stand to attention all day?'

'All day and all night.'

'And she slapped them with her hand? Wouldn't that have hurt her? Wouldn't her hand have got tired?'

'Hand, whip, belt, stick, whatever was lying around. One prisoner she slapped unconscious with the blotting pad on her desk.'

'Blotting paper! Sheesh!'

'Not the paper, the pad.'

'The pad? Double-sheesh!'

I feigned some of my surprise. It oils the wheels of sociability to act the ignoramus. Especially when the other party might up and bite you should the whim to do so take him, or when he happens to be a religious fanatic and you happen to be the sort of Jew who humours religious fanatics, perhaps because you're hiding one in your own heart. Though I knew nothing like as much as Manny knew about these flowers of German woman-hood, I had garnered odd items of information about them on my ownio, from war comics which other kids brought to school, from odd articles in Jewish newspapers which Tsedraiter Ike passed on to me when no one was looking – for in our house the *Jewish Chronicle* was underground literature – and of course from Errol Tobias, though he was inclined rather to harp on the one string. But the minutiae didn't stick for me the way they did for Manny. I would like to think that was because I had other things to think about. I suspect, however, the real reason I lumped these Morys and Binzes and Greses together was that their cruelty was all expressed against women. If I understood what I was hearing correctly, it was women prisoners Aufseherin Binz rode her bicycle into. Women to whom Schwester Vera Salvequart administered her little white powder potions of death. Women at whom 'The Grey Mouse', otherwise known as 'The Beast of Belsen', widened her Asiatic eyes and aimed her revolver or her whip. Many years later I read some of Irma Grese's own descriptions of herself at her trial in Belsen in 1945 and was struck by how prettily she remembered that whip, like a girl recalling her first toy. 'Cellophane paper plaited like a pigtail – it was translucent like white glass.' But she never, as far as I was able to deduce, brought it down on a man. There was nothing inhumane about my preference; I wasn't indifferent to the sufferings of women prisoners in the death camps, some of whom might well have been distant relatives of mine, women who would have married an Ike had they lived, or even a me had I been so lucky, nor was it that I felt more keenly, man to man, the indignities visited on my own sex. It was simply that there was a terrible inversion of the nature of things in the idea of a woman beating a man, of power and cruelty being deflected so perversely from their usual course. And if that inversion happened to be your bag, then Ilse Koch was the person to go to.

It was to her I went, anyway. Visiting her, not in reverie or fantasy – I have never been a great fantasiser (no need of it) – and not even in those unprotected moments between waking and dream, but as one might visit a sick person in hospital, not always certain which is the reality – the world of the healthy, or the world of the dying.

3

Ilse Koch. The Bitch of Buchenwald. My Ilse!

All our Ilses.

Was it a camp injunction, on pain of a beating or a bullet, never to look, never to see her, never to notice the shadow she cast, high in the saddle of her subjugated horse? Or was the prohibition biblical, all in Mendel's head? It didn't matter. He who looked was lost, and Mendel looked.

Through his closed eyes he could see her. Smell her through the smell of the horse she rode. Did it denote fear or love, that dungy smell? How would Mendel know? But her touch was lighter in fact than he would always imagine it later, lying on his bed, his knees drawn up to his chest. The faintest inflection of her heels, that was all it took, and the horse would understand what was required of him. Love. After the fear, the love. You became the perfect instrument of her will, for which you loved her.

She knew he was looking. They all looked, contrived to see without being seen to see, frightened, fascinated. The Camp Commandant's wife, out for her first ride of the day, her cherry-red hair aureoled about her, the thin dress Mendel conjured her to wear, even on the coldest mornings, folding back upon her, into her, like the wrapping on a sticky sweet. And the beaten stallion steaming.

Mendel shuffled in line across the yard and kept his shaven head down. She was on the other side of the fence, alone today. Some mornings she rode in company, with three or four of the wives of officers, openly staring at the prisoners. On his first day, Mendel had crossed the yard naked, to be deloused and disinfected – filthy Jew – shaven of every hair on his body, and they had seen him then. He heard their laughter and decided it was appreciative. His long penis. An animal in a cage, yes, but a fierce, refined, procreative animal. They could laugh all they liked at his unprotected-ness: he knew appreciation when he heard it. But that was months ago. Today there was less of him to appreciate. Less flesh, less sway, less confidence. He was hers for the taking now. Which was why, he believed, she rode past alone more often than she used to.

Through his lowered head he saw her. The lozenge pattern on her dress, like involuted diamonds, similar to one his mother used to wear, for casual but smart, a shopping, striding dress. Filmy for a mother, Mendel had always thought. It was a source of awkwardness for him, the little pained mother-loving Jew-boy with a long refined penis, seeing her coming towards him, or being out with her by her side, her dress fluttering away from her legs then closing in on them again, clinging and then peeling loose. He remembers the sound it made when she increased her pace, a soft sucking, like a kiss in reverse, lips coming away from skin. On Frau Koch it falls differently; because her hips are wider, her thighs thicker and coarser, it pleats less ambigu-ously around her. It is of course impossible that she would ride in this dress. But Mendel has seen her in it, striding on the arm of the Commandant, and this is how he prefers to picture her astride her horse.

She must know its effect on men of education and conscience. Later she will wear the same dress before her prosecutors at the American Military Tribunals in Dachau. Not that Mendel will ever know anything about that.

She is a version of his mother in other ways. On both the skin hangs heavy, their mouths turned down, a pendu-lousness in both their jaws, as though oppressed. For his mother, wherever she is now, this gravity made him weep;

he would have saved her from its cause, had he known it. Strange, then, that in the Commandant's wife the same downward cast of feature arouses him only to a consciousness of his own oppression, and to his desire for it to be increased. Whatever it is that troubles her, let her take it out on him.

For some men there has to be sadness in voluptuousness, and Mendel is one such man.

There has been talk among the inmates for weeks that the Commandant is planning an arena for his wife to ride in, outside the camp, and will be looking for prisoners to help build it. The thought that she will soon no longer ride where he can see or fancy that he sees her upsets Mendel disproportionately. It is because I have concentrated all my thoughts on her, he decides, rather than on my situation. If I lose her, I return to being nothing but a prisoner, and I will act like everybody else, mundanely imagining food, weighing out potatoes before I go to sleep, fantasising about freedom, and then dreading my death by diarrhoea or a beating. To stay alive I must empty everything from my mind except Ilse. To stay my own man I must become – or at least communicate to her that I am willing to become – hers. In my annihilation is my salvation.

His one hope is that he might be employed in the building of the arena. He does not know as what. He has no building skills. He can draw, that's all. He could do equestrian murals for her if she would like them, but she does not look to him like a woman who much appreciates murals. And he isn't sure, anyway, he can draw a horse. Humans are Mendel's only subject. Human desire and disappointment, human perversity, human contradiction. He draws abstractions in the grotesque manner.

On the other side of the fence, riding alone, she surveys him. Don't ask him how he knows, just leave it that he knows. She is thinking about him. As a muralist for her arena? He doubts that. As what then?

Or has she come one last time because she cannot use him, in any capacity, after all?

Is she capable of the poetry of regret?

> Goodbye my little long-nosed Yid,
> I could have torn your skin off
> with my teeth
> and you not raise a finger to stop me.
> But it is not to be.

Does she have such lyricism in her soul?

He confides his fears to the only friend he has made in the hut. He would get a better hearing, he knows, from any of the communists he has seen being led out of the camp to work in the quarry. Communists understand the ways in which what respectable society calls deviancy liberates the mind. But the Jews and the communists, though they are held to be the great twin threat to the Reich, are not permitted to mix. The guards prefer to have some grasp, moment by moment, of which degeneracy they are dealing with, and Mendel is not such a fool as to protest that you can be a Jew *and* a communist, which would only end in his being kicked twice. So he has no other recourse but Pinchas, the moon-faced rabbi-to-be – that's if anything is any longer to be – with whom he shares a bunk. Little point, when you are Mendel's age, trying to keep a secret from someone with whom you share a bunk. Besides, you need a friend. That's the one thing every prisoner knows – you cannot get through on your own. You have to pair off, make a marriage. In fact there is a third person in Mendel's bunk, an old Jew from Dhalem, one of the camp's very first inmates, brought here the morning after *Kristallnacht*, but he won't speak. No one expects him to last very long. Don't speak, don't live. But he has outlasted many. The bunk is a whole foot shorter than Mendel and Pinchas, who are not tall men. To sleep you must lie foetally pressed into the back of the other person; to talk, with your faces almost joined together and your knees drawn up and touching, like children, or like lovers. How the old Jew from Dhalem has been able to construct a silent, inviolable universe for himself in one third of this nursery bunk, Mendel is unable to comprehend. By being old, perhaps. Mendel, though, is young, and has to get the verdant concupiscence of youth off his chest. 'If I stop thinking about her I will die,' he whispers to Pinchas in the dark.

'Unless you stop thinking about her, you deserve to die.'

'Are you telling me you don't think about her?'

'The difference between us is that I try not to.'

'And you think that's a significant difference? The difference between a good man and a bad? *Trying?*'

'That's a distinction for you to draw if you wish to.'

'And during those moments when you fail to stop yourself thinking of her, do you too deserve to die?'

'We will all die anyway. It makes no difference.'

'Then it makes no difference whether or not I go on thinking about her.'

'Mendel, she is a foul, evil creature. That riding whip she carries, she uses. And not only on her horse.'

'I know that.'

'There are men here, Mendel, who have been ordered to parade naked before her.'

'I know that.'

'Jewish men.'

Mendel guffaws. 'Does the Jewishness make a difference? Are you telling me that a Jew is more vulnerable in his nakedness than anyone else? Am I the more shamed because they see my genitals than is Branko the gypsy?'

'What you feel, you feel.'

'And shame is shame, Pinchas.'

'You have been taught the story of the uncovering of Noah's nakedness and the cursing of Canaan. You are a Jew. I don't have to tell you. Adam hid himself from the Almighty, saying "I was afraid, because I was naked."'

'Adam wasn't Jewish, Pinchas. There were no Jews in Adam's garden. Jews hadn't been invented yet. We do ourselves no favours by insisting that we feel the humiliations of the flesh more keenly than others.'

'So you agree it is humiliation?'

'Of course I do.'

'Explain to me then why others do not in fact feel it as that. You mentioned Branko the gypsy. I have seen him naked a hundred times. He does not care who sees him. Ask him how often he has seen me naked? Just once, Mendel. And that was not my doing. Branko prances in his nakedness, while I hide myself, afraid. Tell me why that is.'

'I will prance in my nakedness if she demands it.'

'And be beaten?'

'If it's her wish.'

'You know how she will beat you? You know where she will beat you?'

'A beating's a beating. What's one more?'

'She will beat you where you are a man, Mendel.'

'Where I am a man! What does that mean? Why are you talking to me as though you are one of the Five Books of Moses?'

'If you get an erection while she looks at you – God forgive me – she will beat you there. It has happened. Ask Uri.'

'Uri the gardener from Ostrava? Uri the simpleton? He

has an erection every second of the day. Having someone beat it down will have been good for him. It's just a pity it didn't work.'

'I don't believe in your flippancy.'

'Who is being flippant? This is life and death, I know it. If I have to stop thinking about her I will die. Whereas if she strikes me – to borrow your quaint locution – *where I am a man*, I will live. You're a scholar versed in the subtle paradoxes of the Talmud: that shouldn't be too difficult for you to understand.'

'You're mad.'

'You mean I'm filthy.'

'Mad *and* filthy. You want that loathsome pig of a woman – she is even the colour of pig, Mendel, she even smells like a pig – to raise her whip to you there, the site of every Jewish man's covenant with God. Don't you understand how loathsome that makes you? You should keep your voice down. There are men here old enough to be your grandfather who would raise their hand to kill you if they heard you. You are a degraded Jew.'

'We are all degraded Jews.'

'You want it to be worse.'

'Pinchas, there is no worse. And I have no covenant with God. He broke it.'

'That's a blasphemy.'

'And what? I will die from it?'

'There are worse things than death.'

'Ah yes, I know. Ignominy. Well, maybe it is ignominious, Pinchas, to lie to yourself about your desires.'

'There are worse things than death, ignominy apart. You have heard it rumoured, Mendel, just as I have, that of those she orders to parade unclothed before her she selects some who have unusual markings on their bodies, disfigurements of the skin or tattoos, to do abominations with.'

'Not abominations – lampshades. I have, as you say, "heard it rumoured". I have also heard it rumoured that she shrinks heads. And that she can take a hundred lovers in a day like Messalina. And that she couples with her horse. There is nothing I have not heard rumoured in this camp.'

'Then expose yourself to the object of these rumours, Mendel, and find out for yourself.'

'I have no unusual markings on my skin. Nor do I have tattoos. She won't be interested. More's the pity.'

'But you will have an erection at least.'

'I can't even promise that, but by God I will try.'

'Don't bring God's name into this. It's a sacrilege.'

'Sacrilege? Here? Don't make me laugh, Pinchas. There is nothing left to defile here.'

That night, Mendel was sure, Pinchas dreamed of Ilse Koch. For which, in silence, Mendel begged his friend's pardon.

4

'Hard to accept a woman being hanged,' my father said the night before Ruth Ellis was executed in 1955.

'Hard to believe a woman could have done what she is being hanged for having done,' my mother replied.

My father nodded without conviction. *Was* it hard to believe Ruth Ellis could have done what she was charged with doing? Hanging was hard – that much he did know. As to her innocence or guilt, I'm not sure he had a view. He was simply against the death penalty in all instances. That he wasn't standing outside Holloway Prison holding a placard right that minute takes some explaining. He had been at the forefront of the agitation, organising demonstrations, getting up petitions, lobbying MPs. Though London was further from Manchester in those days than it is now, he seemed to be going there every other weekend on missions of mercy, at least once that I knew of to an anti-capital-punishment meeting chaired by Sydney Silverman, at which such notable champions of conscience as Victor Gollancz and Arthur Koestler spoke, and at which I have a feeling that my father, as a Manchester delegate – observer, stirrer? – spoke himself. 'Ha! All Jews I notice,' I recall Tsedraiter Ike saying when he read about this colloquium in a *Jewish Chronicle* he'd secreted into the house. 'Doesn't anybody else care?' 'Nothing to do with it,' my father said. 'It's not a Jewish issue, it's a human issue.' By which he was bound to have meant that Ruth Ellis wasn't a Jewish issue and that hanging in general wasn't a Jewish issue either. But I had a feeling that Tsedraiter Ike harboured a specific Ruth Ellis-centred grudge. He was proud in a general way that Jews stood up for her, because that reflected well on our sense of social responsibility (whatever Beatrice Potter and my grandmother's silks had said to the contrary), but he seemed to think my father had over-interested himself in the case, Ruth Ellis being the sort of woman, when all was said and done, you didn't want Jewish men running after. 'Hm, Ruth Ellis,' he said to me once, 'not the girl for you, eh, my old palomino? Watch those. Peroxide blondes. Crooked seams in their stockings. Red mouths. Always be careful to watch those, hm.'

Which of course – for all that peroxide ever afterwards put me in mind of the single rotten tooth Tsedraiter Ike couldn't get the word around – I haven't been.

After all the work he'd put in, not to be outside Holloway Prison upset my father deeply. He believed in expressing solidarity. A Jew should always show his face where Jewish issues were not. Which didn't mean he was against showing his face where Jewish issues *were* as well. Let Oswald Mosley dare show *his* face in Manchester and my father was the first on the scene, blowing hard, as I imagine him, shadow-boxing in the early dawn, looking to land a left. A feat which he had famously performed during Mosley's 1939 visit to Belle Vue. I knew the story as well as if I'd been there. Expecting trouble, Mosley had erected wooden fences for his protection, this as well as a line of police and several phalanxes of black-shirted bodyguards. Between him and the gallery from which he intended to address his supporters there was also an open-air dance floor and a lake. Which meant, as my father put it, that to get to him you had to swim, foxtrot and body-tackle half of Manchester City's police force. But if he couldn't be reached at least he could be shouted down. And he was spectacularly shouted down. 'You should have heard it,' my father used to tell me, grinning like a schoolboy – but then he couldn't have been much more than a schoolboy himself at the time of the events he was describing – 'there were hundreds of us – that's those of us who got inside Belle Vue, I'm not counting the thousands demonstrating outside – all chanting, "Down with fascism!" and, "One, two, three, four, five, we want Mosley dead or alive!" And then the best bit – listen to this, Maxie – we began to sing, I don't even know who started it, "Pack up all your cares and woe, here we go, singing low, bye-bye blackshirt!"' At which point in the story I was always required to say, 'So you won that one, Dad, you silenced him, you waved him on his way,' whereupon my father would put a finger to my lips and say, 'Not yet, I haven't finished,' and then tell me how he alone, as the meeting was breaking up, swam, foxtrotted, got past the police, and then the blackshirts, leapt over the barrier, shinned up to the balcony, dodged the personal bodyguards, looked Mosley point-blank in the eye, saw his lip tremble, and landed a humdinger on the point of his jaw. 'Crack! And down the mamzer went!' My only trouble with this anecdote being that it bore a worrying resemblance to another my father had often told me relating to Ted 'Kid' Lewis. Not realising his politics – 'What would a boxer know?' – Lewis had worked for Mosley in the early 1930s, and had even recruited a band of toughs from the East End for him – 'Biff Boys' they were called – but once he twigged what was going on he confronted Mosley in his office, told him he was an anti-Semitic bastard, told him he (Ted 'Kid' Lewis) was through running his dirty errands, and landed a humdinger on the point of the mamzer's jaw. But then I'm the hyperbolist in the family and had there been exaggeration in my father's account of his own humdinger, or even plagiarism, he would surely not have told me the original? Maybe there were just a hell of a lot of pugilistic Jews out there in the great years of secular and muscularist Judaism, queuing up to take a swing at Mosley.

The fact remains, anyway, that the next time my father tried to bop a fascist, they were prepared for him and got the bop in first, the news of it only reaching us when a hospital in Notting Hill Gate called – in the middle of one of my mother's kalooki nights, of course – wondering whether we would like to collect a Mr Glickman, residing at our address, who had been ambulanced into their care with a bloody nose and in a condition they could only describe as 'confused'.

'Look at your shirt!' were my mother's first words when she saw him the following afternoon. 'I'm not surprised you're confused. What the hell are you doing in Notting Hill Gate?' were the second.

Had my father been given a nosebleed in the course of trying to disrupt a Mosley rally, my mother might have looked more tolerantly on him, even if it would still have meant her having to go all the way to Kensington to clean him up. But Mosley was living quietly in Paris at the time. Nursing the humiliation of the time he'd been socked in Manchester, we liked to think. So what had my father been up to? Well – he scratched his head. What *had* he been up to? Oh yes, he'd been to an anti-capital-punishment meeting chaired by Sydney Silverman and attended by Victor Gollancz and Arthur Koestler, for one thing. '*For one thing*! And what, pray, was the other?' Well – he scratched his head again. Later, we would date the deterioration in his health from this incident. But at the time my mother thought he was merely prevaricating, a bit ashamed of himself for getting into a fight at his age, and for putting her to all this trouble.

What she was able to piece together, finally, was that he'd taken the opportunity while he was down there to join a few of his old communist friends in breaking up the headquarters of a Nazi organisation which had recently opened for business in Notting Hill. Jews weren't the problem at the time, blacks were. But a Nazi is a Nazi is a Nazi.

My mother knew that. A Nazi is a Nazi is a Nazi — yes, Jack. But what about his old communist friends — did they too have bloody noses? What about 'Long John' Silverman and Elmore Finkel? Were their womenfolk catching trains from every corner of the country and having to miss kalooki?

As it happened, no, because when they were discovered climbing into the windows they ran for it, whereas my father, well, he didn't get to London very often did he — be fair now, indulge him a little — and he felt like staying. If we thought he looked a mess, we should have seen the other guys . . .

This undignified event had taken place only a week or so before Ruth Ellis was hanged and explains why my father wasn't holding a candle outside Holloway Prison. London was out of bounds. He'd been grounded by my mother who didn't want him in another fight, nursing another bloody nose, and maybe worse.

No surprise, then, that he was more than usually tetchy with Tsedraiter Ike who had been pacing the living-room floor for hours, humming to himself, and driving us all to distraction.

'Do everybody a favour and sit down or go to bed, Ike,' he said. 'Anybody would think it was you who was going to the gallows.'

'Yes, well, we all know you'd like that,' Tsedraiter Ike said. 'And you wouldn't be in any hurry to sign petitions to get me off either.'

My father pointed to his chest, protesting his innocence of any desire to see Tsedraiter Ike swing. Although for a moment, I suspect, that was all any of us could picture and long for.

'The thing is,' Tsedraiter Ike went on, 'women are not always what we think they are. They're supposed to be the weaker sex, but they can surprise you.'

We all looked up. Had any woman surprised Tsedraiter Ike? Was it a woman who had driven him tsedrait in the first place?

'Take that Ilse Koch,' he said.

My parents exchanged glances. Ilse Koch? Did Tsedraiter Ike have a girlfriend called Ilse Koch all of the sudden?

'I hope you aren't talking about my friend Ilse Cohen,' my mother said. 'I hope she hasn't been surprising you.'

I could see what Tsedraiter Ike could see – that my parents had never heard of Ilse Koch in their lives. They were of the in-between generation: too old to want to know the gory details, not old enough to know they had to. What had happened in Germany made a lie of the Jewish modernity they'd been cultivating in Manchester and Liverpool; threw them back, if they attended too closely, to a world from which it was essential they could believe they had escaped, woke them to anxieties it was part of their very survival plan never again to acknowledge. Here they had been, the brash, very nearly Gentile inhabitants of the middle of the twentieth century – dancing, hiking, sitting out in deckchairs in all weathers, debating, trade-unionising, speechifying, playing billiards, playing cards, swinging punches, buying televisions, having children you couldn't tell apart from the goyim, giving them goyisher names and even persuading them to cohabit with goys – while all along, only a few hours across the Channel, it was still the Middle Ages.

Hardly surprising that Jews of their sort, positioned where they were and of their age, warmed to Holocaust literature only slowly. Ilse Koch? Who was Ilse Koch when she was at home?

I, on the other hand, was starting from scratch, with Manny as my tree of knowledge and Errol Tobias as the snake. Ilse Koch! I reddened and hoped to God they hadn't noticed.

'"The Witch of Buchenwald",' Ike said. Ike, of course, as a

medieval man himself, was full of reading on the subject, though my father never permitted his books to spill out of his room into the twentieth century where the rest of us lived.

I knew Ilse Koch had two names, 'The Witch of Buchenwald' and 'The Bitch of Buchenwald', and I knew which I preferred. But I wasn't letting on I knew of either.

'Oh, is she the one who made the lampshades?' my mother asked. It's the obvious joke, but she made it sound like an interior design query. And even if she hadn't, it's my obligation as a cartoonist to make out that she had.

My father got up and began to pace the living-room floor in the opposite direction to Tsedraiter Ike. Anyone would have thought a decision had just unfairly gone against him. Another referee counting him out because of a few spots of blood on the canvas. 'We've done all this,' he said. 'We've said all we have to say on this subject.'

Tsedraiter Ike began to make heavy breathing noises, like someone imagining a heart attack. 'You don't believe she made the lampshades? You don't believe she lined up the Jews of Buchenwald to see who had the most unusual tattoos, because the most unusual tattoos made the most unusual lampshades? You don't believe what the Americans found when they liberated the camp? All lies was it?'

'It doesn't matter what I believe. It's history. Let it rest, Ike.'

'Forget it ever happened, you mean?'

'I didn't say that. I said let it rest. It happened. But it happened to gypsies and homosexuals and communists as well.'

'And that makes it better?'

'Nothing makes it better. It happened, now leave it.'

'Easy for you.'

There was an exchange of bitter looks, Tsedraiter Ike's face shrunken to the size of a rat's, the way Ilse Koch the head-shrinker would have liked it, my father's pinched and pugilistic, as though he was about to land one on the referee. 'Like it's hard for you,

Ike!' he said, witheringly. 'Like *anything*'s hard for you! I don't see you at anti-fascist demonstrations getting a bloody nose. You're here, where you always are, hiding behind women's skirts. Talk's cheap, Ike, talk's cheap.'

My uncle turned on his heels. For what was left of the evening we could hear him pacing up and down his room, singing 'It's only me from over the sea, said Barnacle Bill the sailor'. If you could call that singing.

Between my father and my mother (who was hurt on Ike's behalf) a silence prevailed. Call it the 'lampshade moment'. Every Jewish family had it when I was growing up. I am told they still do, and probably always will. *Never again.* But which is the true freedom – saying never again in the hope that never again, or never again saying never again?

I made a cartoon of it once. Two old Jews arguing. One with a bubble coming out of his mouth declaring 'Never again', the other with his fists in the air and an answering bubble, 'If I have to hear you saying never again ever again . . .' But I was unable to place it. I gave it away in the end to the plastic surgeon who wouldn't touch my nose. Hard to get people to laugh at the Holocaust.

Meanwhile revisionists make a startling point. Those lamp-shades Ilse Koch was reputed to have fashioned for her personal use, featuring outlandish Jewish tattoos – pause for a moment and tell us when you last saw a Jew with a tattoo. Proscribed, is it not? Leviticus 19:28 – 'Ye shall not make any cutting in your flesh for the dead, nor print any marks upon you: I am the Lord.' True, the proscription applied in the first instance to funeral rites, separating the Children of Israel from those who practised blood cults, those primitives who believed that flowing blood would keep the dead alive, as would bearing memorials to them cut into your flesh; but when was there a Jewish proscription that didn't supersede its original application? No marks – that's the ruling whose origins have been long forgotten – no marks upon the body. The prohibition become aesthetic finally, as though God knew in advance that tattoos and navel piercings wouldn't suit the chosen people – a fastidiousness in the matter of adornment, however, which didn't make Him think again about tzitzis, sidelocks, wigs, and shapeless dresses like Mrs Washinsky's.

There is an intriguing contradiction in the position of those who question whether anything as terrible as Ilse Koch and her lampshades ever happened, in that they invariably let you know they wished it had.

And that's not all that's intriguing about them. In order to give credence to their denials and demonstrate mastery of the culture of the Jews whose lies they must refute, many of them become scholars not just of Jewish history but of the Jewish religion, making fine distinctions between the authority of Torah Judaism and Rabbinic Judaism, becoming learned in Mishnah, which constitute the oral law, and Gemara, which are commentaries on Mishnah, not to be confused with the Agadah, which are the parables and homilies derived from or illustrative of both; in short devoting their lives to study of the people they cannot abide.

Thus the Tenth Circle of Hell, where the Revisionists and Deniers and Libellers are to be found, not wailing or gnashing their teeth, not trapped for ever in rivers of boiling blood or buried face down in the mud, their torn parts exposed to the never-to-be-satisfied gluttony of Cerberus, but soberly dressed at library desks, surrounded by Babel Towers of Hebrew texts which grow whenever a volume is removed, not a single word of a single page of which must they except from meticulous study, lest that be the very word which will prove the falseness of the Jewish people and their prophets at last.

Consigned in their Jew-hating to an eternity of Jew.

FIVE

You get tragedy where the tree, instead of bending, breaks. Tragedy is something un-Jewish.

Ludwig Wittgenstein

1

I was never bar mitzvah'd. My father wouldn't hear of it. 'You become a man when you've performed a manly action,' was the beginning and the end of the subject for him.

'What, like punching someone in the face?' my mother said.

Taking her at her word, my father bought me boxing gloves for my thirteenth birthday and sparred with me in the garden.

'Hit him!' my sister urged from her bedroom window. Unusual for her to open her window and look out upon the world. Even more unusual for her to come down into the actual garden, a place which would only have had existential meaning for her had she been able to grow shoes in it. Because she couldn't find a single item to wear that suited her, she was wrapped in a sheet. Nothing on her feet. Nothing that would fit or become her feet. 'Go on,' she said, holding the sheet in at her middle, 'hit him!'

In the heat of battle, neither my father nor I bothered to enquire who she was cheering on. Anybody hitting anybody would have done her.

Seeing her sitting there in her bedclothes, calling for blood, my mother came out with four or five decks of cards and a duster. 'Here,' she said, 'while you're watching, shine these.'

She never had enough to do, my sister. My mother likewise. It wasn't that they were lazy, they were simply never pointed at any activity beyond kalooki. My father's fault, partly. Though a modern man as far as belief systems went, he retained something of the temperament of Abraham in his tabernacle. He liked the idle prettiness of women about him.

I've told this story a hundred times, of me boxing with my father on what should have been my bar mitzvah, always changing it according to the expectations of my audience, now having my father knock me out, now having me KO him, now having my mother piling in to separate us, now having my sister putting on the gloves and flattening us both. But always, of course, in the spirit of comic-book exaggeration. KERPOW! BAM! YEEEEKS! YI-IIII!

In fact I remember it as one of the saddest afternoons of my life. A son doesn't hit his father, not even when it's sport. And though my father had often lashed out at me in temper, actually landing a punch with one of those big stinging leather gloves was out of the question for him too. So we went into a bear hug and lumbered around the garden like that, sideways, with our arms around each other's backs and our heads on each other's chests. What he was thinking I had no idea, but I couldn't get past the sensation of unfamiliarity – how little I knew him, how alien and even off-putting the smell of him was, how uncomfortable I felt being this close to him, as though even a clinch was an infringement of the laws of family. I was upset, partly, on my own account, that my father was a stranger to me; and upset on his account as well, that he had a son who was unable to relax and enjoy a bit of man-to-man knockabout in his company; but I was also sad because I could tell he wasn't well. Nothing he said. Nothing in his breathing or in the way he held himself, or in the way he held me for that matter. Just something he gave off, something you see in old dogs sometimes, a weariness to the bone, a disappointment beyond melancholy, as though you accept now that you will never live the life you always hoped you'd live – a lack of interest, finally, in your surroundings, in the company you keep, and in yourself.

And who knows? Maybe he suspected I would have liked a bar mitzvah.

2

It was considered scandalous, where we lived, my not having a bar mitzvah. It was only one up from marrying out.

People invented the most far-fetched explanations for it. My mother wasn't really Jewish and therefore I wasn't really Jewish either. My father had killed someone in a fight years before and no rabbi would bar mitzvah the son of a murderer. My sister was pregnant and the family feared that the excitement of my bar mitzvah would either terminate or bring on the pregnancy. My father was so desperately poor, thanks to the money my sister lavished on a wardrobe she never wore and the huge amounts my mother was known to spend hosting and having her hair done for her kalooki evenings, that he simply could not afford to give me a bar mitzvah.

Not far wide of the mark, that last explanation. Brought up to be a free spirit, with a hearty contempt for the usual Jewish professions of medicine, banking and the law, my father had drifted into local politics, serving as a Labour councillor for the ward of Red Bank for a short time, in the course of which he'd campaigned without much success to turn places of religious worship into gyms and snooker halls, and then drifting out again when he was suspected of promoting, or at least assisting in the promotion of, an illegal bare-knuckle contest between the Irish prizefighting lightweight Colin McReady and the Jewish kick-boxer Shlomo Grynn in a disused warehouse plumb in the middle of his constituency. 'That sound like me?' was how he dealt with the accusation, and he was never prosecuted for it. Otherwise he scraped a living teaching above-board boxing at various Jewish boys' clubs – strictly speaking a charitable activity – supplemented by a little public speaking at sporting dinners – they liked hearing about Maxie 'Slapsie' Rosenbloom the back-pedaller, and the time Ted 'Kid' Lewis, born Gershon Mendeloff, landed a humdinger on that mamzer Mosley's jaw, and for all I know the beating Shlomo Grynn handed out to Colin McReady — further supplemented by occasional work as a driver, dogsbody and odd-job man, even finding employment briefly at the Ritz, where he stood in as a bouncer until they discovered his susceptibility to nosebleeds.

So it's a question, had he wanted to give me a bar mitzvah, where he would have found the money for it.

You didn't have to be rich to be bar mitzvah'd. Not then, anyway. A new suit, preferably with long trousers, for the man-to-be; some fortifying whisky and hard biscuits for the celebrants before they left the synagogue to walk home; and that, not forgetting the cost of tefillin, concluded the affair. Concluded it religiously, at any rate. But a bar mitzvah wasn't just about religion. It was also about giving the family a party. And the party, assuming it to be black tie, was where it started to get expensive. I wouldn't have minded a party. I liked the way, as soon as you became a man, your uncles felt they could slide a cheque from the inside pockets of their dinner suits to the inside pockets of yours. You turned thirteen and all at once you'd become a hoodlum. You'd return that night to the little cot in which you'd been a boy and one by one slit open the envelopes. Hooch money. Numbers-racket stash. You felt — my friends who *were* bar mitzvah'd told me — like Bugsy Siegel.

Party aside, I had a vague sense I should have been put to a religious test as well. It wasn't that I wanted to stand up in synagogue and read the portion of the law specific to the Saturday, measured by the Jewish calendar, on which my birthday fell — I could have lived cheerfully without the davening and the sententiousness, especially I could have lived without the moment when the rabbi pointed his weekly parable (always a parable for simpletons as far as I could tell) to make it somehow relevant to you:

'Once, a group of Polish acrobats came to Mezhibezh to perform at the bar mitzvah of the son of a notorious unbeliever . . .' – but I feared that the not doing it would always leave me with a sense of unfinished business, cast me outside the clan, even identify me with those enemies of the Jewish people I spent so much time drawing and discussing. Not an excommunication exactly, but on the road to one.

Tsedraiter Ike felt the same. At first he said he would coach me in my portion of the law and throw a service à deux for me in his room. At least that way I would be doing my duty in the eyes of God. But over time he let this suggestion lapse, perhaps because he too noticed the decline in my father's health. He did, though, on what should have been my big day, present me with a secret gift of a tallis in a red velvet bag. 'Today,' he said, enfolding me in his arms, 'my old palomino becomes a man – mathlltuf!'

The other person who wanted me to have a bar mitzvah with the works was Shani. So great was her disappointment when she discovered there wasn't going to be a party, she took to her room and threw shoes about for upwards of two hours. This could explain her hankering, the afternoon my father boxed me in the garden, to see someone get punched. She had been earmarking a dress for my bar mitzvah for years, and now where was she going to get a chance to wear it?

'Show me,' my mother said. And when she saw it she said, 'Do you think I'd have let you go to my son's bar mitzvah in *that*!'

Causing Shani to return to her room and pull her wardrobe off the wall.

Wonderful that when it came to clothes they were able to argue in the past-conditional mode, falling out over what it would have been appropriate to wear at an event had that event only taken place and had Shani worn what she had intended to wear which she hadn't because it didn't.

Not wanting me to miss out on everything, my mother offered to throw me a kalooki night.

I pulled a face. Big deal.

'All right, a gala kalooki night.'

I still didn't look excited.

'You won't have to play,' she said. 'You can be guest of honour.'

'And what will that entail?'

'Darling, I don't know. Being made a fuss over and things.'

I thought about it. 'All right then,' I said, 'but only on condition you invite Gittel Franks and Simone Kaye.'

My mother looked at me with feigned disapproval. 'And sit you in the middle, I suppose?'

'Yes, please,' I said.

'I'll give the matter my consideration,' she said.

Gittel Franks and Simone Kaye were our most glamorous relations, that's if they really were relations, and though they had occasionally played kalooki at our house, they had never played on the same night. This could have been because they knew better than to dim each other's radiance; or it could have been because my mother, as a beautiful woman herself, could not take on more than one of them at a time. Gittel was Dodgy Ike's wife. I envied the proud, possessive way, whenever they came to call, he led her in, supporting her under her elbow, as though she too was another gift of doubtful propriety or provenance he meant to leave with us. But then if Gittel looked genaivisheh it was because she was. Ike had ganvied her from another man. As a divorcee – something barely heard of in the Jewish community in those days – Gittel Franks had a reputation if anything even dodgier than her second husband's. I liked her because she wore her hair up in a style which I think was called 'pompadour', a vertiginous tower of rolls and pleats that forced her to carry her head in an imperious manner very much at odds with the rest of her demeanour to which the adjective most frequently applied was demonstrative. She laughed loudly, touched everyone she met, could not describe an event without knocking over a vase, and ever since I could remember had regarded me through the narrow slits of her amber eyes – a Persian cat was what her eyes reminded me of – as though to promise me (on condition I didn't tell my mother) that she would be my present when I grew to be a man.

If Gittel Franks was demonstrative then Simone Kaye was cyclonic. 'That woman!' my father would say, hearing her from the other end of no matter how long a room, and clapping his hands to his ears. 'She looks like a wedding,' he once said to me in an aside. 'Which part?' I asked him. 'All of it – the chuppa, the table decorations, the band, the dancing, the cake, everything.' The secret of Simone Kaye, as I'd discovered, was to encounter her when she was not in the company of other women, to choose an hour in which you had nothing else to do, and to allow her to trap you in a corner for the whole of it. She was a woman who did everything up close. Tough, if you didn't like the smell of wedding cake, but I did. Marzipan in particular. An extravagance of almonds and sugar and egg whites. Of all our 'relations', Simone Kaye was the one who took the greatest interest in my schooling. 'And English? And history? I know I don't need to ask you about art. And geography? *Don't talk to you about geography* – why not, Maxie, tell me why not?' With every question, her lovely, always somewhat startled face finding more and more fantastical contortions of vitality, her orange eyes seeming to start from their sockets, first one and then the other of her nearly Negroid nostrils flaring, her mouth so full and expressive that sometimes you would have sworn that in her need for volubility she had found an extra lip. When I was young enough to be petted with equanimity, Simone Kaye used to pull me to her in order to pinch my cheeks, and would keep me there by trapping me between her knees. Though her legs were not as long as Gittel Franks's or anything like as elegant as my mother's, Simone Kaye always wore stockings that were silkier than theirs, which meant that she whooshed like curtains when she walked. It was almost more than I could bear, as a boy in short trousers, the voluptuousness of this silkiness upon my skin.

And of course the yellow smell of marzipan on hers.

After giving the matter some consideration, my mother said, 'I'll only be able to get them if I make it a charity event.'

'Me being the charity?'

'I'm afraid not. It will have to be Israel.'

Shame. I wanted it to be just me. But I bowed to the greater cause. 'Brave little Israel.' No moral complications in 1956. You knew who the good guys were. Other than a few families of Satmars who thought any Jewish state was illegitimate until the coming of the Messiah, the only person in Jewish Manchester who wasn't happy to donate a tree to Israel, whether or not a tree actually meant a gun, was my father. Logically, he should have been all for Israel, or Palestine as he insisted on calling it. A new start for the Jews. A Bundist in every kibbutz. Readings from *Das Kapital* instead of morning prayers. But he knew what was going to happen. He knew the rabbis were going to creep back in and start erecting shtetls all over again. 'First the bombs, then the shtetls.' He'd tap his forehead. 'Shtetls of the mind. You mark my words.'

So I had my doubts about my mother throwing a charity gala kalooki night in my honour but nominally in support of the state of Israel in our front room. 'What's Dad going to say?' I asked her.

Her turn to tap her forehead. 'Your father won't be told.'

It was a stark moral choice: my father or Gittel Franks and Simone Kaye. Like having to choose between the Arabs and the Jews. In other words, no choice at all.

And it worked. My mother found a night when she knew my father would be out of the house watching a fight, and Gittel Franks and Simone Kaye succumbed to Zionist blackmail and agreed to come. I was out of my skin with excitement. Gittel Franks and Simone Kaye, in our house! At night! Together! But if I was excited I was also frightened. Be careful what you ask for, Maxie Glickman. What if Gittel Franks, knowing this to be my de facto bar mitzvah, the occasion of my official entry into manhood, were actually to slide her slit Persian pussy eyes my way and mean it this time? What if Simone Kaye, forgetting how old I was, or simply in remembrance of things past, pulled me to her and trapped me between her silken knees?

I wasn't sure I could handle either of these immoderacies, but what if I was confronted by *both*!

I needn't have worried. Things never turn out as you expect them to. Be careful what you ask for, but also be careful what you hope for. It wasn't the fault of Gittel Franks or Simone Kaye, neither of whom could have looked more as I'd hoped they'd look had I set their hair, applied their make-up and poured them into their dresses myself. Gittel gilded and narrow, confined in something tight and rustling, as though to minimise the damage she might do, but laughing hoarsely and smashing glasses the minute she arrived; Simone Kaye as creamy as a Chantilly basket, everything on the point of spillage, at her lips the tiniest bubble of mirth. And me between. Sh-boom, sh-boom, as Errol Tobias sang when he was gardening. Something about paradise up above. Which this so nearly was, and would have been had my mother, fearing the competition from both sides, not gone to the trouble of making sure she would outshine them both. What was in *her* hair? Rubies? What shone on *her* skin? Gold leaf? Had my father rolled her in ochre before heading off to Belle Vue to watch two white-faced consumptives chasing each other round the ring? The consequence of her appearance, anyway, was that I was unable to take my eyes off her, when they should have been on Gittel Franks and Simone Kaye, and Gittel Franks and Simone Kaye were unable to take their eyes off her either, when they should have been on me. I also think the cards came out too soon. Gittel Franks and Simone Kaye had not squared up over the same kalooki table before. They needed time to settle down. Yet there they were, almost before the politenesses had been completed, fighting over the rules relating to the discard pile.

'You can only take from there if you lay down,' Gittel Franks said, seeing Simone Kaye's hand hovering where it shouldn't.

'I'm laying down, I'm laying down, don't rush me,' Simone Kaye replied. 'She's such a rusher, this one.'

'Kalooki!' my mother called.

'Huh,' Simone Kaye said on the reshuffle, picking up a card she didn't like, 'just my luck!'

'A silent game's the best game,' Gittel Franks told her.

'Kalooki!' my mother called.

When Gittel Franks was the first down with her cards a look of oriental certainty passed across her face. She folded her hands across her breast in exaggerated modesty.

'Who does she think she's being,' Simone Kaye whispered to me, 'Twankey-Poo?'

I wondered if she meant Nanki-Poo. She waved her hand at me, a gold ring on every finger. 'Twankey-Poo, Shmanki-Poo – you must tell me later how your schoolwork's going.'

Then it was back to winning.

No one else got a look-in. The competition grew so fierce finally, the heat coming off the three of them so tropical, that Ilse Cohen, looking quite plain in such company, had to get up and open all the windows with her good hand, against the efforts of her bad hand to close them again.

Normally the evening was over when the cards were. But on this occasion, for some reason – I suspected my mother must have shushkied something to them about its being a special night for me – the women stayed on for a final coconut macaroon, Gittel Franks retiring to the sofa in order to show her legs, Simone Franks staying at the table, with the intention, I hoped, of entrapping me between hers one last time, where nobody could see. How we got from cards to Suez to the Melbourne Olympics to Gittel Franks getting up and imitating Rosemary

Clooney singing 'This Ole House' — 'Ain't a-gonna need this house no longer / Ain't a-gonna need this house no more' — escapes me now and I suspect was beyond me at the time. Once we were there, though, it was no distance at all for Simone Franks to counter with '*Oh Mein Papa*', the Eddie Calvert trumpet version which she was able to perform to perfection with her third lip, or for my mother (who I was pretty sure had taken Gittel Franks's reference to this ole house personally) to insist that while she knew her taste was more classical than other people's there was still nothing in her estimation to beat 'By the Sleepy Lagoon'.

Taking one thing with another, I decided I was suddenly very weary. Was Gittel Franks going to slit her eyes at me before she left? Was Simone Kaye going to whoosh me between her knees? I didn't want to stay to find out. I couldn't face the disappointment.

The next time I saw either of them was in a cemetery. I haven't seen them since. Thus do opportunities slip through your fingers.

Considering my devotion to Jewish women of a certain age and allure, it remains surprising to me that I never married one. At least not one who whooshed her stockings or fell off her stilettos into a display cabinet of precious china. I can only suppose it had something to do with their taste in music. But that can't tell the whole story because Chloë adored *My Fair Lady*, and Zoë went to *Evita* at least once a month, and I married them.

3

My father found out about my mother's gala kalooki night in aid of Israel. In a moment of inadvertent vainglory my mother had published the amount of money it had raised in the *Crumpsall Jewish Herald* which, in a moment of inadvertent indolence, my father picked up and perused while he was queuing for delicatessen.

'You don't expect to have to read the Jewish papers to find out what's going on in your own house,' he said.

'You don't expect your atheist husband to be reading the Jewish papers,' my mother said, laughing her most unconvincing contralto laugh.

'It fell open.'

'Just at the right page?'

'In a Jewish paper there isn't a right page. If it isn't bar mitzvahs it's Israel.'

'There are the obituaries.'

'Don't be smart with me, Nora. You know my feelings on this subject. Couldn't you have found another charity?'

She fell silent. At last she said, 'It wasn't for charity, it was for Max.'

'Max? What did Max have to do with it?'

I was listening on the stairs, guilty but excited. It aroused me to hear my parents bandying around my name.

Did my mother know I was listening? Suddenly her voice went quiet. But my father's reply was clear enough. 'If the kid was so upset, you should have told me.'

'He wasn't upset.'

'Then what was the problem? Has the Tsedraiter been stirring it?'

'No, he hasn't. There was no problem. Maxie's fine about it. He hasn't been complaining, I swear to you. But I thought it would be nice to give him a little something to make up for it.'

'To make up for what?'

'For it. For there not being an it.'

'You just said he didn't care.'

'Just in case he cared.'

'Without telling me?'

'If I'd told you, you'd have stopped me.'

'So you went behind my back?'

'Jack, you were out.'

'You don't think I'd have stayed in had I known?'

'In the circumstances, no, I don't think you would have.'

'The circumstances being the arming of Israelis?'

'Jack, what we raised wouldn't have bought a bullet.'

'Even half a bullet can kill,' he said, which made so little sense that I wanted to come running down the stairs and tell him so.

The next day he asked me if I was all right. He wanted to be certain that I understood he'd done it – that's to say not done it – for my benefit. I would thank him when I was older. He knew people who were still ashamed of themselves, thirty, forty years after the event, for having acceded to a worn-out ritual in which they had never for a moment believed. When he'd asked them why they'd allowed themselves to be bar mitzvah'd, they all answered the same way – to please their parents. He didn't want to place that burden on my shoulders. 'You know how you'll please me best, Maxie? By thinking for yourself.'

After which I could hardly say, could I, that for myself I was thinking I'd have liked a bar mitzvah.

He had his own doubts, anyway. Over the years I discovered that the family had put pressure on him to change his mind, both Big and Little Ike making separate attempts to shake his resolution, and even one or two of the comrades saying that he was giving religion more importance in the breach than it would ever have enjoyed in the observance. Isn't that the great thing about Jews, Jack – that they can make room to accommodate religion without really meaning it?

Though my mother knew better than to pressure him, the gala kalooki night was a bitter reproach. 'He's eaten up by it,' my mother called to me one evening from her room. She was doing her hair for cards, I was sitting on my bed, doodling Jews in a sketchbook.

'Eaten up because you didn't tell him?'

'No, not eaten up by that, eaten up by you. In case he's done the wrong thing.'

I understood why she was telling me this. She wanted me to

133

make it right with him. Show him I didn't mind. Show him I was undamaged.

So I did. I skipped about the house whenever I thought there was a chance he might see me, like a child out of Wordsworth, oblivious to care and wearing an inane grin of what I took to be unrepining heathenishness. The boy who was happy to be un-bar mitzvah'd.

Hard to believe it worked. If anything I probably made things worse. By not giving me a bar mitzvah he must have thought he'd robbed me of my senses.

But it was the best I could do. Greater intimacy was beyond us. And had we achieved it I probably would have dissolved into tears. As it was, the idea that he was eaten up by what he'd done – his own deed become a devouring creature, like something out of the *Inferno* – distressed me unutterably.

I was sorry to my soul for him. Jew, Jew, Jew – he was sick and tired of the whole business. It was like an illness which he thought he'd beaten suddenly eating at his bones again. And he didn't, to my eyes, look man enough for another fight.

As for me, it was as I'd feared: I became an oddity. The un-bar mitzvah boy. It was unheard of. Everyone had had, or was expected to have, a bar mitzvah, including Errol Tobias, though in his case the party had not been the black-tie affair that even the poorest families favoured, but was held at his home, among the washbasins and hairdryers, and without the services of an outside kosher caterer. What is more – though every Jewish boy knows this is the one thing above all others you must eschew on your bar mitzvah – he invited the inner circle of his onanist association up to his room for their own gala event long before the other guests had left. For which I then expected him, and frankly expect him still, to burn in hell.

A funny thing about Errol, though. For all that his mind was a sewer, he was highly principled, and highly educated in matters of principle, where you would least have expected principle from him. No Jew could change his name or faith, for example, without Errol knowing about it and – in so far as schoolyard chit-chat could be called exposure – exposing him. I don't just mean the Jew at the bottom of our street who went from Friedlander to Flanders overnight; or Montague Burton, tailor to shlemiels, who began his life as Meshe Osinsky; or even the Hollywood Jews whose original monikers everybody knew – Bernie Schwartz become Tony Curtis, Shirley Schrift preferring to be Shelley Winters, Isadore Demsky transmogrified, with the help of a goyisher cleft in his chin, into Kirk Douglas; not to mention Lilian Marks who, by that Diaghilevian *changement de pieds* for which she was renowned, became Alicia Markova – no, Errol had things to say about Heinrich Heine's defections as well, and Gustav Mahler's, and Bernard Berenson's. When the school awarded me the third-form art prize in the shape of a leather-bound *Palgrave's Golden Treasury* languidly illustrated by Robert Anning Bell, Errol put pressure on me to give it back. 'They mean it as an insult, Max,' he told me.

'I grant you the drawings are a bit soppy,' I said, 'but an *insult*!'

'I'm not talking about the illustrations, you putz. I'm talking about Palgrave. Did you know his father was a Jew? Francis Ephraim Cohen. Met a woman called Palgrave, got baptised into the Church of England, married her, and changed his name to hers. Ten years later he's Sir Francis Palgrave. Play your cards right, Maxie, and it could happen to you. You're already halfway there.'

'By accepting this prize? Don't be a meshuggener. Anyway, you can't blame this Palgrave for what his father did. It's not his fault he was born a Palgrave.'

'Yes it is, he could have changed his name back.'

'Wouldn't have sounded any good, though, would it – *Ephraim Cohen's Golden Treasury of the Best Songs and Lyrical Poems in the English Language*?'

'That's because they've brainwashed you into believing a man

135

called Ephraim Cohen can't be a reliable authority on the English lyric.'

A fair point, I thought. But, 'I'm still keeping it,' I said.

Which, I later discovered, Errol was going around saying was only to be expected from someone whose father wouldn't let him have a bar mitzvah.

As for Manny, his bar mitzvah was still to come – some dark Byzantine event in an underground synagogue I'd never heard of, was how I imagined it would be, Manny folded in shawls, invisible among the beards of holy men, and no dancing afterwards, or that ghastly men-only Hassidic jigging behind screens erected to stop the women seeing what would arouse them into sexual hysteria if they did – a whirling blur of humpbacked scholars in their long black coats making old-country Jew Jew Hari Krishna circles around the bar mitzvah boy.

Manny said nothing to me about the fact that my thirteenth birthday had been and gone unheralded. Tact? Or disgust beyond expression? As it turned out, neither. While we were being gossiped about all over town and I was having to make do with an unwanted pair of boxing gloves and a clandestine tallis as my only presents, the Washinskys were having troubles of their own. Asher. Asher and the fire-yekelte.

4

Zoë, my Gentile second wife, a woman who was nothing if not humorous, once told me a joke just after lovemaking.

'How many Jews can you get into a Volkswagen Beetle?' she asked.

'None,' I said. 'No Jew would get into a Volkswagen Beetle.'

I was lying. I had even owned a Volkswagen Beetle myself once, at the behest of Chloë. But now didn't seem the time to mention that.

Over the bedclothes she hit me. 'Why do you always do that, Max? Why won't you let anyone tell a joke?'

Did I always do that? I wasn't aware I always did that. 'Tell the joke,' I said.

'I can't now.'

'You can. Tell the joke.'

She sat up in bed, knowing that the sight of her perfectly equiponderant hand-grenade breasts would always quieten me. Pale gold, her breasts, like melted butter; her nipples very precise, no spillage in the aureole, thus far and no further. We could have come from different planets, Zoë and I, so unalike in body were we. My limbs and members intermingled freely, I flopped about, bled contour into contour, hue into hue; not Zoë – between one of Zoë's parts and another no continuity was discernible. One at a time they must have come into the world, one at a time and alone.

She was the same with words and sentences. Nothing was assumed already spoken. She had to start again from the beginning.

'How many Jews can you get into a Volkswagen Beetle?' she asked.

Tempting for me to do the same. *None. No Jew would get into a Volkswagen Beetle.* But I was too good a sport to ruin a hilarious joke, and poor Zoë had, by her own account, suffered terribly at the hands of Jewish people already. 'I don't know,' I said. 'Tell me.'

'One thousand and four. Two in the front, two in the back, and one thousand in the ashtray.'

5

Would that be funny to a Holocaust denier, I wonder, or would he see it – though emanating from a Jew-befuddled Gentile – as another example of Jewish overstatement? 'We have done the research and can state categorically that it is impossible to get a thousand Jews, or even a quarter of that number of Jews, however passively disposed, into the ashtray of a Volkswagen.'

So we are an immoderate, overemphatic people, much given to exaggeration – so what? I call it giving value for money myself. You prick us so we bleed profusely. You put us to the torch and we burn well for you. Just don't pretend that we invent the conflagrations that consume us.

If it felt like the end of the world to Mr and Mrs Washinsky when they discovered that their elder son was sleeping with the fire-yekelte, that is because it *was* the end of the world.

Not the sex: they could have dealt with the sex. But everything consequent on the sex: that sequence of events written at the start of creation in the book of Jewish time – the pregnancy, the betrothal, the village church bells tolling a wedding which is no less a funeral, the grandchildren baptised in an alien font (the dew of their baby-Jewishness washed clean away) – the depletion, the erasure, the annulment, the extinction in the arms of no matter how welcoming a Gentile future of their hard-won Jewish past. Not negligible, such concerns, when you consider how intrinsic to Christianity disparagement of Judaism has been. Marry a Christian and you marry into your own denial. In the eyes of Asher's parents, he was sleeping with their negation. That it never bothered me, that I couldn't wait to propose to every Gentile woman I met provided her name was suitably accented, does not mean it should not have bothered the Washinskys. I am the perversion here.

Just as Frances Ephraim Cohen, become Palgrave – whether or not I kept his son's *Golden Treasury* – was the perversion before me.

It was the end of the Washinskys' world, joke about it how you like. Yes, they would have said and felt the same had Asher been sleeping with the daughter of the Archbishop of Canterbury,

and then found some saving grace in it. It is not a sin to be prag-
matic in the matter of miscegenation. If your offspring must stray,
better they stray wisely. Instances are not unknown, when all is
said and done, of apostatic sexual union not only not diminishing
Judaism but actually enhancing it. Esther, for example, married
the King of Persia, from which position of influence she was able
to save the Jews from annihilation. But who was Asher going to
save by sleeping with the fire-yekelte, the sooty person who knelt
in front of the Washinskys' grate on a Shabbes morning, tied
newspapers into knots, tossed matches into coals, and was thus,
since they were poor themselves, the nochschlepper to
nochschleppers?

Himself?

Well, to get to that interpretation you need a more Christian
conception of saving than is available to your average Jew.

6

Although 'Asher and the fire-yekelte' was how it was originally
rumoured, the woman with whom he was having the affair wasn't,
strictly speaking, the fire-yekelte at all. She was the fire-yekelte's
daughter. Yes, when her mother was unavailable or unwell, she
did a little fire-yekelting for the Washinskys herself, but fire-
yekelte qua fire-yekelte she was not. Which made a difference,
or didn't, according to where you stood on yekeltes in general.
Remove the age discrepancy and you remove some of the transgression; remove the transgression and you remove much of the
audacity. As a boy transfixed by the idea of the older Gentile
woman, I would have been more in awe of Asher had he plumped
for the mother. But it was certainly audacious enough of him,
given his upbringing, to have let his feelings lead him where they
did; less lubricious, less heroically unchaste, more conventionally
sentimental, more Romeo than one of the Karamazov boys, but
on that account, weighing this against that, still bold.

Don't ask how I know what I know about this sorry business. 'Don't ask,' as Tsedraiter Ike would say when anyone was fool enough to enquire about anything. His health, the state of Israel, the condition of the Jewish people – *don't ask*. Let's just say I picked up some of it at the time it was happening from Manny, though he was by no means a leaky vessel; some of it from Errol Tobias whose mother, as the local hairdresser, was privy to every whisper of impropriety; and more from my own mother later, most of it an extravagant act of backward deduction from the details of Manny's arrest and subsequent trial as they appeared in the local newspapers; to say nothing of what any man will find if he consults his own heart. Nor do I think it too fantastical to claim intuitive knowledge of Asher Washinsky's feelings from his countenance, that mask of ascetic dissolution which I studied with fascination on the few occasions I saw it, so much did I wish it had been mine. Those hollow gouges where other men had eyes – wonderful to draw because they were already made of char-coal in the flesh – told me everything about the intensity with which he loved a woman. Desperate, he must have been. Far gone, to do what was bound to cause anguish to his parents. And far gone indeed, to do it, to be able to *bear* to do it – for that was what was whispered – in their bed!

He had met her – Dorothy was her name, no saving diaeresis, but it could have been un-Jewishly worse, they could have called her Dot – coming out of his parents' house with coal dust on her face. So that was the two of them black-eyed. He saw her and stopped. She saw him and stopped. Then he took out a handker-chief and handed it to her. 'Here, wipe your face with this.' She could easily have surrendered to the same impulse in herself. He was the kind of man you wanted to mend. Picture them then, on the Washinsky path, dabbing at each other's eyes.

I want to dab at mine, thinking of them. She was pretty. I caught a glimpse of her once or twice, briefly, before she became Asher's girlfriend, standing in for her mother at the Washinskys' grate. A blonde, as you'd expect. When the devil seeks to make trouble in a Jewish family he does it as a blonde. But not one of Tsedraiter Ike's peroxide blondes. Golden, like a cornfield. With creamy skin, yellow-green eyes, and, as I understand it, despite her lowly origins, a good brain. Doing A levels. French, German, Latin. The spot of fire-yekelte-ing she had taken on was a favour to her mother and a way of putting away a few shillings for when she went to university. Not that the Washinskys actually 'paid' for the Shabbes services they received. Only lately have I learned that such a thing was infra dig. What you did was put money where it could be found and then you left it to the fire-yekelte to make the appropriate deduction. Ditto giving the fire-yekelte direct instructions. An Orthodox Jew is not allowed to derive benefit on the Sabbath from saying, 'Put the lights on for me, there's a dear,' but must 'hint' at what needs doing, as in, 'Oy, am I having trouble seeing anything today!' Given how smart Dorothy was, it has to be assumed that she knew where to find the money and how to take a hint.

Love at first sight, anyway. *Coup de foudre*. A bolt of lightning striking both their hearts simultaneously, illuminating them and them alone and plunging everything else into darkness. Midnight in the Garden of Love and Traif.

Forbidden meat, that was what each was for the other. And only a fool would deny that their passion was the greater for a little leavening of the *verboten*.

That I too have managed to transpose the Washinskys' scrubby path into a garden of desire shows how wedded to romantic love I still am, despite my own failures at it. Also shows why I should have listened to my first art teacher's advice and softened my palette, swapped my pencil for a brush, and gone to live in Tuscany for a summer. He was a romantic himself, Ted Hargreaves, as he demonstrated when he resigned his post and ran off with a senior prefect from our sister girls' school who, he said, reminded him of Raphael's Fornarina. Were I half the

Hogarthian I have sometimes pretended to be I wouldn't hesitate to lampoon that elopement. Raphael's Fornarina with a hockey stick, for God's sake! But it's no good pretending. Ask other men in my profession to depict a woman in a man's arms and they give you Olive Oyl in Popeye's. Or Flo Capp in Andy's. At poetic best, Lois Lane in Clark Kent's, dreaming of Superman. Ribald in the doing or the withholding. Because I am not by nature a satirist, I picture Asher and Dorothy (and Ted and Sheila, come to that) in a Rubensesque setting, cherubim in the clouds, the silk of their garments rustling, his fingers unlooping curls that fall about her peachy neck, both their faces on fire.

Aflame with the shock of love, that was how I saw them. *Shamed* with it. And Rubens and Rembrandt both found just the colour for that shame. The Dutch flush.

Under whichever sky you see them, they were mad for each other and might have stayed that way had the 'harpies' (a word with which Manny was to surprise me later) not spoilt it for them. It's possible Asher wasn't in it for the long term, I don't know. It's also possible he wasn't a man you could love for ever. Those cadaver good looks might very well consume all parties to them early. Indeed I've heard it said – Chloë? Zoë? – that that's precisely the erotic appeal of Jewish men. It's like throwing yourself on a bonfire. But there isn't any evidence that these two were playing conflagrations. They were a serious pair of kids. Not the sort, either of them, to embark on a friendship, let alone a love affair, lightly. They both had exams to pass. She intended to become a language teacher. He a rabbi; but then a rabbi, too, is a teacher of tongues. And they would both have felt, given their differences, that they had a lot to teach each other.

Because of his people's perceived exoticism and predisposition to pedantry, it's usually the Jew in a mixed relationship who does the explaining. This is why we put mezuzahs on the lintels of our doors; this is why we light candles at Chanukah – Ch . . . no, *Ch*, from the back of a throat, as though you're coughing up phlegm;

this is why we lean at the Seder table. I can even imagine, in this instance, Asher coaching Dorothy in the rudiments of Hebrew, she being a linguist, remember, and quick to learn. But I have no doubt that he wouldn't have had it all his own way. She was a strong-minded woman. When first she saw Asher her heart would have burst, but when she raised her dazzled eyes to him a second time she'd have seen he was somebody who needed liberating. He looked like a man in chains. You could tick off everything he didn't know, everything he was afraid to go near or put his mind to, in the marks about his mouth. His lips were never still, not because he was praying to Elohim, though he was surely doing that as well, but because he was rehearsing answers to uncomfortable questions, spells and divinations that would get him through the terrors of the day. In knowledge is safety, and the first thing she decided to do was acquaint him with a few things – this is the earth, that is the sky, I am a Gentile, and no, you will not feel unclean in the morning for having touched me.

What a time they must have had, learning about each other, sneaking around the backs of both their lives, heads together, eyebeams plaited, fingers locked, meeting in parks and cinemas, kissing in doorways, maybe jumping on trains to escape the environs of guilt, maybe booking into hotels, though there couldn't have been a lot of that otherwise he would surely not have risked taking her home when his parents were away and uncovering her nakedness in their bed.

Except that there is reason to believe he never did any such thing. Years later, after he had changed his name to Stroganoff, Manny vehemently denounced the story of his brother's defiling of their parents' bed as a calumny. Confirming, I must say, what I had always thought. Why would Asher Washinsky, when all was said and done, have taken the fire-yekelte's daughter to his parents' bed when they were out of the house, given that their being out of the house just as opportunely gave him access to his own? More room to thrash about in, you could argue, his bed being narrow, as befitted a yeshiva boy with nothing but Elohim on his mind; but the luxuriousness of more room would surely have been vitiated by the unluxuriousness of the bed being that in which your mother and your father slept, unless that is to betray, as someone who missed out on being bar mitzvah'd, my ignorance of the depravity of observant Jews.

So scrub the bed.

She took him home. Up the hill from the denser thickets of Orthodoxy in the Manchester/Salford lowlands to the more feathery coppices of half-belief in Heaton Park, then up the hill again to where the Gentiles breathed the clean air of the foothills of the Pennines and not a Jew of any sort had been seen since Leo the Pedlar passed by selling pins and ribbons in the 1780s. People came to their windows to look. Passers-by clutched their children to them. A dog, meaning to bark, changed its mind and shrank back behind its fence. Cars slowed down to look. Later, describing the day, local people would remember that their power supply failed, their gas blew out, their paintings trembled and fell off the walls. All agreed it went dark suddenly.

Dorothy held his hand. 'Not much further,' she told him.

'How much further?'

She squeezed his hand five times.

'Five miles?'

'Five minutes.'

She couldn't decide whether she had been away a long time, circumnavigating the globe, and was now bringing home the spoils of her travels, or whether the real prize was this, her sublunary Gentile world, and she was rewarding Asher with it.

As for him, I know what he was feeling. I've been walked up the hill many times myself, now by Chloë, now by Zoë, half-booty, half-apology. Look Ma, look Pa, look what I've found! The frightening part being not knowing if they intend to open your mouth and examine your teeth, or have a quick feel around to locate your tail. But then you could say that's the arousing part as well, allowing that it can be arousing for a rare species to be used for the sexual satisfaction of a more common one. Ask the merman. Ask the minotaur.

I say I know what he must have been feeling, but in truth he was bound to have been far more terrified than I ever was, if only because he quickened greater curiosity. Enough Jew blazed from my face for Zoë to make the future of our marriage dependent on my agreeing to be de-Semitised, but the very fact that she badgered me to have my nose rolled up and put away – that's what 'retroussé' means, by the way, 'rolled up' – suggests she did not think I looked otherwise, absolutely and incontrovertibly, on pain of death, Jewish. Noseless, it's possible I could have got away with being merely Slavic and depressed. Whereas where Asher walked, the whole of the Old Testament walked with him. Seeded like a pomegranate he was with the sorrows and the tribulations of his people, but juicy with the wine of the pomegranate, too, spicy with spikenard and saffron, calamus and cinnamon, his lips like a thread of scarlet.

And people notice you when you look like that. Especially people from cold countries.

Home was where she was taking him, but not to meet her mother. It had been decided by the interested parties, at least those of them who were in the know, that for Asher to meet her mother was, for the time being at any rate, inappropriate on account of her mother being the person who cleaned out Asher's mother's grate, in which capacity he had already met her. So the daughter was taking him home to meet the father. And since the easiest time to arrange meeting the father but not the mother was Shabbes morning, when Dorothy knew the father would be in and the mother would be out, they set a Shabbes morning for it. Odd for them both, odd for the father too, sitting around the fire in Higher Blackley making small talk, while all along their minds must have been on that other fire in Crumpsall Park, tended by one to whom there was no good reason not to allude, yet to whom nobody felt they could.

That Asher's mind would also have been on Elohim, at this moment receiving prayers in Asher's shul, goes without saying.

'Asher will be missing synagogue in order to meet you,' Dorothy had explained to her father in advance.

'And your father, will he be missing the pub to meet me?' Asher knew better than to ask. But the question would certainly have occurred to him, alcohol being almost as big a stumbling block between Jews and Gentiles as the resurrection.

('Put the glasses away, he doesn't drink,' I remember Chloë hissing to her mother.

'What, not ever?'

'Not ever, Mother. None of them do.'

'Afraid that they'll forget which pocket they keep their wallet in, is that it?'

'Shush, Mother! Promise me you'll shush.' But laughing as she said it.

'Crack you a bottle of something, or will I be having fun on my ownio?' was how Chloë's mother greeted me, notwithstanding her daughter's pantomime objurgations.

So I asked if she had a Château Latour 1949 already open – which started our relationship off on the wrong foot. Unless what started our relationship off on the wrong foot was my adding that if she didn't have a Château Latour, a bottle of communion wine would do as well – any vintage that took her fancy, as long as it was genuinely the blood of You Know Who.)

It was a Saturday morning, of course, for Asher, whereas my introduction into Chloë's poisonous little family occurred on an evening in the week, but even so Asher was always going to receive a more sensitive welcome into Dorothy's family. They were charming people. They deferred to what was unfamiliar. On the table tea and toast and little coconut cakes, with no cream or butter in sight, Dorothy and her father having heard that Jews had to be careful when and where and with what and with whom they ate dairy.

Among the many domestic details that struck Asher as alien and not at all what he had expected was the wallpaper, which was in a better condition than his parents' wallpaper, and the carpets, which were far less threadbare than his parents' carpets, and the bookcases, which contained far more books of a non-religious nature than his parents possessed, and the record collection which was more substantial in the Brahms and Beethoven department than his parents' collection, which wouldn't have been difficult as his parents didn't have any Brahms or Beethoven, only Mantovani and Sophie Tucker; but above all he was struck by the atmosphere of cheerful sufficiency in shortage, of which there was not a semblance where he lived, a consciousness of material deficiency seeping through his parents' house like damp.

Dorothy held on to him, not knowing what he thought. Was he missing sanctity? Did he think her family morally trivial for keeping a clean house? Did he judge them as wanting in spiritual values?

She could never have guessed that Asher would be confused by the discovery that the woman who made the fires for his parents on a Shabbes kept a cleaner and pleasanter home than they did. What else, when all was said and done, would he have expected? Wasn't that precisely why her mother was employed – to do for the Washinskys a little of what she did for her own family? That the quid pro quo of fire-yekelte-ing entailed a deeper hierarchical gulf between the chosen and the not, would no more have occurred to her than it did to Elvis Presley, compliantly skivvying for the Fruchters in Memphis.

(And perhaps would not have occurred to me were I not the son of a father who held fire-yekelte-ing to be a species of social condescension, akin to slavery, of which every Jew should be ashamed.)

Dorothy saw Asher heat up the moment her father addressed

him. A shy boy. She loved him for that. Well mannered. He bowed slightly when her father offered him his hand. And she thought she saw a movement suggestive of his wanting to cover his head. Respect. She loved him for that too.

As for Asher, he was surprised and even a little daunted by the fastidious manners of Dorothy's father, the precise way he greeted him, the elaborately courteous, not to say old-fashioned gestures with which he ushered Asher into a chair and made a ceremony — no, more than a ceremony, a demonstration, as though it was a skill he had only recently acquired — of tea.

But what struck him even more forcibly than this was the fact that Dorothy's father was foreign. To be more precise, German.

End of the Washinskys' world.

SIX

Doctor: How's the world of funny books?
Cartoonist/patient: They're actually not FUNNY anymore.
People who read comics now want drama and adventure
more than laughs.

Steven T. Seagle & Teddy Christiansen, *It's a Bird*

1

At the time I would not have seen the relevance of the enquiry,
but it must have been hereabouts in our Jewed-over adolescence
that Manny, the young Manny, asked me, 'When you see German
script, what do you feel?'

The question came without any context or preparation. But
that itself was not unusual. Most of what Manny said he said out
of the blue.

'Queasy,' I told him. 'The same way I feel about the
Katzenjammer Kids. Queasy and depressed. And the paper it's
always printed on makes me feel queasy and depressed as well.
And the covers remind me of coffins. When I see a German book
I see death. Next question.'

'No, you haven't properly answered this one yet. I wasn't asking
you about German books. I asked how you feel when you see
German writing in a letter. Not the Gothic script, just the handwriting, just the words.'

I thought about it. 'I've never seen German writing in a letter,'
I answered. 'I don't correspond with Germans. I don't have
German pen pals. Why are you asking?'

He was in his swimming phase. His arms thrashing as we
walked along the street, his cheeks puffed. Turning his head from

side to side. And practising holding his breath under water. I'd never met anybody so interested in seeing if he could live without breathing. So I had to hang on for a reply until he came back up. 'No reason,' he said at last. Which seemed to me not worth the wait.

'Course there's a reason. You wouldn't have asked otherwise. Are you getting letters from a German? Who?'

Who's the girl, I would have asked anybody else. Who's the lucky Fräulein? But you didn't make those jokes with Manny. Besides, what chance was there of him of all people corresponding with a German of either sex. All schoolkids had pen pals then. Something your French or Spanish teacher organised. I had a Manuel in Barcelona and a Julie in Aix-les-Bains whose letters arrived liked gifts of the heart in envelopes lined with susurrating tissue paper. But Manny was at a school for Jews. I couldn't see his teachers opening up lines of communication with Hildegarde in Baden-Baden.

He went under again, still in the yarmulke which since going to his new school he now wore at all times. I imagined him floating on the surface, his head down, the silken fringes of his tzitzis trailing behind him as though they had issued from his body, like spawn.

'No one,' he said, when he came back up a second time, his cheeks bulging.

'You just mentioned the matter of German handwriting for no reason?'

He was red and panting. Looking away. Did he always look away? When I try to picture him as he was then I cannot see him ever looking at me. I cannot remember what his eyes looked like. What colour or how big they were.

'I found a letter,' he said, 'that's all.'

'What do you mean you "found a letter"? Where did you find a letter?'

'In the street.'

He was lying. You don't find letters written in German on the streets of Manchester. Or you didn't then. Not in Crumpsall Park. But something always told me to lay off him. So far with Manny, and no further. Not because I was afraid of what he would say or do to me – though there was always his rabid bite to be on the lookout for – but because I was afraid of what I could do to him.

'And what did this letter make you feel when you found it?'

'Upset,' he said.

Which it's possible I was meant to follow up on. Be supportive, be a friend. Possible that there was something serious he needed to get off his chest. But I was frightened and a little bit ashamed of intimacy with him. We were going to change the world with our illustrated history of Jewish bitterness, and we spoke of the horrors of the Holocaust together, but when he said he was upset I shied away.

'Know what you mean,' I said.

2

Upset. The very word my father had used on his return from a trip to Cologne with the Maccabeans boxing team, the first leg of what was intended to be a sequence of exchange visits. Much publicised in the local Jewish press, and much inveighed against by many leading members of the Manchester Jewish community who believed it was too early, the boxing trip had originally been envisaged, by my father and Bunny Silverman who were its originators, as a goodwill gesture. It was time to forget the iniquities of the past. It was time to mend some fences. It was time to go and punch the Nazi bastards' faces in.

But there wasn't much goodwill coming off him when we met him in the hall.

'Well, I won't be doing that again,' he told us, no sooner than he'd put his cases down.

He was puffing, fragile-looking, not himself. He could see what we were thinking. 'No,' he said, 'I didn't get into the ring. I'm just upset.'

He didn't look himself and didn't *sound* himself either. *Upset? My father?*

'Did you lose?' my mother asked.

'We drew. We should have won, but we drew. But that's not what upset me.'

Of course it wasn't. I knew what had upset him. Germans had upset him. I'm not saying I shared the views of those who'd written to the papers arguing that the boxing friendly desecrated the memory of the dead, but I was surprised that he had gone. I was surprised, even knowing what I knew about him, that he could face it. Germans weren't for seeing yet. Not for another five thousand years.

'Was it seeing the old ones and wondering?' I wondered.

Myself I blamed the young ones as well. Sins of the fathers and all that. From an early age I took responsibility for what my forebears had done, and burned with shame still for some of the crimes recounted of my people in Deuteronomy. So there was no innocent generation in Germany to my mind. But seeing the old ones would obviously be worse. Scrutinising every face. And where were *you* and where were *you* . . . ?

'No.' He shook his head. He wasn't having any of that 'and how many Jews did you gas?' business. 'Nothing to do with the people. The people are just people. They're like us.'

My sister snorted. Hard now to remember what she was doing out of her room. Did she hope to hear about the boxing? Who had flattened whom? Or was it because she had missed my father and knew in her bones she wasn't going to see much more of him?

'People are the same the world over,' he said. He looked tired. 'How many times have I told you that? It's what's done to the people.'

'So what upset you, then?' she asked. Angry. Always angry. Everything an affront. Always in a party dress or a sheet and always angry. 'The fact that they drive on the wrong side of the road?'

She had already refused to show gratitude for the present he'd made a ceremony (too courtly a ceremony?) of handing her — cologne from Cologne, prettily wrapped and ribboned. 'Yours will probably be Belsen Water,' she hissed to me out of the corner of her mouth.

Always angry, always sarcastic, and always made up for a ball. Maybe had they just let her *go* to a ball once in a while, she would have been sweeter of temperament. But had they let her go to a ball, at her age, they'd have fretted every minute she was out of the house, and been less sweet of temperament themselves.

I say 'they', but it was my father who drove all this fretting and fearing. For her part my mother (the real pagan in the family) wouldn't have minded what Shani got up to, so long as she wore something my mother approved of to get up to it in.

So what was it my father feared?

The same all Jew Jew Jew fathers were afraid of — goy, goy, goy.

What, even my entirely irreligious God-hating top-to-bottom secularised new-Jew-seeking dad who would have doubled my pocket money had I told him I was going out with shikseh triplets? Well, there's the funny thing . . .

But doubtless I do him an injustice. He deserved better than a caricaturist for a son. Had he been luckier he'd have sired a moral philosopher capable of grasping the subtleties of his position. That's if there is a school of moral philosophy capable of grasping why a man who could imagine no greater future for the Jews than that they should be indistinguishable from non-Jews was unable to bear the thought of a non-Jew fondling his daughter.

He didn't fear what the Washinskys feared, that much was certain. He didn't fear depletion of the Jewish stock or obliteration of the Jewish memory. So what was it?

Only recently has it occurred to me that the answer to the question is in the word 'fondling' itself. What he actually couldn't bear was *anybody* doing it. A disappointingly banal explanation for someone committed to understanding human history as a battle between the Jews and everybody else.

He made a face at her as though he were someone her own age. Then reached out to draw her closer. For a moment we all thought he was going to take her on his knee. Nothing unusual in that for some fathers, but Jack 'The Jew' Glickman only pulled a person to him when he wanted to rough them up in the ring. A cold premonition seized me. And I could see that it seized my mother as well.

'No, clever clogs,' he said, running his hands through her hair – something else he didn't normally do – 'it's bugger all to do with them driving on the wrong side of the road, which as an internationalist I am prepared to believe is the right side of the road anyway. What I didn't like was the fact that they spoke German. Laugh all you like, but that's the fact of it. I didn't like hearing the words. I didn't like seeing the words. It was the look of the letters. The letters upset me.'

So there you are. If the look of the German language could upset my internationalist, non-grudge-bearing father, a man naive enough to suppose that people were only what was done to them and whose sins were therefore not indelible, who wouldn't it upset?

But then he was a dying man.

3

Was it to upset me that Chloë kept nagging for a Mercedes? I don't mean for herself. I mean for us. She, me, her mother – if not exactly in that order. A family car.

I was in my middle twenties at the time, barely out of art school. Not only was I not making enough money from my cartoons at the time, I didn't think a Mercedes was seemly for someone my age.

'Too flash,' I told her.

'You mean too foreign.'

'No, I don't. I mean too bourgeois.'

'There you are, you've agreed with me. Too foreign. Too *bürgerlich.*'

'Nothing to do with foreign. We could have a Renault.'

'So we can have French but not German.'

'What's Germany got to do with it, Chloë?'

'With "it", nothing. With you, everything. Why can't you let the subject drop, Maxie?'

'Let the subject drop? I never mention the subject.'

'Five Thousand Years of Bitterness, Five Thousand Years of Bitterness . . .'

'That's not exclusively Germany.'

'No, just the last five hundred years of it.'

So to prove Germany wasn't a problem I relented, or she relented, and we bought a Volkswagen Beetle.

Had a Mercedes been a problem for me on German grounds, then a Volkswagen would surely have been a greater one. Linguistics, partly. But also something Errol Tobias had told me once when we were having to lower the tennis net across the street to allow a Volkswagen to pass. 'If you look at the hubcaps on a Volkswagen,' he whispered from the side of his face, 'you'll see that the VW makes a swastika.' Since we had a Volkswagen there, waiting for the net to go down, I was well positioned to check.

'No it doesn't,' I said. All I could see was VW.

'It's got to be travelling, shmuck.'

So I waited for it to move off. Nothing. Just VW.

'No, it's got to be travelling at exactly fifteen miles per hour. Fourteen miles per hour, you won't see it. Sixteen miles per hour, you won't see it. It's got to be fifteen. German efficiency for you.'

I believed him. But it wasn't easy finding a Volkswagen travelling at exactly fifteen miles per hour. Fifteen miles per hour was a damnably smart speed to pick. Too slow for the main road, too fast for our street. Those Nazis! You have to hand it to them.

But I have managed to find a Volkswagen doing fifteen miles per hour. Once. In Berlin. And the V and the W did embrace into a swastika. I *think*.

When I made the mistake of mentioning this phenomenon to Chloë she said, 'Right, we're having one.'

As I understood it, the *Volk* in Volkswagen didn't carry an umlaut. *Völkchen* and *Völkerschaft*, yes. Volkswagen, no. But Chloë inserted one regardless. To be precise about it, she inserted two, yodelling the spaces between the *v* and the *l*, and then the *l* and the *k* for good measure, as though a double valley of umlauting divided them. On occasions she even threw one over the *a* in wagen, which made three umlauts in all.

Because she knew it annoyed me, we carted her mother around in the Beetle whenever we were up with her or she was down with us; and because *she* knew it annoyed me, her mother sang cod-German songs in the back seat. No sooner did I put us into top gear than Chloë would wind open the little aperture in the roof, which was the signal for her mother to begin. 'I Love to Go a-Wandering' was her favourite, especially the line about 'a knapsack on my back' which she interpreted as 'ein k-näpsäck ön mein bërk'. Carols, too, she liked, in particular '*O Tannenbaum*' and '*Stille Nacht*', employing German noises, nothing more than gargles, where she didn't know or couldn't remember the words.

'Christ the what-is-it again, darling?' I remember her asking Chloë one clammy afternoon as we powered through the Cheshire dales.

'*Der Retter*, Mother.'

'*Retter* meaning?'

'Saviour, Mother.'

'Shh – not in front of Maxie, darling' – this in a stage whisper

— 'it might upset his sensibilities . . . *Christ, the saviour was bor-orn, Chri-ist the saviour was born* . . . Do you people accept the idea of a saviour, Max, or are you above saving?'

'Beyond saving, more like,' I told her.

'Ah, well, ho-hum, what you can't save you can't have, as the actress said to the archbishop.'

'Mother, don't be vulgar!'

'What – what have I done?'

'Actresses and archbishops! Act your age!'

'All right, as the Jewess said to the chief rabbi, then.'

While all along I sat with the dinky volksie steering wheel clamped in my white clenched fists, racking my brain for some county that had the word mutilation or perdition in it, up or down the little wooden hill to which etc. Then it was home, James, and don't spare the horsepower, followed by 'I'll be saying *auf Wiedersehen* to you now – *auf Wiedersehen*!'

To show there were no hard feelings, Chloë's mother bought me a toy rabbi to hang in the rear window of my Völökswägen. What she thought I'd like about it was the way it nodded its head when the car was in motion, just like 'one of those Hassocks you some-times see mumbling to Mecca on a train'.

'I think you mean Hassids,' I told her. 'A hassock's a hairy cushion.'

'Same difference, darling.

'And they're not looking towards Mecca.'

She rolled her eyes at her daughter. 'So touchy your husband's people, Chlo. You can't even buy them a present without their getting aeriated.'

I don't know where she bought the rabbi. She travelled a bit when she could tear herself away from my company, so it was possible she had picked it up in some colony of ex-Nazis hanging out in Argentina. Or a friend could have found it for her, thinking of me, the sheeny son-in-law, in a corner shop in one of the more

Orthodox suburbs of Jerusalem. Meer-sh'arim maybe. You can never tell with tat; bad taste narrows the gap between the sentimental way you see yourself, and the scorn with which others see you. Half of what's for sale in Israel you'd consider anti-Semitic if you saw it anywhere else.

The one thing I knew for sure was that neither she nor her daughter had made it. They lacked both the patience and the aptitude for handicrafts. It's also very unlikely, wherever Chloë's mother came by the nodding rabbi, that she'd have shelled out much for it. 'I'm as tight as you people are,' she winked at me one day. 'Only I'm a tightey-whitey, whereas you're . . .'

She couldn't think of anything.

'A meany-sheeny,' I came back, quick as a flash.

How did she do that? How was she able to lure me into being rude about myself? It was an astonishing gift. She could make you say the vilest things in the hope of saying them before she did.

But as far as the rabbi goes, wherever she got it and however much it cost was finally irrelevant. It was the thought that counted.

4

And among the thoughts it occasioned was this one: it looked like Manny.

A cruel thing to say, as it was a cruel thought to have, but that was the truth of it – the toy rabbi reminded me of Manny, rocking and rolling to Elohim in my Völökswägen's rear-view mirror.

I wasn't, you see, much better than my mother-in-law when it came to respect for the holy.

That was my only reminder of Manny in those day – the days before he broke all the Ten Commandments in the act of breaking one – the only reason I ever had to think of him. What had become of him I didn't know. Not something I enquired about on my occasional visits to Crumpsall Park – whether he'd left home, whether he was still studying at the yeshiva, whether he had indeed become a rabbi, or whether he was tramping the watery pavements like the man with paper in his shoes who popped up all over Manchester, muttering and looking skywards – at one time a famous rabbi himself, people said. Had I seen him in the street I would have stopped to talk to him, of course. Had I bumped into either of his parents on my visits home, or even Asher – though Asher had become a sort of ghost in my imagination by this time – I'd have asked after him and sent him my best wishes. But they didn't leave the house much, Asher never materialised, and I didn't go looking.

When I sold the Völökswägen I remembered to retrieve the toy, faithfully repositioning it where it would be visible in the mirror of the new car. And I did it again with the car after that. A sentimental ritual, though whether it was Chloë and her mother I was sentimentalising, or Manny Washinsky, I couldn't have told you. But after the phone call from my mother apprising me of Manny's crime, it seemed proper to remove what all at once appeared to be a cruelly satiric effigy of him. I didn't throw it away. But I didn't want to see it, didn't want a comical reminder, bobbing about in the back of my car, of someone who had passed out of comical remembrance into something more terrible.

Later, when they locked him up, I would picture him despite myself – for I tried not to picture him at all – as Goya's black-chalked *Lunatic Behind Bars*, his head dehumanised, as pitiful as a caged dog's, staring out at something he could not see, one naked arm out of the bars, the bars criss-crossed like a wooden crate, a creature as much boxed as barred, nailed away for ever, the more heartbreaking for his compliance.

My removal of him from my sight was more friendly. Not me scalding all trace of him from under my fingernails. More an act of piety.

* * *

I still have the rabbi among my possessions, wrapped in a silk handkerchief and folded into a black cardboard box which had originally housed an expensive set of pencils – a gift from Zoë, 'To my juicy Jew Jew boy' inscribed in the lid.

She should have seen Manny's brother.

That Manny Washinsky was not going to have a conventionally happy life was obvious to everyone who knew him. You couldn't picture him settled comfortably in a nice house with a loving family and in a fulfilling job – those being what a happy life comprised in those days. You couldn't even picture him breathing normally. But had someone suggested he would wind up in prison on a murder rap, I'd have laughed and told them they had the wrong person. Right street, wrong person. You mean Errol Tobias, further up and on the other side. You mean Errol Tobias, whose depravity is such that it would be a kindness to the community if you incarcerated him now, the damage he was going to do being only a matter of time. Yet today Manny is the old lag, his imprisoned mind a charnel house, while Errol Tobias performs the functions of an exemplary husband and father, importing wines from Israel and living quietly in Borehamwood.

Whether there are any lessons to be drawn from that, whether Errol Tobias's depravity was only skin-deep, a passing sinfulness which he would grow out of eventually, or whether it's still in there, biding its time, I can no more than guess. But he was the most depraved person I had ever met and it's hard to imagine where in the universe such depravity could have got to had it left him.

His version of the terrible fight he had with Manny – for me a high-watermark (or do I mean a low-watermark?) in the history of his depravity, though for him I suspect it was just another day – began with Manny biting him. When I disagreed, insisting that from where I stood Manny only started biting him when he started pulling off Manny's trousers, he changed the story without a qualm to its all beginning when Manny laughed at him. I wasn't there for that part, which occurred, if it occurred as Errol described it all, at the bottom of the street where Errol was ripping out the Golonskys' garden. Manny had apparently swum past, on his way home from school, flailing his arms, his mouth opening and closing like a carp's, at the sight of which Errol had plainly said something along the lines of – though I'm only guessing – *Fucking freak! Fucking frummer freak!* Not enough to make Manny stop. He was used to being abused. Not by other Jewish boys, it's true, but then Errol Tobias wasn't like other Jewish boys. To have got Manny so much as to look up – and I'm still guessing – Errol must have tried needling him about Asher, maybe at that very moment inventing the calumny (because he surely was its source) that Asher was sleeping with the fire-yekelte in Manny's mother and father's bed. Very likely, in that event, that Manny would have halted, wondered what to do or say, then grinned that ghastly ice-mask grin of his, the one that got him into so much trouble with Shitworth Whitworth, the one that served the single purpose of stopping his face collapsing altogether. Only someone even less self-possessed than Manny could have taken that laugh of evisceration as directed derisively at him. But that was exactly how Errol, by his own account, took it.

I knew him for a belcher, Errol Tobias. He was one of those boys who could roll belches out of his stomach for as long as he believed it amused people to hear them. An unusual gift in a Jew, who is usually at pains to keep his stomach to himself. And for the same reason especially abominated by Jews, who do not want that knowledge of another person's. So I reckon he would have shouted *Your brother's fucking the fire-yekelte* a few more times, then belched in Manny's face, before returning to his massacre of the Golonskys' foliage.

But he must have gone on brooding over what had happened, and nothing good ever came of Errol's brooding. When he followed himself into his head it was always darker there than it was outside. Manny and I were in the air-raid shelter, refining another year of Jewish bitterness among the five thousand that there were to cover – though we never, I have to say, went at it chronologically – when he turned up. It was a shock to both of us. We weren't aware that Errol even knew of the shelter's existence, let alone that it was a hideout of ours.

'This is between me and him,' he said, holding the flat of his hand out to me, like a policeman stopping traffic. 'Me and the frummer.'

I'd been warned about just such a day, when the yoks would come with their white-boned fists and start knocking us about. Tsedraiter Ike had often told me what to do. 'Give them everything. Your watch, any money you're carrying, your yarmulke, everything. And if they call you a dirty Jew, agree with them. Don't even attempt to defend yourself. You're bound to lose. They don't feel pain, remember that. Even if you were to beat their brains out they wouldn't have the brains to understand that that was what you'd done. Unconscious, they'd still be able to beat you up. Cultivate the Jewish virtue of patience. You'll get your own back another time, when you're the judge and they're up before you for housebreaking. Or when you're the surgeon . . .' Even my father, who of course set a very different example of standing up to Nazis, counselled caution when the terrible day, the little local pogrom we all knew was just around the corner, finally rolled round. But what nobody had anticipated was that the yok with the white-boned fist would be Jewish.

And, more ironically still, the very Jew who had made a corkscrew of the neck of Broderick 'The Bull' Chisnall, who until then had been a one-man pogrom of his own.

He pushed Manny to the ground – on to the broken bricks and dirt which we'd barely trodden in, so lightly did we occupy the place – and began trying to get his trousers off.

'Errol . . .' I said.

He put his hand up to me again. 'Just me and the frummer.'

'What's he done?'

'He's done what he's always done – he's sat on the khazi.'

'Errol, everyone sits on the khazi.'

'Not for twenty-four hours at a stretch, they don't. Not eating khazi paper, they don't.'

'But what's it to you?'

'The same as it is to you – life and fucking death. It's because of him that they march us off to the camps.'

'That's shit. It's because of *them* that they march us off to the camps.'

'Yeah, well,' – he almost had Manny's trousers off – 'don't tell me what's shit. He's shit, that's what's shit.'

Manny himself was saying nothing. He had curled himself into a ball, a quill-less hedgehog. He was more concerned to cover himself than to inflict any damage on Errol. And it was only when he could see he was losing that battle that he bared his teeth. Mistake, I thought. You don't bite a mad dog unless you're an even madder dog yourself.

Against Errol's elbow in his windpipe, Manny had no defence. You can't bite when you're choking.

'All right, let's stop this,' I said. Feeble, but what do you do?

'The mamzer bit me,' Errol said. He had fine skin, almost transparent nostrils, which made him appear more dangerous, as though there were some intervening tissue missing in him, some insulative wadding which keeps the peace, prevents internal heat escaping and making a bonfire of everything around. He was too thin of flesh for his own and everyone else's good. He was breathing hard. For a moment I thought Manny wasn't breathing at all. But then Manny had been preparing for just such a moment.

I stood over them, like one of those referees who used to count my father out because of a minor nosebleed. The difference being that I had no authority.

'The little mamzer bit me like an animal,' Errol said, as though

163

to himself. He was diaphanous with rage. An almost violet light seemed to shine through him. 'And now I'm going to show him what we do to animals.'

He had Manny's trousers round his ankles. Manny had gone foetal, trying to bring his knees up to protect himself, his hands on his genitals. Every boy knows this position from his night-mares. Every man too. Go into the male ward of a hospital and that's how you will see the men lying. It's the position in which we expect death to take us.

And what was I to do? If I'd attempted to intervene, to pull Errol off or threaten to get help, he'd have gone even crazier. You don't provoke a man whose nostrils you can see through. As long as I stayed there, I thought, not taking sides, there would be a limit to any damage he could inflict. I didn't want to look on, I didn't want to be a witness to Manny's shame, I didn't want to see his nakedness. But I couldn't risk leaving them alone together.

So now I have imprinted on my mind for ever the picture of Manny failing to cover his private parts, pink and helpless like something not yet born, not at all the colour of the nakedness Dorothy must have fallen for in Manny's brother, and with nothing of a lover's grandeur, least of all when he began to squeal, and then to scream, terrible inhuman wails, because Errol had taken hold of his testicles as though he meant to empty them for ever of their contents.

Not out of love have I ever squeezed another man's testicles, nor can I imagine how I could possibly do it out of hate. If Manny was disgusting to Errol, then how could Errol touch him? Even to inflict humiliation, how could he put his hands on him, *there*?

I have thought about it since. Only the devil could squeeze the balls of a man he found repugnant. Only the devil or a camp commandant's wife.

But what Errol did next I am not sure even the devil could have done. He released Manny's testicles and snatched at his penis, grabbed it as though it were a clump of weeds in the Golonskys' garden, and pulled. 'So who do you think of,' he said, 'when you're on the khazi day and night doing this to yourself? Your mother? I bet you think of your mother. I bet you think of your ugly fucking mother in her long dress. Or do you have a shikseh you like to think about, a little fire-yekelte just like your brother's? Or . . .' He looked up in my direction, treating me to that lewd gentleman's gentleman expression he'd inherited from his father, and for a moment I wondered what I would do if he brought my mother or Shani into this. Would I let him get away with that as well? But it was a quite different confidence he wanted to establish. Ilse Koch. Can't be sure. Can't prove it. He didn't finish his sentence. I just felt that Ilse Koch was in the air between us.

End of event. He belched twice in Manny's face, then was gone. A minute later so was I. Whatever Manny needed to do to recover, I sensed he needed to do it on his own.

What I needed to do to recover I am still trying to find out nearly half a century later. But if I imagined that Ilse Koch thing, if I conjured her out of the horrors of that disgusting scene, grew her like lilies out of manure, what does it say about me?

Manny Washinsky would do an unimaginably evil thing and rot away for it among the criminally insane; Errol Tobias assuredly sups with Beelzebub most nights whatever else he does in Borehamwood; only I have gone on to live a wholesome life, allowing that being a cartoonist, even a marginally failed cartoonist, to say nothing of being a marginally failed husband, does not disqualify a man from wholesomeness. Good citizenship. Kindness to old ladies. Attentiveness to my own mother, who lived to the fine age of eighty-five, all but the first five of them devoted to kalooki. A good boy is what I am. A gutte neshome. Which cannot be said for the other two. Inner life for inner life, though, how much was there to choose between any of us?

5

We were all fucked. There are fifty chapters on the subject in *Five Thousand Years of Bitterness*, subtitled *The Fucking of the Jews*, one for every hundred years of it. Not easy to accomplish in pictures only, though I say so myself, without any of the ameliorating charms of prose. Just panel after panel of unrelieved fuckings-over. Not excluding fuckings-over by ourselves, though most of those I was conscientiously reserving for a further volume. It's important you take responsibility for your own history, but not until you've finished blaming all the other bastards first. Credit where credit's due: we are a self-defeating, self-disgusted, self-eviscerating people, but we couldn't have got there without outside help.

The Jews, of course, were the first to reject this analysis when *Five Thousand Years of Bitterness* was published. Fucked up? Us? Who are you calling fucked up, you sick fucker? Or words to that effect.

You can easily upset the Jews. We are dainty-stomached, with no taste for obscenity (I am a case in point: I weep, thinking of Manny with his trousers off), and a proud sense of reserve, most especially in the matter of having attention drawn to us by other Jews. If someone must depict us we would rather it were a Gentile. *The Jewish Contribution to Civilisation*, by Sir Shaygets St John-Shaygets-Shaygets, goes down a storm whenever it is reprinted. We suck on praise from Gentiles like babies on the tit. In the praise of Gentiles we find justification for everything we have been through. Thank you, thank you – now would you like to see us go through it all again? But Jews on Jews embarrass us. They put us in mind of Ham, the son of Noah, uncovering his father's nakedness and discussing it with his brothers. It isn't just unseemly, it is parochial. If anyone's going to uncover our naked-ness, let it be a goy, preferably one with a title.

So no, if you're wondering, they didn't like my cartoon

contribution to Jewish art, my lot. Neither did anyone else, much. Not in this country, not in America, not in Israel, not even in Germany where no publisher for it could be found. I like to think the timing was unfortunate. Winter 1976 was when *Five Thousand Years of Bitterness* saw the light of day here and in America, the warm pro-Yiddler glow of the Entebbe Raid not yet faded. If you were Jewish you were proud again, just as you had been after the Six Day War in 1967, no longer finding your reflection in the furrowed brows of rabbis and philosophers, but in fighter pilots and one-eyed generals. So the last thing you wanted to be reminded of was five thousand years of loss and jeering. Jeer at a Jew post-1967 and you risked a strafing from the Israeli Air Force. Now, post-Entebbe, anyone stealing a Jew could expect to wake to see commandos in his garden. We took no shit. And people who take no shit don't have to go round making jokes about themselves. Jokes are the refuge of the *Untermenschen*. Hadn't that been one of the declared aims of Zionism — the creation of a people who would no longer value themselves only for the wit they brought to bear on their misfortunes? A people, maybe, who would never have to make a joke again. Least of all against themselves.

The fucked-over Jew — who was he? We don't remember any such animal. And anyone who does won't want to see him commemorated in a comic.

We're a country, we're a nation again. We don't do funny and we don't do fucked.

As for those who didn't care for Zionism rampant, whose world collapsed if the Jews weren't at the bottom of it, well, they too were having trouble remembering any fucked-over Jews. A fortnight of ascendancy and the Jews were back at the top of the pile, once again pulling all the strings that mattered.

Embitterment was out of style. No one wanted to know. Not even the *Jewish Chronicle* liked it. Nor, judging from the silence, did my own mother.

I did, though, receive a card from Tsedraiter Ike, addressing me as 'My Dear Nephew Mendel', and accusing me of *nest-beschmutzing* – not just doing my dirty washing in public, but befouling the nest in which I'd been raised. 'I simply ask you to consider,' it went on in letters only a spider which had fallen in an inkwell could have formed, 'who this is likely to help. Us, or them?'

Well, what else should I have expected? Adorno famously said that, after the Holocaust, poetry wasn't a good idea. He never thought there was need to include cartoons in that proscription.

Now, of course, there is no sooner a catastrophe than there's a comic strip to tell of it. Everything allowable so long as it's tremulous. Cartoon? Fine, just keep the cartoonery out. Just keep it sweet, and substitute a watercolour wash for any angry lines of satire. Wan is how they like it today, pastel-genteel, or comical in the cute sense, faux naif – look, I can barely draw at all! – with an eye to the children's market, which is where the bulk of the buyers are.

Having watercoloured to order myself in recent years, I know whereof I speak. Kosovo, Afghanistan, Rwanda – when their hour came I did them all. Under an assumed name, of course. In fact under two. Alice and Thomas Christiansen, Alice being an anglicisation of . . . but I'll come to Alice when the time is right, and Christiansen being what it sounded. The nearest I have known to what the verdant call a partnership, Alice looking after the story, I the watercolour wash, or the heart-on-sleeve, don't-disturb-the-horses draughtsmanship. I am not entirely ashamed of what we produced. They go on selling by virtue of being pretty and unthreatening, but not so pretty as to hurt my own heart or misdirect the hearts of others. There's even a sense (I'm quoting Alice now) in which they more honestly reflected the melancholy of my nature, the artist I might have been had this or that turned out differently. Had I been born to goyim, for example. But it's hard to abjure your first ambitions, whatever knocks they take. I have gone on polishing *Five Thousand Years of Bitterness* for my own satisfaction, the new fifty-first chapter of which, 'The Jew Royally Fucked', I like to think contains some of the best of my mature work, highly personal much of it, highly symbolical, and, technically, highly sophisticated, as for example, to speak merely of adroitness with the pencil, my sketch of Errol Tobias's devil fingers, and the damage they wrought to poor Manny's self-esteem. A far cry in subject matter from Tom of Finland, but indicative of the mastery I have achieved at last, I fancy, of that explosive tension between the glans penis and everything the rabbis teach of chastity.

In the next panel a beautiful woman of Aryan complexion, with meteors crashing in her eyes.

6

> In through the gate, and out through the chimney.
>   Buchenwald saying

'Frau Koch . . . ?'

She shook her head. 'Gnädige Frau, to you.'

'Gnädige Frau . . . ?'

He had been brought to her. He did not know why. Perhaps she had heard he was an illustrator and wanted murals after all.

'Who told you,' she said, 'that you could look at me?'

He had not dared to lift his head since they came for him. 'I am not looking at you, Gnädige Frau.'

'Not now. Before. When I was on my horse.'

Should he tell her? Should he chance everything and tell her that her beauty was more than he could bear and that like Lot's wife on pain of petrification or worse, he had no choice but to turn and look, and let the fireballs in her eyes

169

destroy him? Or should he deny he had ever raised his face to her? Which was the greater rudeness? To know that, he needed to know her. Otherwise it was all on the roll of the dice. And it might have been decided anyway. Look at her, not look at her, what difference if she already meant to skin him where he stood?

She takes his silence for a confession, and laughs a little laugh. 'So tell me about yourself . . .'

What will he tell her? That he is an artist from Prague or Vienna. That his mother is/was a free-thinking, rationalistic, bohemian Jew from Kovna or Odessa, his father is/was a God-fearing Kabbalistic solicitor from a village outside Warsaw or Budapest. She will be interested in the subtle differences, Frau Koch, will she not? 'Tell me what it means to be Kabbalistic, Mendel. My husband the Commandant and I have always been so curious about your holy books and your little Jewish ways.'

So does he only want her to mother him, after all? He is disappointed in himself. Still without raising his face to hers, he drops to his knees and seizes her hand, putting it fervently to his lips.

That's when he feels the kiss of the whip she carries. The scourge.

'A Jew cannot touch the flesh of a member of the master race,' she tells him.

'No, Gnädige Frau.'

Again she strikes him.

Mendel's heart soars. I am her equal, he thinks. We are in this together.

She orders him to undress.

'Yes, Gnädige Frau.'

She is wearing a glove now, and with her glove she reaches down and takes contemptuous hold of him. He understands what this means. Just as he cannot touch the flesh of a

170

member of the master race, so the flesh of the master race cannot touch the member of a Jew.

Disdained, it rises.

And that is that, for one day.

Back on their bunk, Pinchas wonders what has happened. 'I am her little Yid,' Mendel says.

'For how long?'

'What does it matter? For as long as the hobby amuses her.'

'And when it doesn't, what will she do with you?'

Mendel shrugged. 'Crush me between her teeth,' he said. 'If I am lucky.'

'So you are an artist,' she says the next day, for yes, there is a next day.

Naked, pale in his nakedness, he nods.

'And what sort of artist are you?'

He draws, he tells her, to reconcile his two backgrounds, his rationalist mother and his God-smitten father. Drawing is itself, he explains, a godlike act – making something out of nothing, dispelling the darkness of the original void, letting there be light, and in that sense, yes, can be said to usurp God's function. But the mother in him scorns such nonsense, so he draws satirically, to spite himself. But as a satiric artist is a contradiction – at one and the same time making something of nothing and nothing of something – you could say it perpetuates the ambiguity of his situation.

He hopes she will love him for these paradoxes, but also beat him for them – another contradiction.

It is wonderful standing without his clothes, discussing art with Ilse Koch.

'I have brought you pencils,' she says, the day following, 'so that you may draw me.'

'Gnädige Frau, if I am to draw you I will have to look at you.'

'I will remove a garment a day,' she said. 'You will look only at the part I have exposed. Some days I will put a garment back on. You will never know whether I am going to take a garment off or put one on. Nor will you ever see all of me naked altogether, as I now see you. If you try to assemble me naked in your imagination I will know of it because this will rise. And every time it rises I will beat it, Jew. Do you understand?'

'I understand, Gnädige Frau.'

'Do you have any questions?'

'How do I finish the drawing, Gnädige Frau?'

'You do not. You erase it every night and start again every morning.'

He has another question, if he dare ask it. What if this, his penis, does not rise? Will she not consider it . . . ?

'An insult? Yes. No Jew dare look upon German woman-hood limp.'

'But day after day, Gnädige Frau, and while I am concentrating on my drawing . . .'

'Treat me with disrespect and I will shoot you, *nicht*?'

Discontentment courses through his body. If they could distil melancholy and inject it into you with a syringe, this is how you would feel. Or if you finally came face to face with Elohim and found him to be common. A Northern German with a snub nose.

It is prosaic to be threatened, and doubly prosaic to be threatened with death by shooting. Is that all?

Will Ilse Koch, too, prove to be an anticlimax? In general the Germans have been a terrible disappointment to the Jews. They have not lived up to Jewish expectation. Such music! Such writing! Such an elaboration of myth! All for this! The great bathos of National Socialism. You would expect that where there is art there is refined imagination. But maybe the imagination is all on the side of those who love the art, not those who make it. So am I, Mendel wonders, going to be Frau Koch's superior in the refinements of cruelty as well?

His charge is not banality. It is not banal to do what they are doing. This camp is not banal. It is supremely ambitious. The end magnificent in its completeness, outdoing all previous attempts to bend creation to man's will. No wonder the nation is so enthralled. Forget not knowing. They all know. They can smell exhilaration in the wind. And that isn't all they can smell.

But the means!

Shoot him, indeed! And then what? A lampshade. Well, that too smacks of grand conception. Take human skin and do so little with it. As insults go, it is magniloquent. But why shoot him when she can have him, as she has her horse, as a live instrument of her desire? Own him, still living, as she owns her property. Make a household object, a utensil, of the living man, not the dead skin. But then he already is her property, is he not? Every Jew in the camp, every gypsy, every communist, is her property. So he must mean something else. Something which demeans with more exactness. He does. He would like to be tiny in her grasp. He would like her to lift him to her lips, like Goya's Saturn devouring his own progeny, her hands become his ribcage, her eyes wide with forbidden knowledge. He would like her to laugh at his smallness, and then, like the giant, to close her mouth around him. He would like to be her food. Jewish food. He would like to give her kosher pleasure as she rolls him around her mouth, and himself unkosher pleasure as he is swallowed and disappears into her stomach. He would like to hear her moan a little from the inside, first with pleasure, then with grief at what she's lost.

A voluptuousness that has not occurred to her, and would no doubt shock and appal her, deviant as she is said to be.

He would enjoy that. He would enjoy taking Frau Koch's breath away.

And he has barely started yet. Hardly put his foot on the first rung of the ladder downwards into hell. Because where everything is permissible . . .

Shoot him, indeed!

In a flash, as the melancholy sluices through his body, he understands that she is conventional, a child of a conventional people, and will be bound to disappoint him. Through the blank clouds, Elohim with his snub Schleswig-Holstein nose regards him incuriously. This is no person-to-person accident. It would not have been otherwise had Ilse Koch been a different German woman, and he, Mendel, a different Jewish man. It is a fact of history. Another Jew let down by another German.

His penis falls limp. She strikes him with her whip and he cries out. Not from the pain but from the never-to-be-satisfied longing.

SEVEN

Chinese Husband: Honollable wife, I have heard you are
   having affair with Jewish man.
Chinese Wife: Honollable husband, I cannot think where
   you are getting these bobby meises from.

1

And beyond staring into the end of the world, what did Asher
Washinsky do when he realised that Dorothy's father was
German?

He cried.

But he cried only because Dorothy's father cried first.

And Dorothy?

She of course cried at the sight of them both crying.

Manchester has enjoyed long and noble relations with Germany,
both commercial and cultural. Not counting the signed photograph of Frankie Vaughan which stood on Shani's bedside table,
and Geraldo & His Orchestra's version of 'By the Sleepy
Lagoon' which it was my mother's custom to put on the gramo-
phone and play at low volume when people turned up for
kalooki, ours wasn't a musical family; but even we took pride
in the Hallé Orchestra without knowing that its founder was
born in Hagen, Westphalia, and had briefly been a friend of
Wagner's, before moving to comfier accommodation in
Greenheys Lane, in the south of the city, not at all far from
where today stands Hillel House, the hall of residence for Jewish
students attending Manchester University. That Charles Hallé
was able to start and fund an orchestra of the Hallé's quality
was due largely to the enthusiasm, munificence and artistry of

the German community with whom he mixed, some of it German Jewish, some of it just German. A similar consideration – the presence of family, good business connections, articulate and convivial company from the homeland (though the city's Schiller Institute with its skittle alleys and billiard room and gymnasium and male-voice choir was not yet established) – brought Engels to Manchester.

Dorothy's father was related neither to the Hallés nor the Engels. But he was a Beckman – poorly and distantly related to the Manchester Beckmans, a discreetly high-bourgeois family originally from Düsseldorf which had owned a small engineering factory in Salford since about the time the Hallé played its first Beethoven symphony. A *very* poor and distant relation, for when he was sent over to meet his Manchester mishpocheh it was in the capacity of driver for one of the junior directors. A hundred years earlier and he would have risen in the firm and looked forward to a still more distant Beckman being sent over from Düsseldorf to drive *his* car. But this was 1937. Not a good time for a German with little English to be making his way in the world – not this part of the world anyway. When war broke out he was interned in Huyton, a camp on the outskirts of Liverpool, where he learned philosophy and Bible history and a few words of Yiddish from the other internees, most of whom were Jews. It's feasible, though it was never discussed, that he did a bit of fire-yekelte-ing himself while he was there, in return for Hebrew lessons. Whether or not, he grew proficient in compassion, and by the time he was released in 1944 was a confirmed Judaeophile. Had he been acceptable to a Jewish girl he would have married one. Any one. As an act of atonement partly, for he was ashamed of his country's crimes and believed that fewer of them would have been committed had he not left it when he did, but also from inclination. He liked how Jewesses looked. When he imagined kissing a Jewess he imagined licking out a jar of damson jam. In the event, all Jewesses being closed to him, he married lime marmalade. The daughter of the respectable working-class family with whom he lodged, who had their own doubts about him as a German, but learned to judge him, in that English way, on his individual merits. Of those, industriousness and honesty – as evidenced by the little notebook he carried to write down every expenditure and debt – and the fact that his trousers always had a perfect crease in them, and that he liked double cuffs on his shirts, and that his fine gold cufflinks had his initials engraved on them – *AB* – struck them as adequate guarantees that their daughter would be well looked after. And she was. Not provided for to any high degree – Albert Beckman's Germanness counting against him when it came to driving for anyone not a German, and for anyone who was, come to that, since there were some things, if you were German, you didn't want to advertise – but cherished and indeed improved. The work he encouraged her to do for Jewish people, for example, was without doubt helpful in balancing their weekly budget, but it was also something he taught her to think of as a mitzvah – not just a good deed but an opportunity for them both to employ a word he'd originally picked up in Huyton and liked the sound of.

'See it as a mitzvah!'

Mitzvah. No sooner did he shape the letters with his mouth, and with his mind shape the concepts of commandment, meritoriousness and charity which a mitzvah encompassed, than he felt he'd made a small recompense for a wickedness of which it was not finally for him to say that he was entirely innocent.

So when he heard that his daughter was in love with a Jewish boy, the son of a family his wife made regular expiation to on his behalf, he shaved twice, put on his best shirt, attached the double cuffs with the links his mother had given him for his fifteenth birthday, laid out an English breakfast, and waited for the hour of reckoning to arrive.

In comes Asher, not just the damson jam but the damson orchard entire, and is it any wonder Albert Beckman's tears pour from him like waters from the rock Moses smote when the Israelites were thirsty?

I know how I would draw the scene were I making a cartoon of it – Albert Beckman, double-shaven and double-cuffed, square-jawed in the manner of Dick Tracy, but with his head bowed and his hands to his temple, standing in a cloudy puddle of his own tears, and from his lips a bubble of exclamatory remorse: 'Forgive me, my little *Judeler*! I am the Auschwitz German! Can you ever find it in your heart to forgive me?' And Asher, purple as an aubergine, opening his arms and saying . . .

An anachronism, of course. People were not calling themselves the Auschwitz German in those days. Not least as Auschwitz itself had not yet acquired its terrible symbolism, outstripping even Belsen and Buchenwald as the *ne plus ultra* of concentration camps. But as a cartoonist who likes the future remembered in the past, a historian of essentials not of time (Haman lives – that's my point), it pleases me to anachronise. And once you have actually been collared by a would-be Auschwitz German, backed up against a wall by someone who wants you, as a Jew, to fumigate his country's past for him, you don't lightly forgo the opportunity to make an Auschwitz German of them all.

The circumstances in which the phrase was first delivered to me were these:

I was travelling with Zoë, in one of her Jew Jew phases, visiting museums and synagogues and sites of camps in Poland, Czechoslovakia, Lithuania and God knows where else. Not Novoropissik, though. I'd given my father my word I would never go back there and my word to him was sacred. Had Zoë known of such an undertaking she'd have found out where Novoropissik was and bundled me on to the first train, or the first horse and cart, that went anywhere near it. Although my father had died long before I met Zoë, she was at daggers-drawn with him. 'I don't think I'd have liked your father,' she told me when she first saw his photograph. When I gave it as my opinion that he wouldn't have liked her, she was deeply insulted. 'He didn't know me,' she said. I couldn't be bothered taking her through the rigmarole of rationality – 'And you didn't know him' etc. No point. Going on his photograph, Zoë adjudged my father to have been another one of those Jews who would have rejected her affection and suggested she go to Berlin and be a prostitute. In my father's case she couldn't have been wider of the mark. 'Now there's what I call an English rose!' he'd have enthused. 'Look at the complexion! Look at the dainty shnozzle!' (In one of his unconscious reversions to the muddy language of Novoropissik he might even have added 'Kuk the ponim on her!' – the ponim the face, but always a little face, a face viewed affectionately, in my father's usage.) 'What are you waiting for, Maxie? Go ahead and marry the girl. Then at least my grandchildren will look like choirboys.' But I didn't tell her any of that either. With Zoë you had to assume that both sides of any coin offended her equally.

The business of going to Berlin to be a prostitute so preyed on her mind that we took a detour from our Jewish-sites-of-horror pilgrimage to see what working as a prostitute in Berlin would be like. We stayed in a modern hotel *auf dem Zoo* and hung around the strip joints and video booths at night. When we couldn't find any prostitutes we went inside to watch the porno, twin cabins with a communicating hole. Not something a man is supposed to do with the woman he cherishes, watch porno, but these were special circumstances. When aren't the circumstances special? A few years earlier I'd persuaded Chloë to accompany me to *Love Camp 7 – All the youthful beauty of Europe enslaved for the pleasure of the Third Reich* – at a ratty cinema in Amsterdam. 'I can see this is something you have to do, so let's just go in and get it over with,' Chloë said at the time. When we returned to England she changed the cinema into a live sex theatre and complained to her mother that I'd not only forced her into it but made her go up on to the stage and take part in unnatural sex acts, threatening to throw her into the canal if she refused.

'But sweetling, you're married to him,' her mother reminded her. 'Isn't that enough of an unnatural sex act already?'

'I know, Mother,' Chloë wailed. 'But it was that or the canal.'

'And was the canal in question the Herengracht, dear?' An enquiry that filled me with dread lest the Herengracht concealed some terrible *jeu* to plague me with.

Very clever of her. To this day I cannot hear the Herengracht mentioned without tremor cordis coming on me. The price she made me pay for debauching her daughter.

The next time I was in Amsterdam it was with Zoë. 'No,' she said, as I kicked my heels outside a row of video cabins. I respected her firmness. A honeymoon is a honeymoon. Besides, the most tempting vid on offer was *Ilsa: She-Wolf of the SS*, which I took to be about you-know-who and which, on that account, I couldn't watch with Zoë a mere fumble through a hole away. Some things you don't mix up. Not even when all you're mixing up is one Nazi she-wolf with another. I liked to think I had grown out of Ilse/Ilsa anyway, though it interested me to discover that others hadn't. I made a mental note. On my ownio, and as a caricaturist of derangement, I thought I should find a spare hour to look into it.

Berlin came later, but even in the adjoining filth-boxes *auf dem Zoo*, *Ilsa: She-Wolf of the SS* appeared not to be available. German delicacy.

'You choose,' Zoë said. Which presupposed there *was* choice. In fact, Aryan porno only has one subject: regression. What excites them is to see adults returned to the condition of messy childhood. You wet the bed when you shouldn't any longer, you poop your pants when you're in your thirties – and that's the turn-on. The land of Dürer and Goethe. And before these people the whole world trembled! No Nazis on the bill of fare however. Just Norbert in a rubber nappy and Solvig going for her weekly enema. We plumped for Solvig, the eroticism consisting not so much of her lying with her toches in the air on a hospital bed in a field with the Bavarian Alps in the background, as the time it took the enema to kick in. They are monotonous in their appetites and patient in their perversions, the Germans. They wait and wait. Too monotonous and patient for Zoë who was out of there long before the attendant physicians, or whoever those men in leather aprons were, had finished inserting the syringes and clyster pipes necessary to the operation, all the while pleading, '*Ja, komm, komm, oh ja, Scheisse, Scheisse, ja, komm . . .*'

'If this is what being a prostitute in Berlin is like . . .' Zoë protested.

I stopped her, offering it as my view that a prostitute did more than watch shit-and-piss videos with her husband sitting in the adjoining cabin.

'I know that,' she said, 'but if they expect me to do that to them . . .'

'They're Germans, what else do you expect them to expect?'

She was angry all over again with the Krystals, the Jewish family who had originally betrayed her, for thinking that pissing and shitting on Berliners was something she was cut out for. So we strolled down the Kurfurstenstrasse where prostitutes were said to work, in the hope of discovering a more noble version of the calling. But Zoë saw no one with whom, in her words, she 'could empathise'.

I pointed out a handsome foxy-featured girl in fur coat and with feathers in her hair. Pure Kirchner, I thought. Her face a perfect triangle of bilious green.

'Too tarty,' Zoë said.

'Zoë, she's a prostitute.'

'Yes, well, I'm not.'

The next day we were in Theresienstadt, 'the village which the Führer gave to the Jews', and where more than thirty thousand, in their ingratitude, contrived to die. Zoë, as usual, more moved than I was. Anger was what I felt. Towering rage. I already knew some of Malvina Schalkova's edgy, determined-to-be-domestic drawings of existence in Theresienstadt, the sort of thing I might have done had life treated me more cruelly, had I not had the leisure to cultivate sarcasm, and I knew some of the children's drawings of the ghetto too, executions, nightmares, apprehensions, maybe, of the next stop, which was Auschwitz. So I was in a temper to be enraged before I arrived. I take unkindly to the slaughter of artists. Futile, I accept, to be kicking stone so many years after the event – unless you happened to think (as I did) that anything under a thousand years was no time at all. That, anyway, was what I did, while Zoë watered the unholy ground with her little fairy tears.

Only give *me* the chance, I thought, to shit and piss on a Berliner!

The day after that we were in the Jewish cemetery in Prague. 'Such dear sweet tombs,' Zoë said. 'But how close together they are. Why do Jews enjoy being piled on top of one another like that?'

We went to a nearby café and talked about the golem. She wondered what it meant that Jewish myth demanded a monster in the image of Adam, life breathed into clay. Was it a metaphor for Jewish arrogance? Or was the golem no more than the ideal Shabbes-goy, primed to do the dirty work and ask no questions? I told her what I knew, which was that the golem had been fashioned in an hour of need to apprehend mischief-makers who left deceased Gentile babies in the ghetto with the aim of getting people to believe they were victims of a Jewish blood cult.

'Like me,' she said.

I looked bemused.

'Like me. I'm the victim of a Jewish blood cult. They clasped me in their embrace, they sucked me dry of blood, then they cast me aside.'

'There is no end,' I said, 'to Jewish wickedness.'

She touched my hand.

An hour later we were drinking with a couple of German

Lutherans she'd picked up in a bar. Theological students, one young, one of unfathomable age. Because they were gay and she was drunk she allowed them to take liberties with her, stroke her hair, squeeze her knee, then talk about the Holocaust. She signalled me to them with a sideways motion of her eyes. Jew boy. Be careful what you say. They couldn't believe their luck. They'd suspected as much, of course. But this was not a part of the world where you could take such things for granted. Half the world, east of Prussia, looks Jewish, until it starts to look Chinese. One more Pilsner each and they were apologising to me. The one of unfathomable age wanted to kiss me.

'It's all right,' I said.

'Oh, Maxie, let him,' Zoë urged me. She had turned tearful, but also high-coloured. She loved it here, at the crossroads of history. She was glimmering. When she took my wrist I could feel the excitement in her fingers. It was as though a great peace treaty were on the point of being signed, and her pen was going to do the signing.

So I let him — Lukas, he was called, Lukas Kirsche or Klein, a fellow with thin hair and bad skin — I let him kiss me.

How was I to know that the kiss would turn into a collapse? One minute I was offering him my cheek, the next he was in my arms, sobbing. Outside, revellers were passing, throwing their shadows on the walls of one of those interminably baroque edifices from whose windows some Czech or other had been throwing himself for five hundred years. Two men dressed as Mozart, in cocked hats and white tights, squeezed on to the end of our bench. In the back room of the bar a fiddler was playing Janáček.

Culture. Everything that wasn't kalooki. I should have been delighted.

Zoë was looking at me with the German in my arms as though I were her child. 'Oh, Maxie,' she said.

Lukas, through his blubbering, had begun to make words I

recognised. 'Oh, oh . . . I am the Auschwitz German,' he said. And then, having at last said it, couldn't stop. 'I am the Auschwitz German . . . oh . . . oh . . . I am the Auschwitz German.'

I wasn't sure what to do. Pat him, of course, but after that what? Hand him over to the authorities?

At last, his friend – Dieter, was it, or Detlev, Deadleg? – said, 'He wants you to forgive him.'

'Why, what's he done?' I asked.

'Not what has "he" done, what have "we" done.'

'Ah, not that,' I said. 'Not more of that.'

I didn't of course mean I thought it was time we put all 'that' behind us. I meant I didn't want to hear any collective-guilt shit from their mouths. Didn't want them getting off on it. Didn't want them thinking they could be released from it in a bout of Pilsner-fuelled remorse. In my time, in my time, when I'm good and ready you'll be released, until then sweat, you fuckers.

Zoë threw me one of her silent pleading looks. Be kind. Be kind, Maxie, be kind.

From Lukas, indistinguishable now from my shirt, more of the Auschwitz German.

'Forgive him,' Zoë said.

'Zoë, on whose behalf would I be forgiving him? He's done nothing to me.'

'It's not "he" . . .' his friend said.

'I know,' I said, 'it's "you".'

He smiled at me, a long, slow, sad smile, and touched my other shoulder.

'In which case,' I went on, 'why aren't *you* asking for my forgiveness?'

Not a wise remark, that. A second later I had the two of them crying into my neck. 'We are the Auschwitz Germans . . . oh, we are the Auschwitz Germans.'

'Forgive them,' Zoë said.

'I can't. I don't have the right.'

'Make the right,' she said. 'Make the right for me.'

'You aren't Jewish, Zoë. I can't do it for you.'

'I would have been Jewish if they'd have let me.'

'But you're not Jewish, however much you'd have liked to be. You're not the injured party.'

Now she was crying openly. 'I *am so* the injured party!'

I looked into her glistening goyisher eyes, into their unfathomable grey. Sometimes you have to make the leap. The gulf is so enormous that unless someone does something reckless it will never be bestrid or overarched.

'I forgive you,' I said. 'I forgive you both.'

And didn't add, 'Consider it wholesale, two for the price of one.'

That night Zoë sobbed in my arms and told me she'd never been more moved by anything in her life.

2

It must be assumed that Dorothy, faced with a comparably emotional scene, felt the same.

Asher's feelings are harder to imagine. Had it been his brother Manny in his shoes – but that's an impossible hypothesis. Manny was not a lover. Whatever else in the way of genes and religion they had in common, they did not have in common the wherewithal to make a woman lose her heart. No point wondering whether Manny would have acted differently in the face of the same temptation: the same temptation could never have come Manny's way. And our characters are as much determined by the temptations we are able to invite as by the principles we are taught.

Guilty, frightened, at the edge of his nerves, but sweetened by the sweetness he inspired, which is another way of saying in love with himself because he was beloved of so many, Asher must never have felt more feverishly alive. As a giver of pleasure and as a keeper of secrets, he was at the centre of more people's universes than he could count. Whatever his Jewish loyalties, however powerfully his Jewish education worked in him, insisting on renunciation, urging the debt he owed to family, to his people, to the very principle of survival, nothing could have been louder in his ear than the sound of his own blood roaring through his veins.

'I will not,' he said to Dorothy, 'say anything to my parents. Not yet.' Or words to similar effect.

She thought he meant he would not say anything to them about her German father. But what he also meant, he explained, was that he would not say anything to them about her.

She was distressed by that. 'Are you ashamed of me?' she asked.

'No, I am ashamed of myself,' he said.

'For what? For falling in love with me? For allowing yourself to fall in love with me?'

'No, for not having the courage to tell them.'

But it's possible he *was* ashamed of himself for falling in love with her. There is a potency in the idea of the shikseh that is hard to throw off, no matter however many of them you fall in love with. A shikseh answers to some capacity for lowness in yourself. Not the woman, the word. But once the word has done its work, the woman herself is for ever marked by it. In this regard it is no different to the word Jew, used disparagingly. When Tsedraiter Ike cautioned me against marrying a shikseh, any shikseh, because she was certain one day to call me dirty Jew, he was acknowledging the authority vested in both words. So Jews and Gentiles are alike in this: we appoint each other to stand for a terrible tendency to moral baseness in ourselves. As a Jew, of course, I don't hear in the word Jew what the Gentile hears. And when I do hear it for myself I become what is known as a self-hating Jew. For some reason we know less about that condition as it affects Gentiles. But that doesn't mean it isn't there. Take Zoë. She was a perfect example of the self-hating shikseh.

Ashamed of his feelings for Dorothy or not, Asher cleaved to her. A man can hold more than one position when it comes to the woman he loves. And she – though she was always watching, always aware that she was watching, as if the minute she took her eyes off him he would be gone – she cleaved to him.

They went on meeting in secret. Parks, cinemas, graveyards. Boating lakes where they could row shoulder to shoulder, taking an oar each. Fairgrounds, he winning goldfish for her on the rifle range, she (the bolder of the two by miles) dragging him on to wheels and caterpillars and dodgem cars, and then the Tunnel of Love in which neither did anything to either because they were not separate but a thing indivisible. They walked a lot, where no one could see them. Saw sunsets, watched the moon come up. The streaked sky their passion, the moony chastity their devotion. They took buses to the country. Looked at horses, ran from cattle, bought postcards which they didn't send. Visited stately homes in Derbyshire, ruined abbeys in Yorkshire. They hung over stone bridges and stared into water running over pebbles. They kissed in tea shops and on benches in little railway stations. It was like being on the run. And when that got too much for them there was the kitchen of her house. Her bedroom was of course out of the question. The regulation decency of the times determined this. There were some things an eighteen-year-old girl was not encouraged to do at home. But the moral inequality of the arrangement as it stood must also have played a part in the Beckmans' thinking. If their daughter wasn't good enough to be taken to meet the Washinskys, there had to be limits to how welcoming they could be of him.

When they weren't able to be together they wrote. He could post his letters directly to the Beckman house, whereas for him to receive hers he had to have a poste restante address in the city centre. Few things in life are more exciting than waiting in a queue at the post office to collect illicit mail. Asher loved it. Sometimes he wondered if it wasn't more fun getting Dorothy's mail than seeing Dorothy. She was a clever girl and missed nothing. She kept her letters hot. One day she wrote to him in German. Basic German of the sort she had been teaching him in return for Hebrew, but still German. She knew the effect that would have and enjoyed imagining him opening the envelope, seeing '*Liebling*' and going up in flames.

He read the letter in a coffee bar, then threw it in a waste-paper bin, then retrieved it, then folded it into his wallet, then took it out of his wallet and threw it into a bin again, then realised someone might find it and see to whom it was addressed, then retrieved it, then stuffed it into his shirt, then tore it up and threw the several pieces into several bins. After which he felt so guilty about Dorothy that he begged her to write to him in German again, whereupon he felt so guilty about everybody else that he thought his heart would stop.

'God will strike me down,' he said to his own reflection in the mirror of the public toilets to which he'd gone to flush away the second letter. 'God help me,' he muttered to himself when he queued at the post office, waiting for the third.

Was he the luckiest boy in the whole wide world, he wondered, or was he the most accurst?

Lucky at least, as Manny reflected long afterwards, to be offered the choice.

'Now it's your turn to write to me in Hebrew,' Dorothy suggested.

But he couldn't. He could talk Hebrew to her but he couldn't write it. 'It's a sacred script,' he explained.

'And cannot be employed upon a profane object?'

'I don't mean that,' he told her.

But what if he did?

'You know what the problem is,' she told him. 'Reciprocity. *Gegenseitigkeit*. You can't even play at being together.'

Once he took her on a train to Birmingham where he was in part-time religious employ — so it was true, he *did* teach at a Midlands Talmud Torah! — and hid her in a commercial travellers' hotel on the edge of the city. She had hoped that she would be able to watch him at the blackboard, but he explained to her that that was out of the question.

'Because I'm not Jewish?'

'Because it's not allowed.'

'Well, at least let me walk with you to the school. I can't picture it. I can't imagine what your pupils look like.'

He shrugged. 'They look like me. When I was younger.'

'All the more reason I'd like to see them.'

He shook his head. 'It's not allowed.'

'It's not allowed for me to walk you to your school? That's rubbish. You just don't want them to see me. You're ashamed of me – the fire-yekelte's daughter.'

'It's got nothing to do with your being the fire-yekelte's daughter.'

'Just with my being not Jewish.'

Jew, Jew, Jew. Not Jew, not Jew, not Jew.

'We get caught up in your interminable fucking drama, whether we are or we aren't,' as Zoë once said to me.

I didn't reply that there were some women who got *themselves* caught up in our interminable fucking drama, probably for fear of inciting her to get herself fucking out of it again.

You might not always want to be with them, but they beat being on your own.

3

'It's making me ill,' she told him.

He melted before her. 'But I love you.'

'And I love you. But it's making me ill. So long as you're in front of my eyes I feel I'm with you. But the minute you're not there I feel I don't exist for you.'

'You never don't exist for me. I think about you every minute.'

'That's not the same. You might be thinking about me, but

when you're elsewhere you become a person who isn't with me and doesn't know me. It's not being your secret I mind – at least as your secret I'm an important part of you – it's being of no account. Never to be mentioned, always to come second to your family.'

'You don't come second.'

'No, I come third. Or even fourth. How can I feel I know you unless I know your family?'

He told her that it would kill them. That he would have to tell them slowly. First his brother. Then, his father . . .

'Then?'

Could he tell his mother? His father he imagined storming and raging. He could accept that. But his mother? He imagined her in tears, on her knees, clinging to his legs. Don't do it, Asherla, don't bring this shame upon us.

'I know,' he said, 'it's a bit primordial.'

'A bit?'

He shrugged. 'She's my mother.'

'Oh yes, Jewish boys and their mothers!'

Unless that was Chloë or Zoë speaking. 'Oh, yes, Jewish boys and their mothers!' They both hated my mother.

Also a bit primordial. Of them, I mean.

He would have looked helpless, hands by his side, a little boy lost. Standing on the railway station with his suitcase by his side, waiting for the Auschwitz Express – Jew Jew, Jew Jew. 'Please don't take me from my mother!' Whatever your religion, you're born knowing the day will come, born wondering if it will be today or if it will be tomorrow – the separation, the choice, her or her, your mother or your mother's mortal enemy, the other woman. But if you're born Jewish, the other woman is your people's mortal enemy as well; as in this instance, not just a Gentile woman, not just the daughter of the woman who makes your fires on a Shabbes, but – is he mad or what is he? – a German! How many sins? Go on, Asher, add up the offences.

The poor girl. How could she know how many offences she amounted to?

'I want their approval,' she told him. 'I want your mother and your father to love me for loving you.'

He pointed to his chest. Made a dagger of his hand and plunged it between his ribs. 'It doesn't feel right for me, either,' he said. 'Here! It doesn't feel right, here, without their approval.'

'What doesn't feel right? You mean you don't feel right about me?'

'Everything. Nothing. None of it feels right.'

She stared at him, a chill about her heart.

'My mother and father loom very large in my life,' he told her, as though she didn't already know.

'Yes,' she said. 'That's why I want them to loom very large in mine. And why, so long as they don't know about me, I feel I don't loom very large for you. Take me to meet them, Asher.'

Did she want the brutal truth? Did she want to hear him say *Not a hope in hell, Dorothy*?

And so it descended into the usual. 'You're not the only one with feelings because you're Jewish, Asher.'

Tears in his eyes. He the more emotional of the two. But silent. The silence a goad.

'I'm not nobody, Asher. I'm not a nobody because I'm not Jewish.'

A movement of his shoulders. Meaning what? That he knew she wasn't nobody but there was nothing he could do about it?

Until finally – 'You people!'

Whereupon Asher could empty his conscience of its guilt, accuse her of being an anti-Semite, and go home to his family.

4

'I bet you didn't know,' Manny said to me on one of his rare visits to my house, 'that Germans iron their underwear.'

He had just visited the bathroom, which seemed to explain the association. But it was also clear that he was looking for something to say to cover his embarrassment. Not easy for Manny, going to someone else's bathroom. His own bathroom was trial enough, what with the number of times he had to test that the wash taps were really off before he left, and the amount of flushing of the lavatory he had to do, but someone else's imposed a near-intolerable burden of conscientiousness on him. I was not a tap-twiddler myself. I did not believe that if I was not super vigilant, and then doubly vigilant of the effects of my vigilance, the sink or cistern would overflow, flooding the house or drowning its inhabitants in ordure. But I was similarly delicate. It was how we'd been brought up. For a people refined in the matter of the body's exigencies, and respectful of others' privacies, a visit to an alien bathroom constituted a transgression. In my case it was often (and still is often) accompanied by extreme sadness, as though the neatly folded towels and the scented tissues, the new soap in the soap dish, the eau de cologne, the considerate rows of scissors, tweezers, nail files, represented an innocence of which I was the defiler.

Whether I am describing a philosophical dismay which is peculiarly Jewish I can't be sure. But though we never discussed it, I knew that Manny was beset by it no less than I was. So if it is Jewish, it isn't specifically Orthodox or liberal Jewish. It is of a Jewishness which predates theological finessing.

Either way, it has to be said that Errol Tobias didn't share it. Errol would have set up a branch of the Crumpsall Park Onanists in any bathroom that had a door to it, and even the door was optional. Years later, when I stayed with him for one night in Mill Hill – this was prior to his move to Borehamwood – I was shown into a guest bathroom papered with photographs torn from pornographic magazines of women with their legs open. 'I like a bog to be a bog,' he told me. 'Enjoy!'

But then Errol was the exception that proved every rule.

As for Germans ironing their underwear, that's one of those things you aren't sure whether you know or not. It seemed of a piece with everything else I'd read about their methodical cruelty, but whether it had cropped up in *The Scourge of the Swastika* I couldn't remember.

'So how do you know this?' I asked him. 'Did Ilse Koch – may her name be wiped out – iron hers?'

He threw me a strange look. 'I just know it,' he said, rubbing his fist in his hair. He had been reading about the importance of getting blood to the brain and reckoned that massaging his scalp with his knuckles would facilitate this. Then he suddenly asked me, 'Can you keep a secret?'

'Depends on the secret. If it doesn't threaten the safety of my family I will keep it.'

'It threatens the safety of *my* family.'

'Then I'll keep it.'

'It's someone Asher knows,' he said, lowering his voice. Not counting the German letter he claimed he'd found in the street, this was the first allusion Manny had made, in my hearing, to Asher's troubles.

'Asher knows a German?'

'He knows a girl who knows a German.'

'Asher knows a *girl*?'

Disingenuous of me. Everyone knew that Asher knew a girl. And everyone knew a lot more than that as well. But I didn't want my knowledge to upset him.

'It's her father. Asher says he irons underwear in the kitchen, in front of him.'

I pulled a face. The same face, apparently, that Asher pulled.

We are finicky, we Jews. We no more want to see other people's underwear or bathrooms than we want them to see ours. It was a matter of honour in our house not to leave even the most innocent item of underclothing lying about. It is possible I idealise, but I do not recall once coming upon a slip of my mother's where it should not have been, nor my father's vest, if he ever wore a vest. The same principle operated at the Washinskys' which was in every other regard a rubbish dump. The first time Manny took me home he asked me not to look at anything. 'My mother isn't well,' he told me. 'That's why nothing has been done today.' But 'doing' wasn't the problem. From the way the place appeared you could only guess that when the Washinskys ripped their clothes off at night they threw them on the floor in rage and left them there. Shirts, shoes, trousers, dresses, hats, keys, loose change, books, pens, pieces of paper – whatever had been about their persons was spilled and forgotten as though God had advised them the very moment they were naked to clear their minds of everything else and make ready to appear before Him. Yet even here, God or no God, not a single item private to the Washinskys' wardrobe was left where you could find it. If I close my eyes I can picture their house as though I had been in it only this morning, the dumps of bed linen, the piles of towels, the tangles of disregarded clothing, the torn siddurim, but no articles of underwear do I espy. It's possible they stuffed them into pillowcases. It's possible they burnt them. It's possible God took them. It's conceivable they wore none. Whatever the explanation, the same fastidiousness that operated in the gleaming godless palace that was our house operated in the sad site of superstition and neglect that was theirs.

And this applied to discussing the subject as well. So other than pull the same face as Asher, there wasn't much of a response I was able to make. Germans ironing their underwear in front of you – ugh!

If Manny had wanted to confide in me about his brother, or about the girl, I didn't exactly make it easy for him. It's possible I was too similar to him to be much use as a friend. There I was, lost inside the refined unspokennesses of my own head at a time Manny might have wanted me to help him get out of his.

5

It finally fell out as it was bound to.

They were seen. The irony of it is that they were probably arguing at the time. As they thought, hid in hugger-mugger, each accusing the other of being a racist. Maybe even deciding to call it a day. No matter. They were seen and they were reported. Whether with diabolic intent, or with inside knowledge of the relative mental strengths of the Washinskys, whoever was the bearer of the news bore it to Mrs Washinsky first.

And Mrs Washinsky's initial impulse was interesting. She decided to keep it from her husband.

'This will kill him,' she told Asher, who had always thought it would kill *her*.

They were sitting in the kitchen – as I conceive it, the debris of a dozen meals around them. Which you can be certain is me cartoonifying them again. The house was as one of the rubbish dumps of hell, but they were particular about food. They had to be. The Lord had ordered it. Merely to separate what was flaishikeh from what was milchikeh – not just the meat but the meat-associated from not just the dairy but the dairy-associated – occupied half a day. And that's not to mention the amount of salting that went on. 'I'd get nothing else done if I had to keep a home that was even ten per cent kosher,' my mother used to say. By 'nothing else', she was thinking of kalooki. And Channa Washinky kept a home 110 per cent kosher. Hence the rest of the house looking the way it did. Kosher ruled the roost. Kosher was king. Separating this from this – habdalah, keeping apart what didn't belong together, the great act of discrimination at the centre of Jewish thought as well as Jewish diet – made it virtually impossible for the poor woman to lift a finger to anything else.

Couldn't the fire-yekelte have helped? Couldn't the fire-yekelte have done a bit of general cleaning up – making the beds, dusting the furniture, taking the towels off the bathroom floor – after she'd swept the grate? She did, she tried, but a fire-yekelte, too, was a thing apart, and besides, this was not a good time to be bringing up the fire-yekelte.

Eerily, to Asher, his mother brought up nothing. She didn't charge him. She didn't ask how much of what she'd heard was true. She didn't take him through the sacrifices both she and countless generations of Jewish mothers before her had made so that he, Asher, could with impunity find a Jewish woman who would in turn be mother to generations of Jews to come. She simply conjured her husband's presence – his ghost in advance of his dying, as it were – and told Asher who would be held responsible.

It was good psychology. A boy mindful of the sacredness of his father's life cannot prevaricate, cannot lie or make excuses, when the ghost-to-be is in the room. It was also – depending where you're coming from – good morality. It asserted the primacy of his father's life over everything. Asher would be a father himself one day, all being well. And would expect to receive the same respect from his son. Thus, without saying much, without even having recourse to the J-, let alone the G-word, did she play the continuity card.

She was a problem for the cartoonist, Channa Washinsky. I keep wanting to put her in a sheitel, the wig that every Orthodox Jewish wife is supposed to wear in order to prevent a man not her husband from lusting after her in his heart; but in all honesty, although they are usually easy enough to pick, on account of their making the wearer look tipsy and slow of wit, like some catatonic Netherlandish doll, I am not able to say whether she wore one or not. I want to make her pallid as well, but again without justification. I saw a photograph of her not long ago, and not only was her hair her own – it was too fine and lifeless to be anything else – but her complexion was halfway to being swarthy. Which shouldn't be at all surprising, given Asher's Levantine colouring. So why can't I, why *couldn't* I, see her as she was?

Caricature is a methodology for telling a greater truth – that's where I stand – but even I accept that what the artist caricatures, the ordinary eye must recognise as just. So why couldn't I be just to Channa Washinsky? Why couldn't I, to cite another example of my determination to distort her, not see that she had rather fine dark eyes, a little sleepy it is true, but poignant in their thwarted lustre? A sentence of Zoë's returns to me. 'Unless a woman is made up to the nines, dressed to kill, smelling like the perfume counter in Harrods and beckoning you with her little finger which must have gold on it, you don't notice her – do you know that?' 'I noticed you,' I reminded her. 'Of course you noticed me – I was spotlit, fuckwit, standing on a stage, imitating Marlene Dietrich, in six-inch heels and a see-through gown that was slit to my vagina . . . I'm speaking metaphorically.' Point taken. I didn't notice Manny's mother because she wasn't anybody I wanted to see. She wasn't immodest.

But even in the matter of modesty I must try to be true to her. Modesty was not then what it is now. On the night before her wedding Channa Washinsky would certainly have immersed herself in the ritually cleansing waters of the mikveh. Even my sophisticated mother, Leonora Axelroth, about to be the wife of a notorious non-believer, visited the mikveh without telling him that one time. Thereafter, if she wasn't sheiteled, it was unlikely that Channa Washinsky would have fussed about her body religiously at all. We were coming out of the dark ages in those days, not going back into them again. The laws of modesty have been around a long time, the obligation on a Jewish woman to make herself appear pleasant in a quiet way, to avoid brightly coloured or tight-fitting clothing, to choose her decorations with moderation and discretion, to be sure not to 'make a tinkling with her feet' (Isaiah 3:16). But the great love of the vividness of the world which Jews enjoy (the shadow side of our longing to be invisible) kept even the reticent tinkling. *Kept.* Past tense. Half a century later we are born again, and with born again comes clean again. Except that there's nothing more unclean, is there, nothing lewder, nothing more likely to lead the mind to thoughts of what is *im*modest, than the modesty consciousness of the fanatical. (See the little comic book on mikveh practices I published privately a few years ago – if you can find it.)

Whatever problem she poses for the cartoonist, Channa Washinsky posed even greater problems for her son. Not the least of these being that he was all at once smitten by her. It's often at this time that men fall in love with their mothers all over again, whether or not their mothers make a tinkling with their feet. Maybe the mothers have been waiting patiently for this very opportunity. Wheel out the opposition and watch me chop her into tiny pieces. Sometimes they do it with exaggerated vitality, as my mother did. You bring another woman into your life and suddenly your mother is a Busby Berkeley Musical Extravaganza. But sometimes they do it by being exquisite in their reserve. This was Channa Washinsky's method.

And it worked. Worked in the sense of making Asher appreciate her, anyway. He didn't know she could be so self-possessed. He didn't know that she could vest such authority in herself. As for working in the other sense . . .

A week later she raised her eyes to him. Not beseeching. Beyond beseeching. Well?

He hadn't done it. It would take him longer. It wasn't as easy . . .

Then her words came. 'I don't blame the girl. I don't blame her mother or her father. I blame you. I'm not saying I don't understand you. I'm saying I blame you. I don't wish to argue the rights and wrongs of it with you. In your eyes what you are doing might appear right. But had you stopped to think for a single minute how this was going to affect us, you wouldn't have done it. There are a hundred things you could have done to hurt us, Asher. There are hundred things I have imagined you doing. But this was never one of them.'

This. How much did she know?

Could he ask her? Could he go though his transgressions, counting them out on the fingers of both hands, until he came to one she hadn't heard about?

Imagining the worst, that she still wasn't in possession of everything, he took the coward's option and said, 'It will blow over, Ma.'

'If it will blow over why did you let it start?'

'Oh, Ma, *start* . . .'

'If it's so unimportant to you that you think it will blow over, it can't be important enough to let it kill us.'

Us. Kill us. He was responsible for them both now. This was more how he thought it was going to be. She'd be screaming soon. Tearing gouges out of her flesh. The week before, he'd been close to sacrificing Dorothy to her. What was Dorothy with her stretched-forth neck and wanton eyes compared to the dignified woman who'd given birth to him? Now that his mother threatened melodrama, he was once again besotted with Dorothy – the sweet, the calm, the melodious Dorothy.

Is this cynical of me, to suppose that Asher could operate only dialectically – one woman rising in his estimation as the other one descended? I don't mean it to be. This, as I recall, is how it feels to be a boy in the throes of his first big passion. Especially if he's a Jewish boy with dialectic in his soul. This or that. Meat or milk. Jew or Gentile. Wife or lover. Your life or your father's. Choose.

'All I ask,' he said, 'is that you don't say anything to Dad yet.'

'Until it blows over – is that what you're asking me?'

'Or until I decide to tell him myself.'

She put her hand out to him, as though the ghost she'd been seeing were his now.

'You are not to do that,' she said. 'Promise me you won't do that.'

So he promised.

But later that same week his father got to hear about it anyway, and had what was diagnosed in our community as a double stroke. One on discovering his son was sleeping with a shikseh. One on discovering that the shikseh was a German. By our understanding of medicine, it was the second stroke that saved him from the worst effects of the first. Sometimes the news can be so bad that you go on living. Especially when going on living is worse than death.

The doctors said that Selick Washinsky had suffered a minor stroke. There you are! That was how terrible things were.

I remember the ambulance coming for Manny's dad. How could I not? Twenty minutes later another one was coming for mine.

6

Under the body of his father, a boy lies.

It is hot. The boy can hear flies buzzing and dying. He thinks he can smell them too – decomposing flies. He doesn't know how late in the day it is, or even whether it is the same day. His father is lying on him, his chest on his face. The boy understands the intentionality of this. His father doesn't want him to see, but more than that he doesn't want him to be seen. Nor does he want his breath to be heard. No word was spoken between them but he is lying as he knows his father wants him to lie, in utter silence, seeing nothing, barely breathing.

They are in a pit, in a clearing in a forest, in the shtetl of Butrimantz in the south-west of Lithuania. When the shooting started his father pushed him into the pit and then fell on top of him. When the shooting stops, the sounds in his father's chest stop as well.

The boy listens but can hear nothing. Only the flies. He listens for so long that if there were other boys lying, breathing silently beneath their fathers, he would hear them. He is the only boy

alive in the pit, maybe the only boy alive in the whole of Lithuania
— who knows, he may be the only boy alive in the whole world.

He hasn't got the strength for what is required. He is over-
come by sadness. To what end must he exert himself? To what
purpose?

A contradiction, as terrible as the pit, assails him. He owes it
to the love he bears his father not to live. He owes his father
death. But his father gave his own life so that he, the son, should
live on. So he owes his father life as well.

Someone explain to the boy how he can repay his father by
living and not living at the same time.

No one can explain this to him. There is nobody who knows.
There is nobody alive.

When they start throwing soil into the pit, he makes a decision for life. Thus it happens: we want what we cannot have. He
pushes his face into his father's neck, takes one deep breath, then
closes his throat and nose. Everything goes black. This must mean
that there was light before and he was seeing it. The light perhaps
of the same day. Perhaps of the same hour. It's conceivable he
has been lying here no time at all, a matter of minutes, no more,
seeing light he did not recognise as light. But he sees nothing
now.

The boy is Manny Washinsky.

Living on the pockets of air in his father's jacket and shirt, he
survives his own burial, escapes the pit in the dead of night, hides
in the forest for weeks on end, criss-crosses the Lithuanian/Polish
border, and finally finds his way to Kaliningrad where partisans
smuggle him on to a boat bound for Hull. Subsequent to that he
has lived with his uncle Selick in Crumpsall Park.

This was the story Manny began to put about soon after his
father was released from hospital.

'I'm glad your father's better, Manny,' I said.

'He's not my father,' he replied.

'Who is he then?'

'My uncle. My father's dead.'

And that was when I got to hear about the pit in Lithuania.

Out of some motive too base to investigate, I told Errol Tobias what Manny had been saying about himself. 'It's bullshit,' Errol said. 'The Nazis cleaned out Lithuania in 1941. Your meshuggeneh friend wasn't born yet.'

'How do you know that?'

'How do I know when your meshuggeneh friend was born?'

'How do you know about Lithuania?'

He tapped his forehead. 'By fucking reading. Probably the same fucking books as your meshuggeneh friend's been reading. Ask him. Ask him about the *Einsatzgruppen*. Ask him when they'd finished.'

They were all reading. Every Jew I knew. All swallowing bile. Even Errol Tobias who could have passed as a member of the *Einsatzgruppen* himself. All storing up their rage. The only person I knew who wasn't by his fourteenth birthday an expert on the Holocaust (whether or not we called it by that name yet) was me. But I had enough bile in me already. And what I didn't know I could imagine.

And what I could imagine I could draw.

Errol had one other point to make about the miracle of Manny's escape from the pit before leaving the subject. 'I bet the creep got the idea for that from the time I beat him up in that air-raid shelter of yours,' he said. 'His father lying on top of him, me sitting on his face stopping him from breathing. I bet he wanks about me being a Nazi, the freak.'

'Or about you being his father,' I said. Which caused Errol to pretend to beat me up.

Of course I knew that every word Manny had said about Lithuania was preposterous, but the fact of his bothering to lie at all made me suspect that some essential aspect of it could be true, that while he was too young to be a survivor of the war, he was just possibly someone other than we thought he was, and certainly not the brother of Asher, for example, whom he resembled in absolutely no particular.

But then the rows between his brother and his parents (real or imaginary) began in earnest, terrible screaming contests, some of them so blood-curdling that on a couple of occasions Tsedraiter Ike had to go over and hammer on their door to make certain Selick Washinsky was not having another and this time more serious stroke. At which time it occurred to me that Manny's pit story wasn't a description of the past at all, but of the future.

7

The reason it was Tsedraiter Ike who did the neighbourly thing and not my father was that my father wasn't up to it. He had gone into hospital on the same day as Selick Washinsky, and even shared a ward with him for forty-eight hours, before they let him out with a warning: 'Take it easy.' In those days that was all they could do for a worn-out heart, before bypasses and transplants – prescribe rest and quiet and as many pills as he was prepared to swallow.

'What about boxing?' he'd asked the doctor.

Not quite a family friend, Dr Shrager. Though he chose to act like one. 'Over my dead body,' he said.

'What about being Jewish, speaking of dead bodies?' This to needle Shrager, who did Jewish in a bigger way than my father thought a doctor of medicine should.

'What *about* being Jewish?'

'Do I have to die Jewish?'

'No one's talking about dying, Jack.'

'Well, I wasn't, but *you* are.'

'Just take the pills.'

'And if they don't work they'll bury me the same afternoon and have some rabbi mutter mumbo-jumbo over me.'

Similar mumbo-jumbo to that from which he'd preserved me on my thirteenth birthday.

How much all that thirteenth-birthday stuff had contributed to the breakdown in his health I cannot say with any certainty. But I do recall, in the period after his discovering the real reason behind my mother's gala kalooki night, a strange passage in which, around me particularly, he alternated needless irritation with an unaccustomed, not to say uncomfortable, solicitousness. One occasion stands out above the others. I had been in the habit, when it was too cold to go on drawing in the air-raid shelter, of bringing my sketchbook back home, being careful always to keep it out of the way. All discussion of Manny's and my cartoon history of the anguish of the Jewish people had stopped the day my father recommended I get another interest – boxing, say – a year or so before. Just how serious his objections would be if he learned I was still at it, I didn't know, but it seemed prudent not to put him to the test. He asked no questions, I told no lies. So I shouldn't have been such a fool as to leave it where he could see it – Freudian? well, I accept it sounds Freudian – a caricature of Ilse Koch à la Hank Jansen in full riding gear and with swastikas on her saddle inspecting a line of naked Jewish prisoners with hard-ons. (Unless that should be, as Errol always insisted, hards-on.)

'I don't mind the sexual fantasy,' my father said. 'You like a big toches on a woman – that's your business. At your age I was no better. But I'll tell you what I do mind . . .'

I was covered with embarrassment. 'I know,' I said, 'I know – the swastikas. And the private parts.'

He looked at me in astonishment. 'Why should I mind the swastikas or the private parts? The only time I'd mind a swastika is if you came home wearing one. And we've all got private parts. What I mind, Maxie, is the look on the faces of those Jews. Why have they got no fight in them?'

Well, I couldn't tell him, could I, that in my book acquiescence, when you knew what you were acquiescing to, was a sort of fighting.

He shook his head. 'Look,' he said, 'if you're going to be an artist, be an artist. But do me a favour' – and here he reached across and grabbed my wrists, a restraining officer, handcuffing me with his fingers – 'just don't make every Jew you draw synonymous with suffering.'

I wanted to protest that he hadn't taken adequate cognisance of their hard-ons/hards-on; that their hard-ons/hards-on, artistically speaking, stood for the virility of the Jewish people in the face of adversity. You know, a cartoonist's way of saying you cannot keep us down. But there are some conversations you don't have with your father, particularly when he's taken you into custody. And even more particularly when he's unwell.

It must have been about a fortnight after this conversation that he complained of pains in his chest and the same ambulance which had earlier in the day come for Manny's father, came for mine.

Back home, gulping tablets, he became a chair person, falling asleep in the middle of a conversation, or begging to be excused from taking an interest in anything that wasn't happening in his chest. 'My ticker,' he'd say, apologetically, touching it and looking somewhere else.

Eventually it became another member of the family – Jack's ticker. The person other people came to see. His old communist pals visited most days, determined to cheer him up, to get him back to the firebrand he'd been, but they were themselves down in the mouth, not to say shamefaced, after the invasion of Hungary. Elmore Finkel took me into the garden to ask whether I thought it could have been that act of betrayal that had made my father ill. 'Disillusionment is a terrible depressive,' he told me. I shook my head. My father had never been under any illusions about Russia. Russia for my father was Novoropissik. The past, not the future. I was proud of him. Only moral and political infants do disillusionment. Only people foolish enough to have illusions. And my father was not one of those.

But he was tired. Soon, to our great consternation, he didn't even want to see his chums. We noticed him begin to wince when he heard them on the path. I suggested that we lock the door like other people, but he wouldn't hear of it. Our door had always been open to everybody and he wasn't going to close it now. Increasingly, though, he treated them as though they belonged to another existence, pointing to his chest, saying, 'My ticker,' and signalling them to leave almost before they'd arrived.

Three months later it stopped ticking altogether.

'You know, I envy you,' Manny said, not long after. 'I wish I didn't have a father.'

EIGHT

Man has the right and the privilege to declare himself
to be in disagreement with every natural occurrence,
including the biological healing that time brings about.

Jean Améry

1

The revelation was my sister. In the last weeks of my father's life
she was never out of his sight. Following my mother's lead, I was
acting as though everything were as normal. We ate at the same
time, made the usual amount of noise, and dropped in to see my
father propped up in his bed the way we would on an ordinary
Sunday morning. He was lying in, that was all. He was taking a
breather. But not to Shani, he wasn't. To Shani he was dying and
she didn't want to lose a moment of whatever time was left to
her to be with him.

She wept openly in his company, sitting by his bedside, stroking
his hand. Once when I went in to see him he was holding her in
his arms the way he must have held her when she was baby, kissing
and smelling her hair, crooning over her. His shaineh maidel he
called her – his lovely girl. I couldn't believe my ears. Shaineh
maidel was grandparent Yiddish, maybe even great-grandparent
Yiddish. When I drew shtetl Yiddlers that was what I had bubbling
out of their mouths – shaineh-maidel talk. No one used that
expression any more, except in self-parody, least of all my father.
So was that why they'd named her Shani? Had my father crooned
into her baby scalp and called her his shaineh maidel the moment
he first saw her, his lovely girl, his beautiful daughter – and was
she therefore the child of his Jewish sentimentality, Shani because

he had never clapped his eyes on anything prettier in his life, and there was no other word to describe her?

You howl when you hear your dying father remembering when he first held his baby in his arms, regardless of whether that baby was you or someone else. And that was what I did, I ran out of the house and howled the rest of the day away in the air-raid shelter. Was I jealous of Shani? I'm not sure the question is even worth asking. Jealousy and envy are so constituent to our natures we might as well factor them into every consideration of our dealings with one another and not refer to them again. But beyond that, beyond that mole of inwrought meanness, I don't believe I was put out. My father hadn't named me after anything beautiful, but I did bear the name of a boxer he admired, and boxing had certainly been as important in his life as beauty. Yes, I howled for me because I would soon be fatherless, but otherwise I howled for him, and, though it goes against the grain professionally for me to say this, for the love he bore his daughter. Call that *my* Jewish sentimentality. He adored her. She was his shaineh maidel, which meant that he adored her with some part of himself that was mysterious to me, and must have been equally mysterious to him. Was it *his* father who was talking through him, or his father's father before him? I had never known either, but I howled for them as well.

She never left his side. There were complications. Pneumonia? I don't know. I couldn't bear to take in the physical facts of his illness. Nor could my mother. We closed our ears when the doctor spoke to us. It wasn't my father's death we were in denial of but the truth about bodies. And not just our bodies, *all* bodies. We didn't want to know how they worked. Offered the choice between ignorance and knowledge, we chose ignorance. Shani was different. Shani took in every detail of what was wrong with him, saw to the medication, told him what to expect, cleaned him up, changed his pyjamas, turned him in his bed, everything. And all without a single expression of petulance or complaint.

Gone, the angry fretful girl who had locked herself away all day, unable to reconcile her eyes to her appearance, gone as though she had never existed. Unable to comprehend what we were seeing, my mother and I exchanged wide-eyed stares of astonishment when we passed on the stairs, but otherwise said nothing. It was as though we didn't want to speak in case we broke the spell. It's also possible we were too ashamed to speak. Ashamed of our incompetence and squeamishness, but equally ashamed of the bad opinion we'd had of Shani. She wasn't who we thought she was. Not simply unlike herself, but a different person entirely.

The only one who didn't seem surprised by this was my father. At an hour when Shani would normally have been immured in her bedclothes, there she was, taking his temperature or delivering him his breakfast. And *dressed*. Dressed not in a sheet either! 'And how's my beautiful daughter this fine morning?' he would say to her, as though she'd been ministering to him with precisely this efficiency every morning of her life.

She sponged his face, emery-boarded his nails, shaved him — though until the final days he wasn't so weak that he couldn't have shaved himself — even cut his hair. He behaved like a child throughout these procedures, submitting to her, as he had never submitted to the decisions of any referee, with the sweetest compliancy, smiling, gazing up at her, and sometimes laughing to himself.

'Why are you laughing?' she would say, gently pinching his cheeks.

'So that you will do that.'

She could barely catch her breath. 'You're trying to make me cry.'

He would smile at her, his turn now to touch her face. 'I'm not. I wouldn't make you cry for the whole wide world.'

But sometimes, usually in the late afternoon when she'd finished her tasks, they wept openly together. And then he would call her his shaineh maidel again. Which only made her weep the more copiously.

Whether he wept with my mother, I don't know. That would have happened, if it happened at all, in the night. What occurred between them had always been subject to the strictest blackout. No jocularity, no ribaldry, in our house in the matter of intimate relations between man and wife. They could have been a rabbi and rebitsin, so decorous were they. Indeed, I am hard-pressed to think of any rabbi I have ever met who was as instinctively modest as my father. Never once, for example, did I see him naked. I have photographs of him in the ring, with his chest bare and his chin out and his nose about to bleed, but even in these he is wearing shorts up to his neck and down to his ankles. My mother the same, and I don't mean with regard to the chest and the shorts. I cannot recall ever having seen her anything but dressed and made-up for the day, and certainly never in a bathrobe. I can only guess, then, at what it must have been like for them in the night, organising their goodbyes, with my father so respectful of her, and she so unwilling to approach the failing of his body. But black circles were appearing around her eyes, and she was beginning to fall absent, forgetting what she had to do, and on occasions who she was talking to.

To me, my father was soldierly. I had to be a strong boy and look after my mother and my sister. Unfortunately I was rarely able to be soldierly in return. No sooner did he say those words – 'You're going to have to be a strong boy, Maxie, and look after your mother and your sister' – than I would begin my howling again. I do no better remembering the words today.

He asked for me one evening, gave me his hand to hold, which I hadn't done since I was about six, and told me to fight the good fight. When I asked him what he meant he said he didn't know but I should fight it anyway.

I said I would.

He released his hand from mine, then squeezed my fingers.

'I've worked out what it all adds up to,' he said. 'It adds up to my family.'

Howl, Maxie! Except I knew I didn't dare.

'That's what I'll take,' he said. 'That's what I'll settle for. A long shlof and my family.'

'Gai shlofn,' he used to say to me when I was small. Go to sleep, but also sometimes meaning put a sock in it. I loved the word. You could hear peace in it. After life's fitful fever, he shlofs well.

'Shlof now,' I said, 'you look tired.'

'I mean a longer shlof than that,' he said with a little laugh. 'A much longer shlof than that, Maxie.'

It was almost Christian. A long sleep in the arms of the Lord. But then it's from us the Christians learned it. The shlof that passeth understanding.

But waiting for the Lord was becoming harrowing.

'Do you know what,' my mother said to me in the final days, 'I think I'd have preferred it if he'd died in a road accident.'

I tried to smile at her.

'Do you think that's terrible of me, Maxie?' she asked.

'No, I don't. I know what you mean. It's the saying goodbye.'

She looked distraught. 'But our Shani has been doing it for weeks.'

This was the first mention we had made of it. 'I know,' I said. 'It's amazing.'

She stared at me, her eyes wild. 'Where do you think she gets it from?'

I'd already decided that. 'From him,' I said.

Shani was with him when he died. I cannot say whether they planned it that way. I doubt it. I am sure he would have wanted all of us there, but then again he knew who the strong ones were and weren't.

She came out of his room, a whiter white than you would have thought a living person could be. My mother sank to her knees when she saw her.

'He's gone,' Shani said. 'He was very good. Very good. He asked me to comb his hair. Then he told me to say that he loved you all, then he closed his eyes.' She shrugged her shoulders. 'And that was that.'

She seemed ever so slightly disappointed, as though there should have been more.

In a strange way I felt there had been too much. *Loved us all.* That wasn't how my father spoke. No love talk. At least not away from the blackout which was his love affair with my mother. But then I didn't know what fathers said when they were taking leave of their families. And it was always possible that Shani had made it all up to spare us the fact that what he'd really said was, 'My shaineh maidel', and taken her into his arms one final time.

These Jewish men!

2

Selick Washinsky's stroke affected Asher in ways he would not have expected. In expectation of such an event – and he had antici- pated it often – he had seen himself running to the hospital and begging his father's forgiveness. Thereafter there were alterna- tive versions of the story. Sometimes he would promise never to see Dorothy again. Sometimes he would no sooner beg his father's forgiveness than he would further beg him to give Dorothy a chance – 'If you only knew her, if you would only meet her, you would love her, Dad.' To which reasonable plea, in one version, his father would listen patiently. And in another would respond by having a second stroke.

What Asher had not made provision for was his own intran- sigence. No, he would not budge. No, he would not give in to blackmail. For his part, Selick Washinsky's mistake was to have had an insufficiently serious stroke. He didn't look ill enough when Asher went to visit him in hospital. Jack Glickman in a neighbouring bed looked far more sick, and Jack Glickman didn't have a son who was seeing a fire-yekelte's daughter – that much he knew, leaving the son out of it, from the fact that the Glickmans didn't run a kosher house and therefore didn't need a fire-yekelte. His father wasn't looking well, Asher accepted that, but when had his father looked well? As soon as he saw him, Asher decided it was a trick. Jewish fathers could throw strokes the way other men could throw a switch. There was nothing wrong with him. He just didn't want his son marrying the daughter of the woman who made their fire and who also happened to be German. Well, that was tough shit. Asher kissed his father on both cheeks and handed him a box of kosher chocolates.

'What's this,' his father asked, 'a mockery?'

To which Asher replied, 'No, Dad, the mockery is you.'

'He's faking it,' he told Dorothy. 'It's not real. He made it happen.'

'But he is in hospital,' she reminded him.

'He *was* in hospital. By now they'll have let him out.'

She couldn't see how this helped them. If anything the situation was worse now. If a man could fake a stroke to stop his son being with her, it didn't mean he was less upset than had his stroke been real. It might mean he was more upset. She could see where this would end – with Selick Washinsky dying and Asher saying it wasn't real, even as they were throwing pebbles on his grave.

'So what are you going to do?' she asked.

'Tell them to geh in dred.'

'And what does that mean?'

'To go to hell.'

'I know what the words mean, Asher. You've used them to me enough times. What I'm asking is what effect they will have.'

'It will have the effect of making them realise that unless they want to lose me for ever they will have to accept you.'

She puffed her cheeks out. Sometimes she thought she knew Jewish families better than he did.

Asher didn't tell his parents to geh in dred. They told him. Leave the girl or get out. There was nothing more to say.

In fact there must have been plenty more to say, otherwise Tsedraiter Ike would not have gone round there to see if Selick Washinsky were having another stroke. But that was what it boiled down to. Leave the girl or never be seen by us again. Leave the girl or accept that you are an orphan. Leave the girl or be as good as dead to us.

Asher made the mistake of saying, 'Isn't that a bit extreme, Dad?'

I happen to know that because Manny, finding it harder and harder to keep what had been happening to himself, told me, some time later, a little of what ensued. They had been drawing him into it for weeks. No avoiding it. 'You talk to him, he's your brother, get him to see sense,' coming from his parents; 'Speak up for me, they'll listen to you, tell them it'll blow over if they give it time, but this way . . . explain to them,' coming from his brother. Manny hadn't mentioned any of this while it was happening. Not a word. I'd be surprised if he said much to any of the parties either, despite what they asked of him. He was not a person who responded well to pressure. Demand anything of Manny and he'd hold his breath for half an hour. Try to get his attention and he'd be off down the street, practising his breast-stroke. He knew what he was good at. He understood his own tolerance level. When someone wanted help he swam away from them.

But after Asher's 'Isn't that a bit extreme, Dad?' he was willy-nilly a participant. When your father and your brother are wrestling on the floor, you cannot just stand there holding your breath, even if you are Manny Washinsky.

'A bit extreme!' Selick Washinsky had shrei'd – shrei being a

Jewish scream, something only Jews can do. 'Me! A bit extreme! You go to bed with a German girl, a child, you take advantage of a *child*, the daughter of a woman who works for us and who we respect . . . You come to my hospital bed and call me a mockery . . . You spit in your mother's face, you bring disgrace upon your family, and you call me a *bit extreme*!' He was bouncing on the balls of his feet, his hands tearing at air, as though it was the word itself he wanted to attack – extreme, the word *extreme*, if he could only get at it, and when he did get at it he would rip it apart letter by letter.

'Selick, Selick, stop it! Selick, you've just come out of hospital,' his wife had cried, trying to calm him, to come between him and that word.

'Extreme! A bit extreme!' And then, because there's nowhere else a shrei can go, and because he had decided at last where and where only the word was to be found, he had leapt at Asher's throat. 'I'll kill you. May the Almighty forgive me, I'll kill you . . .'

And had he been possessed of the necessary strength he would have.

Maybe this was the fight that brought Tsedraiter Ike across, maybe it wasn't. Apparently there were any number of scenes like these. This one, at least, was terminated when Manny piled in on top of his brother and his father, lashing out at both of them, and having what he described to me as an epileptic fit.

'You are an epileptic?'

'No. I just had this fit. My legs went stiff, I couldn't stop my arms shaking, my face turned to ice and I was foaming at the mouth.'

Rabies! So I'd been right to be worried the time he bit me. If he'd bitten me that bit closer to my thumb who knows what the consequence would have been.

'Have you ever foamed at the mouth before?'

'Never.'

And no doubt he thought he would never foam at the mouth

or be otherwise unrecognisable to himself again. Which just goes to show how little we know about ourselves.

How did it happen, how did Elohim allow it to happen, that a boy as hesitant and introjective as Manny Washinsky, a boy so unprovocative and – not to be unkind – *invisible*, could have found himself entrammelled in so much violence? How many times was it that I'd either seen or heard about him doing battle on the floor? Here am I, the son of a boxer, by profession a scratcher-out of eyes, a brute without a heart, if Zoë was to be believed, and to date I have never found myself in anything that remotely resembles a fight, not even an upright almost shaping up to be a fight, let alone a down and dirty horizontal wrestle.

At least not with men. And even with the women, I always ran before a blow could be landed.

Was it simply Manny's bad luck? Did these misadventures just befall him? Or was there something in his nature that sought them out?

Not hard to imagine, whatever one makes of Manny's fit, what must have been going through Asher's mind. His father trying to kill him, his brother foaming at the mouth, his mother yelling 'Stop it! Stop it!' and throwing salt on the combatants, as though to kosher them into stopping. Is any woman worth all this? Asher must have asked himself. But the opposite thought, too, must have seized him: who wouldn't run to any woman to escape all this? And with each thought the corresponding image – Dorothy, lovely but insubstantial, just a girl, to be relinquished; and Dorothy, the girl who loved him, who wouldn't raise a finger to harm him, and with whom every moment was as an eternity of peace.

Whether or not it was the salt that did it, a kind of peace was restored here too. The parties withdrew. Nothing was said. Each waiting for the other to make the next move. Briefly, Asher gave way to the crazy fantasy that the hours of silence denoted the beginnings of a change of heart on his parents' part. They would come to see that his happiness was paramount. Little by little they were growing to understand that he would be no less Jewish for being with the fire-yekelte's German daughter — who was, when all was said and done, only *half*-German, don't forget that — but on the contrary that he would be the *more* Jewish as a consequence of being with her, for was it not a Jew's responsibility to be happy and to glory in the variousness of the world which Elohim had made? It was possible, yes it was possible that on their own and in the quiet of their confabulations they would come to see that. For their part, his parents were less sanguine. You can't leave a Jewish boy with a non-Jewish woman and expect him to come to his senses unaided. That is not how it happens. The Jewish boy doesn't have the seichel, the nous, and the non-Jewish woman doesn't have the charity. How can she have? She has laid her hands on the one thing non-Jewish women prize above all others. She has got herself a yeshiva bocher. Sidelocks, fringes, yarmulke, the lot. The prince she has been dreaming of all her life. You can't even blame her for her cupidity. What woman wouldn't do the same! So all the silence of Selick and Channa Washinsky denoted was a change of plan. They had tried holding him responsible for killing his father, now they would try holding him responsible for destroying their marriage.

'You know what your father is saying to me,' Channa told her son. 'He is saying that it is my fault. That the reason you are as you are is because I have brought you up badly, that his children are a bitter disappointment to him due to my misguidance. He believes that the twenty years we've been together are wasted.'

'But that's nonsense . . .'

'Is it? Isn't the value of our marriage in our children? Aren't you the proof of whether it has been successful or not?'

'And you're saying that it's not? And that your children are the reason?'

'Well, you're the clever one, Asher. You tell me. You tell me how proud of you we should be.'

It was at that moment, and I have it from the horse's mouth, that Manny came home from school. As to how much he had heard about the bitter disappointments which he too, it seemed, had caused his parents – 'Enough,' was what he told me.

Which was pretty much the way he felt about Asher as well. Enough. Enough now. 'You're ruining everything,' he said. 'You're not my brother any more. Why don't you just go.'

'See!' Channa Washinsky said. 'See what's happening to this family.'

'Yes I do,' Asher said. 'I see exactly what's happening to this family.' And with that he bolted. To hell with everybody. And that included Dorothy. He was meant to be meeting her that evening. Her father was cooking for some relatives she wanted him to meet. But to Asher that felt too nakedly manipulative in its long-suffering. *I can't meet any of your family, but I introduce you with pride to all of mine.* Fucking Germans. Fucking Germans with their fucking devious remorse. No thank you. He'd done with relatives, Jews or Germans. For two weeks he stayed with a friend in Birmingham. They prayed together, the rocking rhythm soothing Asher's heart. They went to a couple of midweek football matches together where they prayed again. On Friday evenings they went to the synagogue. Midway through the service on the second Friday Asher thought of Dorothy. On the Shabbes he caught the train back to Manchester, energised by the transgression, and walked the three or four miles from the station to her home. Not so many people came out to stare at him now. They were used to him. And besides, he had lost his juice. He no longer looked like a pomegranate on legs.

Dorothy was not there. For a moment Asher thought she might have been standing in for her mother and putting in a little fire-yekelte-ing at his parents' house. But the likelihood now was that not even her mother went there any more. Albert Beckman was short with him. 'You cannot expect her to wait here for you for ever,' he said.

'I don't,' Asher said.

'My daughter is very upset because she hasn't heard from you. When you last spoke you told her you were coming to see her in an hour. We were all expecting you.'

'I am sorry for that,' Asher said. 'And I can imagine how Dorothy must have felt. It's been very upsetting for me too.'

'We made sacrifices for you,' Albert Beckman said, not looking at Asher.

'Sacrifices?' Asher racked his brain. What sacrifices?

'We took a risk on you.'

Asher preferred risk to sacrifice, but he wasn't sure what the risk was either. 'You make me sound like a danger you braved,' he said. 'What was dangerous about me?'

'Not you in yourself. The situation.'

Asher rolled his eyes. *You think the situation has been risky for you? You should try it from my end!* But he knew there was nothing to be gained from comparing risks, or from comparing sacrifices, come to that. The German owed the Jew. The Jew owed the German nothing. That was where Asher stood. That was where I make him stand. But he also knew how little was to be gained from saying that. So he simply stated what he thought – 'The situation is between me and Dorothy.'

'Yes, but it is never as simple as that.'

'Where is she?' Asher asked.

'She has gone away.' And though her father appeared to regret the words he'd used, and even, Asher thought, wished he could take them back, he wasn't going to tell Asher where she had gone to. Or when she would return.

Asher walked home in tears, before realising he no longer thought of it as home and shouldn't have been going there. His father was sewing in the window and pretended not to see him. His mother started when he entered. 'I hope you are here to tell me it's all finished,' she said. No preliminaries. No other matter on their minds. Was it over or wasn't it. Was he seeing her or wasn't he. The spirituality of his family reduced to that. To a shtupp. Was he or wasn't he still penetrating the German girl?

'It looks like you might have your wish,' he said.

'What does that mean?'

'Dorothy can't take any more.'

'What does that mean?'

'It means that I've been sent packing.'

'And what do you intend to do about that?'

'There is nothing I can do. I have to accept it.'

'Good. If that's true, I will tell your father.'

'Tell him what you like. Just don't tell him I'm happy.'

'And just don't you tell him that you're not. We've had enough of your unhappiness, Asher. It's been in the house with us for months.'

'It will be with me for a lot longer.'

She sucked her teeth at him. 'I hope you're not asking me, Asher, as your mother, to be sorry about this?'

'About "this", no. I'm asking you, as my mother, to be sorry for *me*.'

She looked at him, as he thought – as he told Manny that he thought – with hatred for him in her eyes. 'Well, I can't be. If she doesn't want to see you, that's for the best. You'll get over her. You're a child. At your age feelings don't run so deep.'

Having said which, and having told her husband the good news, her hatred turned once again to love.

But she was wrong on several points. It wasn't for the best. At Asher's age feelings did run deep. And he didn't get over her.

3

When I reminded Manny Stroganoff that as Manny Washinsky he had once said he envied me not having a father, he claimed to have no recollection of it. But he gave no sign that he cared whether he'd said it or not. It was as though I were describing events in another life . . .

I would not yet reintroduce Manny in his Stroganoff incarnation were there any way of avoiding it. In this, a comic strip is preferable: you can foreshadow more suggestively when you are not at the mercy of linear narrative, you can prefigure the future in the clouds of the past, you can intimate a likeness of that which has not yet occurred. Turn to the earliest pages of *Five Thousand Years of Bitterness* and you will swear you can make out Hitlerian storm troopers, or at the very least a moustache suggestive of the Führer, bobbing on the waters of the Red Sea. That's how I would prefer the older Manny to make his presence felt – not here just yet, never here just yet, but always waiting to happen.

From which it will be evident that I didn't want to see him again, whatever the inducements offered by Lipsync Productions and whatever the promises I'd made to the sisters Bryson-Smith. Why? Because I couldn't imagine how you talked to someone you used to know quite well who had, since you saw him last, murdered both his parents. The comedian Tommy Cooper once performed a sketch in which he found himself sitting opposite Hitler in a railway carriage. Not knowing what else to do he buried his face in a newspaper. But his conscience would not leave him alone. Conscious of the moral inadequacy of silence, he would from time to time look up from his newspaper and hiss. *Ssss!* I took this to be a profound exploration of the impossibility of ever expressing outrage sufficient to a monstrous crime. *Ssss!* I'm not saying I equated meeting Manny with meeting Hitler, but wasn't it required of me to demonstrate some reprobation, however feeble – *Ssss, Manny, ssss!* – before asking him how life otherwise had been treating him?

There was reason to believe Manny felt as awkward about our getting together as I did. At first he denied all knowledge of me. And if he didn't know me he couldn't, as a matter of simple logic, want to see me again, could he? Then he said he did in fact vaguely remember my name but wouldn't discuss his past with me for anything less than a million pounds. I stayed out of this,

221

leaving all negotiations to Francine and Marina, the progress of which was reported to me on a regular basis by a succession of trainee PAs with improbably throaty voices, not one of whom had the most basic grasp of who Manny was and what he had done, still less of where I fitted into the picture, but who relayed the latest manoeuvre by either party as though their working and creative lives depended on it. Eventually, they found a price which they could afford and Manny was prepared to take – fifty pounds was my guess – and couriered me a train ticket.

That a further six weeks elapsed before our meeting was my fault. I couldn't face it. I had not supposed when I agreed to what was after all an excavation of my own past as well as Manny's that he would have returned to Manchester on his release. Stamford Hill was where I imagined him, Stoke Newington or Hackney, in some charitable home for broken-down old Jews with a criminal past. I'm not saying that seeing him anywhere would have been easy, but in situ, so to speak, in the environs of our innocent childhood, where we played ball, drew pictures, and huddled, breath hot on each other's necks, over *The Scourge of the Swastika* – that took a bit of preparing for.

I'd made a booking in a pizza restaurant off Deansgate and had he not been at the table before me I would never have recognised him. I'd thought a lot about who I was going to find, obsessed about him even, partly I suppose because you dread marking in those you haven't seen for so long the imperceptible changes in yourself. And not just the changes, but the emotional expenditure, the history of unachievement, the waste. On the one hand I'd imagined him as one of those neurasthenic Jews out of Otto Dix, the brains showing through the forehead, the skin white with the over-interiority of the Hebrew. On the other – and this was a conscious corrective to that expectation, considering where Manny had been for the last however many years – I was ready for a hardened lag, head shaved, shoulders widened, a man with a closed face and flattened ears, thick about the neck, much like Broderick

'The Bull' Chisnall had been before Errol Tobias felled him. Had I drawn the person I was going to meet, combining these two versions, he'd have come out as The Mekon, Lord of the Treens, Dan Dare's green-faced genius antagonist, on the body of the Hulk.

Ssss!

The one description I would never have got to on my own was dapper. Dapper-deranged. He looked like someone out of H. G. Wells, a draper's assistant who had gone too long without advancement, or a railway clerk working in a station where the trains no longer ran. Still the boy's skull, smooth high brow and small vulnerable neck, topped with a little hair, like an omelette, yellowish in colour, with a diminutive quiff. And a wan moustache which looked no less foreign to his face than the outcrop of baby fluff had, forty years before. Nor was he dressed as I'd imagined he would be. But that was the fault of my imagination which had stopped, like a clock after an explosion, at the sepulchral uniform – white shirt, black suit, fringes, homburg – of an Orthodox Jewish boy as seen by an un-Orthodox Jewish cartoonist. It had crossed my mind to put him in rolled-up jeans, brown suede shoes and a green polo neck pulled tight across the chest, as worn by someone Errol once introduced me to sotto voce – Merton Friedlander, at the time the only Jewish boy any of us had ever met who had been to borstal. Stealing cars. Think of that. A Jew stealing cars! A Jew in borstal! But Manny would not transliterate into clothes like Merton Friedlander's. Now here he was in a dogstooth jacket, a Viyella shirt, a dull silvery, diamond-patterned tie and grey trousers. The clothes of a man who had never been anywhere and to whom nothing had ever happened.

He was half the size I'd remembered. Had he always been small, or had they shrunk him in there? Had they lobotomised half his frame away?

Normally when you meet someone you haven't seen for a lifetime you register the shock at the beginning, then little by little become reacquainted with the familiar. With Manny it was the opposite. He had been better than I'd expected at first, but with every minute that passed he seemed worse. There was nothing of him. And what there was seemed of another place. What did he keep smiling at on the restaurant ceiling? Why did he push his jaw out as though he wanted to chin away every word I said to him? Where was he?

We didn't shake hands. I took my cue from him. He didn't want to. Indeed, for the first half-hour it was difficult to discover anything he did want, other than food.

Watching him having trouble cutting his pizza, then having to resort to biting into it directly from the plate, it occurred to me that he might never have eaten pizza before. Carrots served with potatoes where he'd been. And maybe at weekends, or when they changed the chef because the previous one had been knifed, potatoes served with carrots. When he was last out and about there weren't any pizza restaurants in Manchester. When Manny was last at large – that's if one could think of Manny ever being at large – pizza hadn't even been invented.

'The place must look very different to you,' I said.

'Here?'

I made a little world with my hands. Meaning the restaurant, Manchester, the universe. The everywhere to which, if he needed any questions answering, I was happy to be his guide and mentor. In loco parentis was how I felt; the man to his boy.

'I've had seven years to get used to it,' he said.

What did he mean, seven years? Had they moved him up here from wherever he'd been, and let him out for walkies, like a dog?

He read my confusion. 'I've been a free man' – this, talking of dogs, accompanied by a strange, quick barking noise, as though a dog might laugh – 'for seven years.'

'Seven years!'

'That's when I came out. Seven years ago. Didn't you know?'

What I didn't know was where to look. The fuckers! That

fucking writer and those fucking film girls, why had they sold him to me as hot property, a man that very hour released whose story we needed to pounce on before Hollywood beat us to it? Seven years! Jesus Christ!

But of course the fault wasn't theirs. If I was Manny's friend, why hadn't *I* known he'd been out so long? Why hadn't my mother or Shani, who still lived within the ghetto walls and read its newspapers – why hadn't Tsedraiter Ike, come to that, who vibrated like an old cello with every ghetto shock or perturbation – why hadn't any of them told me that Manny had been released? Or were they, too, in their kalooki, like me in my cartoons, happy to know nothing of this particular item of intelligence, content for it all to stay where it belonged, and where *he* belonged, behind bars. Whatever his original sentence, however much of it he'd served, we'd put him away for life.

He smiled into his fingernails, deriving satisfaction from my embarrassment. Something like mirth, or the corpse of mirth, rattled in his neck.

'I'm not arguing with you,' he said at last.

He was a gift for a cartoonist – never still, the expression on his face never matching what he said, and what he said interrupted by so many half-coughs and clicks and other muffled ejaculations – as though he were punctuating his own lapses of concentration in his throat – that only coloured stars and broken bits of typeface exploding out of his mouth could capture the demented carnival of his conversations. One sound he made, though, I feel I have to try to render in language. It was somewhere between an exclamation of impatience and an invitation to forgetfulness or sleep – a hush almost, but more jittery, and more sibilant. And with something of Tommy Cooper's displeasure with Adolf Hitler in it. 'S-sssch' is the nearest I can get to it with letters. Like someone stuttering on the word 'shit', and then giving up.

I'd said nothing when he told me he wasn't arguing with me, partly because I hadn't understood him. So he went on without waiting for me to catch up. 'I am of the opinion I should have stayed in longer myself.'

'That's not what I was thinking. Or think,' I assured him.

'S-sssch . . .' he said, while I waited. 'A life for a life.'

'Nor is that what I think.'

'Isn't it? Why not? But I'm glad to hear it. It's not what I think, either. I think they should put you away for a short time, for appearances' sake, then let you out no matter how many lives you take. Like H-horst S-ssschumann. You couldn't count the numbers of people he killed, but he was out and about in a year.'

'Was he someone you were in with?'

He laughed through his nose – more a bark than a laugh. 'Horst S-ssschumann? You don't know Horst S-ssschumann? That's a pity. I've a feeling you would have liked him. Many people did.'

I didn't only not know who H-horst S-ssschumann was, I didn't know how much of that was his name, how much was stutter, and how much of it was Manny's hushing one of us either into sleep or vigilance.

'Why would I have liked him?' I asked, keeping it simple. 'What were his qualities?'

'An enquiring mind. A love of science. And a curiosity about Jews. All three took him to Au-auschwitz to run their mass sterilisation programme. There, he X-rayed the testicles and ovaries of Jewish men and women the age we were when we last met, then castrated them to make sure the X-rays had worked. Sometimes, on the assumption that they were as interested in his scientific findings as he was, he would carry out these experiments in view of the next patients. If you happened to survive the burning from the X-rays you'd die from t-terror or s-ssshock. I think that interested him scientifically as well – the amount of s-ssshock to which you could submit a Jew.'

'May his name be blotted out,' I said.

He looked at me as though I were a moral simpleton, stuck in some childish game of expunging our enemies from human speech, a ploy which hadn't worked when we last tried it and certainly wasn't going to work now. He'd changed, that was what he wanted me to see. He'd had a long time to consider tactics. Now he loved the enemies of the Jewish people. And wanted them remembered evermore.

'S-ssschumann's name wasn't blotted out, I am pleased to say. After leaving the mass sterilisation programme he worked as a doctor all over the world. No less conscientiously than he'd worked at Au-auschwitz by all accounts. You should be sorry you were never able to consult him yourself. We both should be. He had a good bedside manner with Jews. Finally, after twenty years of good work, the Germans found him, brought him back and put him on trial. A series of events which, as you might imagine, he found very distressing. Fortunately they discovered he had – ha! – h-high blood pressure, and released him halfway through his trial. No l-laughing matter, h-high blood pressure. So they let him go. Which I call justice.'

My turn to bark. I would have adopted Manny's crazy circus of verbal emissions had I dared. *H-high b-blood pressure? S-sssssssch! The f-f-f-f-fucker!* But I didn't know whether they were an affliction brought on in anticipation of Nazi nomenclature or his throat's refusal to accept his decision to love his enemies. Either way, they served the function of denying the f-f-f-fuckers decent articulation.

'Well, the consolation is that they are released into the torments of hell,' I said.

'Is that what you think happens? Ha! Well, you might be right in some cases. It's possible we will run into a few of them in hell when we get there, or at least when I do. But not any of the doctors in charge of the Nazi sterilisation and extermination programmes. After being released into a comfortable life here on earth, they will probably be in heaven now. S-ssschumann lived until he was seventy-seven, quietly in F-frankfurt. Klaus E-endruweit, accessory to the murder of thousands of the mentally ill, was still in medical practice when I was inside. S-some of them are digging their gardens or cradling their great-grandchildren while we speak. And I'm pleased to say that those who did die enjoyed obituaries from their profession of a s-sort we are unlikely to get from ours.'

Ours? Which profession was Manny in? I wondered.

List-maker of murderers – did that count as a profession?

Eerie, all this. As though time had not happened anywhere but on our faces. If I kept staring at him would the years fall away, would we be back in the air-raid shelter, I with my pencil in my mouth, making Donald Duck noises, Manny running through the names of our eternal enemies, enumerating their crimes, biting their specialities into my flesh so that I would never forget them? Not much had changed, considering all that had happened to both of us. Not much of an advance, despite Manny's apparent conviction that by pretending to love our enemies we could achieve some sort of moral victory over them. H-horst S-ssschumann – what a great bloke! And yet it was strangely consoling to be back doing what we were doing. I was impressed that he had continued with his studies while he'd been out of circulation. There was something wonderful about it, Manny locked away all those years still pursuing in his head those who'd persecuted us. It was what he was for. His conscientiousness was a lesson to us all. And who was to say that this wasn't what I was for as well: to listen to what he told me, to be his pupil – no matter that I saw myself as in loco parentis to him – to study at his feet.

One question I wanted to ask him about his cataloguing – whether he now included his own name, E-emanuel Eli W-w-washinsky, among the roll-call of unpronounceable killers of Jews?

But there were some smaller questions to be asked, before the greater. Where he lived now, for example, what he did for money, what he did to pass the time, how he had found the courage to return to Manchester where not everybody, surely, was unaware of his existence. But even they seemed premature. 'Pizza OK?' was the best I could do.

He nodded, but gravely as though in response to one of the questions I hadn't been brave enough to put to him.

'So why Stroganoff?' I asked at last. It was my way of trying to get him to make a declaration of friendship. *In memory of the old days*, I wanted to hear him say. *In memory of us*.

But all he said was, 'I needed another name.'

Why that should have distressed me as much as it did I am unable to explain. I had been careful not to think of him as a friend even in the days when he *was* a friend. And he had never shown me any warmth to speak of. It was a bit of a shock, nonetheless, to discover that time had no more softened him to me, than me to him.

We both looked at our food for a while, then suddenly he asked, without a stutter or any other impediment to speech, 'How's your father?'

'He's dead, Manny. You know that.'

He made a peculiar motion with his lips, half as though licking them to make them moist, half as though flicking something away.

'He died years ago,' I reminded him. 'In your time. After the funeral you said you envied me not having a father. I have never forgotten that.'

'Don't remember,' he said.

He was holding his left hand tightly in his right, the thumb of the one squeezing all colour out of the knuckles of the other. He protruded his jaw – a weak man's resolution. But again, he wasn't arguing with me. If he said that about my father, he said it. At the time to which I was probably referring he could, frankly, have said anything. The remark would have been directed at his father, not mine. He believed he had rather liked my father. And my mother. Whereas his own parents he did not, at that time, like. He had turned against them. Grown ashamed of them. Had I lost my mother he might have said he envied me not having one of those as well.

Strange. I had been thinking it would take us a thousand meetings for us ever to get anywhere, for me to find the form of question I felt I had any right to ask, for him to concentrate his attention long enough to answer me. Now here we were, in the very thick of things after only fifteen minutes. Manny grown ashamed of his parents. At this rate we would have the gas taps on before coffee.

And wouldn't Francine be pleased.

What he told me came out haltingly, and much of it was addressed to someone who wasn't there, and certainly wasn't me. But what it amounted to was this:

4

After his outburst against Asher, he had fallen into one of those fits of despondency well known to people who act out of character. It had been exhilarating at first, losing his temper, making something happen, even if that something was Asher's running away from home. Good. Excellent. Asher needed time to clear his head. And Manny needed not to hear his family screaming at one another. But when days went by and Asher did not return, Manny's spirits deserted him. What if he had succeeded only in throwing his brother into the fire-yekelte's daughter's arms? Worse – if anything could be worse – what if his brother had grown desperate and thrown himself under a bus? Was this to be the consequence of Manny's single deviation from the laws of his own undemonstrative nature – the loss, one way or another, of his brother? But then, when Asher returned, Manny was exhilarated again. He had done some good after all. Asher had sorted himself out, come to his senses, and was now back where he belonged, trailing between home and the synagogue, without the girl. Wonderful, for Manny, to see before his eyes, as the very proof of his effect, the family reunited.

Or it would have been wonderful had they – 'they' meaning

his mother and his father and himself and maybe even Elohim – taken a little longer to pass from heartache to happiness. It was too sudden. Wounds don't heal that quickly. Not if they are real wounds in the first place. No – I tried him with this – no, it wasn't that he had wanted Asher to be kept longer in purgatory. Absolutely not. His eyes fluttered like trapped birds. Yes, he could see that his feelings were open to cynical interpretation. Why should Asher be rewarded with the fatted calf for going off the rails, while he, Manny, the good boy who had gone nowhere, was rewarded with nothing? Unjust, the jubilation which always awaits the return of the prodigal. But that wasn't the cause of his depression. His mother and father were the cause of his depression. The fact that their affliction could turn to rejoicing in a second. The screaming, the emergency ambulance, the fisticuffs, a son raising his hand to his own father, Manny himself driven into an epilepsy to which he had not hitherto had any idea he was disposed – hadn't any of it meant anything?

What's the worth of rage that cools so quickly? What does it tell you about the cause? As a matter of seemliness, if nothing else, Manny believed his parents should have thought twice before trumpeting their relief with such blatancy. Should have thought twice before showing it to each other, but more importantly should have thought twice before blaring it at Asher. Was there not bad taste in that? Was it not gross of them to suppose that Asher would concur quite so promptly, if at all, in their felicity? And was it not cruel of them not to wonder how things were in Asher's heart?

Manny talked about Asher's heart as though it were an empty bed. Someone had lain in it beside him, and now she was gone. Manny could see the impression her body had made. He had been a lonely boy himself and was now an even lonelier man. Perhaps it was this that made him exquisitely aware of Asher's loss. Never mind that the girl was German. It had surprised him, he told me, to catch himself not minding, because he had at first minded a great deal. A German was a German. A person you could not forgive and should not go near. But he got to the humanity of not caring what she was via the impression she had left behind her in Asher's heart. The impression was without religion or nationality. The impression – the sad, simple indentation – humanised her.

And by contrast dehumanised his parents who would not notice, or care, that it was there. For this, and without any prior warning signs in his theology, Manny, in his depression, blamed the faith of his fathers.

God, good. God, I was sure, would take us where I wanted to go. Wherever that was. Talk to me about God, Manny.

'It wasn't a fully-fledged religious crisis,' he said, a queer blue smile irradiating his face. 'I wasn't intelligent enough for one of those. I just started to have my doubts.'

'I remember,' I said. 'I remember you questioning the Unquestionable One. I suspect I wasn't sympathetic.'

He didn't appear to care whether I'd been sympathetic or not. 'Illogical doubts,' he went on. 'I didn't have the nerve to reprove God for His brutality, so I took what some would see as the easier option of wondering where He'd gone.'

'You think He should have interceded for Asher?'

'Of course I didn't. Asher had to make his own mind up.'

'Which he'd done . . .'

'Not really. Asher just got pushed around. He should have been braver. But it was upsetting to see him put in that position. I had originally agreed with everything my parents felt about him. In certain moods I still do. But in the end they should have let him go. The Jewish people were not going to perish because of Asher.'

'My dad would have said that the Jewish people would have been the better for Asher taking himself a Gentile wife.'

'Yes, but your dad didn't always say what he meant.'

'I don't follow you.'

He wasn't going to help me. He looked bored suddenly. He had even stopped gripping his left hand with his right. 'Sorry,' he said, 'it's the head. It gets tired.'

He got up to go to the lavatory. Would he come back, I wondered, and tell me that Germans ironed their underwear?

I was distressed to see that he shambled like an old man.

And was then struck by the thought that he hadn't s-ssschushed me in a while.

5

Before we parted, he grew more forthcoming about God, more forthcoming about Asher anyway, which by Manny's roundabout route amounted to the same thing.

Asher had not settled back into the life of his family. He was in torment. Manny's word. *Torment*. He could not clear his mind of Dorothy.

'You make her sound like an infestation.'

'That's your interpretation. But it was not her doing. Asher did not *want* to clear his mind of Dorothy.'

'This is Asher being a free agent again. Not God's fault.'

He hesitated. 'Not God's fault that Asher wanted to go on thinking of Dorothy. But you have to ask yourself whose fault it was that he felt he shouldn't.'

'Did Elohim ever tell us, *specifically*, to stay away from Germans?' I asked.

'He probably thought He didn't need to, having warned us off everybody else.'

I don't know how to do justice to the bitterness of that remark. It was thrown off, an aside almost, but had it been a well you could have sunk a bore a long way down before reaching bottom. Was the bitterness on his own behalf? Had Manny fallen for someone he shouldn't, and had he too been warned off in the end? It felt unlikely. Manny sentimentally entangled with *anyone*, allowed or not, was beyond imagining. So was that the cause of the vexation I heard – that with him the warnings against wandering off weren't even necessary, so good a job had his parents done on him, so love-proof had they made him, for fear the love would go in an unacceptable direction?

Rather than have the love go in an unacceptable direction, let there be no love!

As usual there was no clue in the expression of his face. His blue eyes – much bluer than I'd remembered – offering to be serene this time, not fluttering at the windows, just seeing beauty, perhaps angels, in the firmament. So maybe the example of Asher was explanation enough of Manny's anger.

Asher was in torment. He could not forgive himself for the almost accidental way in which he and Dorothy had broken up. He owed her feelings more consideration. He owed his own feelings more consideration too. He had acted like a coward, a nobody, a nishtikeit in her language and in his. How terrible, to think it would be as a nishtikeit that she would for ever think of him, if she thought of him at all. He couldn't decide what was worse: her contempt for his memory, or her crying over it. What did goodness teach? Where was Judaism on this? Does the good Jew suffer the obloquy of one he has loved in preference to having her suffer the grief of loving him still? Whose tears are the more precious? Where does it teach you in the Talmud to weigh the emotional consequences of betraying a German girl?

Over and above all this, he quite simply missed her. The one remedy for that – taking his chance and seeking her out again – was not to be entertained, regardless of whether she would even consider agreeing to see him. He could not start that war all over. He could not engage her affections again when he knew he would eventually have to forfeit them for the same reasons. Thus her dear face, whose image he carried in his heart like an ache, became entwined with the idea of impossibility. And when you think of a woman as impossible to you, denied you by forces in the universe over which you can exert no control, you have succumbed to romanticism in its most morbid and irresistible form.

He wept every night for her, and Manny heard him.

Then in the morning he would go to the post office in case she had written to him, which of course she had not. But on the way there, and on the way back, a hundred times in each direction he thought he recognised her. He grew gaunt and papery and more gouge-eyed even than he'd been before, but not once did his mother or his father think they had been wrong or wonder whether, for his sake, right *or* wrong, they should reconsider their ruling. They remained obdurate and relieved, and Manny saw them.

Then, when Asher did not recover his spirits, they sent him to convalesce in a home for weak-chested Jews in Cheshire, and Manny watched him go.

That was why Manny grew to hate his parents, and to lose his faith in G-god. The way he talked, the two were interchangeable.

6

Had my mother believed in God to start with, she too might have lost her faith in Him when my father died. As it was she turned to kalooki.

Though my father had expressly asked to be spared a Jewish funeral — I don't want any of that machareike, he had said — it turned out that he had made no provision for any other sort, so a Jewish funeral was what he got. I think his Yiddish was at fault with machareike which he employed to mean fuss, but strictly speaking means contraption. I suspect the impatiently onomatopoeic qualities of the word confused him. The sound of something being made of nothing. It still perplexes and distresses me that he should have felt that way about his own death. But this might be the paradox of heroic atheism: you rob yourself at the last of the grandeur to which you believe your freedom of mind entitles you. I have, for this reason, made no provision for a secular burial myself, even though I too can't stand all the machareike. Insidious, the old religion, the way it bides its time with everyone, knowing that when you want the big party or the big send-off, you'll be on the phone.

I wept like a baby throughout my father's funeral so didn't notice whether the send-off was big or not. It began – this much I do remember – with my father's comrades lining up outside the house, not sure what to do with their hands, some in hats or yarmulkes, some not, 'Long John' Silverman carrying a prayer shawl under his arm, Elmore Finkel bearing what looked like a gift for my mother tied in a black bow – just in case (how would he know?) a funeral gift was appropriate – all of them respectful but somehow emasculated in their blackest suits, each wishing me, as is the Jewish custom, 'long life'. That could have been the trigger for my tears. Their capitulation to Jewishry for this one hour hurt my head: I couldn't decide whether it was ennobling or enfeebling. What would my father have thought? Wouldn't he have preferred to see them in their hiking boots, grinning raffishly at the trappings of a faith they had no truck with? Wasn't there a comradely farewell that would have become them, and honoured him, more? The rifles of the revolution, maybe? The singing of the 'Red Flag'? A fusillade of anti-clerical jokes? Or did the death of one of their number necessitate a reversion to ancient custom? Was that, after all, the greatest respect they could show him? In which case . . .

In which case futile. Futile all of it. My father's life, my father's principles, every word he'd spoken to me – futile. Not what the rabbi was saying, but who cared about the rabbi? He was futile too. So what did that leave? The mere brute physical fact of my father, his unthinking bulk – and I knew where that was going.

I wouldn't look. Where it went I know but didn't see. That way there was – that way there *remains* – the possibility it went somewhere else.

I was meant to recite Kaddish at the graveside, the great booming lamentation for the Jewish dead, but I botched it. Tsedraiter Ike had transliterated it for me. *Yisgadal veyiskadash*

236

. . . Those dreaded words. Like the tolling of the final bell. You hear them in synagogue when you are young, chanted by orphans and bereaved brothers, and you wonder when your time will come and whether you will be up to it. Well, the time *had* come, and I wasn't. *Yisgadal veyiskadash shemey rabo, Be'olmo di'vero chir'usey.* Botched, but not the time for blaming my dad for never teaching me the Hebrew or its meaning. *May His great Name grow exalted and sanctified — Amen — in the world He created as He willed.* Tsedraiter Ike helped me through. He was just about the only man there who had any inkling of what we were doing or saying. My father's friends looked at the ground or moved their lips at what they hoped were the right moments. Of no use to him whatsoever now. Die and any atheist friends you have are blown away like the leaves from winter's trees.

As though to compensate for his shortcomings at my father's funeral, where his sole concession to the solemnity of the occasion had been to remove his ironic spectacles and dab twice at his eyes, Rodney Silverman wrote me a sweet letter the week following, telling me how he had always admired my father, what a fine and upright man he was, and how he had thought of him recently when he saw Rembrandt's painting of Abraham sacrificing Isaac. 'It is a most terrifying portrait of the eternal Jewish father,' he wrote, 'his hand completely covering Isaac's face, manhandling it in a way that suggests the boy's life is his to do with as he pleases. In this way it denies the rights of the mother absolutely. But look again, Max, and you will see that Abraham's action is in fact loving. The reason he covers his son's face so completely is that he wishes to spare him the sight of the knife going into his heart. Your father was an Abraham. If he sometimes appeared brusque or brutal with you, it was only because he wanted to save you from the cruelty of the world. But you are the artist, so I don't have to explain any of this to you.'

He also sent me a gift. While on one of his many visits to

America on union business he had come across a comic book called *Impact* #1 which contained an illustrated story he thought would interest me. 'Master Race' written by Al Feldstein and drawn by Bernard Krigstein. These Jews! Feldstein and Krigstein! Where would any of us be without these Jews? Rodney Silverman didn't say that, I did. What Rodney Silverman said was that he thought 'Master Race' was pretty good, and he thought I would too . . . Continuing heartfelt condolences and all good wishes, Rodney.

He was right. I did think it was pretty good. Noirish, I suppose we would call it now, futuristic in its line, the sequences of panels cold and filmic, vertiginous in their perspective and their morality, the wicked falling from the height of their wrongdoing in a series of incontrovertible frames, the good almost static in their icy vengefulness, never to be satisfied, existentially inconsolable. The story – though the story is secondary to its illustration – depicts Carl Reissman, a commandant of a Nazi death camp who somehow managed to escape before the Russians arrived, losing himself 'among the streams of refugees that choked the roads and highways before the advancing allied armies . . .' Also surviving the camp is one of Reissman's victims. In a flashback he swears, 'I'll get you, Reissman. I'll get you if it's the LAST THING I DO!' It is this nameless survivor who one day sees Reissman as he travels on the New York subway. The two men, torturer and victim, recognise each other. The survivor chases the ex-Nazi down a platform which is emptied of every other living soul. It is just one-to-one, as each of them has no doubt a thousand times imagined it one day would be. In his haste to escape, Reissman is drawn falling in slow motion, like Lucifer being hurled from heaven – or does he hurl himself? – under an approaching train. Black-hatted, black-coated, cadaverous, expressionless, the survivor is left watching the train rage past, every face in every window as blank and pitiless as his own.

'What happened?' people gather from nowhere to ask. 'Ever see him before?'

'No,' the survivor answers, averting a head which in the shadows looks almost shaven. Then, in a narrow panel of unrelieved gloom – the survivor's coat blacker than the darkness of the Underground, his back completely turned now – he delivers his final line, as though to no one: 'He was a perfect stranger.'

Did Krigstein see himself as the survivor, at the mercy of the cruelty of strangers? Did I see myself as Krigstein? Perhaps because I had just lost my father I adopted him from a distance. At one and the same time I identified him with my father, with Rodney Silverman, and with the artist I aspired to be. It wasn't hero worship. Outside of Rembrandt and Goya and Rubens and one or two others of similar stature, I didn't do heroes. And it wasn't as though I wanted to draw like him. There were no visual jokes in Krigstein. He was too quiet for my taste. Too stark. But something troubled in him spoke to me. So that I wasn't too surprised to learn, years later, not only that he had been an agitator for the rights of illustrators and cartoonists – a union man, which was probably what Rodney Silverman saw in him – but that he'd grown to be desperately unhappy in what he did, and considered himself to be a serious artist who had squandered his genius on a trivial form. The eternal Jewish conundrum. Do you dedicate your talents to God, who never laughs, or do you make a clown of yourself to win the love and admiration of mere mortals? Eventually, Krigstein gave up illustrating comic books in order to return to painting. According to critics who knew what they were talking about, the serious paintings he produced in his later years were leaden compared to his comic-book illustrations.

Hard, once the imp of high-art ambition leaps on the back of a cartoonist. Or vice versa.

Had I ever met Krigstein I'd have told him that his expressionless survivor, surveying the emptiness of his revenge, haunted me as much as any image of moral futility I'd encountered in high art. But I doubt he would have thanked me for that.

7

My mother took in less of what had happened at my father's funeral than I did. Even while my father was still alive she had begun to turn away. Shani did the looking for her. Shani did the arranging. Shani did the welcoming, the comforting and the good-byes. I hadn't realised, until the day my father was buried into the Jewish faith, how tall Shani was. It's possible this was the first time I had ever seen her upright and in shoes. Very fine she looked, buttoned and veiled, having found an outfit that suited her, and an occasion on which to wear it, at last.

We sat shiva for not quite as long as we should have done, my mother picking up the threads of my father's testiness. 'Enough of this machareike,' she said, sending back the foreshortened stools and taking the coverings off the mirrors. Tsedraiter Ike was scandalised. He loved sitting shiva. 'The only time you can ever get him to go out,' I remember my father saying, 'is when someone dies.' We used to marvel at Tsedraiter Ike's knowledge of the houses of the dead. Where did he get his information? Was there some publication that came for him in a brown, or would it have been a black, wrapper? Was he on some hellish guest list? Or did he just go out into the street and follow his nose? He was never happier, anyway, than taking chopped fish round to some grieving family and wishing them long life. Only the principal mourners rend their clothes, but Tsedraiter Ike would have sat on a low stool in a torn jacket for all eternity had it been permitted. And here was my mother curtailing an opportunity for a shiva of which he had been at the very centre.

What I think stopped him putting up more of a fight was grief. For all that he and my father had never seen eye to eye on a single subject, my father continually reminding him that he was toler-ated only out of deference to my mother, and that he couldn't count on being tolerated for ever even then, Tsedraiter Ike was as devastated by my father's death as any of us, and as a consequence had developed a new habit of vigorously shaking his head, as though in mortal disagreement with Somebody. When my mother shortened the shiva period, he registered his complaint by sitting it solo in his own room. He knew what was owing to the sacred memory of the dead, even if we didn't. Where we had abbreviated, he extended. Day after day we didn't see him, just heard him davening. My mother indulged him for a while then called him down. 'Ike, what are you doing up there? Trying to kill yourself? That won't bring Jack back.' She berated him for being ghoulish, and ordered him back into normal clothes and the routines of the living. He didn't argue with her. He knew which side his bread was buttered, prayers for the dead or no prayers for the dead. 'It's only me from over the sea, said Barnacle Bill the sailor,' he sang as he withdrew, nodding, from her presence.

Thus did my mother take over from my father the responsibility of making Tsedraiter Ike feel unwanted. It suited him. He needed someone to make him feel that.

At the same time she informed me that she was about to resume kalooki.

I looked at her as Hamlet looks at his mother in every production of the play I have ever seen. That it should come to this: but two months dead, nay, not so much, not two . . . Not even one month in my father's case. Not two weeks . . .

'Are you upset with me?' she wanted to know.

'Ma, it's a bit soon.'

She sat me down at the kitchen table and stretched her hands out so that they were touching mine. Not holding, just a light rhythmic tap of her fingers on my fingers. 'Your father asked me to promise him that I would marry again,' she said.

I was discomforted by the intimacy. We didn't go in for this kind of talk in our house. None of the Jews I knew did. Whatever Gentiles surmise, sometimes enviously surmise, of the closeness of Jew to Jew, of the hothouse which is the Jewish family, the home life of Jews is in truth marbled with the finest traceries of reticence. Yes, we live in each other's pockets, often long after the historical necessity to do so has been removed, but you can live in each other's pockets and still be strangers. It took death to acquaint me with Shani. But since my mother had brought up the subject of her marrying again, I had no choice but to ask, 'And will you?'

'What do you think?'

'Well, if you're up for cards, why not a husband?'

'They're not exactly the same thing, Maxie. Your father asked me to promise him solemnly that I would find another man – he even suggested a couple of names . . .'

'Who?'

'Little Ike and Liverpool Ike, if you must know.'

'But they're Jewish. Surely he'd have wanted you to take a Catholic. Or at least an atheist. And if he has to be a Jew, what's wrong with "Long John" Silverman? Dad loved "Long John" Silverman. And "Long John" Silverman has always drooled at the mouth for you.'

She inclined her lovely head. No point denying what was undeniable, and, let's face it, due. 'Maxie, "Long John" Silverman has a wife of his own.'

'Big deal. Get Little Ike to run away with her.' Little Ike, for the record, being known, despite his size, as something of a runner with other men's wives.

My mother curled her mouth at me. 'Very funny, darling. Marital musical chairs. But you know how bad I'd be at that. Everyone else gets a seat, I'm left standing.' She paused, surveying herself marooned at the party, only her on her feet. Then she shook herself out of it. No self-pity. It was her great strength. She refused sadness. 'None of it's of any relevance just now, anyway,' she went on. 'I refused to make the promise your father asked for. I don't want another husband. I cared too deeply for your father to suppose I can care deeply for someone else. I don't intend even to try. I don't want to care deeply, in that way, for another man. It's foolish, I accept that, to pretend to know how I'll feel ten or fifteen years from now, but I hope I will be saying the same to you then.'

'Well, I don't,' I said. 'But just for the moment . . .'

'You'd like me not to play kalooki?'

Against the hosts of other men lined up waiting for my mother – she was a beauty, don't forget, and the more beautiful, I thought, for being a widow, with lovely lugubrious ovals, like ashen teardrops, looped beneath her eyes – against the Little Ikes, and even the Big Ikes for all I knew, a game of kalooki, when all was said and done, did not represent the greatest of derelictions. But then it wasn't a matter of one or the other, was it? For a little while at least, it was open to her not to take another husband *and* not to play kalooki. 'Or is that,' I asked, twisting the corners of *my* mouth this time, 'too much to ask?'

She had a way of nodding her head – not shaking it from side to side as Tsedraiter Ike had taken to doing, in apparent disagreement with Someone – but as though to concur in everything you were saying while not really listening to a word of it. 'No,' she said, 'it isn't too much to ask, and if you'd rather I didn't, then I won't.'

'What does Shani think?' Shani, the new arbiter of right and wrong, the new Moses Maimonides in our family. Guide us out of our perplexity, Shani.

'Shani thinks I should ask myself what your father would have wanted.'

'You know what my father would have wanted. He hated kalooki. He believed it was the name of a shtetl.'

She looked hurt. 'You're wrong there, Max. That was just his teasing. He had no desire to play himself, I grant you, but he liked it that I played. He said he'd rather know where I was, that he'd rather have me sitting shuffling a kalooki deck at home with my friends than see me dolling myself up to go to shul, or busy-bodying myself in Jewish causes.'

'I thought kalooki *was* a Jewish cause.'

'Only when I made it one to get you your gala night.' No mistaking the reprimand. As though to say this was a poor way to thank someone who'd delivered me Gittel Franks and Simone Kaye.

I inclined my head in acknowledgement of that, then scratched it. 'So you'd really be getting back into kalooki for Dad, is that what you're saying? You're really doing it as a favour to him.'

'You know what your father was like. No fuss. No sentimentality. Life is for the living. You could make fun of me, Maxie, if I came home tomorrow with a new prospective husband and said I was marrying him for your father. But I have no intention of doing that.'

It was a trade-off. I can bring a Mr Murdstone back, or you can leave me to my kalooki. You choose, Maxie.

I threw up my hands, much as my father would have done. 'Play your cards,' I said.

Thereafter, though there were no further conversations on the subject, I thought a great deal about what she'd said to me. She was frightened, I could see that. She feared she would be rudderless and didn't want to go down the usual route of finding another man to rudder her. Fair enough. More unsettling was the bold implication – for such I took it to be – that by returning to kalooki before decency allowed she was at a stroke reinstating the provocatively secular regime of my father. The unbeliever is dead, long live the unbeliever! Continuity – that was how she was selling it to me and no doubt to herself. Get kalooki back into the house, quick, and it would be as though my father had never left us.

On the face of it, the logic was hard to follow, but once followed, hard to fault. I was even prepared to be admiring of it. My mother, the heroine of the unconventionalities. No wonder my father had loved her.

But what if she were simply shallow?

BOOK TWO

NO BLOODY WONDER

NINE

1

Manny had no more recognised me than I had recognised him that first time we got together again at the pizza restaurant in Manchester. But he didn't tell me that until the second time we got together again.

'You're different,' he'd said, without quite looking at me.

'Well, it has been half a lifetime since we last saw each other,' I'd reminded him.

'We ate together last week.'

'I thought we were talking about before that.'

'Thirty-eight years.'

I had no idea when he was counting from. 'Not surprising then.'

This time he did half look in my direction. So blue the eye he showed me, so much bluer than I'd remembered, that for a moment or two I seriously wondered if it were glass. The consequence of a prison fight? Or of an operation to extract the patricidal section of his brain? But then he showed me the other eye, and that too was the colour of the sky. 'No,' he said, 'something's different. Your nose is different.'

He was right. My nose was different. Not different in the way that Zoë in her time would have liked — not smaller, but then again not exactly bigger either. The adjective is hard to find. But Manny probably put his finger on it. 'It seems to have spread across your face more,' he said, with a cruel indifference to my feelings which I at first attributed to the hardening influence of incarceration, until I remembered that he had always been like that. Not rude, just unaware of politeness.

Not without its ironies, what had happened to my nose. Not without ironic implications for Zoë, anyway. When Zoë wasn't pestering me to get it shortened she was complaining about the noises I made through it when I breathed. Not much I could do about that, I told her, short of giving up breathing altogether.

As always she gave consideration to whatever I suggested, the sweetest of quizzical expressions lighting up her impeccable and soundless features.

My own theory was that my breathing, which I freely acknowledged could be over-audible at times, was a consequence of the same condition that gave me nosebleeds, the epistaxis which I had inherited from my late father.

'And did your father also snore like an express train?' Zoë wanted to know.

'Whether he did or he didn't,' I answered, 'I believe my mother slept like a normal person and therefore didn't notice.'

This was a reference to what I considered to be the *ab*normality of Zoë's sleep patterns, a matter of some contention between us, since she believed she slept the way a person was meant to sleep, that's to say stretched between waking and unconsciousness like piano wire, her eyes wide open and every millimetre of her flesh aquiver to the faintest rustle, let it be breath issuing from my nostril or the wind fluttering a sweet wrapper three streets away.

'There is nothing wrong with the way I sleep, were I only allowed to,' was how she made the point to me.

'Same here,' I said. 'Do you not suppose I would sleep more soundly and therefore more silently myself if I didn't have to lie there, awake even when I'm not, listening to the sound of you not sleeping?'

'You're so Jewish,' she said. 'You're so fucking illogically, argumentatively Jewish.'

Which I suppose was just another way of making my point, that we are a dialectical people.

We resolved our differences in the end. She sent me to an ear, nose and throat specialist. Who sent me to an otolaryngologist. Because I was uncertain what one of those would do to me I checked him out with Kennard Chitty, the plastic surgeon Zoë had unearthed a year or two before with a view to getting him to harmonise my face with hers. It was Chitty who had refused to lay a scalpel anywhere near my nose because of the patriarchal associations it held for him, he being of the opinion that a Jewish appearance was the noblest on earth, wanting only the true conviction that came with Christ. 'Jesus must have had a nose like yours,' he'd told me, 'so it would be unchristian to change it surgically in any way.' We'd become friends of a kind, with him buying a set of my Old Testament cartoons to hang on his consulting-room walls, along with other odds and ends, and I allowing him to invite me to his Christmas parties and shtupp me with cheaply printed literature explaining how it was only by learning to love Jews that Christians would finally save the world, but first the Jews had to consent to becoming Christians. All that apart, he told me not to worry about otolaryngology and even recommended a treatment he'd read about for someone with my condition. Sphenopalatine artery ligation it was called, which excited Zoë when I mentioned it because she assumed it meant I was getting surgery after all.

'While they're at it . . .' she began.

But I had to explain to her that it was surgery from the inside not the out, and that if she thought I'd be coming home from the otolaryngologist retroussé, she'd do well to think again.

Here's the irony I talked about. In the end the otolaryngologist advised against ligation in my case – some issue with the septum nasi which I was not capable of grasping – and put me on a regime of what can only be called 'packing', all manner of materials being stuffed into my nose over a long period, the eventual effect being that it took on the appearance of being larger rather than smaller, even if Manny's description of it spreading all over my face was exaggerated. I did bleed less frequently, as a result, and I snored less too. But it was a cruel blow to Zoë who found it harder than ever to look at me.

2

My memory draws a blank when I try to picture Manny and me after my father died. I see no air-raid shelter, recall no further talk of the Brothers Stroganoff, retain nothing of any conversations we might have had about the Nazis. He came to my father's funeral with his father, that much I know. I see them standing together, to one side, both in long black coats. But no Asher. Shortly afterwards Manny delivered himself of that sick nonsense about his envying me not having a father, but I cannot see the place or remember the circumstances in which he delivered it. Then there was his crisis of faith or whatever it was which I spitefully threw back in his face; though that, too, will not locate or define itself. Otherwise a black hole. We didn't fight, we didn't in any of the usual ways fall out, we simply stopped.

Sex stopped it partly. At fifteen, Errol Tobias started going out with Melanie Kushner, a South Manchester girl with a woman's breasts, and that was that – goodbye to the carefreeness of childhood. No more *Scourge of the Swastika*, no more breaking a religious man's windows, no more spluttering circle of onanists. 'Won't be needing you now,' Errol had announced at a sort of extraordinary general meeting of the latter, called, as it were, to wind up the company's affairs. All over. We were in business for real, suddenly. Or at least Errol was. For the rest of us there was some serious catching up to be done and we weren't going to manage that with meshuggeners like Manny Washinsky hanging around. I became one of the boys, that's why I lost touch with him. I hit the town.

And Manny? No idea. He didn't exist.

Not entirely true. Something comes back to me, dimly, in the reluctant half-light of shame. Me and a girl, hand in hand, leaving the Library Theatre, an Arthur Miller, I think, always Arthur Millers at the the Library Theatre, me and Märike it must have been, stepping into the wintry dark, stopping for a kiss on the steps of the Central Library itself, this is how we kiss in Kobenhavn, this is how we kiss in Manchester, and then there, sitting in an old raincoat, on the cold stone, scratching his face, giving the air of waiting for somebody, but obviously not, Manny Washinsky, not looking my way. How old would I have been? Nineteen? I was already at art college, I am sure of that, because I had met Märike, if indeed it was Märike, at a college dance and was bringing her home to meet my mother. So this was probably me showing off the sights of Manchester to her. Theatre, Library, Mother, Art Gallery – *now* will you put your hand inside my trousers? Showing off the sights of Manchester to her, but also showing off her to Manchester. Oh, to have been able to show her off to Errol Tobias, but he was married already, a child bridegroom, and living in the South with pictures of women exposing their vaginas on his toilet door. So poor Manny, sitting there, thinking his own thoughts, had to suffice. There were losses and gains to this. No points for showing her I knew Manny. But points aplenty for showing Manny how intimately I knew her. Why that should be, when Manny was now as nothing to me, and no measure of anything I any longer valued, I cannot explain. Some imp of malice or uncertainty, though, some hunger for validation, explain it how you will, made me make him notice us. See what you're missing, Manny. See what I've got and you haven't. I even effected a cursory introduction – Manny, Märike; Märike, Manny. He didn't get up from where he was sitting. Just nodded his head, then looked away again. Whether he was feigning indifference, or genuinely didn't care who I was with, I am unable to say for sure, but at the time I feared the latter. He was otherwise absorbed, as incurious about me as I had been about him, but more self-sufficient than I was, it appeared, since I had set about attracting his attention, whereas he hadn't shown the remotest interest in attracting mine. Elohim? Was that the explanation? Was Manny back on friendly terms with Him? I decided yes. He had the look: not transfigured with light – that had never been his way – more as though returned to antiquity, in the process of turning back into the mud out of which the first man was fashioned. In which case, fine. I could live with losing to Elohim. But just between me and myself, I felt a clown.

Consistent with his appearance at the time, Manny had no recollection of the encounter when I mentioned it to him in the course of our second attempt to get reacquainted. Steps of the Central Library, night-time, I with a very lanky Danish woman, bit like a giraffe? Ring no bells? No. Not a tinkle. And he thought he would have remembered the giraffe. As for whether he had indeed returned to God whenever that was, 1961 . . . 1962 – that was like asking a man when he had stopped beating his wife.

'And now?'

He put his lips together as though he were going to whistle a tune. But no sound issued from them.

I waited. Had he forgotten what he was going to say? Had he forgotten what his thoughts were on the subject? That could easily happen, I imagined, when you were locked away. Your mind could just empty.

But he hadn't lost his thoughts, he was just organising them. 'If you're asking me whether I believe in God,' he said at last, 'you're asking the wrong question.'

'So what's the right question?'

'There might not be one. But belief isn't optional. You can't choose it.'

'It chooses you, is that what you're saying?'

'Not exactly, no. People think they can believe if they feel like it. They can't. It's a privilege, not an entitlement. Yes, I think

God probably does exist. But I have lost the right to believe in Him.'

3

The effect of Errol Tobias's betrothal to Melanie Kushner, the girl with woman's breasts, was to helter-skelter me through my teenage years. Long before I was ready for it, Errol fixed me up with one of Melanie's friends – Tillie Guttmacher, a super-Jewess with wrestler's shoulders, a furry upper lip (not all that unlike Manny's) and Cleopatra eyes. The idea was a foursome, then we'd pair off.

We met at a cheap curry restaurant in Rusholme, Errol believing in the aphrodisiacal qualities of vindaloo. 'Maxie's an artist,' was how he introduced me; then, after a stage pause – 'a dick-artist.'

The girls laughed. At a nearby table a man whose face I thought I recognised paused from apportioning rice to his two female companions to stare our way. He had prim yet fleshy lips, a lisper's lips I thought, which he shaped into a little prune of disapproval. He appeared to be making a mental note, so as to avoid having any contact with one in the future, of what a dick-artist looked like.

I have to say dick-artist was new to me as well. It's my belief that there was no such existing expression, that in the late 1950s we weren't even talking bullshit-artists yet, and that Errol, who had a genius for this sort of thing, had coined it. I can't pretend I was grateful. It bore so little resemblance to reality that I took it to be a sarcasm. I didn't believe that Tillie Guttmacher was much enamoured of it as a description of her date for the night either, for all that she had shaken her head and laughed, the gypsy hoops ringing at her ears. Perhaps because my mother never allowed a coarse word to pass her lips, and Shani had only ever cursed her wardrobe in nursery profanities, I entertained a rarefied idea of what constituted the sensibility of a Jewess. It even crossed my mind that Tillie Guttmacher had laughed her big laugh only to conceal the fact that she didn't have the first idea what a dick, let alone an artist, was.

It is sometimes said of Jewish men that they go to Gentile women for sex so as not to disrespect their own women. This was never the case with me. I would willingly have disrespected a Jewess had I thought there was the remotest chance she'd have understood my intentions. The shock of finally discovering that Jewish women put out for Gentile men with even more alacrity than Jewish men put out for Gentile women was what precipitated a series of irritably lewd cartoons I once drew, a sort of *Rake's Progress* set in Stamford Hill, where every strumpet was a Jewess in a sheitel, but which no reputable publication was prepared to take, not even *Playboy*, despite my offering to redraw the location to make it look like Crown Heights.

Tillie Guttmacher apart, I had a further reason for being angry with Errol. I had suddenly worked out who the man at the next table was. Isaiah Berlin. *Sir* Isaiah Berlin, for I had recently seen a photograph of him in the newspaper receiving his knighthood.

I nudged Errol. 'Isaiah Berlin,' I whispered.

'Geezer!' Errol said. 'Why would Isaiah Berlin be eating a curry in Rusholme?'

'Shush,' I said. 'He can hear you. He's already heard you call me a dick-artist, thanks very much.'

'Who's Isaiah Berlin?' Melanie Kushner wanted to know.

I waited to see if Tillie Guttmacher might be able to help her out, but no.

Errol screwed his eyes at me disgustingly. *Birds!* they said. *What else do you expect from Jewish birds?*

He was loathsome but you had to hand it to him, he was educated. Had I told him Freddie Ayer was sitting next to us, or Karl Popper, he'd have known who I was talking about. 'Philosopher,' he told the girls, who seemed offended by the word.

'Otherwise known as an ideas-artist,' I helped out.

'Except,' Errol said, 'that that isn't him. You're confusing him with someone else.'

'Who?'

He thought about it. 'Bronowski.'

I looked again. The big spectacles, the half-benign, half-disapproving face, the slightly angelic but ironic mouth, the lugubriousness. 'That's not Bronowski. It's Isaiah Berlin.'

'In Rusholme?'

'Well, if Bronowski could be in Rusholme, why can't Isaiah Berlin? He'll be visiting the university.'

'And having a curry while he's here?'

'Why not? He's got to eat, hasn't he?'

'A fucking biriani?'

'Errol, do me a favour, keep your voice down.'

'I can't stand this. We're here to have a nobbel and you've gone all ungelumpert. Go and ask him if you think it's him. Then we can all relax.'

'What's "ungelumpert"?' Melanie asked.

'What it sounds like – acting like an awkward lump.'

'Excuse me, I'm not ungelumpert.'

'What are you then?'

What was I? 'Curious, that's all.'

'So satisfy your curiosity. Go and ask him.'

'Errol, are you mad!'

'Then *I* will.' And he would have – *Are you Sir Isaiah Berlin? I thought as much. Then let me introduce you to my friend Maxie Glickman, dick-artist* – had the vindaloos not arrived to save me.

Whether or not vindaloos were aphrodisiacs as Errol claimed, they did have the effect of making women go hot around the neck, which had the further effect of making them undo at least one of the buttons on their blouses. Tillie Guttmacher, who had as much reason to be proud of her chest as Melanie Kushner did of hers, undid two. Already red with the make-up of the Nile when she arrived, she had begun to glow like a volcano. After every forkful of vindaloo she took her napkin and fanned her face and throat with it, but that only made the volcano burn the brighter. At the moment it became apparent that she was about to fall off her chair, Errol dug me in the ribs. 'Blow on her, Max,' he urged me.

I had never blown on a woman before. But an emergency was an emergency. I made a bellows of my lungs, puffed out my cheeks, and sent such a crosswind Tillie Guttmacher's way that I stirred a maelstrom in her plate – rice, sauce, pickles, bits of pappadom, all swirling in a hurricane that blew itself out finally on and down her unbuttoned blouse. At which moment Sir Isaiah Berlin raised his heavy head and pruned his lips in my direction for the final time.

I had not read any Isaiah Berlin. I was a bit young for his urbanity of thought. But I knew two things about him. One was that he had written a book on Marx, and I knew that because I'd heard 'Long John' Silverman speaking to my mother about it in unflattering terms. According to 'Long John' Silverman, Isaiah Berlin was the wrong person to write that book because he lacked instinctive sympathy with Marx's view of history. 'I'd like to write a book one day,' had been my mother's response to that. 'And I would like to read it,' had been 'Long John' Silverman's response to her. The other thing I knew about Isaiah Berlin was that he'd written about Tolstoy. So profound an impression had his description of the aged Tolstoy at Astapovo made on one of my English teachers, David Brennan, that he would recite it to us at the close of almost every lesson, his eyes brimming with tears – 'At once insanely proud and filled with hatred, omniscient and doubting everything, cold and violently passionate, contemptuous and self-abasing, tormented and detached . . . he is the most tragic of the great writers, a desperate old man, beyond human aid, wandering self-blinded at Colonus.' The passage had the identical effect on me. I couldn't breathe while David Brennan was reading it. The sound of my swallowing filled the classroom. Had Brennan asked me to comment on it I'd have collapsed into sobs. Me, of course – it was me Berlin was writing about, me as I would be at the end, the most tragic of the great cartoonists, omniscient and doubting everything, Jewish and yet not, a torment to myself, beyond human aid.

On the strength of that sentence, if nothing else – and I couldn't care less whether or not he lacked instinctive sympathy for Marx's view of history – Isaiah Berlin was a hero to me. But by virtue, as I understood it, of his being a well-connected Jew, he frightened and bewildered me as well. How could you be a well-connected Jew? Who could you be connected *to*? No Jew was well connected where I came from. It was a contradiction in terms. For this I both hated Isaiah Berlin and craved his approval. By 'his' I meant that of people like him. *Other* well-connected Jews. Win their approval – I say nothing of admiration or friendship – and you would thereby, magically, become well connected yourself. But what chance of that after Errol, in his hearing, had introduced me as a dick-artist and got me to blow on Tillie Guttmacher's chest? Of Sir Isaiah Berlin's connections, how many were dick-artists?

In fact, as the smallest amount of research into his circle reveals, quite a number of them were. But they didn't call themselves that, there was the difference. And what you call yourself determines how people see you. A. J. Ayer couldn't keep his dick in his pants, but he called himself an iconoclast and libertarian. Just as Goya, the greatest of cartoonists, knew to present himself to posterity as a painter, satirist and historian. The secret of reputation: call it big and they'll think it big.

Whether or not Isaiah Berlin in later life remembered me from the curry restaurant in Rusholme I have no way of knowing. But he never responded to my publishers when they sent him an advance copy of *Five Thousand Years of Bitterness*, a work which, given what he wrote about Tolstoy, you'd have expected him, if not to endorse or even like, at the very least to understand. Other well-connected Jews of his calibre the same. Not a peep. Mine was not, that was all I could deduce – since not every one of them had come to hear of me first as a dick-artist – their idea of serious discourse on a Jewish theme.

<h1 style="text-align:center">4</h1>

The clap!

We went back to Errol Tobias's house, ostensibly to remove the curry stains from Tillie Guttmacher's blouse, crept about among the washbasins and the hairdryers, made free with the reclining chairs, and she gave me the clap. A carelessness to repay a carelessness.

My first sexual encounter with a Jewess, which also happened to be my first sexual encounter of any kind, and it poisoned me. Hard to square this with my going on imagining Jewish women as sexually inaccessible, I know, but I was somehow able to delude myself that the sex I'd had with Tillie Guttmacher I hadn't, and that the clap she gave me I contracted through some other agency. It didn't much feel like sex, in the dark and the discomfort of the salon, with Tillie complaining about her blouse, and Melanie laughing, and Errol egging us on and quite possibly, for all I could see or recognise to the contrary, manually busying himself between us. And what didn't feel like sex surely couldn't give you any of the diseases that were the punishment for sex. I'd caught the clap off Errol, I decided. Off Errol's hands, off the seats of Errol's mother's salon chairs, off the words Errol spoke, off the air Errol breathed, off Errol's pestilential contiguity.

Alvin Shrager, the doctor who had attended my mother in both her pregnancies and my father in his final illness, and who therefore saw me as a sort of ward of his practice, reprimanded me for bringing an infection into his surgery that was not of a kind either of us had any business with – 'A boy like you shouldn't be coming to me with this,' were his exact words, which made me wonder what a boy like me *should* be coming to him with – and confirmed that it couldn't have been a Jewish girl who infected me. 'What you get for going to prostitutes,' he told me.

'She wasn't a prostitute.'

He made that Merchant of Venice weighing motion with his hands, as though to suggest that in the scale of things, a lapse was a lapse and a trollop was a trollop. He'd just told me I had the clap. Who was I to be making nice distinctions of morality?

'I'm telling you,' I said. 'She wasn't a prostitute.'

'How do you know?'

'Because I didn't pay her, for one thing.'

He removed the pipe from his mouth, laid it on the desk next to his stethoscope and threw his head back. 'There's more than one way of paying,' he laughed. 'And you've paid all right.'

Then he took his pipe up again and bit on it. These days doctors don't smoke while they're treating you, but Shrager was what was known as an old-fashioned family doctor even then. He breathed an almost solid fuel of bile and pipe tobacco into the faces of his patients.

The need rose in me – inexplicable in the circumstances – to defend the reputation of Tillie Guttmacher. I was a snap of the fingers away from giving Shrager her name and, had I known it, her address. *She's a Guttmacher, of the Didsbury Guttmachers! Now what have you go to say?* But I settled for something almost as conclusive. 'She's a nice Jewish girl,' I said. 'The nice Jewish girl every nice Jewish boy is supposed to marry.' I would have liked to add that she could have been his daughter.

He arched an eyebrow. He was famous, Alvin Shrager, for his shaggy eyebrows. Shani believed they were false. My mother thought he simply roughed them up every morning, before surgery. Craggy wisdom was what I thought – the mamzer wanted

259

to give the impression of reflection seasoned in experience.

Out of the depth of which experience he came up with a gem of unpleasantness, even by his standards. 'Think on,' he said, 'where else might you have been?' The most unpleasant part being that I had been asking myself the very same question.

I laid out for him the topography of my uncleanness: the school lavatories with their cracked wooden seats, the school shower, a club in town where the urinals overflowed and the washbasins were green, the Temple Cinema known with good reason as the fleapit, the number 35 bus, Tsedraiter Ike's towel, the changing rooms in Halon's man's shop in Withy Grove where I'd tried on a pair of trousers, the trousers themselves previously tried on by God knows who else, the chairs in Errol's mother's salon, Errol's conversation, my own mind . . . Could a boy get the clap from his own imagination?

Shrager sucked on his pipe. 'You can't catch what you've got from any of those,' he told me. 'Who else have you had sexual relations with?'

I opened the palms of my hands to him. He had that effect on me. He made me feel guilty about whatever ailed me. Not just the clap, a cold as well, a sore throat, a bad stomach, an ingrowing toenail. All my fault. 'No one,' I said, ashamed to admit it, because that was clearly another thing I bore the fault for – being a virgin until Tillie Guttmacher had her way with me while she was waiting for her blouse to dry – that's if she really did have her way with me.

He pointed to a chair. Sit. While I sat he filled another pipe. At any time the ritual of pipes infuriated me. That was another of the ways I denoted cartoon villainy when I was denied a big nose – a pipe. Only a very bad man would subject others to that tyrannous time warp where all of creation must wait on the filling of a pipe. But I had further reason to be impatient. I was suffering from a debilitating disease of particular incidence to artists, a disease that had wrecked the lives of Cellini, Manet, Lautrec,

Gauguin, to name only the ones who sprang to mind, and instead of beginning treatment immediately, before it wrecked my life, a life that had barely begun, Dr Alvin Shrager was sticking a thumb in his pipe bowl and preparing me a lecture.

'If what you're telling me is true, and I've no reason to doubt you, it sounds like you've been unlucky. I've been a doctor in this town for more than thirty years and I have never once treated an unmarried Jewish woman for what you've got. Very occasionally a married one who's contracted it from her husband, and who isn't pleased about it, I can tell you – but a single Jewish girl—'

'From Didsbury,' I put in.

He closed his eyes so he could continue. 'But an unmarried Jewish girl – never! Well, there's always a first time you'll tell me, and there's a bad egg in every batch. And you'll be right. Just a pity you had to find her. But this I can tell you, young man – and I'm telling it you out of the respect I bear your father, olovhasholem, and your mother who I hope is well – don't go fancying yourself as some Lothario. What she did with you, whoever she is, this nekaiveh, she'd do with anyone.'

'No one would have sex with me who didn't want sex with everyone, is that what you're saying?'

'Max, no decent woman has sex until she's married. And there's a joke that no decent Jewish woman has sex even then. You've been given a warning. Or at least part of you has been given a warning. Respect your body, and women will respect you. Yes?'

No, I said in my heart. But I wanted my prescription. 'Yes,' I said. 'Yes, doctor.'

As I was leaving he called out 'Max!', then when I turned he winked at me through a fog of tobacco. 'Don't forget,' he said, 'stay away from those shiksehs.'

In fact I have exaggerated what was wrong with me. It wasn't the clap, it was crabs. But the clap sounds better. More artistic. More Hogarthian.

I don't otherwise exaggerate Alvin Shrager. He was round, brown, boiled, evil-smelling, florid, smug, religiose, a disgrace to medicine, a shame on my mother and father who had stayed with him because he was 'our doctor', a shame on me who continued to see him for the same reason – because he was 'our doctor' and therefore 'had' something on me or owned me in some way – and an offence to Judaism. Many years later, I gave him a whole page to himself in *No Bloody Wonder*, my follow-up to *Five Thousand Years of Bitterness*, among the enemies of the Jewish people who happened to be Jewish, not with the self-haters and the apostates and the Jews who changed their names, but alongside the Jews who harmed Judaism by being overzealously Jewish where Jewishness had no business showing its face. Needless to say, this page didn't go down any better than the others, especially with Shrager's daughter Toyba who threatened to sue my publishers unless they promised to remove the carica-ture from future editions. An empty threat, but one which my publishers were of course only too delighted to take seriously, knowing there would be no future editions.

As a satisfactory addendum to this episode – and it will explain Toyba Shrager's hypersensitivity as to her family's good name – Alvin Shrager's other daughter Lipka enjoyed a period of noto-riety for a while, even appearing for two weeks running on the front page of the *News of the World*, wearing a belted leather coat, dark glasses and a hunted look. She was denying all charges, of course, but you could tell from the leather coat, which she wore as a second skin, and from that prioressy air which women at her end of the market often carry, that she was lying. She was the one all right, she was the Mayfair call girl in the kisses-for-secrets scandal, whispering information garnered from high-ranking Arab clients into the ears of Israeli diplomats, and, I am afraid to say, vice versa.

Some nice Jewish girls give you crabs, some croon to you of

troop positions – as Dr Shrager said, it's just a matter of luck which you fall in with.

As a further satisfactory addendum to *that* episode, the public disgrace hurried Shrager into a grave nothing like as early as I'd have wanted, but certainly much earlier than he did.

5

I presented Manny with a signed copy of *No Bloody Wonder* on our second attempt at reunion. Better that, I thought, than *Five Thousand Years of Bitterness* which had originated in a joint endeavour, never mind that he had washed his hands of it so many years before. I had nothing to apologise to him for – not in the matter of publications anyway – but people can behave strangely in the presence of a book, especially a book they had once had a hand in but which doesn't bear their name. Fortunately, he wasn't the publication junkie I am. He appeared indifferent to my authorship at any rate, and barely thanked me for the gift. Summarily, as though performing a duty he couldn't himself see the point of, he looked the front cover over, licked his lips, then idly, even rudely, flicked the pages. Unimpressed is one word. Contemptuous is another. 'I would have expected you to have moved on from this kind of thing,' he said, without any challenge in his voice, as though I must already have come to such a verdict about myself without his help.

'I'm a better drawer than I was when we sat and planned the predecessor to this in our shelter, Manny,' I pointed out. Miffed was one word for how I felt. Fucking furious were two others.

A better drawer was I? As a courtesy to that assertion he flicked through a few more pages, but obviously didn't see it.

'They're still cartoons,' he said.

'You mean not realistic?'

'I mean not serious. Not considered.'

I pedalled backwards from the punch. Maxie 'Slapsie' Rosenbloom would have been proud of me. But where had Manny learned to hit like that?

Don't answer.

'The lines could not be more considered,' I said, catching my breath. 'If you look, you'll see that the lines are highly formal. And my intention could not be more serious. For a cartoonist I am serious to a fault.'

'Then maybe you should stop being a cartoonist.'

Oooof!

'What is it you don't like, Manny? The hyperbole? The extravagance? Surely you still don't find this stuff blasphemous.'

He did me the justice of thinking about it, though it was hard for him: his attention wavered, his eyes were always halfway to somewhere else. 'You seem to have embraced ugliness,' he said at last.

'Ugliness has its way with all of us,' I said. And let him take that how he liked.

'Isn't that all the more reason to try to find beauty? You seem to be in an argument with beauty.'

'How can I not be in an argument with beauty? I'm a cartoonist. More to the point, I'm a Jewish cartoonist. As an Orthodox Jew yourself, or as a one-time Orthodox Jew – I don't presume to know what you are now – you should approve of this. Leviticus 26, Manny, "Ye shall make you no idols nor graven image." I happen to take that prohibition very seriously. Not in its sensuous applications but in its ethical ones. It is not good to lose oneself in art. It is idolatrous. Lose yourself in art and you end up not knowing where you begin and end. It is a mistake to fuse with the image. Well, you can't fuse with mine, Manny. It won't let you. It won't allow it. If by ugliness you mean the ceaseless mockery, through a visual medium, of all the seductions of visual media, then yes, OK, have it your way, my drawings are ugly.'

Not that I wanted him to think I was passionate about what I did . . .

We were in a kitchen, I wasn't sure whose and didn't think it was appropriate to ask. He had invited me there, somewhat obstinately and with a certain degree of domestic pride, I thought, in the face of my offering an outing to any bar or restaurant he fancied. It was as though he felt that I needed to understand his needs – neither to underestimate nor to overestimate them – and to see the manner in which they were satisfied. It was a terraced house, modest, but well kept, furnished with stripped pine and inexpensive third-world rugs, situated in those heights looking out over Heaton Park, not all that far, if my Manchester geography hadn't deserted me, from where Asher would first have met his German mishpocheh. I took it to be a small home, perhaps paid for by the social services and local Jewish charities, for Jewish men who had killed their parents and served their time in prison. A quiet act of consideration, not to be bruited abroad, at once of benefit to the men themselves and to the Jewish community they'd disgraced.

It would have been interesting to know how many more were billeted there. And what they talked about together when their visitors had left. But I didn't enquire. There had always been something about Manny that inhibited curiosity, and on his home turf, if you could call it that, I felt I was obliged to spare him questions of a personal kind. Gas taps yes, who his friends were now, no.

His hands were on the pine table in front of him, the left holding the right, pressing the knuckles white. For a moment I wondered if he was another Ilse Cohen, himself a victim of Alien Hand syndrome, one more person who couldn't control the waywardness of half his will. Another hysteric. He saw me looking at him, and changed hands.

'Other Jewish artists have answered the challenge of Leviticus 26 differently,' he said, at the very moment I was thinking of changing the subject.

265

You have to be prepared, when you're talking art to Jews who once wore fringes, and wear them surreptitiously still for all you know, for them to mean the junk you find for sale in the lobbies of the Red Sea hotels – rabbis fashioned out of silver wire, sentimental woodcuts of old Jaffa, menorahs encrusted with Eilat stone. (Coincidentally, there was an Eilat-encrusted menorah in the kitchen where we sat, in an open cupboard alongside bottles of vinegar and olive oil.) With Jews, philistinism flourishes in direct proportion to Orthodoxy. You can see it on the bookshelves of the holy. Everything is written by God or Enid Blyton. But Manny had educated himself in the years he'd been away, he had given himself back to the world, and by 'other Jewish artists' I at once knew that he meant Rothko. Don't ask me how I knew, I just knew. There is a Rothko face that people pull. They go dreamy. Rothko reminds them of some long sojourn somewhere else. It's possible Manny had a reproduction Rothko hanging on the wall of his cell, or wherever they put him, and he was recalling his days there. Where are they now, the Rothko snows of yesteryear?

Mark Rothko. Born Marcus Rothkowitz, as Errol would have known, and once upon a time a yeshiva boy, like Asher Washinsky, and like Manny himself. So why did he change his name? And why, like Errol whom I would much rather not be like, do I hold it against him that he did?

Or is what I hold against him that he made his equivocal Jewishness lovable to Jews and non-Jews alike by taking all the joking out of it?

When non-Jews love a Jewish artist I'm suspicious – let's leave it at that.

'Yeah, yeah,' I said to Manny, without mentioning any of the above. 'As by painting exquisitely expiring spiritual abstracts. Fading even as we look at them, like the flesh which houses us. Very beautiful, I grant you, and in their own way biblical, I grant you that too. But precisely for the reason that they seduce us by their beauty, are they not any sort of riposte to Leviticus 26. They are still graven images. They might not be images of prancing gods in animal or human form, but they are idealised images of the soul. And therefore they remain idols in whose shape we worship a sentimentalisation of ourselves. Abstraction doesn't solve it, Manny. Abstraction's a con. Only ridicule solves it. Only mockery keeps you the right side of idolatry.'

He quarter turned his eyes towards me, showing me something (though it was very hard to be sure) much like mockery in return. It was a queer thing for me to be doing in his or whoever's little kitchen, haranguing him with my views on art.

Only afterwards did it occur to me that as far as he was concerned, at least, we weren't discussing art at all. We were discussing my fitness, as a man of comedy and exaggeration, to interpret his story.

Given the choice, he'd have gone for Rothko.

Tough. Given the choice, I'd have gone for Rembrandt. But you don't get to choose who tells your story.

At the time, feeling that the fault for the haranguing was mine, I reached out to touch him, apologetically. But he started from the contact. Not knowing what else to do he reached for the pages of my comic history again, and alighted on the caricature of Shrager.

'My d-doctor,' he said, passionlessly.

His stutter had returned to us. Evidently doctors brought it on.

'Shrager? Was there anyone whose doctor he wasn't? But I'm flattered you recognise him' – through the maze of unconsidered ugly unseriousness, I was going to say, but satisfied myself with the bad-taste jest of stuttering his name instead, as though he were one of Manny's Nazis. 'Dr A-alvin S-sssch-shrager. Another evil man of medicine.'

Manny didn't respond to my needling. There's a chance he didn't notice it. He disagreed with my estimate of Shrager, though. 'I'm not aware that he gassed children in order to be able to experiment on their brains.'

He'd abandoned the lumbering pretence of loving our enemies.

He was back where I preferred him, in the realm of unequivocal hate.

'I grant you that,' I said, 'but he still played around with mine.'

Manny fell quiet. Then suddenly he remembered something which struck him as more cheerful. 'He tried to interest me in your sister once.'

'He what?'

'He asked me to take your sister out. Asher told me he'd asked him as well.'

'Shrager asked you and Asher to go out with Shani?'

'Well, not *asked*, s-suggested. And not at the same time.'

'I'm assuming not at the same time, Manny. But on whose say-so did he put that suggestion to either of you? What made him think . . . Christ, Manny, Shani was years older than you for starters.' And you were a frummie freak, I wanted to add, upon whom she would not have looked had her life depended on it. Family – family first.

'He said he thought it would be a good idea. He said he thought your father would approve.'

'Well, that's a joke! Hard enough – excuse me – to imagine what Shani would have said about it, but my father! In the first place my father would not under any circumstances have gone telling Shrager what he wanted for Shani – why would he for God's sake? – and secondly what he wanted was a well-to-do left-wing atheistical goy with a double-barrelled name from some cathedral town in Hampshire.'

'Perhaps he changed his mind. He talked to my father a lot when they were in hospital together. He said he was worried for your sister. What would happen to her when he died. He wondered about Asher. My father even mentioned it to Asher, but Asher, as you know . . .'

Yes, Asher was in love with someone else. And Manny, presumably, was at that time still in love with God. So sorry, Shani, looks like you missed out on frumkie bliss!

I did not know what to make of any of this, except that it was profoundly insulting to my sister, my father, and to me. Which left only my mother, and who was to say that Shrager hadn't suggested Manny or some other epileptic creep of medieval Yiddishery as a husband to her?

But just because it was insulting didn't mean it hadn't happened. Anything was possible. Without doubt my father had begun to entertain some strange notions in the last months of his life, and maybe finding himself in a hospital ward in a bed next to Selick Washinsky, where they were both equal in the hands of the Almighty, softened his attitudes. I had also to accept that when it came to Shani, his lifelong views about the need for Jews to shed their Jewishness were already pretty soft – vaporous, vapid, like the bubbles he blew from the clay pipe he once bought me as a Christmas present. Karl Marx, presumably, was the same with his daughter. *What is the object of the Jew's worship in this world? Usury. Only not in your case, my darling daughter. From everything I say against Jews, assume that I exempt your dear self.* Takes some explaining, all that. But it's what Jewish daughters do to their Jewish fathers. They make monkeys out of them. And if it tells you anything, it is that my father was mistaken on another score: Jewishness is not what you get when you lock people in a ghetto, Jewishness is what even the harshest Jewish father sees when he looks into his baby daughter's eyes. Shmaltz.

But then my father knew that too.

Shmaltz! He pronounced it with the fiercest disdain. Which just goes to show that you can know the name and still not be able to resist the substance.

6

Whatever my father's fears for her, Shani had not needed anyone to keep an eye on her, or to find her a nice Yiddisher beau. After my father's death, several of the bachelors or widowers among his friends, including some whose first choice would have been my mother – let me frank about this: everyone's first choice would have been my mother – took the early steps to wooing her. Chocolates, flowers, invitations to rambles, dances, even kalooki evenings in other people's homes. And one or two who weren't bachelors or widowers, I am afraid to say, essayed the same. But she kept them all at arm's length. She was a changed person. If I were to put what was changed about her in a nutshell, other than that she now dressed every day and found shoes to fit her, I would say that she had decided to occupy my father's place in the world. Not only to fill his social and secretarial role about the house, paying bills and looking after guests while my mother went her merry way kalooki-ing, and Tsedraiter Ike sucked at his single tooth and dribbled into histories of Israel, and I cartooned and got the clap – but actually to supplant him. There was something epic about it, something that would have reminded me of Greek tragedy had the omens been bad, but in fact no great collapse of dynasties was in the wind, no gods had been enraged other than Elohim who had never been much pleased with us anyway, and the House of Glickman felt, if anything, more secure than it had for a long time. So I suppose I meant Greek only in that it seemed archetypal, Shani moving into the space my father had vacated, as though one of us was bound by some elemental law of family to do it, and actually shouldering the burden he had dropped, thinking like him, talking like him – a touch brusque, determined to be watchful of sentimentality, the shmaltz as she had now taken to calling it – and keeping alive the principles of anti-religiosity by which he'd lived his own life and protected ours from fanaticism.

This was what made Manny's recollections of Dr Shrager's matchmaking so preposterous: a Jewish man, never mind a Jewish boy, was the very last of Shani's wants.

It would have been neat of her to fall in love with a goyisher boxer with a broken nose and low-caste cauliflower ears, maybe a lad my father had once trained and seen a gloriously bloody future for, but she didn't. She fell in love with a sailor. Mick.

'Mick!' Even my mother, who was the inverse of her late husband when it came to Shani and me — wanting me to have a Jewish bride if I had to have a bride at all, someone called Bathsheba or Hepzibah at the very least, and with a complexion to match the Arabian silkiness of her name, but not caring who Shani took up with provided he treated her well — even my mother drew the line at a Mick. 'He isn't Irish?' she pleaded not to hear. 'Please say he isn't Irish.'

'Mick Kalooki is his name,' Shani said. 'Draw your own conclusions.'

My mother made a bouquet of her hands and thrust it at my sister. 'Don't toy with me, Shani. On your father's life, tell me the truth. Is he or isn't he?'

'On my father's life you shouldn't be asking me that question, Ma. You know what he'd have said. *A man's man for a' that.*'

'That's Scottish,' I put in. 'He's not a Scotsman, is he?'

You can never tell who's going to be the last straw in a family. A Hottentot, a German, a Jew as outlandish as I must have looked to the protected eyes of Chloë's light-heartedly Jew-despising mother. In our family it was an Irishman. No idea why. Something to do with the Irish epitomising what we meant by a bates, the male equivalent to yekelte only worse, the proletarian drunkard whom we feared, in the abstract, more than any other being because we did not understand from the inside the workings of a mind befuddled by alcohol and could not calculate what it would do. If you want to understand a culture, look at how it goes about subverting itself. Carnival contains everything you need to know about Catholics; and Purim, the most carnivalesque of all Jewish festivals, renders up the Jew. At Purim even the holiest of men are required to get so drunk that they will not, for a whole day, be able to distinguish Mordechai from Haman, the friend from the enemy, the saint from the sinner. Behold then why Jews fear alcohol: in alcohol we lose the one quality that guarantees our humanity – our ability to distinguish good from evil.

They will tell you, the anti-Semites who collect my cartoons and show them on websites much visited by extremists with too much time on their hands, that our disdain for non-Jews, measured by the size and hostility of our vocabulary for them, is proof of our belief in our inherent superiority. Bad psychology, my farbrenteh friends. Your reasoning is as flawed as your hearts. Colourful language did never yet proceed from confidence. The confident are languid in their contempt; what fuels the vivacity of our mistrust is fear. All those goyim and batesemeh, all those yekeltes and shaygetsim – what are they but characters in a recurrent nightmare, the Grand Guignol of our waking terrors? Not just our enemies, blind with drink, but that to which we might ourselves be reduced if we do not keep our wits about us. If the Jews felt easier in their chosenness they would be sweeter to get along with. As it is, they start in fright whenever an Irishman who isn't W. B. Yeats or Oscar Wilde (and they aren't all that sure about Oscar Wilde) approaches them with a glass in his hand.

'An Irish son-in-law,' my mother wailed. 'What have I done to deserve an Irish son-in-law?'

'And a sailor, Mother,' Shani reminded her. 'So the house will stink of rum as well as whiskey.'

In fact he was purser on a luxury liner, came from a good cheese-smoking family in County Cork, had been educated in England, so didn't sound like a tinker, and by any standards other than ours would have been counted teetotal. Although Shani had tried to keep the details of her meeting him a tight secret, and would have liked us to imagine her haunting the docks in the early hours of the morning, looking for seamen, it came out that they'd fallen into conversation in Radiven's, the kosher delicatessen at the bottom of our street. He was in Manchester seeing relatives, and could not forgo the opportunity to buy a pound of chopped liver and a packet of matzohs, food he had acquired a taste for as a boy when his parents took him to stay with Jewish friends in Dublin. He had already got what he wanted when Shani walked in, whereupon he realised that what he really wanted, to go with his chopped liver and matzoh, was a beautiful Jewess to serve it to him.

He had a day in town before his train left for Southampton and persuaded Shani to spend it with him in Heaton Park. How far you can fall in love in a single afternoon in a park, depends partly on the park and partly on your physical and mental availability. In Jane Austen's words, 'He had nothing to do, and she had hardly anybody to love.' The 'he' in question, incidentally, also a sailor. Though the 'she' a long way from being a Jewish girl from Crumpsall Park with a thousand pairs of unworn stilettos in her wardrobe. It had happened that way at any rate – love in a single afternoon – for Asher and Dorothy. It had happened that way for me and Zoë, for me and Chloë, and for me and several others. And it happened that way for Shani and Mick. By the time they separated in body they were engaged in spirit. He wrote to her every hour from his boat, she replied with cables to Aden and Colombo and other places Shitworth Whitworth correctly supposed we could not point to on a map – Shani, this was, who had never previously sent a postcard to anybody in her life – and so we became aware that something very serious was taking place in Shani's heart long before we met the cause of it.

Whether she had so arranged it that when he was next on leave he would turn up at our house in his purser's uniform just as one of my mother's kalooki evenings was about to kick off, I can only guess. But if she hadn't, she was damned lucky. He took the gathering by storm. Handsomish and certainly well formed, if not exactly dashing or imposing, but in naval whites, with the colour of the high seas in his cheeks, an unshaveable dimple in his chin and a proven way with red-nailed matrons, he would have made a big impression had he merely popped his head around the door, said *Hello, ladies* and left immediately. That he should have been a card-player, to boot, that he should have loved kalooki in particular, being expected to play it every night in the saloon of the *Oriana* with the wealthier version of just such women as were gathered here tonight, that he should have been able to take his place at my mother's table as though he had never parked his trim behind in any other seat, and be expert enough to keep everyone on their toes but not so expert or indiscreet as to win every hand, and that he should have declined the peach brandy my mother kept for rabbis and alcoholics – well, an angel sent by Elohim could not have managed things better.

'So you're Mick,' my mother trilled, when her other guests had left, while in the shadows of the hall Tsedraiter Ike rolled his shabby little fingers into fists and called upon the Almighty to intervene.

TEN

1

Little by little I fancied I was getting Manny to relax. Whenever the trainee PAs at Lipsync Productions had nothing better to do, they would contact me, mentioning meaningless deadlines for outlines, citing the names of impossibly stellar directors whose windows of opportunities would soon be closing, and cut-off dates beyond which we would be plunged into the perilous uncertainties of another tax year. I told them Manny couldn't be rushed. I explained that there was difficult, even intractable matter which could be coaxed out of him only gingerly, if he was not to take fright and bolt. The word 'intractable' usually got them off the phone and Francine on it. Was there anything *she* could do, she wondered. Had she been a man I'd have deduced from her tone that she meant like breaking both the bastard's arms.

'Time will do it,' I said. 'Leave him to me a little longer.'

What was I up to, I could hear hear her thinking. *What's your little game, Maxie Glickman?*

It was always a little shivery getting Francine in person on the phone. She had a way of making you feel she was taking a moment off from tea with Henry Kissinger, or a Bellini with Berlusconi, to talk to you. If you listened hard you could hear them breathing at her elbow. The other thing you could hear if you listened hard was Francine's beauty. It had an audible quality, like temperature. You can hear heat and you can hear cold; in Francine's case you could hear the strained patience in her green eyes, and the challenge that was so important an element in her mellifluous looks. I could not have drawn her from her voice, but I immediately remembered how it felt to be in her company. Above all, the sensation of having let oneself down. But whether that was because I didn't measure up to her, or disliked myself for trying, I couldn't decide.

As for Manny, with whom for very different reasons I felt something similar, the truth was that after four or five meetings I still hadn't said a word to him about there being a scriptwriter at my elbow wanting to empty my mind of that of which I'd emptied his. Of course he knew the basis on which we'd been meeting, and wasn't naive enough to suppose I'd be spending this much time in his company simply for the love of it. But getting his story down on paper hadn't come up as an issue between us. And the business Lipsync was most interested in — the gas taps, the gas taps, Max — was not proving to be as imminent as I'd first thought. My own fault. I'd got him on to theology and art. I'd made him teleologically self-aware. Now he thought twice before he mentioned God, and God, I felt, held the key to it.

However, so long as no one rushed either of us, I saw no reason not to believe we would eventually get there.

It might have been my imagination, but I thought he found it easier to talk when he was out of Manchester. He seemed to like coming off the train at Euston with *The Times* under his arm and being surprised to see me waiting for him. It must have felt to him as though he had business to attend to. And I was beginning to prefer it when he came to me. A trip north inevitably incurred family obligations which I didn't always have the mental strength to honour. Jewishly, it didn't feel healthy up there any longer either. The air was not bracing. There were no Jewish ramblers left. If there were still Jewish atheists in town they were lying low. The sky had darkened. People were waiting for the Messiah. My mother's kalooki nights went on almost as before, but I noted that she suspended play on the High Holy Days and even on some of the Lower Holy Days, a respectfulness she would not have dreamed of exercising once upon a time. 'Frummers got to you again, Ma?' I would say when I called in and found the tables empty. But there was no teasing her. 'Without the frummers as you call them, Maxie, we wouldn't be here.' See! They'd slipped into the vacancy left by my father and blackmailed her. They'd made her feel that it was they who had kept us going for five thousand years, the lungs and bellows of the Jewish people, precisely so that Jews like her could lead their frivolously irreligious lives unimpeded. Left to her, there'd be no Jews. That was the package of obligation they'd sold her. Left to her – and me – we'd have died out. Someone the spitting image of her might have persisted, paying for her hair to be sculpted, painting her nails and playing kalooki, but she wouldn't have been Jewish. So she owed them.

Made no sense to me, but I wasn't living there, breathing in the tainted air.

Made no sense to my poor father either, I'd have staked my life on that, and he *was* still there.

Occasionally I'd visit his desolate grave in Failsworth, a blasted Jewish cemetery for the privilege of lying in which my mother had been paying a burial board functionary a penny per week per person by my calculation since Cromwell let us back into the country. *Failsworth* – it describes what happens to your heart when you get within a mile of the place. But that's the way of it with Jewish graves and graveyards: they are of necessity sites of failing strength and failed imagination. After death, nothing.

I hadn't fought when my father's grey slab went up, commemorating the bare bones of his existence in Hebrew script. I hated the look of Hebrew characters almost as much as I hated German. On a grave they reduced the inmate to nothing but an addendum to Jewish history, a mere slip of an ancient tongue which alone enjoyed eternity. But we hadn't been able to come up with a satisfactory alternative. My mother could not abide the idea of burning him, I knew of no country churchyard with an enclosure for amateur boxers with names like Jack 'The Jew' Glickman, and Shani believed that burying him in the manner his father and his father before him had been buried was, though unsatisfactory, best.

So much for his attempt to change the course of Jewish history.

For which failure on our part — because that was how I saw it: *our* failure not his — I apologised each time I went to see him.

And each time there seemed more to apologise to him for.

2

It wasn't only being out of Manchester that appeared to relax Manny's tongue. It was being out full stop. He didn't move well, but as long as he felt he wasn't under pressure to get anywhere, he liked wandering around. Sightseeing. Shopping. Hanging about, or zikh arumdreying, as it pleased him to call it, laughing to himself about the expression, as though it delighted him to remember a Yiddishism he'd had no reason to employ for years. There was no zikh arumdreying where he'd been. He'd shlumped, but that was different. Zikh arumdreying implied active, even ingenious hanging about, whereas a shlump just quietly rotted into the earth.

I'm not saying that he grew suddenly garrulous crossing the river on bridges that hadn't been there when they first put him away, or hobbling along the King's Road like a Chelsea Pensioner, but he would comment on what he saw — people's dress, the numbers of foreigners in the streets, everybody wired up to some item of technology or another — so that I at least became privy to his sudden negligences and parentheses. It was as though the city acted as a chaperone between us, releasing him from the fear of unwonted intimacies, while making small talk easier. Not ideal, given that it was intimacy I was after — and I could hardly seize upon the iPod as a pretext for bringing up double homicide — but as I kept telling them in Wardour Street, just give me time.

One Saturday morning I picked him up off the early train from

Manchester and took him to the British Museum. I thought he might like to mooch around the new courtyard, and otherwise wander where his fancy took him. How we got to Ancient Egypt I am not entirely sure. More by accident than design, I think, since as Jews neither of us was able to get excited by pharaohs or the mummification of their priests. I hadn't cared for mummies even as a pre-adolescent when all that bandaging is supposed to speak to some regressive sexuality in a boy, and never warmed to them thereafter, for all that they were demonstrably a species of cartoon – panels of naturalist narrative criss-crossed with garrulous strips of hieroglyphics, not an inch of space left undevoured. Noisy, vivid, the bright colours of life refusing the monochrome of death, one hyperbolic assertion of history and nature tumbling over another. My bag, you would have thought. Done with me in mind. That they left me cold and even slightly queasy I can only ascribe to instinctual Jewish resistance to plaster and paint, to bandages and gum, to extracting the internal organs of the dead, and to what I understood of the principle of *ka*, the life force which was said to live on and expect feeding after the individual had died. We Jews draw more cut-and-dried distinctions than that, clear our dead away much quicker. Among Jews it is possible for you to have a heart attack after dinner and be in the ground by breakfast. Hasty but clean.

And there's no *ka* hanging around hoping for a hot meal after. Habdalah.

The older I get, the more enamoured I grow of the principle of Habdalah. Keep the meat from the milk, keep the holy from the profane, keep the living from the dead.

And the goyim from the Jews? As an incorrigible mixer, and with the bruises to show for it, I am still thinking about that.

Seeing me holding back from the mummies, Manny shuffled to my side. 'Ugh,' he said, and shuddered.

Funny, the difference an unwelcome corroboration can make to your evaluations. Who was Manny to be shuddering at a once great civilisation, for Christ's sake, when he'd grown up in a house of rags no better than a mausoleum itself?

'I suppose you don't much care for this guy either?' I enquired, moving him on ill-temperedly to a small painted wooden Bes, the dwarf fertility god — smirking, naked, phallic, prancing, laden with musical instruments.

One of Zoë's favourites, Bes, whenever we'd encountered him in a museum on our travels.

'You know there is something of Bes about you, Max,' she liked to tell me, 'if we discount the fertile, the naked, the phallic, the prancing and the musicality.'

She loved a joke, Zoë, as I loved her for making them. 'So all that leaves,' I would say . . .

'. . . is the smirking dwarf. Exactly.'

But there was a more serious point she wanted to make. 'Don't you wish you had a Bes in your pantheon?' she asked me once, I think it must have been in Charlottenburg, on our seeing how she would hack it as a Berlin harlot. By 'your' she meant not belonging to me but belonging to the Jews.

'A pointless question,' was my answer. 'We don't have a pantheon. We have Elohim, full stop. I think that's wiser myself. One God or No God. Start letting everybody in and you end up praying to a hunchback with his dick out and tambourines in his hands.'

'I thought you were a musical people, Max.'

'We are. But when we discover a musical gift in ourselves we don't take all our clothes off and start dancing. We apply for a job as first viola with the Israeli Philharmonic.'

'And go mad with living in your brain. You'd be healthier with more than one sort of god, Max. You'd be more various in your interests. In your case you might even *get* an interest. And you'd certainly look better . . . all of you.'

Which of course was exactly what I wanted to say to Manny. Had you made a bit of room for Bes in your heart, Manny, who knows – you might not have had to play the Holocaust around and around in your head, or stutter into your fingernails, or gas your parents.

He didn't engage with me on Bes. Maybe he was thinking what I was thinking. But he did stop and look long into a case of bronze and limestone deities, half-animal, half-human – a squatting antelope, a leering jackal, a cat-headed goddess slinky as a nightclub singer, knowing and obscene. Irresistibly disgusting, all of them. And impossible, for a cartoonist anyway, not to admire. Easy enough to take or leave a painted sarcophagus, but I couldn't, professionally, resist comic gods and goddesses who mocked the spiritual, could I?

'Do you think this was what Moses found our people dancing around when he came down Sinai with the tablets in his hands?' I wondered, gesturing at a ram-headed deity.

'No. That was a gold calf made from women's earrings.'

'But an animal god, anyway. Something sickening and slightly wonderful like this, wouldn't you say? I can see why they danced. He makes you swoon. Look at his obscene, wide-apart ears, and those extended arms, like a curtain opened on himself – behold, see what's beneath, see what animality is incident to your graceful humanness. You can't say no to it, Manny.'

He sent his blue eyes twinkling into the ironic distance again, something he hadn't done all morning. With a quick dart of his tongue, he wet his lips then touched his moustache as though he feared he might have licked it off. 'What I was taught,' he said, still looking away, 'was that the children of Israel danced around the calf because, like children, they thought Moses had gone for ever. They were desolate and wanted to worship something they could see.'

'Agreed. Something palpably indecent. Something which answered more to what they recognised as the complexity of their natures. Something that wasn't words and interdictions.'

Odd that I should have been playing the devil's advocate.

I knew where I stood on the question of gods. Four-square behind words and interdictions. But sometimes Zoë's voice spoke through me. This can happen in a marriage, even long after the marriage has been dissolved. You open your mouth and lo! – your long-lost spouse's voice comes out.

'That's an interpretation,' Manny said, also ventriloquising, I thought. 'It isn't the one I was taught.'

Lost him. Lost him again to our invisible God, in whom he had forfeited the right to believe.

He was looking at nothing now, wanting to be gone, wanting the morning to be over. To spite him I lingered longer than curiosity demanded, taking in whatever obscenities I could find – a squatting baboon with a penis the size of a cartoonist's pencil, a jeering hippopotamus-headed god, another jackal, a turtle, a second inebriate Bes clanging his cymbals. And not a word of the Law to be heard.

3

It might have been something or nothing, but Manny engineered a queer encounter outside the museum. We had agreed we would have lunch together, but first I needed to visit the comic shop opposite. If it's funnies you want, Bloomsbury's the place to go. Since a comic shop could not possibly interest Manny and the morning was warm, we agreed that he would sit in the sun and wait for me. That's what nutters do – they sit in the sun and wait. I left him to find his own slab of concrete, which is never easy given the busloads of foreign schoolchildren who gather here to eat their sandwiches and discuss Egyptian art. To my surprise – a surprise I cannot justify – he chose to sit himself, very deliberately it seemed to me, between a Muslim gentleman who was reading a newspaper, and two children who were surely his, busy playing with their Quetzalcóatl keyrings, Rosetta Stone mouse mats, and countless other items of swotty tat bought from the museum shop. What surprised me more when I returned was the sight of Manny, who I couldn't trust to purchase his own bus ticket, engrossed in convivial conversation with the whole family. Not only that, he knew their names.

'Mr Nasser Azam,' he said, 'my friend M-max.'

Mr Azam rose to shake my hand, inclining his head slightly. I did the same. He would have introduced his children, but Manny got in first. 'This is Tamoor – am I pronouncing it right? – and this is Zahra. Tamoor and Zahra Azam. This is my friend Max.'

Great names, I wanted to remark. Tamoor and Zahra, great names for a comic-book hero and heroine from another galaxy. The other thing I wanted to remark was how beautiful they were, eyes like the fishpools in Heshbon, their heads like Carmel and the hair on their heads like purple, and indeed how exquisitely they smelled – frankincense, myrrh, calamus and cinnamon, like the gardens of Lebanon – but one ethnic minority cannot marvel over the exoticism of another without offence.

'We have been comparing notes,' Mr Azam told me. He too was succulently beautiful, his hands – always the first thing I look at – a lustrous, ochreous brown, the fingers extraordinary in that they appeared to be flat-sided, faceted even, the crescents of his nails as thrilling in their perfected nakedness as Ilse Cohen's used to be.

'Notes? On the museum?' I feigned alarm. 'Has Manny told you that he and I have been disagreeing about the gods of ancient Egypt?'

He shook his head, laughing. 'Well, we,' he said, 'have been comparing our views of Abraham.'

'Amicably, I hope.' Which was an asinine thing to say, but then I wasn't versed in the etiquette of Abrahamic discussion Jew to Muslim in plein-air Bloomsbury.

He bowed. Of course amicably.

'Presumably Zahra,' I said, 'is a variation of Sarah, Abraham's wife.'

Again he inclined his head to me. If I were wrong, if Sarah and Zahra were polar opposites, he certainly wasn't going to tell me.

My head was spinning. Where had Manny found the savoir faire to strike up conversation with the Azams? I had only been away ten minutes. How come he had hit it off so well with them, utter strangers, in that time? And how come he had dared venture, so soon, into the minefield of Torah and Koran? Was it chutzpah, or stupidity? Had all those years of being locked away dulled him to the sensitivities of Jews and Muslims in the matter of one another's mutually confuting faiths?

I was also strangely touched that he had introduced me as his friend. 'Friend' had not been in the air between us much. It was on the basis of our friendship that we were doing whatever it was we were doing – making notes towards a film of Manny's ruined life, were we really embarked on that? – but the word itself had not previously been used, at least not by him, and it made a difference. I was no less touched by Manny's engrossment in the children. As I stood there, not quite knowing what to say to their father, Manny examined Tamoor's and Zahra's toys, laughed at a snowstorm on the pyramids, helped them with a metal puzzle which had baffled the holy priests of Mesopotamia. They were huddled about him, attentive, like acolytes around a senior boffin, apparently oblivious to his oddities. It seemed to me, too, from the way he bent over them – though this was only a surmise, a cartoonist's reading of the body's longings – that he wanted to touch them, that he would have liked to gather them to him so he could breathe in the incense of their hair, but knew he couldn't.

They gave him their email addresses when we parted. God knows what he intended to do with those. He watched them go, dark into the great white city, waving longer than I thought was necessary.

Over a minestrone and bruschetta lunch, his eyes suddenly filled with tears. He wiped them with his serviette, but there was no staunching the flow. I grew embarrassed. There were people at adjoining tables watching, wondering what I'd done to him.

At last he said, 'They didn't remind you of anybody?'

'Tamoor and Zahra?' I thought about it. And then I realised that yes, yes they did.

Asher.

4

Sometime in my first or second term at art school I received an invitation to dinner on *Oriana* notepaper, disappointingly post-marked Manchester, not Surabaya or Trincomalee. Chloë, whom I'd just met – though I couldn't be certain she'd met me – would have warmed to a candlelit spread in Surabaya. 'I like exceptional men,' I had heard her telling a group of her friends in the refectory, and what could have been more exceptional in 1963 than a man who took his girlfriend to dinner in the South China Sea. The sender of the invitation was Shani's Mick – Mick Kalooki, as we'd taken to calling him after Shani's joke – and the venue to which he was inviting me was any restaurant of my choice, with a good bottle of wine thrown in. A PS requested that I make no mention of the invitation to Shani.

I wasn't sure how I felt about this. After mulling it over for a few hours I decided that the invitation couldn't possibly bode ill to Shani, not given its bon vivant spirit (by 1963 standards), and not unless the man was a bounder, which he wasn't. More likely it presaged a desire to get to know the family better, either with a view to making Shani an offer she couldn't refuse, or as a prelim-inary to moving in with us – or with *them* rather, as I had already moved out – so that he could be at the kalooki table before anybody else. Fine by me so long as it was fine by Shani and my mother. Mick was a nearly permanent fixture already. He had left his seafaring the year before, folded away his purser's uniform to the disappointment of every woman over fifty in Crumpsall Park,

285

and opened up a barber's shop right next to Radiven's, the deli-catessen he rated above all others in the world, and he was a man who could be said to know the world. Whether he could be said to know barbering was another matter, but he had barbered a bit at sea before becoming a purser, and though seamen were less fussy about their hair than dry-land Jews, barbering was, by his own admission, the nearest thing he had to a civilian profession. Eventually this would cause friction with Errol Tobias's mother who did a little moonlighting with men's hair when women's busi-ness in her salon was slow, but in the beginning Mick's transition from sailor to hairdresser, as from bird of passage to fixed star in Shani's affections, was smooth. He snuggled up a bit close for my taste – he could make you feel there was more of him inside your skin than there was of you – but I liked him well enough at a distance of two hundred miles. My fear, on getting the invi-tation, was that he meant to snuggle up even closer. But for what reason, since he was already a combination of brother, son, husband and lapdog to all of us except Tsedraiter Ike, who had detested him at first sight and never wavered, I couldn't imagine.

We met in a Jewish restaurant in Whitechapel, ate saveloys with boiled potatoes and drank a wine of no known varietal type. The restaurant wasn't my choice. I'd suggested a nice little Italian I knew in Soho, next door to a strip joint on one side and a clip joint on the other – now I come to think of it, probably an earlier incarnation of the very place where Francine Bryson-Smith would lunch me into Jewing up the tragedy of Manny Stroganoff – but Mick didn't think Soho was suitable given that he was my sister's boyfriend. And besides, he wanted to eat kosher.

I quickly discovered he wanted to talk kosher too.

'So what's a nish?' he asked me.

'A nish? I don't know of any nish.'

He pointed to the word in the menu.

'Oh, k'nish! The *k* isn't silent. In fact it's noisy. You rock on it – k'nish.'

'K'nish.' He practised it, pushing his face forward. 'K'nish. K'nish.'

'That's good,' I said. 'And it means dumpling.' I didn't tell him, for the same reason that he didn't want to meet me in Soho, that a k'nish was also a vagina.

By this stage he had brought a pen and notebook out of his pocket. It was odd. He knew the lexicon of delicatessen nosh backwards – the bagels, the challas, the kes, the wursts, the apricot and almond rugalach, and of course the chopped herrings and chopped livers in all their subtle variations. But Jewish restaurant food was different. Nobody had taken him, that seemed to be the problem. Nobody wanted to take him. 'If we're going to eat out we're not going to eat that pap,' my father had always said, meaning we were having Indian or Chinese full stop, and that tradition had been kept alive by Shani. The only person in the house who might have been up for a kosher meal on the town was Tsedraiter Ike, but he did all his dining away from home in houses of the dead. And would not have entertained the company of Mick anyway. Thus this poor Irish sailor, thinking he had gained admittance to that penetralium of mystery, a haimisheh Jewish family, was reduced to dragging himself down to Whitechapel to dine Yiddler-wise with his girlfriend's younger shikseh-doting brother who, to tell the truth, wasn't all that keen on the pap either.

'I think I know what kreplach are,' he said, keeping with the *k*s, 'but how are they different from kneidlach?'

'Well, kreplach are like little ravioli, as you know, whereas kneidlach are dumplings, only rounder in general than k'nishes. But I'm not an expert.'

'You have a lot of words for dumplings.'

And a lot of words for vagina, I thought, remembering pirgeh and peeric and pyzda and pupke – unless Errol Tobias who had taught them to me had made them up out of devilment.

'Isn't there something called kochleffel?'

'Yes, but you don't eat it. A kochleffel is a busybody. A stirrer. You want to watch it when Shani starts to call you that.'

He beamed at me. 'So lovely.'

'Shani?'

'No . . . I mean yes, of course, but I was talking about the language. Such a lovely language, Yiddish!'

Indeed. But then I hadn't told him what k'nish meant in slang.

I was prepared, this once, for Shani's sake, to take him through every dish on the menu, but I had to stop him when his curiosity grew more philosophical and he tried to get me on the difference between shmendrik and shmerrel and shmuck and shmegege and shmulky and shlemiel and shlimazel and shvontz and the hundreds of others – the rich roll-call of dishonour in which a people who prize intelligence above all things register the minutest distinctions between ignorance, simplicity, folly, buffoonery, ineptitude, sadness and sheer bad luck.

'Just one thing more,' he said, after he'd paid the bill. 'If you had to choose between shmendrik, and shmerrel and shmegege—'

'No,' I said. 'No, I can't. There aren't enough hours in the day.'

He laid his hand on mine. 'Let me finish. If you had to choose one of those to describe *me*, which would it be?'

I was horrified. 'Mick, why are you asking me that? You are none of those things.' For a terrible moment I wondered whether Shani or my mother had been abusing him. And then I realised. Tsedraiter Ike – himself named after a weakness of the brain that was nearly but not quite the same as that suffered by a meshuggener. Tsedraiter Ike, I felt sure, had been undermining him in Yiddish, no doubt spitting the words at him through the letter box when he arrived for kalooki. And no doubt spitting them at him again from his bedroom window when he left.

'Take no notice of a word that wicked old bastard says,' was my advice. 'My father, who was a good judge of character, and who it's a great shame you never met, wanted to throw him out of the house.'

Mick smiled at me, not bothering to pretend he didn't know who I meant. 'He's a momzer, yes?'

'Mamzer. Momzer's London Yiddish.'

He looked alarmed. 'You're telling me there's London Yiddish *and* Manchester Yiddish?'

'And Glasgow. And Leeds. And Dublin, too, presumably.'

He rolled his eyes. 'Oy, oy, oy – I'll never master it.'

'Just don't try to rush it,' I said. 'It takes five thousand years.'

Though he'd paid the bill he didn't want to leave.

'Just a coffee.'

Fine by me, but I had to stay his hand before he could ask the waiter to bring him cream. 'They can't serve you dairy after meat,' I told him.

He punched the side of his face, and took his notebook out again. 'Sorry,' he said. 'I did know that, but it didn't feel like meat.'

'It never does,' I reassured him.

Funny, how protective of him I felt, though he was older than me by a dozen years or more. He was a sweet man. Much the sweetest Irishman I had ever met. I could see why Shani liked him. I'd have kissed the dimple in his chin myself had I been a woman. Shani was very lucky, I thought. We all were. He was an addition to our little family. But I was worried for him. No one should want to be that Jewish. Certainly no one who wasn't Jewish to begin with. The shaygets who would be Jew . . . it felt self-harming, pathological in the way that explorers who'd lost their way and cheerfully ended up as tribesmen with bones through their noses seemed pathological. Had I suggested circumcision I'm sure he'd have agreed to it. That's supposing he hadn't taken that drastic step already.

I shook his hand warmly when we parted – a 'you're one of us now' sort of shake – but he insisted on hugging me, this a good twenty years before hugging between men had been normalised. Such goodwill, I thought on the bus home. We enjoy such goodwill from so many. Do we make it all up, this anti-Semitism? Is it a fire in us we need to feed? Could we possibly have called the Nazis down on us because we couldn't exist without them?

For an hour or so I felt as though I had woken into a different universe, where everything was love. Had someone asked me to empty my pockets into his I'd have agreed to do it. All men were brothers. There wasn't a person anywhere who didn't wish me well. I was lucky I made it home in one piece. Certainly lucky I didn't fall off the bus. These moments can rob you of your balance.

But the next night I started going out with Chloë, and I was firmly on two feet again.

5

Why I fell for Chloë Anderson when she enrolled in art college in a Chanel suit and French high heels with two cameras carried diagonally across her chest like small arms is not a question in need of an answer. You couldn't not. You couldn't not if you were me, anyway. The shoes had something to do with it. As the son and brother of women who between them owned every pair of shoes that had ever come off a shoemaker's last, I understood the poetry of shoes. But Shani, at least prior to my father's death, no sooner put something on her feet than she looked like a mill girl off for a Saturday night eating fish and chips out of a newspaper in Blackpool. She clomped, she teetered, she clickety-clacked, often not even making it down the stairs before realising she couldn't go out in what she was wearing, returning to her room and hurling her entire wardrobe against the wall. My mother the same. Despite the classical attenuation of her ankles – the heel narrowly incurved, the ankle bone itself a perfect sphere, and with a glisten on it, like sucked caramel – my mother had only to put on a heel higher than her thumb and she metamorphosed into a fine piece of ass, the sort of dame that gave a Chicago mobster cachet.

Whereas Chloë . . . Chloë in shoes was all paradox. Austere and yet with daggers for feet, the convent girl and the street-walker, slightly scuffed and yet somehow scuffed to plan – how did she do that?

She made me sorry for Shani and my mother even as I fell for her. Sorry for all Jewish women if I am to tell the truth. No instinct for ambivalence, you see. No double meanings.

When the daughters of Israel tinkled their feet for their menfolk, their intention was solely to give pleasure. Chloë too was in the pleasure business, but at the depriving of it end.

She was the first of the conceptualists, possessed of no manual dexterity, no sense of the ridiculous, and no patience to make art. So out of place among us did she look that everything she said and wore were taken to be ironic statements. Only a highly sarcastic and anarchic individual – that was the reasoning – would dare turn up at an art school looking like someone answering an advertisement in the *Lady*. In fact she was a deeply, even anarchically conservative woman. I like to think I was the only one who understood that. But that was just about all I understood.

She was furious when I met her. Her mouth in a perpetual arctic downturn, no matter that she was engaged in convivial conversation; a quiet, simmering rage narrowing her grey eyes, and issuing in a sniffle which never quite became a cold but which never left her in the all the years I knew her. That I wasn't the object – the *sole* object – of this ferocious froideur, I now accept. It felt pretty personal the first time I encountered it, however. An icy blast directed at the softest chamber of my pulpy Jewish heart.

But I wasn't just in it for the insult. Or at least not just for the insult to me. What doubly attracted me the first time I clapped eyes on her – along with the armed cameras and equivocating shoes – was the look she had of having been insulted herself. There was something smutty, or do I mean smutted, about her. Someone had demeaned her. Why it is necessary, in order for me to fall in love, for one or other of us to feel slighted, I don't know. My instinct is to put the question the other way round: how do people manage romantic attachment where there is not some history of disdain, some evidence of ignominy to stimulate the passions? I suppose none of this is necessary where sex is perceived as a natural activity, continuous with civility and good manners and all the other arts of social refinement and consideration. But that doesn't sound like very satisfactory sex to me. Sex, surely, once we've put the animal state behind us, is an aberration, and therefore, for it to be sex at all, must thrive on imbalance and reversal, on usurpation of the decencies, on disregard for what is usually owing. As civilised beings we cannot do without respect; as sexual beings we cannot do without the opposite. All of which might not tell you anything except that *The Scourge of the Swastika* fell into my hands too early.

Fell into my hands too early, *too*.

As I was later to discover, there was an immediate occasion for Chloë's rage. Someone *had* demeaned her. A short time before I met her, on the eve of her applying for a place at art college, the man with whom she had been living since she was a schoolgirl pushed her head into the kitchen sink and anally ravaged her. 'Took her cherry' was how she put it, her other cherry having been taken long ago. But the pretended lightness of expression did not belie the gravity of the crime. Nothing stayed light for long in Chloë's mouth. In this instance she made you think of every sinister nursery rhyme you had ever heard. Cherry evoked merry but there was murder in the rhyme. She would kill him for it. Or if not him, someone.

She was two or three years older than the rest of us, having left home and gone to live with this man – a painter of people's pets by trade and a rugby player by inclination – instead of pursuing her education. Her mother had not stood in her way. It sounded to me as though she had been sweet on him herself. He was her type. Hazily blue-eyed, square-necked, Cheshire-born, and tickled when she said she would be saying goodnight now, goodnight. James. Jim. Which would also have been her idea of a good name for a man. None of your Maxie-Shmaxie nonsense. James, Jim – whatever Chloë's mother thought of him – had anally ravaged Chloë as a way of expressing his discontent with her decision to go to art college. Goyim do that. They get upset, see red, hit the roof and take it out on you anally. Prior to that, their life together had been unmarked by violence – unless you call rugby violence, which I do. But importantly he hadn't raised a hand to her. In return for which she did his washing, removed pieces of other players' bodies from his teeth, photographed the team in action and repose, and, because he had an ambition to paint flesh as well as fur, took her clothes off for him. None of these being activities she could regard as 'hers', she informed him at last of her intention to study photography, 'for herself', whereupon he told her that was retrograde to his desire, filled the sink and had his way with her from behind.

'The mongrel didn't even have the balls to look me in the eyes,' she told me in due course.

'Well, he hardly could, could he?' was my response.

'And what would you know?' was hers. Meaning I wasn't man enough to anally ravage her myself. Which indeed, as a Jew, I wasn't. I'm not saying that the sodomising of women is unknown among Jews. But it's not a favourite. Hygiene partly. Also the obstacles it places in the way of conversation. You can grunt your satisfaction but you can't quietly discuss things, and Jews, who are a verbal people, like to talk during coitus. (For me, oral sex still means conversation.) But above all it's the superfluity that bugs us, nature having already provided a vagina.

We have earlier discussed Habdalah, the keeping apart of that which should not be confused. But in this case it's the aesthetics rather than the morality of Habdalah that's decisive: the laws governing art and form, giving due place to this or that, honouring the beauty of things in their separateness and season. Aesthetics. It's all aesthetics with Jews.

These are considerations to which violence, of course, is blind, and if Chloë when I met her was in flight from violence, she was also still, in some essential part of herself, in thrall to it. She admired strength, almost in the Nietzschean sense, until she was the victim of it. That's the catch with *Übermenschen*. They're fine until they start giving it to you from the rear. But she was backed into a corner of her own psychological making. She chose me because of all the people she encountered at art college, I (along with Aaron Blaiwais and Arnie Rosenfield) reminded her least of the brute she no longer wanted to be with, but precisely because I (we) reminded her least of the brute she no longer wanted to be with she was unable to feel good about herself in my (our) company.

Was it to turn me into somebody else, or to make me see who I really was that she showered me with gold in the first years of our marriage? A gold signet ring to go with the gold marriage band, two gold watches, gold cufflinks, gold studs for my dress shirt, a gold bracelet with my initials engraved, and nearly – had I let her – a gold necklace. 'I can't believe how little it takes to release the Arab in you,' she told me, and photographed me in the attitude of a pasha, or what she took to be the attitude of a pasha, cross-legged on a Persian rug with my hand stroking a stuffed saluki and all my gold glinting.

Coming back from a shooting assignment in the Middle East she bought me a jubbah and had me wear it around the house without underwear. The scarf of the Palestine Liberation Army which she picked up on the same trip she had the sense not to give me until our relationship was already in tatters. But more than once she snapped me with a towel on my head, marvelling at how masculine it made me look.

This wasn't a passing photographic fancy. She believed she was possessed of a sort of moral X-ray vision in relation to me, seeing behind the merely incidental Novoropissik sojourn of however many hundreds of years, to my origins in sun and sand. In this, her ambition bore a striking resemblance to my father's. He wanted me out of the shtetl one end, she wanted me out of it the other. For both of them, the enemy was the life-fearing Ashkenazi Milquetoast who buried himself in holy books and mumbo-jumbo to escape the notice of marauding Cossacks. As indeed he was the enemy for me. So if Chloë was prepared to forgive me the last couple of thousand years and return me to my desert setting – as a sultan, a caliph, a sheikh, whatever she wanted to call me – provided it didn't entail my actual living in a desert, I was up for it. And yet no sooner did I embrace the part, padding about in my jubbah and Ali Baba slippers, sipping mint tea, jingling my jewellery and letting my belly grow, than she accused me of being a crass vulgarian, an Oriental souk Jew with the taste for trumpery of a market-trader from Walthamstow.

'A bit rich,' I complained, 'considering that I didn't own an article of jewellery until I met you. The way I look is how you've made me look.'

'*Made* you.' She sniffled her contemptuous sniffle. 'The victim is always willing, Max.'

I knew the reference. I'd heard it enough times. Cartier-Bresson, her hero, on the photographer seeking to capture the inner silence of the willing victim. The reason, as a cartoonist, I hated photography. All that silence shit. Not that I cared much for the willing victim as a concept either. None of my victims was willing.

'My willingness,' I said, 'is just marital courtesy.'

She had, as I have said, no sense of the ridiculous. She couldn't bat a joke back. 'You should be fucking grateful to me,' she said, 'You should be on your knees.'

'I'm *on* my knees. I'm always on my knees. I'm just not sure, in this context, why.'

'Because I've made you look how you were always intended to look, that's why.'

'And what's that?'

'Preposterously vain.'

'Which I thought you liked.'

'Well, you're better than you were.'

'And how was I?'

She struck a pose, feet pointing outwards, tongue lolling, Catherine wheels spinning at her ears, suggestive of a Novoropissik simpleton with sidelocks.

Suggestive, in fact, of Manny Washinsky.

Had the parody not been so inaccurate – I was the art school goyisher housepainter when she met me, more like Hitler as a boy than Manny Washinsky – I might have turned nasty. There are parts of Cheshire where a woman can get herself sodomised on a smaller provocation. Even by a man who's on his knees.

But that was our contract. She jeered at me for not being what she was in hiding from – a cherry plucker – and I took her jeering as evidence of my superiority to it. A superiority, I don't deny, which looked at from another angle wasn't much of a superiority at all. I wasn't a bully, but didn't that, by the merest switch of logic, imply I was a coward, a man of intellect and introspection only because it wasn't open to me to be anything else, all mental cunning because mentality was my sole possession?

'But then again,' I recall Chloë's mother saying to me one scratchy Sunday Cheshire afternoon, after I'd cleaned them both up at Monopoly and Scrabble and most other games besides, and then apologised for myself by making slighting reference to my lack of muscularity – 'but then again' – Chloë's mother's favourite expression – 'you are such brainboxes, darling. It really is no cost

296

to you, admitting you're all coward-cowardy-custards in your bodies when it's really only the brainbox you value. What say you to that, Chlo?'

'Agree with every word, Mumsy. Do you know what they're calling it now?'

'What's that, my precious?'

'Reading books and things . . . Being brainboxes . . .'

'Tell me.'

'Hermeneutics.'

'Never!'

'I tell you truly, Mamma.'

'Sounds so . . . you know what, doesn't it? Hymie Neutics. Shall we call him Hymie Neutics?'

'It would serve him right for always making it so plain.'

'Making what so plain? His origins?'

'Well, those too. But I was thinking of the contempt he shows us.'

'For not having a brainbox the size of his?'

'And for not being Freud or Einstein ourselves, Mamma.'

Helène wrinkled up her nose. 'Do you think Frankenstein was one, Chlo?'

'One what, Mamma?'

She tapped her nose. 'You know.'

'Could be, Mamma. Why don't you ask him?'

'Maxie, darling, was the monster one of yours?'

'Frankenstein was the name of the scientist, Helène,' I told her.

She rolled one eye to heaven and another to her daughter. Was there no end to the over-subtilising of these people? 'The scientist, then, darling. Was *he* one?'

'I am not sure there is any evidence to suggest such a thing.'

'No, but what do you think in that great big whirling brainbox of yours? What's your conclusion, Maxie? Yea or nay?'

'Well, I'm not sure that he made any money out of his creation, Helène. Does that help?'

She smiled sweetly at me. 'Well, money, I have to say, darling, was the last thing on *our* minds, wasn't it, Chlo?'

Leaving me to curse myself for falling on her chintzy fist and knocking myself out yet again.

There it was, anyway. Mercantilism and mentalism – if they couldn't catch me with the one they'd nail me with the other.

As for what Chloë was doing going near someone in whom both found their personification – and when I protested my innocence of materialism at least, she pointed to the photographs she'd taken of me in a voluptuous Arabia of the senses – only the science of perverseness explains it. No doubt we both had problems in the area of what popular psychologists call self-worth. We corroborated each other's damaged self-esteem. We stayed together for the time we did because, Jew to Gentile, Gentile to Jew, we were a confirmatory insult to each other.

As the years roll by I understand more and more why Tsedraiter Ike sang, 'It's only me from over the sea, said Barnacle Bill the sailor.' It's only me. A phrase my mother has also started to employ when she telephones me. *Only me*. Not anyone of worth.

6

In the light of that song, Tsedraiter Ike's resistance to Shani's fiancé, a one-time sailor, takes on an interesting aspect. Of course Tsedraiter Ike was always going to oppose an Irishman on religious grounds, whether or not Mick now knew the difference between a kreplach and a kneidlach and could rock the *k* in k'nish. But I too was gone among the Gentiles – gone among the anti-Semites in fact – and though he berated me for it, tutting when he saw me, and dropping the 'old palomino' from his conversation, he didn't turn on me as ferociously as he turned on Shani. So the sea could have had something to do with it.

But it takes a bit of winkling out.

We had no sailors in our family. No Bills, no Barnacles. My

father did once say that in another life he wouldn't have minded sailing single-handedly around the world, but he got a nosebleed the one time he took us rowing. And neither Ike nor my mother had what you could call a strong stomach. A short car ride and both of them turned the colour of mould. So a heaving deck in the middle of the Atlantic was no place for any of us.

But we hadn't just sprouted in Crumpsall Park like mushrooms. Our origins were elsewhere and we had to have got from there to here somehow. And since we came before there were planes, it stood to reason that at least one of us had been on a boat. Was that why Tsedraiter Ike sang 'It's only me from over the sea, said Barnacle Bill the sailor' – because he remembered being shipped over from one of those shit-heap Eastern European shtetls in his mother's belly? I don't find it hard to believe you can remember how things were for you before you were born. Myself, I go back four, five thousand years. Part of it's fake memory, I grant you, prompted by old photographs and stories handed down from one generation to the next. But some of it I remember as though I'd been there. Abraham, Joseph, Moses, Esther. And if I remember it as though I'd been there that's because I was. It's not only the sins that are visited upon you if you take the details of your antecedence seriously. Start admitting guilt from five millennia back and you'll be privy to the good times too. The golden calf, for example, no matter what Manny insisted it was made of and stood for – what a hoot of a fucking night that was!

Tsedraiter Ike knew about the sea foetally, that's my view. The wind howled, the rain spat, my grandmother sat huddled in a lifeboat in case any of those bastard Cossacks had slipped aboard at Arsopol or Voznosenski Isnosenski, and Tsedraiter Ike, lurching in her watery belly, learned about Barnacle Bill. There's even a chance my grandmother herself conversed with Barnacle Bill in hiding. According to my mother, who would open the door on the subject about an inch every ten years, her mother was a flirtatious, not to say highly sexed woman, with little or no erotic respect for her husband, from whom I therefore imagine Tsedraiter Ike to have got his looks and personality. And something of a sexually unpleasant nature definitely happened on the crossing – or if not on the crossing itself then in the period they had been housed in Brody, trying to find whoever had sold them and then robbed them of their tickets – because immediately on landing my grandfather vowed that for decency's sake he would see the child born and then have nothing again to do with either of them.

'You are refusing to have anything to do with your own child?'

'How do I know it's mine?'

'How does any man know his child is his?'

'By not marrying a slut, that's how.' Only he wouldn't have said slut. He'd have said kurveh or zoineh.

'I talk to a sailor and you call me a slut?'

He pointed to her belly. 'You call that talking?'

She threw her head back and laughed, showing him throat. No woman should ever show a Jew her throat unless she wants him for a slave for life or an enemy for longer. Midianite women showed the Israelites their throats whenever the two peoples encountered one another in the desert, and short of wholesale massacre the Jews have had no defence against the gesture ever since. It was witnessing my grandmother's throat that got my grandfather into this mess in the first place. 'Did he fondle your breasts like this?' my grandfather wanted to know. 'Did he put his hand up your skirt, so?'

'Did who?'

'The sailor.'

'I talked to the sailor for five minutes. You were there.'

'I wasn't there the whole time. I had to be sick overboard. Twice I left you to empty my kishkies into the North Sea. And what about in Brody? You weren't even *carrying* a child when we first arrived in Brody.'

'Then I admit it. In the time you were emptying your kishkies

I let him fondle my breasts, then I let him put his hand up my skirt where he encountered no resistance to speak of, and here I am, twenty-four hours later, big with his child.'

'I could kill you,' my grandfather cried. 'I could hack you into a thousand tiny pieces, you trollop.' Only he wouldn't, not having any English prior to this, and having landed in Hull only that morning, have said trollop.

In the end – and I tell the story exactly as my mother told me her mother told it to her – it took an immigration officer to separate them. 'Not a promising start,' he said, eyeing each of them in turn, then leading them out of the queue. He was a lean Englishman with no colour in his face but for the two stains of grey which marked the whereabouts of his cheekbones. Such men, cruel with the unhurried coldness of the English, have been turning back my people for centuries, and had my grandmother not shown him her throat, on the off chance that it might work as well on anti-Semites as on Jews, we might all of us have been turned back for ever.

'You're going to have to do better than this,' he told my grandfather while he fondled my grandmother's breasts. 'Name?'

My grandfather answered him in whatever Eastern European mishmash he spoke. 'I am Igor ben Whateverov. I am from Novoropissik. But I have spent the last thousand years in Brody trying to find the thief who stole our tickets.'

'Do you know the Axelroths?' the immigration man asked my grandmother. 'They're from Brody.'

She shook her head, letting the hair fall from her turban.

'They are very nice people,' he said. 'They sell vegetables near me. Would you like to come into this country as an Axelroth?'

'*Was?*' My grandfather cupped his ear. *Was*, pronounced *vas*. The sound old deaf Jews made throughout my childhood. *Vas?* For that habit alone he deserved to lose my grandmother. 'The Axelroths? *A finster auf* the Axelroths!' A curse on anyone from Brody.

Apparently my maternal grandfather in full curse was a comic spectacle.

The official laughed, his colour high suddenly, my grand-mother laughing with him. 'That's what we'll call you,' he said, taking out a pen. 'Finster. But not Igor. You wouldn't want to be called Igor in this country. Let's agree to Ivor, yes? Ivor Finster it is then.' And with that he stamped their papers and slipped his address into my grandmother's burning little hand.

Six months later my grandmother was living in the village of Swine in the East Riding of Yorkshire with John Skinner, Immigration Officer, as his wife, and Ivor Finster was training to be a cabinetmaker in Crumpsall Park.

Ten or eleven years down the line my grandmother miraculously conceived again. This time there was no argument who the father was. John Skinner. He did not live to see the baby born. Not wanting to spend what was left of her life bringing up an after-thought child alone in Swine, she contacted Ivor Finster, who was now relatively comfortably off, and offered a deal. For the sake of the children she would resume relations with him in Crumpsall, bringing up the boy – his boy, Isaac – as a Finster, but Leonora – my mother – as a Skinner. She owed that to the man who'd given her a new life in Swine. My grandfather – except that it was now looking as though he was my great-uncle, not my grandfather – agreed in all particulars but the last. He could accept no Skinner as a child of his. He suggested reverting to their old name. What about Whateverov? My mother offered a compromise. Axelroth. *A finster auf* anyone called Axelroth, my great-uncle said. But he was lazy and lonely and they shook on the deal. Maybe they even slept together on it. And let people say whatever they chose to say.

It took me some time to digest what my mother was telling me, that's if I have digested it yet. 'Hang on,' I said, 'just hang on a minute.' I was so confused I had to count relations back-wards on my fingers. But whichever way I counted, it came out the same. One of my grandparents was a Skinner. A Gentile.

Which meant, assuming that my poor father had no skeletons in *his* cupboards – though those assuredly were buried with his own skeleton now – that I was only three-quarters Jewish.

'If any of it's true.'

'What do you mean if any of it's true? How can you not know if any of it's true?'

'My mother was a colourful woman with a vivid imagination. And my father kept things to himself. You didn't always know where you were with either of them.'

'Is that your actual father you're talking about now?'

'Well, I only knew one, Max.'

'And you never asked him about the other? You never asked why you had a different name? You never talked to your mother about him? You never thought of visiting his grave in Swine?'

'I think you've forgotten, Maxie, how young I was when they all died. I was the child of old parents, Max. We made our own way in those days. There wasn't anybody to ask.'

'But you've had time to do a bit of checking since. Weren't you curious?'

'Time?' She regarded me with wide-eyed astonishment. 'What time have I had?'

'Ma, you've done nothing but play kalooki for the past half-century.'

'You, too,' she said, 'have a vivid imagination.'

'Are you saying I've imagined the kalooki?'

'I'm saying that I'm rather hurt you think that's all I've done with my time. How do you think you and your sister got brought up?'

'Under the kalooki table.'

'That's not amusing, Max. I don't appreciate you making a cartoon of your family.'

'Ma, how long is it since you finished bringing us up?' I didn't add the further question, 'So how do you explain what you've been doing with your fucking life since?'

303

Which was where we left it until the next time I made the journey up to see her. Our conversation must have been preying on her mind because she reopened it almost the moment I arrived.

'It's not as though you're made any less Jewish by all that,' she said – looking rather exquisite, I thought, in the lugubriousness she'd adopted for the conversation – 'though God knows why any of it should matter to you, given your record of marrying out. But you're still playing with the full deck, if that was what worried you. My mother was Jewish. I'm Jewish. End of story – you're Jewish. How much more Jewish do you need to be?'

'It's not need we're talking, Ma. It's curiosity. If it happened we should know about it. I've never understood all this secrecy. Who we are, where we come from, what we were really called. All this starting again, always starting again, for what – to hide a quarter of Gentile blood?'

'Well, they do it, Max. They've all got some old Jew in the background they're desperate to keep hidden.'

'The worse for them if you're right. But you're not right. Not any more. Now they can't wait to brag about it. Now you're no one if you can't produce a pedlar called Shmuel who inseminated Aunt Harriet on his way through Harrogate. Time we got our own back. You think you're exotic? Look who inseminated *our* aunty – a shaygets called Skinner from the Humber! It's nothing to be ashamed of, Ma, a quarter of Gentile blood. Or a half, in your own case.'

'Who's ashamed, Max?'

I took a moment to think about that. Who *was* ashamed?

'Did Dad know about it?' I asked, changing tack.

'Of course. That's to say he knew my mother's version of events. I'm not sure he believed it all. As I've told you, your grandma liked to spin a yarn.'

'Ah, so it's Grandma suddenly. Hardly ever heard a word about her, almost never seen a photograph, no word until now about where she came from – Russia, somewhere, Novoropissik, who knows, who cares, fargess es – and now she's my bobbeh, my bubbeleh. How come neither of you ever mentioned it before?'

'Me and your grandmother?'

'You and Dad.'

'We didn't want you unsettled.'

I thought about it. Was I unsettled? Yes, a bit. A quarter unsettled.

'So where does that leave Ike?' I asked, still working people out on my fingers.

'Oh, he's completely Jewish too. Even more completely Jewish than us.'

'No, I meant, who is he to you by the latest calculation?'

'My half-brother. Same mother, different fathers. It's not all that weird, Max.'

'And he knows?'

'Of course.'

'And you don't think that's what sent him tsedrait?'

'What?'

'The secrets, the shame, the dread of anyone seeing the inside of our lapels.'

'No one's ashamed, Max. There are just some things it isn't necessary to talk about in front of the whole world.'

'As I do, you mean?'

'Well, you haven't exactly been a private man, Max, splashing ink everywhere.'

'Ma, I'm a cartoonist.'

'The world's full of cartoonists. They don't all spill their kishkies for the world to see every five minutes.'

It was the same phrase my venerable ancestor had used on the crossing from the old country. Was it something in the family genes, then, spilling our kishkies in public places? – allowing that to be a fair description of what I did, which it categorically wasn't. But I'd had this out with my mother and Shani too many times to go through it all again. They had their thoughts, I had mine.

305

I believed Five Thousand Years of Bitterness was a story I couldn't tell enough. They thought there were other subjects.

So I returned us to Tsedraiter Ike. 'And being the son of a sailor – wouldn't that send you tsedrait?'

'What sailor?'

'Barnacle Bill.'

'You're the tsedrait one,' she said, waving away the ludicrous idea, before wondering if I'd stay for a hand or two of kalooki later.

But it would explain Tsedraiter Ike's otherwise irrational aversion to Shani's fiancé, wouldn't it?

And the apologetic song he sang. Only me, from over the sea.

ELEVEN

1

Asher.

So how was Asher?

Gross of me, to pounce on Manny's tears? Perhaps. But he'd been leading me a merry dance. Now inviting me in, now pushing me away. His right, of course. His ruined life. But he did know what we were about. He had agreed the deal.

And Asher was not a forbidden subject. Not even his late mother and father were forbidden subjects. Manny had alluded freely to them all in the course of our 'reunions'. It was just that I felt he was teasing me with them, punishing me with them even, bringing them out of his own volition on to the open stage of our conversation, then fading them, turning the lights down on them, the moment I let my curiosity show.

'So how is Asher?'

A risk. I did not know whether he was in communication with Asher or even whether Asher was still alive. Of Asher alive or dead since Manny made an orphan of him I had not heard a word. But sometimes you have to take a risk. And there was something about the intimacy of the tiny restaurant, serving home-made Italian soups and bruschettas to museum types, that emboldened me.

'In love is how I imagine him,' he said, as if speaking from a long way away. 'Always in love.'

'So he fell in love again, then, after Dorothy?'

'Asher was never out of love.'

'Were there many?' I asked, smiling. My appreciation was genuine. I like incorrigible romanticism in ageing men.

'You misunderstand. Asher was always in love with the same woman.'

'With Dorothy?'

'Always with Dorothy.'

Such statements break your heart. The flame that never dies. For a moment I wondered whether Lymm and all the rest of it had been a blind, a family subterfuge, a bit like Tsedraiter Ike, to hide from the Jewish community the fact that the great rabbinic hope had been living embowered in bliss with the fire-yekelte's half-Germanic daughter in a little goyisher cottage in rural Cheshire. And if that were the case, had they been bowered together in bliss all the time poor Manny had been banged up, and were they bowered in bliss still, this very minute, a little grey-haired couple with eyes only for each other, while Manny and I, neither of us remotely blissful, traipsed the streets of London in half-silence?

Impossible, of course. This wasn't that sort of story. Families who put their children's happiness before everything else don't end up getting gassed in their own beds by one of them.

'What happened to Asher?' I asked. 'What happened after he was sent away?'

He looked at me evenly – for him. A little surprised, I thought – as indeed was I – by the directness of my question.

'There's a rabbinic saying,' he said, '"Happy is the man whom God chastens . . ."'

I waited. Here we go, I thought. Here we go again. But I made my face into a question mark. Yes? Happy is the man whom God chastens . . .

'". . . so he can study God's law."'

'Study is a punishment?'

'No, it's a mitzvah.'

'Then why the talk of chastisement?'

'You have to think of it as a chastisement filled with love. God tries the righteous. There is no point trying the wicked. They would not endure it. There's another saying – God's rod comes only upon those whose heart is soft like the lily.'

'So God broke Asher's heart to make a better student of him, is that what you're saying?'

'God breaks all our hearts. Asher wasn't the only one man whose heart was soft like the lily.'

Amen to that, I thought. But I wasn't meant to be thinking of me. Asher, remember Asher.

'I take it from what you're saying, then, that he returned to the yeshiva?'

He nodded.

'Where he pined for Dorothy?'

He rocked in his chair, his attention beginning to drift away. 'He did and he didn't.'

What was that supposed to mean? Did study blot up the pain? Did Asher find a more suitable woman to love, one with her dress down to her ankles and babies round her feet? One in whose fetid embrace he would try without success to forget the silvery loveliness of Dorothy's? But before I could frame the question a little more nicely than that, Manny surprised me with a show of what sounded like irritation. 'They met again,' he said.

'Asher and Dorothy?'

'Yes – s-sssch – they met again . . .'

'Asher and Dorothy met again!'

'Yes.'

'And . . . ? And . . . ? And . . . ?'

But he couldn't continue. His tears were back, a weeping of a sort I'd never seen before, more a saturation around his eyes than a shedding, almost an inundation from without, as though the tears were falling not from his eyes but into them.

2

They met again.

Which could have been something or could have been nothing. But if nothing, why the tears?

And if something, how *big* a something?

A week or so later, over an early-evening catch-up drink in Francine Bryson-Smith's club – another overcrowded joint at the end of a disreputable West End lane – we discussed progress.

'Well and not well,' I said. 'There was an upsetting morning recently when he saw Asher—'

'Where?' She was excited. Whatever the state of Asher's heart, he had gone to ground, eluding even the appetence of Christopher Christmas's researches. Dorothy the same. Apart or together, alive or dead, they had vanished. So any sighting of either of them was, to Francine, a promise of a storyline.

'Oh, not in a real place. It was more Asher's ghost – My brother, methinks I see my brother – which he actually beheld in the faces of a couple of beautiful children.'

I could see that she found it hard to associate any brother of Manny's with the idea of beauty. She even wrinkled the tip of her nose, which I'd noticed when I kissed her was cold, like Chloë's.

Angry women have cold noses – that is just something I happen to know.

'How do you read that?' she wondered.

'I read it that he was upset.'

'No, but did you get the impression he knew where his brother was?'

Plot. All anyone was interested in – fucking plot! Who cared where Asher was? How did Asher feel to Asher – that was the only story that interested me. How fractured was his heart? How many scorpions feasted on his mind? Could he still believe in a God who chastened him for his studies' sake? And Manny, the tears that had appeared on Manny's face like a flood rising from a multitudinous sea beneath – what did they denote?

Careful. If I wasn't careful, plot hunger would be gnawing at my innards next. But it made a difference, suddenly, knowing that Asher and Dorothy had met again. I could see a sequence of events. That Asher's doomed affair with Dorothy had been somehow instrumental in the turning of Manny's mind, and thus instrumental at the last in the dooming of them all, I had always known. The whole community had known that. Thus do seemingly long-buried events wreak their havoc in the end. *Oedipus Rex*. But now effect appeared to be more intimately related to its cause. They met again and something happened. They met again, told Manny about it, said be happy for us, rejoice, our love is born again, and Manny in his happiness for them gassed the rest of the family . . .

Why not? Hence Manny's tears. He knew his actions had ruined Asher and Dorothy's second chance?

But I wasn't ready to spill any of this to Francine yet. Don't ask me why. A feeling of propriety, I think. Propriety in both senses of the word. It wasn't seemly to tell her. And it was my business, not hers.

'He said nothing to suggest he knew anything of Asher's whereabouts,' I said, 'but that could have been because I wasn't thinking along those lines. I was struck by his tears. So far he hasn't shown anything you could really call emotion, unless catatonic schizophrenia is an emotion—'

'You think he's schizophrenic?'

She looked worried, as though schizophrenia wasn't a subject Lipsync Productions touched.

'I don't know. I just use these terms irresponsibly. They're all poetically interchangeable to me. Scientifically I've no idea what he is. He barks, he twitches, he spits out broken letters, he stutters over the names of Nazis—'

'Why do you think he does that?'

'It might be like not pronouncing the name of God. Some names are too holy for language, some are too foul. That's my guess. But all I meant was that he's been dead-batting me and suddenly the sight of him in tears made me wonder if he was gearing himself up to talk candidly.'

She agitated the ice cubes in her drink. 'And was he?'

What are you keeping from me, Maxie Glickman? What's your little game?

'Yes. Except that he seems to have jumped a stage since. He hasn't told me anything about what he did. Only what they did to him for doing it.'

'Well, we want that.'

'Of course we do. My only worry is whether it means he's blotted out the crime in favour of remembering the punishment.'

'Maybe he's one of those who have to come at things backwards.'

'Are there such people?'

She threw me a ravishingly intelligent smile. Miss Margate, DLitt. 'Aren't you one?'

'Me? Well, sideways perhaps, speaking as a cartoonist now. But I don't know about backwards.'

She was still smiling. 'Thought it was a trait,' she said, then seeing I wasn't up to speed, blew the thought away with a cuff of her hand. Blue-red fingernails, I noticed, even as I was wondering about the word 'trait'. A trait of mine? A trait of cartoonists, a trait of *my people's*?

'But anyway,' she continued, 'he's talking?'

'Yes. Beginning to. In fact I'm thinking of moving him into my place for a few weeks so as not to lose the flow.'

She ignored that, presumably afraid I was going to ask her to contribute to his keep. 'And what he's saying to you is interesting?' she went on.

'Well . . . Incarceration stories have never grabbed me much, I have to say. The mind has always been prison enough for me. But yes, I'd say interesting . . .'

'Such as?'

She was bringing our drinks session to an end, signalling the waiter, scratching impatiently at the air with her blue-red fingernails. Which was also a sign to me to make my 'such as' briefer even than brief.

I felt rushed. 'Such as' – now I was scratching at air – 'such as the metal missionary pot . . .'

3

They slide a pot across the cell floor to him.

Eat, they say.

The pot is black, made of metal, the sort cannibals stew missionaries in. It contains potatoes and carrots in a watery gravy.

He eats.

After he has eaten from the pot he is told to defecate into it.

She has her coat on, we are in the street, and she is flagging down a taxi, so I can't elaborate much on this.

When they next bring him food it is in a pot he recognises. The missionary pot. It has been emptied but it has not been cleaned.

Eat, they say.

She makes no comment until she is in the taxi. Then, giving me the glimmer, she says, 'Did you ask him if the food was kosher?'

Ways of Saying Kosher When You're Not Jewish – an idea I had once for a cartoon series. Needless to say, no takers. Surely that would need to be a verbal joke, if a joke at all, was the universal view. Not so. The inclination of the head important, the size of *o* the lips form, the knowing aftermath on the face, the movement of the hands, the invitation to collusion and of course the interrogative glimmer. A veritable challenge to the caricaturist and the historian. How would Luther have said the word kosher? How would Haman? How would Hitler?

I can't say I held out much hope for a positive response from the *New Yorker*, but I'm still at a loss to understand why *Private Eye* or the *New Statesman* didn't bite.

4

They slide a pot across the cell floor to him, towards his bed.

Eat, they say. No other word. It isn't an order. It is barely a suggestion. It's just a sound. He can eat or not. The decision is his. It's his stomach.

The pot is black, made of metal, the sort cannibals stew missionaries in. It contains potatoes and carrots in a watery gravy. He eats.

Now shit, they say.

This is the fuller version.

It is also the cell version. Another time he tells it to me he is in a sort of ward, and he is lying on a shelf.

A *shelf*! Well, what do I know?

In this version, because the room is populous, they say his name. Eat, Scooby-Doo. Shit, Scooby-Doo.

It sounds affectionate. Could they have liked him?

'Why "Scooby-Doo"?'

'He's a dog. A cartoon dog. You should know that.'

'I do know that. I'm asking you why they called *you* Scooby-Doo.'

'Rhyming slang. Scooby-Doo, Jew.'

'Did they all call you that?'

'Who's "they"?'

'The other prisoners.'

'Patients.'

'Forgive me – the other patients.'

Had I said patients to begin with he'd have corrected the word to inmates. When I pick up on inmates he changes them to victims.

'Yes. Scooby-Doo was their invention. The g-guards learn it from them.'

'Guards?'

'Wardens.'

On another occasion they are nurses.

Does he mind being called Scooby-Doo?

'It's not the worst of my worries,' he tells me.

The worst of his worries, in this version at least, is that they will not feed him again until he defecates and defecating in these circumstances is beyond him. He has never before — at least not since he was an infant — had to defecate into anything that isn't a lavatory bowl. He doesn't know how he is going to manage a pot. Nor has he ever defecated in the hearing, let alone the sight, of other people. At school he would have to go to the lavatories at odd hours to be reasonably certain no one else was there. Or wait behind until everyone had gone home. The activity of voiding his bowls within a hundred miles of another living person was and always had been a torture to him. So defecating into the pot in the company of other men is not going to be easy.

My own view is that it would be impossible. That one would sooner explode. But then I have so far been spared extremity. More than that, I have gone to great lengths to avoid extremity. Not to find myself in an extreme circumstance — Chloë and Zoë excluded — has been the principal study of my life. It has kept me quiet. And law-abiding. It would have stopped me turning the taps on my parents, for example. But not everybody remembers how terrible the lavatories are going to be before they commit a crime.

After he finally succeeds in filling the pot he is instructed to empty it. I don't ask how long this has taken him. A week? A month? A year? Nor do I ask him where he empties it. Ask a question and you might just get an answer. Shortly after his success, they — the guards, the wardens, the nurses — return with his food in a pot he recognises. His pot. It has not been washed. The next time he tells me the story they don't bring him food, they bring him back his faeces. But what they say in all instances is the same.

Eat.

Not for me to have an attitude but I find it hard not to express

315

surprise that things are quite so primitive in Her Majesty's mental hospitals.

Once, when I do raise a question along those lines, he turns on me in irritation and tells me he is not describing life inside any kind of hospital I might have encountered.

Well, what do I know? For all my experience to the contrary he could be remembering what it's like inside a yeshiva.

Or wherever it was in Lymm that tubercular Jewish boys were sent to.

And I am taking him to be exercising a degree of poetic licence, anyway, ordering his recollections in a fashion that can only be called metaphorical.

If I'd had the appropriate psychological language – something a touch more nuanced for him than catatonic schizophrenic, or frumkie – I might have been better positioned to decide whether he was actually meting out to himself, in memory, the punishment he thought he deserved. A life for a life, but with what do you pay for two lives?

5

I had offered him the use of a granny flat I'd had built as an extension just before Zoë left. Part of our trial separation. Got all you need, I'd told him – private entrance, galley kitchen, tiny living room, *your own lavatory*, no reason for you ever to come out. I hadn't expected him to accept. Just because he was talking didn't mean he'd turned sociable all of a sudden. Any more than it meant he had decided to like me. Nor, to be honest, had I wanted him to accept. But if he was meting out punishment to himself, then maybe it was time I meted out punishment to *my*self. My punishment was him. This thing of darkness I acknowledge mine, etc etc.

He turned up with a few things in a cardboard suitcase of a sort I hadn't clapped eyes on since the 1950s. I didn't doubt it was the same suitcase that bore his belongings when they put him behind bars. Something in the sentimental way he carried it.

He took the keys from me without meeting my eyes. Then he asked whether he would need change for the gas meter.

Could that have been a hellish joke?

I decided probably not. He was simply pointing out the difference, I decided, between his circumstances and mine. But if it was a joke then I wished Zoë had been around to hear it. She enjoyed that sort of humour.

No one had slept in the granny flat since Zoë left. We exchanged farewells there. 'Goodbye, Bollocky Bill,' she said, extending her hand. Every time we reached the point of breaking up Zoë would offer me her hand, an action so piteous in its finality – reduced to this, a mere formal handshake, we who had rolled all our sweetness up into one ball – that we both dissolved into tears and fell in love with each other again. Not this time, though. This time we meant it.

'Bollocky Bill' was what she had called me, despite my scant resemblance to a Bill, bollocky or otherwise, in the early days of our marriage, before the romance went out of it. 'Bollocky Bill from over the hill.'

No relation, that I knew of, to Barnacle Bill, although Barnacle Bill does become Bollocky Bill in saltier versions of the ditty. Mere coincidence. 'Bollocky Bill from over the hill' was pure Zoë coinage. The charm of nonsense had eluded her as a child, and the discovery in her maturer years that she could make rhymes and limericks and doggerel of her own – actually and of her own volition put nonsense into the world – gave her enormous pleasure. If the nonsense could at the same time comprehend an insult or two to me, her happiness was complete. Another man might have begrudged her this; I could not. The more particularly as she viewed these forays into verbal play as proof that we had not entirely destroyed in her the creative genius she could have been. 'We' being the Jews.

But this is not to say that Bollocky Bill didn't proceed from an impulse even deeper in my Jew-besotted wife. I would not have put it past her, for example, to have detected my Bollocky/Barnacle Gentile ancestry long before I knew of it myself, discerning, in that uncanny way of hers, the Bill closeted behind the mask of Max. Yes, she married me to reconnect herself to that Jewishry from which, as a girl, she had been so brutally repulsed, but she also looked forward to a time when I'd have my nose off and look the goy I had it in me to look.

With Zoë, prognostication waited upon the iron of her will. What she foresaw was what she would make happen. She espied a moustache on my face and she made me grow one. Ditto the beard. Ditto the long hair. Ditto the rainforest eyebrows.

'I'm not able to see out of here,' I complained in the early days.

'What do you want to see?'

'The world.'

'You've seen the world.'

'Zoë, I'm a fucking artist. If I don't see the world, we starve.'

'An artist! You! Don't make me laugh, Max. If anyone's an artist in this relationship, I am. You're just a cartoonist. Which means you don't see the world at all. You only see your own sick view of it. What you do, you can just as well do blind.'

There wasn't much of a future for us, anybody could see that. Fucking Bollocky Bill the sailor could see that. But I'd been brought up to do what women told me. Zoë wanted to find out what the whores looked like in Berlin, I took her to see what the whores looked like in Berlin. Zoë wanted me to forgive the German people, I forgave the German people. Zoë wanted me blind, I went blind. Very nearly I acceded to the nose job.

When she said she was an artist she was right. I'm not referring to her abusive ditties or the calligraphy which she only ever put her energy into fitfully, when friends wanted wedding invitations written for example, or she needed to inscribe some instruction to me in eyeliner on the bathroom mirror –

Don't say God fucking help me every time you take a leak, or *Try imagining there isn't something in the middle of your face stopping you from getting close enough to read this.* No, Zoë's artistry didn't reside in anything she actually produced, any more than Chloë's did. She was an artist by virtue of the power vested in her fancy. She was an artist in her disenchantments. It's open to any old soul to imagine herself hard done by, let down or disappointed; Zoë's sense of being obstructed by the universe — personally spited, as though it were a face-off between the divinity and herself (a Jewish divinity was how she always saw him, a divinity with specifically my features) — was of an epic inventiveness. She could have been, she could have done, she could have achieved — *anything*! She had been set down among us for that sole purpose, to astound us with her gifts, to change the language and conception of woman, to make Zoë the very currency of intelligence and beauty the world over. Forget celebrity: Zoë pre-dated celebrity and exceeded it in ambition. Nothing short of imperishable legend could answer to her sense of destiny.

In this, as in all things, she was encouraged by the devotion of parents to whom she had been a late and unexpected gift, a miracle almost, as Isaac was to Sarah. Together, just the three of them — her father a retired art teacher who rarely spoke, her mother an embroideress and potter who smiled at stars and squirrels — they strode the heathland heights of North London, Zoë papoosed to one or other of their chests, listening to their heartbeats and gathering intimation there, like Wordsworth's pigmy poet, of all that nature had in store for her. They pointed out wild flowers to her, taught her the names of birds and butterflies, explained how you could tell a tree by the configuration of a single leaf, and, when she was ready, stretched out their hands so that she could see, over the rooftops, beyond the Finchley Road, the silhouetted golden city where she would make her name. As what, was immaterial. She was already a prodigy by virtue of being born to them

319

at all. The rest would follow as surely as the wheeling night followed the deep slow satisfactions of the day. But they were careful not to leave it only to chance. For her fourth birthday they enrolled her in ballet classes. For her fifth birthday they bought her a little artist's easel. For her sixth birthday a violin. For her seventh birthday they gave her singing lessons and sent her to acting school. And so on and so on, this showering of opportunity through the long summer afternoons in which she otherwise rowed on lakes and walked her dogs and smiled whereat her mother smiled and rolled down grassy banks laughing in her silent father's arms, until – a genius in happiness as well as everything else – she reached the age of nine, when the Krystals moved in next door.

At first it seemed that they too were presents from her parents. Or another Annunciation, like the one that presaged her amazing birth. Behold, my child, the Krystals, the angels for whom you have been waiting, through whose supernatural agency you will be brought before the breathless courts of public notice.

'You can't imagine how much I loved them,' she told me. 'They shone, they glowed, they sparkled. The first time I saw them as a family they burned my eyes. It was as though a giant candelabra had been installed next door, and whenever I passed their window or looked out of mine, there it was – blazing light!'

No mention of wings, but wings they clearly had.

They owned a factory making plastic bowls and mop buckets, everything for the kitchen, though nothing made of plastic ever turned up in their kitchen, that's if they even owned a kitchen, which was highly unlikely given that angels have no stomachs and as a consequence no need of food. A library, that was what Zoë remembered most vividly about their house, the rows of bookshelves holding books unlike the books her parents showered on her – the ballet books and how-to books and I-spy nature books with pictures of snails and flowers and empty pages to press flowers of your own in – no, no books of that sort on the Krystal shelves, but Freud, Kafka, Gombrich, Wittgenstein (unless she was imagining Wittgenstein because of his name's spitefully clever-clever all-mind-no-nature Jewish resonance), books with words in, words being the only thing her all-providing parents lacked, along, of course, with that which words enabled: worldliness. Celestial worldliness.

'It was as if they moved in another dimension,' she told me. 'Neither the inside as I knew it, nor the outside as I knew it. They inhabited somewhere else.'

'It's called Jew-space,' I explained.

'Now, to my cost, I know that. Then, what did I know? What you have to remember is that I only ever saw my father in an open-necked shirt or a windcheater with a bobble hat. One for in, one for out. Footwear the same. Carpet slippers for in, walking boots for out. What else did he need? Where else was he going? Then suddenly there appeared these other-dimensional men in suits that seemed made of silver foil, wearing shoes in whose reflection I could see my face.'

'We don't polish them,' I wanted her to understand. 'You buy them pre-lacquered. There are Middle Eastern shops on Bond Street that sell nothing else.'

'What, with the reflection of some gullible shikseh already burned in? How many pairs do you own, Max?'

'I don't know any gullible shiksehs . . .'

'Why don't you shut the fuck up and let me tell you what I'm telling you. This is my story, not yours. It's enough the Jews did this to me, without another Jew providing the fucking footnotes. What was I telling you?'

'Shoes you could see your fucking face in—'

'Don't swear at me. Why must you always swear? And without laces, these shoes! Can you imagine how amazing that was? My father squandered his life doing up his laces, foot up on a little kitchen stool, starting again each time to be sure the ends were even, a little tug after every hook, remembering to tuck in the

321

tongue, then twice around the ankle before being tied in a double hitch. That's how I defined a man. A person with his head between his knees, roping up his feet. Now here was this laceless breed, who in a single movement could slip their feet into their shoes and be gone. And ties! Before the Krystals came I doubt I'd seen a tie. And certainly not silk. Wool, maybe, for when my father came to a school speech day. Or to keep his trousers up at home. But the Krystals wore ties so refulgent, Max, they danced.'

I needed no convincing. Mine too. Once I was out of art school and no longer having to look like a goyisher housepainter, my ties leapt like Nureyev upon my chest. Never mind fringes and yarmulkes, a dancing tie is also a prescription of the Lord's.

But Selwyn and Seymour Krystal were scarcely older than she was when they blazed for her through their window that first time. Ten, eleven. Were *they* in Jewish showbiz business suits already?

'They were men, Max. They shaved. They had deep voices. They had the *charm* and confidence of grown men.'

'And you fell in love with them?'

'Of course. How could I not? But I wasn't just in love with the boys. I adored the whole family. I am not going to say they were warm – I've had it with warm Jews, Max. And it's a cliché anyway. It's how you like to see yourselves. Loving. Generous. *Gemütlich*. Fuck all that. What they were was hot. Hot in the words they used. Hot in the jokes they told. Hot in the hurry they were in to top one another's stories. Conversation was like a race. They didn't drowse away the days as we did, they consumed them, they burned time. It was like a mission – to grow up, to move forward, to get somewhere. I was exhilarated by them. They came through my life like a train and I had to jump on . . .'

Until they pushed her off.

Her breasts grew, but not too much, and Leila Krystal took fright. Poor Zoë. Of this part of the story at least, I believed every word. Oy gevalt, a gorgeous little shikseh with hand-grenade breasts and features so diminutive and precise she looked as though a fairy god had pinched them out of Plasticine. What chance of Selwyn and Seymour resisting that? She knew her boys. They weren't rompers or wenchers. Gentile girls with rosy cheeks and udders to their ankles came and went without causing any lasting damage. But this brittle and unblemished piece with a haughty, pointed nose and icy, tragic purpose in her eyes – no, the moment they noticed what she had grown into they would not resist her. She would call to them in their brief sleep from across the river and they would plunge into the freezing waters though they knew they could not swim. They had no choice. The ancient music sang in their bones. It was a compliment to Zoë of course, but you couldn't expect her to take it as one. Leila Krystal had been born with one foot in Berlin and another in Vienna, her mother had been born with one foot in Prague and another in Budapest, cities where beauty was understood to be a commodity you were a fool not to trade in if you had it. Telling Zoë to put on fishnet stockings and walk the Kurfurstendamm (or words to that effect) was not unappreciative advice. And who's to say it wasn't right, that this was not the big thing Zoë had been waiting for. Her calling. To be the whore to end all whores. After which, it was anybody's guess . . . A royal title? The movies?

I even put that to her once. 'Maybe Leila Krystal was your angel after all,' I said. 'Maybe she was showing you your destiny. And you blew it.'

'Only a Jew would have put her mind to what I had between my legs and seen a business opportunity in it,' she said, slapping my face, 'and only another Jew would have thought she was doing me a favour.'

She agreed with Hitler in the matter of Jews and prostitution. Hitler believed prostitutes were a Jewish invention, and Zoë swung between believing that every Jewish wife was a sort of prostitute to her husband and every Gentile woman was a prostitute in the eyes of every Jewish man. But they had it wrong, Zoë and Hitler both. There was nothing specifically Jewish in turning sex to your advantage commercially. The practice had attained a high level of refinement in what had once been the Austro-Hungarian Empire. It just so happened that in our journeying through this Gentile agglomeration of states, a number of us picked up the local way of thinking.

Thus Zoë's myth of exile, anyway. It was like listening to the Kabbalah. A paradisal unity shattered, the vessels broken, the holy sparks scattered far and wide. A war waged between true primordial light and its imitators. At the end of which – and this you don't find in the Kabbalah – poor little Zoë standing outside the gates of the garden, and the angel Krystal with his flaming sword, barring her from re-entering for ever. A myth of exile which she was bound to repeat, not only with me but *to* me, charging me with it whenever we fell out, for the reason that I was on the continuum of Jewish treachery which had precipitated it, and was therefore, in my own person, one of its primary causes.

Strange to say, I accepted this guilt. Just as I held every German alive or dead accountable for Germany's misdeeds, so did I shoulder responsibility for all acts of wickedness perpetrated or still to be perpetrated by Jews on Gentiles. A hard theology, but at least consistent. Bearing Five Thousand Years of Bitterness entailed bearing Five Thousand Years of Culpability.

Another way of putting that is to credit Zoë with the gift – oh yes, she was loaded with gifts, and not all of them went unexploited – of getting me to know what it felt like to be inside her head. I would watch her standing at the window after one of our fights, and I could hear the sea raging behind her eyes. She would try to look out of herself, notice something happening in the street, a person getting into their car, a mother wheeling a baby, but everything that wasn't me, wasn't her, wasn't the Krystals, would be swept away. Although she claimed she could remember every poisoned word Leila Krystal had said to her on the afternoon of the great betrayal, and every movement of Leila Krystal's bejewelled hands – 'Here, child, sit here,' patting the tapestried cushion on the deep-sprung buttercup-yellow sofa, and then two fingers on the point of Zoë's knee, as though she couldn't trust even herself to make more fleshly contact with the girl than that – the story never came out quite the same way twice; but that was beside the point, because the poison, like the sea, was cumulative, each dosage increased by the memory of how it was the last time she remembered. To get through today meant getting through last week, and getting through last week meant getting through the week before. It was beyond her. It stretched too far back. The sea of her shame – the multiplying shame of so many failures to throw off shame – crashed in her ears. Had Leila Krystal appeared before us and Zoë plunged a knife into her heart, the noise in Zoë's head would have been a mitigating circumstance. Not that it would have stilled the sea. Had she been able to quell the shame she would have been left with hatred, and had she been able to quell the hatred she would have been left with pain. Go all the way back, past the week before and the week before that, and she could only hope, at best, to come upon the little girl – for that was how she saw herself, no matter how luridly Leila Krystal apprehended her and feared her, just an unsuspecting little girl – whose starry, dazzling universe of love and optimism was about to be smashed into a thousand tiny fragments.

It had happened, could never be made not to have happened, would always go on happening – I was the living proof of that, another shatterer of stars, another stealer of Zoë's rightful glory – and only a brute would not have wept for her. Yes, she passed it on, made herself so vivid to me that for years the sea in her head became the sea in mine, though I have to say she was not herself made any quieter by the companionship. We simply suffered it together, until finally she saw that as the latest and most diabolical Jewish trespass upon her of them all – my attempt to muscle in on her sorrow.

After which there was only one thing she could say to me.

'What's the difference between a Jew and a pizza?'

'I don't know, Zoë. What is the difference between a Jew and a pizza?'

'Pizzas don't scream when you put them in the oven.'

6

They give him a postcard to send to his family. On the front is a photograph of a railway line.

'Here, Scooby-Doo, write to your parents.'

'Do you have other ones?' he asks.

'Other ones?'

'Different pictures.'

'No. What's wrong with this picture? We all like it, don't we?'

They all agree. They all like it. All things considered it's their favourite.

'What about stamps?'

'You don't need a stamp. We'll post it for you.'

'What about a pen?'

They give him a pen. Roll it in through the cell door, throw it on to his shelf, pop it into the glass by his bed.

He recalls marvelling that they would do this for him. A postcard, for God's sake! Yesterday they were getting him to eat his own shit, today they are providing postcards. What do they mean by it? He closes his eyes and opens them again, expecting the postcard to have gone – but no, it is still there.

An hour later they come to collect it.

'Written to your parents yet, Scooby-Doo?'

'I can't think of anything to say,' he says.

'Tell them about the weather. Tell them about your friends. Describe your day. Tell them what you do. Tell them how much you think about them. Say you wish they were here.'

But he can't. For some reason he can't think of anything that would interest them.

When they come to collect his postcard the next time they see he has addressed it, but otherwise left it blank.

'I would like this to go by the next post,' he tells them. 'There is some urgency.'

'But you haven't written anything.'

'I haven't anything to say.'

They scratch their heads under their caps and look at one another. 'We are not sure that it's allowed to send a blank postcard.'

'I don't think the post office will mind,' he says.

They laugh. 'It's not the post office that's worrying us. It's *we* who are not allowed to post a blank postcard. Who knows – it might be code. You might be conveying secret information.'

'I would use words for that.'

'Oh, would you!'

'If I wanted to, but I don't.'

They scratch their heads again, then one of them has an idea. 'We'll have to get you another postcard,' he says, 'so that we can watch you leave it blank. That way we'll know if you're up to anything.'

'Such as using invisible ink,' a second says.

'Or leaving it blank in a particularly suggestive way,' puts in a third.

'Why don't you do it for me?' he wonders.

They suck their teeth. 'Oh no. We can't write prisoners' postcards for them. We'll be accused of painting too rosy a picture.'

'Not if you leave it blank.'

They think about that. 'No,' they say at last. 'Then we'll be accused of being uninformative. You'll have to leave it blank yourself.'

They come back with a new postcard for him and smile between themselves when he fills in the address.

That's the moment he realises what they are up to. The reason they have given him a postcard to write to his parents is that he has no parents. The address he writes — s-sssch — is obsolete. They don't live there, no one lives there, any more.

S-sssch.

It is the same with his suitcase.

Twice a week they get him to sign for his suitcase. His signature is an acceptance that they are holding it for him with his permission.

'What's changed since the last time I signed?' he asks.

'You have,' they tell him.

'But what bearing does that have on my suitcase?'

'We want your signature before you forget.'

'Forget what?'

'Forget that you have a suitcase.'

'But if I forget, then it doesn't matter, does it?'

They accuse him of solipsism. Just because he doesn't apprehend his suitcase with his mind doesn't mean his suitcase doesn't exist. 'The suitcase is still there, even if you aren't,' they say.

'And why is that important?'

'It's important for our records. We need to know who the suitcase belongs to.'

'It belongs to me.'

'Not if you suddenly decide to deny it.'

'And why would I do that?'

'It's something people do who have lost their minds.'

'I don't know why that would worry you.'

'Because then we'd have a suitcase on our hands we couldn't account for.'

'Destroy it.'

They make a tutting noise in harmony, like a glee club. 'We couldn't do that. Too much paperwork.'

*   *   *

And how, I asked, was that the same as the postcards?

He was surprised I didn't see it. Because in both instances the efficiency of the system was on the line. And in the end that was all that mattered – the efficient working of the s-system. How well organised everything was, right down to the smallest detail, how much care they took, how much pride they showed in their work. And how hurt they would be when that was not appreciated.

It's when they come in with an iron and ironing board, get him to strip off his uniform and then order him to press the yellow star which adorns it, taking particular care with the six points, each of which must be smooth, and then when they begin beating him with their rifle butts because one of the points is not smooth, that I decide to say something.

'Why are you messing with my head, Manny?'

'People don't know how beautifully made those stars were—'

'Stop it, Manny.'

He looked away, up at the broken ceiling rose I was always promising Zoë I'd get fixed. His eyes were bluer than cornflowers. Confronted with such an expression, Shitworth Whitworth would have clobbered him for dumb insolence.

Had he been deliberately messing with my head, or was his own head so messed up that he no longer distinguished between what he'd read and what he'd experienced, where he'd been and where he had always feared they would take him?

'Do you want to know what actually happened?' he asked me, an hour later.

I made no reply.

'I lay on my bed and tried to find a justification for every crime that had ever been committed against Jews.'

'For twenty years?'

'Why not? I could have taken longer.'

'And did you succeed?'

'Yes. We deserved everything that had been done to us.'

'And did it make you feel better to think that?'

'Yes, it did. It's always better to feel you've played your part. Anything's better than being a victim.'

'And what do you think now?'

'I think anything's better than being a victim.'

'So you don't ever think of yourself as one?'

'As a victim? Me? How could I be? I broke the Ten Commandments.'

'Only one of them, Manny.'

'You can't break only one of them. Break one, break them all.'

'You told me that when we were kids.'

'Well, it's not going to change, is it?'

'So you reckon you got your desserts?'

He thought about it. Then he did something unexpected. He took off his jacket and rolled up his sleeve. He wanted me to see the numbers tattooed upon his arm.

TWELVE

Once he has served her, that's the end of him as man.

Ilsa: She-Wolf of the SS

1

Round about the time they were hauling Manny off to Belsen or Buchenwald or wherever he believed they were taking him, a young American film director, Don Edmunds, was handed the script of *Ilsa: She-Wolf of the SS*. 'This is the worst piece of shit I've ever read,' he said. When the producer peeled off $2,000, Edmunds relented. Maybe I can find something socially significant in it, he conceded. He shot the film in nine days on the abandoned set of *Hogan's Heroes*. Waste not, want not.

Errol Tobias must have told me this. Otherwise there's no explaining how I come to know it.

The film itself – more cartoonery than porno: hence my interest – I first happened upon in Amsterdam as I have already explained. That being my honeymoon, I never went to see it. We observe the decencies, we Jewish husbands, whatever else there is to say against us. But the memorandum I made to myself on a small folded-down corner of that honeymoon, to look into *Ilsa: She-Wolf of the SS* when I had a spare and more seemly hour on my ownio, turned out to be unnecessary. Before such an hour could be found, the she-wolf looked into me. The circumstances take a bit of unravelling. Errol had something to do with this as well. When did Errol *not* have something to do with the under-belly of my life? Zoë too. Errol and Zoë. Two people who could not have loathed each other more.

Why I didn't keep them apart is a question I have often asked myself. But it's possible that without Errol, Zoë and I would have never met. Or at least never got together. And there's also an argument – though it's a trifle far-fetched – that without Zoë, Errol and I would never have resumed our friendship.

We differed, Zoë and I, as we differed over most things, in the matter of how and where we made each other's acquaintance. She said it was in a crowd on Oxford Street watching a young Chinese man threatening to throw himself off the roof of Selfridges. I said it was when she was a kissogram at a party at Errol's. I remembered the person threatening to throw himself off a roof, only I remembered him as African. She remembered Errol – finally, and with a little coaxing, oh yes, she remembered Errol – but had no recollection of being a kissogram.

It was a disagreement, partly, about the nature of the word 'met'.

'I *saw* you that day in the crowd,' I admitted. 'I could hardly not have seen you. But we didn't meet.'

'You stared at me, appraised me with your eyes, like a length of cloth you fancied for a suit, then asked me what I was doing afterwards.'

'*Actually* asked you, or *appeared* to ask you?'

'I don't accept the distinction.'

'And when you say I asked you what you were doing *after-wards* . . . did I mean after the African jumped?'

'Chinese. After he jumped or after he didn't jump. You didn't specify. But there was a growing feeling in the crowd that they'd been cheated of their time and that he wasn't going to jump, so you could have meant after they'd dispersed.'

'I remember the disappointment. The impatience even, as though he was letting us all down by not carrying out his threat. You would have thought we'd paid good money for front-row tickets. If you're going to fucking jump, fucking jump, I remember hearing someone say.'

'That was me.'

'Before or after I asked you what you were doing afterwards?'

'Both.'

'And what did you say?'

'I said I didn't need another Jew in my life.'

'Did you say that *actually*, or did you *appear* to say it?'

'I don't accept the distinction.'

'Well, listening to your argument, it seems to me we didn't meet.'

'No. We met, I just didn't go to bed with you.'

'A pretty unsatisfactory meeting, then. You're lucky I didn't threaten to throw myself off Selfridges' roof in the African's place.'

She had nothing to say to that except, 'Chinese.'

The other version of our meeting, *my* version, begins in a pub out in the sticks somewhere near Borehamwood. I was lost. Trying to find Errol Tobias's new house. We had stayed in loose contact with each other, chiefly by virtue of Errol's needing to drop me a postcard once or twice a year to tell me what so-and-so's real name had been before he or she had changed it. 'Just a quick line to let you know that Mike Nichols was born Michael Peschkowsky, the mamzer. Don't do anything I wouldn't. Errol.' Or 'Long time no see, you meshuggener. Bet you didn't know Jane Seymour was Joyce Penelope Frankenburg. Worth a shtupp whatever her name. Go in health. E.' And once he surprised me as it were on my own doorstep. 'Here's one for you, Max. Max Gaines, publisher of the first ever comic books . . . Maxie Ginzberg. But then you probably knew that. All Maxies are Yiddlers.' This time, though, he had rung to invite me to a party. It was his fortieth birthday and he wanted old friends around him. The Bishops Blackburn Onanists reunited. To see how many – his joke – had gone blind. Kätchen, my girlfriend at the time, was reading me directions. Kätchen the blind navigator – my joke. It was when

333

we drove past this pub for the third time, Kätchen by now upside down in her seat trying to orient herself on the map, and I turning left when she said right, and right when she said left, on the assumption that every instruction she gave needed to be reversed, that we accepted our relationship was at an end.

'I'll drive you home,' I said.

'You aren't capable of finding my home,' was her reply.

'I'm just the driver,' I reminded her.

'Drop me at the pub,' she insisted. 'I'll pick someone up.'

'Ask me before you do and I'll describe him to you,' I suggested.

As it turned out, we both picked someone up. Zoë was dressed as Marlene Dietrich, sitting on a small round table, drunk, in a top hat and with her skirts up, showing suspenders and frilly French knickers. Not a sight you expect to see in a Hertfordshire pub. And the surprise for me was doubled because I recognised her at once. Where I recognised her from I had no idea. But I knew the fraught oval of her face as well as if it had haunted me in a dream. Once I placed her – and that was much later in the evening – I wondered if the agitation she caused me could simply be ascribed to the memory of a man throwing himself off a roof. The chances were, however, that it pre-dated that. I'd been waiting for her.

She was causing a bit of a sensation, titillating the drinkers and deliberately embarrassing the man she appeared to be with, a bit of a sensation in his own right, I gathered, on account of his being a twopenny-halfpenny actor in a onepenny-halfpenny television soap. No person of sound mind, seeing what she was up to, would have gone near her. But she was in lewd and angry spirits, her brittle body giving off sparks, the demureness of her countenance belied by or belying the promise she was holding out. And since when was a sound mind any defence against the Blue Angel?

She heard me asking for an address. 'What do you know? That's where *I'm* going,' she called over.

So, it turned out, were most of the people at the bar. It wasn't the fault of Kätchen's navigating that we were lost. Everyone was lost. In fact Errol's house was just a hop and a step away, but set back in a field that was invisible from the road, so that in the end a visitor had no choice but to go into the pub and ask the way. What had kept them, as it would surely have kept me, was the sight of Zoë in her underwear.

'It's not a fancy-dress party, is it?' I'd asked her.

She looked me over. 'Well, you obviously think it is,' she said.

I explained that I was an old Crumpsall friend of Errol's, and that in old Crumpsall we dressed for parties exactly as I was dressed, as though to carry a coffin. What was her excuse?

A good one, as it happened. She did not know Errol from Adam but had been hired to be a kissogram.

'Then let me deliver you,' I said.

I waited at the bar while she put on a coat and shook her actor friend's hand. 'Goodbye, Bollocky Bill,' or something similar. Zoë's heartbreak shake.

She wouldn't kiss me in the car.

'What kind of girl do you think I am?' she asked.

'A kissogram,' I replied.

'An actress,' she corrected me.

'Got it,' I said. 'An actress.'

'Yes, well, don't forget it.' Meaning don't go mistaking artifice for reality. Don't go thinking a naked thigh entitles you to naked thoughts. But also meaning, I thought I detected, don't go losing your heart. But it was a bit late for that. I already had.

Fifteen minutes later she was sitting on Errol Tobias's knee, under a sticky oil painting studded with Eilat opals of a holy man from Safed, singing – Zoë, not the holy man – 'Falling in love again, what am I to do . . .'

'Well, you could suck my dick for starters,' Errol laughed.

From the other end of the room came the sound of Errol's wife putting her fingers down her mouth and pretending to throw up. 'Yuk, Errol!' Melanie Kushner as was. Melanie Kushner, the girl with the woman's breasts, whose friend Tillie Guttmacher had given me the clap. Now a matron with a matron's breasts, three children to bring up, a shrine to Jewish shlock buried in the English countryside to maintain, and the moral decencies to uphold. 'Yuk, Errol!'

'Be fair,' Errol shouted back. 'It's my birthday.'

The disconcerting thing was that for a moment or two it looked as though Zoë might just take Errol at his word. She had that air – a woman who, by the paradoxes of a nihilistic intelligence, believing in nothing, was capable of anything.

In the end, the chance to show off her gift for cabaret – wasn't that what Leila Krystal had spotted in her as a girl, the licentious *liebeslieder* strumpet with tragic eyes? – overcame all other temptations. 'See what the boys in the back room will have,' she sang, and though I was later to be her husband and must therefore be accounted biased, I have to say I had never heard it sung, and never will hear it sung, with more sexual challenge.

I believe she did the Weimar lingerie with more vitality and wit than the original as well. It doesn't fall to every woman to pull off suspenders and frilly knickers. In order not to look desolate in that haberdasher's nightmare of ruffled silk and taut elastic, or not too trussed up in it, come to that, you need to give a suggestion of aloofness. But then again not too much. You have to show that you can do irony *and* corruption, funny *and* sad. A skill Zoë had off to a tee.

The rest of the evening was, for me at least, as a brief descent into hell. Devils clutched at me from every side. First Errol, asking how come I knew the kissogram and what about a swap. And when I asked him who the fuck with he said with Melanie who the fuck did I think with and did I have any objection to that. To which the answer was, well, any number, Errol, of which the fact of her being your wife, the fact of her unattractiveness, the fact that her friend had once given me clap (all right, crabs), the detail of her consent to a swap not yet having been asked for or given, to say nothing of my not being in a position to swap Zoë even had I wanted to, having only just met her, were but the first that sprang to mind. Then Melanie herself, arriving in the nick of time, for I couldn't of course say any of the above to Errol, with the kind offer of showing me around (as I hadn't yet seen it) the sick fantasy of ormolu and alabaster they called their house – a house which Zoë, collaring me next, referred to – with commend-able restraint I thought – as a palais de drek of a sort that only a Jew could want to live in, before dragging me into one of the bathrooms, the one with a Venus rising from the Dead Sea painted on the door, and giving me my kiss at last. Only we hadn't prop-erly locked the door – this being Errol's house, it was likely there were no proper locks on bathroom doors – and were discovered in embrace in the Romano-Israelite bath by Kätchen and Zoë's actor boyfriend, who had hitched up in the pub, decided they would come along to the party since that was where their part-ners had headed off to and they were so far from anywhere else, and were looking for a Roman bath to embrace in of their own. Fuck you, Zoë's boyfriend said, I wasn't sure to whom; fuck you, Zoë said in return; fuck you, Kätchen said to Zoë, and before I could say fuck you to anybody, Errol burst in, utterly unsurprised to see any of us there, but mouthing to me with an exaggerated roll of his Mephistophelian lips the question *WELL?*

Should I have told Zoë of Errol's proposal? Hell or no hell, did I owe her the truth? My friend wants me to swap you for his wife. I hate his wife, I hate him, I hate it here, I've only just met you but I love you – so what do you think?

No, was the answer. No I should not have told her. But I did tell her.

'Why?' she asked me.

'Why does he want to swap?'

'Why are you telling me?'

'Because . . .' Why *was* I telling her? 'Because I was afraid you'd think me a coward if I didn't. Because if I didn't tell you there would be an untruth between us from the start. Because it's funny.'

'If it's funny, why aren't you laughing?'

'Because it's not *only* funny. Because it's horribly depressing as well.'

'Try being more courageous, Max. That is your name, isn't it? Max? I always like to know a man's name before he trades me for his best friend's wife. You should have the balls to come clean. Either say you want it or you don't.'

'Want what? The swap? I want the plague more.'

'Then why did you bring it up?'

'I told you.'

She showed me the full sadness of her perfectly defined face, knowing she had nothing to fear from the closest scrutiny, knowing that wherever my eye lit, it would be pleased with the clarity of what it saw. Had I ever before seen a face less blurred, or one in which the relations of part to part were so chaste? Yes, as a matter of fact I had, in a crowd in the moment before a man fell from a roof. But that wasn't the first time either. The first time was in Siena, five hundred years or so before. A Sano di Pietro Madonna, that's who she was, without a baby to feed but otherwise with all the cares of Christianity on her shoulders. As for the sadness, it adhered to her face as an immutable law, as though perfect beauty must always expect an impossible perfection of appreciation, and so must always be disappointed.

And if you're a Madonna, the people who disappoint you the most, of course, are Jews.

'But what you told me was not the truth,' she said.

'You think I have a secret agenda? You think I want to roll between Melanie Tobias's fat breasts?'

'Well, who am I to say? But no, since you ask me, no, I don't think that. I think you want to disparage me.'

'Why would I want to do that?'

'You tell me. You're the pervert. Because you'd like me to do

338

a turn with you and your friend – how does that sound? Because you fancy a gang bang. But because you're ashamed of saying that's what you want, you plant the suggestion and then run away from it, hoping I will do the rest. You can't help yourself. You see a Gentile and you see sex.'

'Let me stop you there,' I said, gesturing at her naked Berlin thighs.

'Oh, don't be so fucking gross! At whose behest do you suppose I am dolled up in these ludicrous clothes? I play the slut you pay me to play. You aren't the first and you won't be the last. I seem to excite something in you people.'

'*We people?*'

'What – is it supposed to be a secret? Look around you, Mister Max. We're in a bordello designed by a rabbi who's lost his faith or his reason. It's like a whorehouse in Tel Aviv in here. If you were thinking that this was a good way of keeping a low profile, think again.'

'It's not my house, Miss Dietrich. And I didn't pay you.'

'You might not have paid me but you're happy enough to get an eyeful. And whether it's your house or not, you sure as hell don't look out of place in it.'

'That's because it's you who's doing the looking. *You* people only see what you want to see. You think we look at you and see a prostitute, but it's you who look at us and see a pimp. You aren't the first. And you sure as hell won't be the last.'

She appeared sorry for me, suddenly. She put her hand up to my nose. The merest touch at first, perhaps in fear that I might pull away, but gradually a more exploratory caress, ascertaining the soundness of the bone, the thickness of the cartilage, then feathery again, the movement of her finger tips almost trancelike, slowly tracing every contour, as though we both might find peace in it.

'Nice,' I said. 'Very nice.'

She seemed surprised by my docility. 'Would you let anyone do this?'

'Explore my nose? Only you.'

Finally she pinched my nostrils together and stepped back.

'It's very fine,' she said, 'but it will have to go.'

2

'Once he has served her, that's the end of him as a man.'

Interesting that in the movie none of the She-Wolf's victims is specifically Jewish. Why would that be? Good taste?

For months after that party Errol never left me alone. He was on the phone to me almost daily. What had happened to our friendship? Why were we seeing so little of each other? Was I aware that Yves Montand's real name was Ivo Levi and Simone Signoret's Simone-Henriette Kaminker? How long had I known the kissogram?

Eventually, because I couldn't face the hike to Hertfordshire, I invited him to lunch at my place in Belsize Park, the house I had once shared with Chloë, the house outside which we had parked our Völökswägen with the rabbi swinging in the rear window. He turned up in powder-blue pants and canary-yellow sweater with a flamingo-pink suede blouson hanging loosely on his shoulders. The warmth of the day explained his outfit partly. But I knew what explained the rest of it. Desire.

You could smell it on him. The thin, needling fetor of cold semen.

He was disappointed that it was only him and me for lunch. I watched him counting the cutlery and weighing up the salad. At every noise he started, hoping it was her. The kissogram.

'You live here on your own now, then?' he asked me more times than was polite.

'Since my divorce, yes.'

'Did I meet that one?'

'I don't think so.'

'Would I have liked her?'

'No.'

'Would she have liked me?'

I looked him over. The devil, presumably, doesn't change. As he was when an infant imp, so as a hundred-thousand-year-old demon. No healthy principle of growth. Errol the same. The bones still as cruel as ever, the skin still so fine a purple light seemed to shine through it. There is a sort of thinness that denotes abhorrence. An extremity of distaste which we expect to find in puritans and ascetics. The mystery of Errol Tobias was that he was capable of such fastidiousness of expression even while he rolled in shit. 'No,' I said – though he alone of all the Jews I knew was not particular from which direction he took a woman, which versatility Chloë might well have smelled on him – 'no, she wouldn't have liked you one bit.'

He laughed through his nose, pleased at the effect he might have had on my ex-wife, had he only met her. 'What's happened to us, Max?' he said, his face wrinkled into sentimentality. 'Why have we seen so little of each other?'

'London. London's like that. And anyway, look at us. You live in a palace . . .'

'Well, this isn't exactly a shit-heap. Belsize Park, for fuck's sake.'

'There's Belsize Park and there's Belsize Park,' I reminded him. 'And neither is Borehamwood. I live on a main road, I've got squatters dossing either side of me, I don't have two acres of garden, I don't have a tennis court, or a marble-pillared porch—'

'—or a swimming pool.'

'Exactly. Or a swimming pool.'

'But so what? You draw cartoons, I import wine. Sometimes I have a good year, sometimes I have a bad year. It must be the same for you. Maybe next year will be a good year.'

'Errol, this year *is* a good year.'

He wiped his mouth and took a look around. There was

something in the way he examined my work that told me he was putting his mind to how I could run my business better. First there'd be an exposition of the problem as he saw it. Then there'd be a game plan for the future. Then he'd present me with the bill for his services which he'd waive for a night with the kissogram.

'How much do you get for one of these?' he asked.

'No, Errol, we're not doing this. Sit down and I'll bring you cheesecake.'

'Could you do my family?'

I shook my head. I didn't do portraits.

'Could you do the house?'

I shook my head again. Ditto houses.

I did cartoons, full stop. And he wouldn't want anyone or anything he loved — not that there *was* anyone or anything he loved — in one of those.

He was frantic. There had to be something he could give me. In return for which . . .

'What wine do you drink?' he asked me.

'Errol, how can you ask me that? I drink whatever wine's put in front of me. So long as it's sweet. We drank Mateus Rosé with our curries, don't you remember that? And we found that somewhat on the dry side. We were wonderfully above wine. That's something I've been meaning to ask — where did it all go wrong for you? How come you became such a gantse wine-macher?'

'To tell you the truth it was a piece of mazel. First I met Melanie who had an uncle in the business. Then the Israelis captured the Golan and planted vines on it. Plus, you know me, I read a few books on the subject. And this is the result.' He opened his arms wide to show me the fruits, then remembered he was in my shabby sitting room/studio, not his palais de drek in Borehamrigid. Zoë's joke.

'How's your mother?' he suddenly asked me.

'She's fine. She has her kalooki, and of course her grand-children. How's yours?'

'Fine, too. She's still working. She must be the oldest hairdresser in the country. I've offered to buy them something down here, but they say they know no one. I tell them they know me and Melanie and their grandchildren, but they say they can't come and stare at us all day. So they stay in Crumpsall. How's your sister? Did she marry that yok?'

I clicked my tongue at him. Of all the Jewish fear words for the Gentile, yok is the most hateful. There are contested derivations of the term. Some say it denoted a citizen of York, where an angry and unlettered mob chose to believe the usual rumours and in the year 1190 massacred 150 Jews. Others see it simply as goy spelled backwards, with the final consonant unvoiced. I favour the former explanation. Goy is too neutral ever to have mutated into yok. A Jew can feel affectionately to a goy. But in yok you hear the baying mob. The lowest form of humankind. It expresses an indelible loathing. And that before it suffered comminglement with Errol's noxious spit.

'Do me a favour, Errol,' I said. 'Don't call him that.'

He backed off. 'OK. But we had a little quarrel with him in our family, don't forget. He moved in on my mother's business.'

'Errol, he cut about fifteen people's hair in a year. All men. I'd hardly call that *moving in.*'

Fine. He wasn't arguing. Not to meet my eye he began circling the room again, scrutinising my cartoons as though conscious that he hadn't done his best by them the first time round.

'Tell me something,' he said at last, 'do you ever worry what the goyim think?'

'In what sense? Do I worry that they miss the joke? Of course they miss the joke. They're goyim.'

'I don't mean that. I mean do you ever worry that you're telling them too much about us?'

'What, by blowing the lid on what we're like? You think they don't know? My position, Errol, is that they managed to detest and fear us well enough before I came along.'

343

'Don't you think they'd show us more respect if we showed ourselves more respect? For example, look at this . . .'

He extended his hand to a small drawing – one of a series illustrating Jewish jokes which I'd unsuccessfully pitched, when I was hard up, first to a publisher of greetings cards and then to a Christmas cracker company. It showed two stereotypical old Yiddlers sheltering under a tree and looking up at a bird which had defecated on them. 'And for the goyim they sing,' one of the men was saying.

'Yes,' I said. 'I'm looking.'

'Well, why's that funny, Max? What's amusing about Jews always seeing themselves as being shat on? Isn't it time we outgrew that?'

'It's time we outgrew making lists of Jews who change their names, but some of us do it, Errol.'

'I don't publish those lists for all and sundry to read, Max.'

'Ah, so it's not my shitting on those poor old Jews that bothers you, it's my doing it for the entertainment of the Christians. The accusation is not *Masochismus* but *Nestbeschmutzing*. Well, as far as charging me with *nestbeschmutzing* is concerned, let me tell you that others have got there before you. There isn't a Jew living who isn't guilty, in the opinion of some other Jew, of fouling the nest. Unless you take a vow of silence or wire your jaw you're a *nestbeschmutzer*. And if you do take a vow of silence or wire your jaw you're suffering from *Judische Selbsthass*. We either love ourselves too much or hate ourselves too much. To a Jew there is no acceptable way of being Jewish. Every other Jew does it wrong. And I can't say that aloud either in case a Christian hears. Which is the best joke about us of the lot. I must remember to find a Christmas card company to send it to.'

He made a placatory gesture with his hand, almost, but not quite, patting me on the back. Even though he hadn't touched me I could feel the skeletal outline of his fingers on my spine.

'Make fun of what I'm saying all you like,' he said, 'but there

344

are people out there ready to seize on everything we say against ourselves. Have you read *Did Six Million Really Die?*?'

'Why would I? I can tell there are no laughs in it. And anyway, I don't read books that have questions for titles. I like authors who know the answers.'

'This author knows the answers, believe me. *No, Six Million Did Not Die.*'

'Don't tell me. Five million, was it?'

'Too few to count, Max. And of those that did, most were victims of the Russians, illness, or an unwillingness to accept emigration. We're a pestilence on the face of the earth, and in a well-regulated world six million of us *would* die every afternoon, but as it happened, and in this particular instance, they didn't harm a hair of our heads.'

'Yep. I know. And this is the thanks we give them – inventing the chambers and the ovens.'

'Exactly. And claiming compensation for Jews who couldn't possibly have died or there wouldn't be so many of us left controlling the media, bankrupting the planet and stealing land from poor Arabs.'

'You shouldn't be reading it, Errol, it will make you ill.'

'Someone has to.'

'I agree with you. And better it's you than me. But I don't see what this has to do with my shitting bird.'

'They make their history by seizing on every instance of one Jew differing from another. They'd see you dead tomorrow, but if they can quote you against your own people they will make you a hero for a page. They'll even invite you to one of their conferences and be photographed with their arms around you. "Look – they're such liars, these Jews, that even Jews don't believe them!" They're besotted with us, Max. If you state that 260,000 Jews lived in the Baltic States before the German invasion, and I put the figure at 260,001, they'll use us to confute each other. They monitor everything we say and do.'

'Then they'll be monitoring this. Are you sure you're not becoming paranoid, Errol?'

'From you! Five Thousand Years of Fucking Bitterness!'

'That's not paranoia. It's history.'

'Well, they deny it, Max.'

'Well, let them. It will work in our favour in the end. If they're so determined to disprove all our complaints about the past, they have a stake in giving us nothing to complain about in the future. Think of them as the guarantee of our children's future. See it as having free bodyguards.'

He fell into an armchair and grinned at me. 'It's good to see you again, you meshuggeneh Yid,' he said.

I fell into an armchair opposite. 'Good to see you, too,' I lied.

'So?' he said.

'So?'

'So tell me about the kissogram.'

3

Did I want to defile Zoë as she claimed? Was it the case that I no sooner looked at her than I saw the whore of Babylon? And could it really have been my buried wish to have her get it on with me and Errol both – a stubby shikseh passed like a roach from Jewish hand to Jewish hand?

Honesty demands I be scrupulous about my dark unconscious, whether or not I thereby give ammunition to Gentiles on twenty-four-hour Jew-degeneracy watch. Beholding her bare-thighed on Errol's knee, outlola'ing Lola Lola – a joke she didn't quite get herself – did I not wonder how far, for veracity's sake, she might go? And when Errol put it to her that she might go so far as to suck his dick, did I post-date my dread that she might into an expectancy, an assumption – all right, all right, into a longing – that she would?

No. Yes. No.

But dreads do have a way of fulfilling themselves. And the time came when yes, God forgive me, yes, I did behold Zoë, or at least when I with good reason *imagined* I beheld Zoë – by then become my wife, a woman I had undertaken to honour and protect, Zoë Glickman, the mother-to-be of my children, except that we would have no children – yes, when I came as close to beholding as you can come to beholding without actually beholding, whatever it was I thought that I beheld.

Which answered, all things considered, to that longing I did not dare acknowledge?

Yes.

No.

Yes.

But yes or no, it didn't happen all at once. And that it did happen at all (*if* it did happen at all) was so contrary to any desires I recognised on the upper levels of my person that I reject as wicked libel Zoë's assertion that it was just another act of Jewish machination practised upon her innocence. First Leila Krystal, now me – no sooner did we see her trusting beauty, Zoë the unspotted, golden as the corn she came through, than the need was on us to befoul it.

Reason not the need, Zoë. Need never entered into it. Any befouling came as surplus to desire. And its object was me, not you.

Self-befouling, *nestbeschmutzing*, all the cunning cartoonery of the heart – we are too busy with ourselves, Zoë, to have time to worry about demeaning you.

Despite his continuing curiosity, I didn't bring Errol and Zoë into each other's company again for several years. Our friendship had been rekindled and we kept it up *à deux*, meeting each other halfway, as it were, in East Finchley, or Hendon, or other last outposts of the city where we had heard rumours of a new salt-beef bar or similar having opened. I am not sure why either of us persisted. It certainly wasn't for the food. Nor was it for the company, come to that. I always groaned when the time came to get ready and do the trek, and I never doubted that Errol felt the same. But we must have felt we were honouring something in our past, even if we couldn't have given it a name.

Though he never failed, the minute we met, to ask after the kissogram, and I never failed, the minute we parted, to send my love to Melanie, we otherwise avoided home talk. That way I didn't have to tell him I was getting married or invite him to the wedding, and he didn't have to involve me in whatever ceremonies of the hearth clicked off the years in Borehamrigid. Mainly we talked the emotional politics of being Jewish as we individually saw it: the philistinism of Hertfordshire and Crumpsall Jews (me), the shrinkage of the Jewish population due to intermarriage and name-change (Errol), the continuing silence of English Jewish intellectuals on Jewish matters (me), the refusal of Jewish readers to take Jewish cartoonists to their hearts (me), and of course Israel, about which there was good and bad to say, though Errol – again bearing remarkable similarities to Tsedraiter Ike who, after the Six Day War, had succeeded in getting half of Crumpsall to boycott the *Guardian* – never ceased wondering how as a Jew I could submit cartoons to papers which only saw the bad.

Plus we talked the Holocaust that wasn't.

In this respect, at least, we recaptured something of the feverish excitement of our youth – Errol inducting me into the salacities, not of the Swastika as Scourge this time round, but of the Swastika as Scourgee, were such a word to exist, the Swastika as Bemused and Slandered Bystander, the Swastika as Boon could we only see it, the Swastika as Benediction. The horror clocks might have stopped in Manny's head, but elsewhere cruelty was evolving nicely. No need for anything so crude as Ilse Koch's lampshades any more, no sadism so precise and graphic you could not have told it apart from your dreams, or told those dreams apart from fears of dreams to come, no, something far more subtly inhuman was afoot now – the gaze of insolent incredulity, denying even those who'd died the factuality of their death. The jeer of the SS militiamen that even if a single Jew survived, no one would believe him; Primo Levi's nightmare, the recurring nightmare of all the prisoners he knew, that were they to get home alive, not only would those dearest to them not give credence to their stories, they would refuse to listen, they would turn away from them in silence – these terrifying apprehensions of the limits of human sympathy, wherein, for his offence against metaphysical good manners, the victim becomes the perpetrator, these horrors had become realities.

'Only partial realities,' I said, trying to look on the bright side. 'There are a strictly limited number of these cranks kicking about, surely.'

'That's how forgetfulness starts,' Errol said.

I didn't know how forgetfulness started. But I accepted that even a single instance of it amounted to such wickedness that Elohim would have been within his rights to put a torch to us once and for all.

I'll show you fucking forgetfulness, you fuckers! Or however Elohim talks.

Looking back, I'm not sure that many people were then aware that a revisionist movement was gathering momentum. A few people who made it their business to be in the know (like Errol) had noticed that the German academic world was quietly realigning itself away from guilt, but that movement for reimagining German history which became known as the *Historikerstreit* had not yet publicly declared itself. Its chief architect, Ernst Nolte, was yet to oppose plans to build a memorial in Germany to Jewish victims of the Nazis, and yet to be caricatured by me, giving the Nazi salute (well, why not!) while declaring that 'To remember completely is just as inhuman as to forget completely', as though anyone had granted him the right to be exercising the slightest choice in the matter. And as for the now infamous whitewashes by more populist writers, English and American – they were still

349

to come. But Errol was in advance of his times. He knew so much that I sometimes wondered whether he wasn't in the pay of Mossad or some other secret Jewish agency dedicated to rooting out and hunting down our enemies. Were the wine-buying expeditions a blind? Did he go to Golan four times a year not to taste the grapes but to collect his instructions? I was the beneficiary of his knowledge anyway, that's if you can call knowing the name of every neo-Nazi slimeball able to find a publisher a benefit. But I too had a job to do. And it rarely happened that I left Errol without another tormentor of the Jews to add to my jest book of hellhounds – Alexander Ratcliffe, leader of the Scottish Protestant Party, early refuter of the Holocaust, and not averse to posing in Nazi regalia; Austin J. App, lover of literature, apologist for the Third Reich, and author of the *Eight Incontrovertible Assertions*, the most self-fulfillingly incontrovertible of which being that the Jews who died in the camps were criminals and subversives; Maurice Bardeche, a French critic with a Monsieur Hulot pipe, creator of the myth that gas was used only as a disinfectant, but blaming Jews for what happened to them anyway because they had supported the Treaty of Versailles; Paul Rassinier, another ruminative Frenchman, debunking the genocide with mathematics, totting them all up, the Yemeni Jews, the Polish Jews, the Turkish Jews – $(1.55 + 2.16)/2 = 1.85$ – as though algebra could refute witness, moving the figures about the globe until every Jew supposed to have gone missing in Auschwitz turned up in Tel Aviv or Rio; and so on and so on, the roll-call of infernal pedants, each egging on the other, none of them arguing from the impossibility of such cruelty, or belief in the essential goodness of the human heart, only the impossibility of the numbers, the failure of practice to live up to ambition, all of them bent on saving Jews from the gas chambers so that they could kill them again in their minds . . .

'You've got to listen to this,' Errol laughed one afternoon in a quasi-kosher café somewhere north of Muswell Hill. 'I've just been dipping into a book called *Imperium*. An anti-Semitic rant hundreds of pages long by a man called – and you're going to love this – Francis Parker Yockey.'

'Yockey by name . . .'

'. . . and Yockey by nature. Dead right. I knew you'd like it.'

'I don't believe you, Errol. You've run out of revisionists so you've newly minted this one.'

'Newly minted? Him? He's the fucking *father* of revisionism! *Imperium* came out in 1948, and even then he was saying there was no evidence of any gassing, the photographs were frauds, the Jews were a shagged-out people anyway, and blah blah blah.'

'What I don't get is why they aren't delighted it happened. Why, instead of doing the arithmetic of impossibility, they don't celebrate the mathematics of achievement. So many dead in so little time, hosanna, hosanna, hosanna!'

'Well, you'd think so with Yockey in particular, since he believes in anti-Semitism as a wholesome organism resisting the disease which is Jewish life.'

'Meaning that the body of society has a sanative responsibility to destroy Jews?'

'Exactly.'

'A bounden duty?'

'Nothing less.'

'In which case three cheers for Auschwitz, Buchenwald and Belsen.'

We'd have drunk to that, clashed our glasses of Russian tea, cut our hands open maybe, bled all over each other, chewed our fingers off in the frenzy, had we not remembered in time that we were in the Netanya Falafel Café, Friern Barnet.

4

And then, out of the blue, he suggests a charity kalooki night, his place.

'In aid of what, Errol?'

'In aid of a Holocaust Denial Fellowship.'

'You want to give them a fellowship?'

'Not the deniers, shmuck. We want to fund a lawyer to investigate ways of criminalising them.'

'And you think kalooki's the way?'

'Every little helps.'

'I'll contribute a comic strip.'

He looked disappointed.

'Fine. I'll write you a cheque. But no kalooki. My family plays kalooki, I don't. Not playing kalooki was how I learned to understand I wasn't my mother.'

'What about the kissogram? I bet she plays.'

'She doesn't play any games. It's against her religion. She plays the flute, the harp, the violin, the piano, the cello — all to concert level — but she doesn't play kalooki.'

'I'll teach her.'

'Errol, we're not coming. It's too far. I get lost.'

So he left a message on my answerphone, repeating the invitation. To both of us.

'Who's Errol?' Zoë wanted to know.

'You know perfectly well who Errol is. We met there.'

'What do you mean "there"? Is Errol a place? Besides, we met in Oxford Street, waiting for a Chinese to jump off a roof.'

'We met at a pub next door to Errol's. You were a kissogram. And he was African.'

'Errol's African? Never met him. And I have never been a kissogram. You've got the wrong gal, pal.'

'Palais de drek, Borehamrigid — ring any bells?'

She shook her head. Always pretty when she shook her head. Her nose like a little bell itself.

'Nope. But are we going?'

'Nope. You don't play kalooki.'

'How do you know I don't play kalooki? What is it, anyway? A Polynesian stringed instrument?'

'Well, if it were, you'd play it beautifully. It's a card g
You don't play cards.'

'Only because I was never taught.'

She turned it into a reproach. The things I never taught her!
The number of doors these Jews she had the misfortune to get
mixed up with slammed upon her genius!

I could have left it at that. She would have forgotten. But something – a little worm of perverse honourableness gnawing at my
heart (or was it some other part of me?) – made me tell her what
the kalooki evening was in aid of. After which there was no question but that we would go. Wherever she stood at any moment
on the Jewish question in general, Zoë was rock solid on the
Holocaust. It was Zoë, on our Jew Jew trip to Eastern Europe,
who had wept over every killing site, not me. Yes, she had
persuaded me to accept the apology of the German people, but
she would not have done that had she not believed the German
people had something to apologise for. It occurred to me as we
filled flasks, packed sandwiches, wrote wills and motored out to
Hertfordshire, that the fellowship should go to Zoë. The great-
ness that had always been in store for her, that special thing she
had been appointed to do before she died – was this not it: to
strangle with her bare hands every freak found crawling over
what was left of Auschwitz with a set square and calculator?

It's possible the same thought crossed her mind. She was highly
excitable when we arrived, murderously elegant in the European
introspective mode – Simone Weil, Hannah Arendt, Simone de
Beauvoir *and* Jean-Paul Sartre – in a black polo-neck sweater and
plain long black skirt, neither her wrists nor her ankles showing.
Zoë funereal, showing respect to the Six Million Dead.

'How do you do,' she said to Errol, extending her goodbye
hand as though to insist she had never clapped eyes on him before.
'What a beautiful house you have.'

I made a face at him not to let on he knew her. He wrinkled
his nose at me. *The devil knows what little fibbers women are, Maxie.*

Then he wrinkled his nose at Zoë.

I hadn't believed a word of Errol's story about raising money for a Fellowship in Holocaust Denial Denial, and so was surprised to see the make-up of the gathering.

'Christ, who are these people?' Zoë whispered to me. 'They all look the same.'

'They are the same,' I told her. 'They're all in charity.'

'How can you tell?'

'A cartoonist's trick. You have to scrutinise their faces very closely. The men all look as though they have something to repent – you can see it in the melancholy brackets round their eyes. And the wives have all got their tits out.'

She corrected me – 'No, *all* the wives have all got *all* their tits out. But why?'

'It's an unconscious expression of their givingness. Somebody says charity and they think of giving suck.'

'And this applies to all charity-givers, does it?'

'Only Jewish ones. The tit part anyway. Jewish women give more tit than Gentile women. It's their way of saying sorry to their boy children for subjecting them to circumcision. In fact the whole shebang is about saying sorry. The Jews are a highly apologetic people.'

'Oh, Jew Jew Jew!'

I shrugged my shoulders. It wasn't my fault that Errol Tobias had assembled half of fucking philanthropic Elstree.

Put the swearing down to Zoë. But also put it down to half of fucking philanthropic Elstree. If Zoë agitated me into near sociopathic philo-Semitism, fucking philanthropic Elstree agitated me, no less nearly, into its opposite. The stain of Crumpsall on me, was it? Something I believed they saw, whether they did or not? My origins in poor-house, atheistical Judaism? Yes, I was paranoid, without a doubt. But I didn't imagine the men with the bored, sad hoodlum eyes asking me what I did, as though they found it hard to believe from the look of me that I did anything, nor their expressions of the profoundest indifference when I told them 'cartoonist', nor their wet-nurse wives thinking that they might just have seen, at some time, somewhere, something or other I might have done . . .

The thanks you get for chronicling their Five Thousand Years of Persecution.

As usual, Zoë when they asked her told them she was a concert pianist and opera singer.

'You're wasting your time with that stuff here,' I whispered to her. 'If you want to impress this bunch tell them you're in fucking *Evita*.'

'I thought Jews were supposed to be cultivated.'

'Not these Jews. Different Jews.'

'Oh, Jews Jews Jews!'

Though she understood nothing of the principle of cards, Zoë threw herself into kalooki, won a hand, believed she had a natural genius for the game, lost a hand and left the table.

When I next saw her she was sitting on her own, weeping, in a small anteroom which I remembered Melanie describing, the night she showed me around the house, the night of Errol's demented proposition, as The Library. Most of the bookshelves were taken up with family photographs in rococo frames – the Tobiases grinning by the Dead Sea, the Tobiases grinning at the Wailing Wall, Errol sniffing Israeli grapes on the Golan – and those shelves that didn't hold photographs held glass paperweights which Melanie collected for want of anything else to do. But there were a few rows of books in gilt bindings – some in Hebrew, the sorts of books you were given for your bar mitzvah, assuming you were given a bar mitzvah, and a number of popular classics, a brown leatherette set of Dickens, for example, which a national newspaper once distributed to every family in Crumpsall, plus about two dozen Reader's Digest condensations. I had expected The Library to be given over to Errol's research interest, Yockey and his chums, and at first took these to be the reason for Zoë's tears. She had opened Rassinier, I reasoned, come upon $(24.8\% + 28.8\%)/1.85 =$ fuck you, and felt the ground go beneath her. But she did not have Rassinier beside her on the camel-hide and onyx couch, she had a collection of Errol's porno.

5

She hasn't shot him yet. That's something.

He has seen almost every part of her naked, and so is able to put an image of her together in his head. But she has forbidden him to do this.

'How will you know, Gnädige Frau?'

'I will know. I will see it on you.'

'But how am I to stop myself?'

'That's for you to work out.'

They have not yet discussed what will happen when she has no part of herself left to show him.

It occurs to him that she is saving something special for him. The climax. The 1001st night. When, in the moment before she shoots him, he is permitted to see the parts assembled, and to draw what he sees.

As always, her vanity makes her coarse. As his degradation makes him subtle. Does she not understand that the parts have become greater than the whole? Mendel's parents bought him jigsaw puzzles for his birthdays. They would do them together as a family, the three of them standing round the oval walnut dining table, not speaking, leaning across one another for a piece, their faces creased in concentration. The Tyn church. The wild crocuses in Lazienki Park. The Neris river on ice. Mendel remembers the disappointment of finishing. Now what? What's to be done with a completed jigsaw puzzle? They would leave it there for an hour or so, a disconsolate monument to the futility of human endeavour, then his mother would sweep the pieces back into the box so that she could set the table for dinner. Finding a piece on the carpet or under a chair, Mendel would marvel at the curiosity it rekindled. Where did that piece go again? Was it light on stone? Was it a crocus leaf licking the foot of Szymanowski's flowing sculpture of Chopin? – the statue Mendel remembered the Germans blowing up not many months after they marched into the city. Why would they blow up a sculpture of a composer? And what did the piece denote? So many questions attaching to such a tiny, foolish shape, endlessly intriguing in its male and female symbolism, on the face of it no different to every other piece, but in fact unique. Once in place, though, once its mystery had been plumbed and the questions as to its function answered, all interest in it faded.

The Germans could not abide a statue of a Polish composer to remain standing in a once Polish, now a German park. Was that because they too felt the anticlimax of completion and wanted matter returned to its component parts? Were they doing to humanity what they had done to Chopin?

If that were the case then Frau Koch was out of step with her co-iconoclasts. Not knowing that Mendel was more than satisfied to look at her in fragments, she believed he must be waiting to see her recombined. She was building up, she thought, to Mendel's big day, not knowing that every day that Mendel feasted like a slave on whatever scrap she threw him already *was* his big day.

Perhaps Frau Koch wasn't out of step in that case, and all Germans felt the same. They were not dismantling humanity for the pure joy of destruction but simply clearing the pedestals for the day when Germany perfected would be put on show. Behold the Godhead.

So they were not able even to pursue the logic of their own nihilism.

Frau Koch's unimaginativeness would be a trial to Mendel were it not, by the laws of his own subtlety, a further inducement to abasement in him. There would be nothing rare and strange about submitting himself to the whims of a woman of quality. Men do that every day and call it love and marriage. But to give oneself without modesty or restraint to a woman who possesses no qualities whatsoever – unless you count the coarseness of her intelligence a quality – there is satisfaction beyond words in that!

He is enjoying erasing his drawings at the end of every day. It lends purpose to his nights, imagining what he will see, what he will be drawing, what shape he will have to go grubbing for, in the morning. The anticipation of starting again, as though he never was and never more will be, excites him. The transience turns out to be voluptuous. *Einmal ist keinmal*, the Germans say. What happens only the once might just as well not have happened at all. Which is a clue to the force for repetition and self-commemoration that drives them. Mendel reads *einmal* differently. *Einmal* is the yellow of the crocus. *Einmal* is finding where the jigsaw piece goes. *Einmal* is seeing his mistress only one part at a time, and never that part again. *Einmal* is ecstasy. *Einmal* is art.

She wishes to discuss art with him. She is confused by what he has told her about caricature. He has told her that art is not the rendering of what is outside art. That art sees but remakes what it sees, in that way causing something to appear that wasn't there before. But to draw a caricature is to acknowledge dependence on something previous to the work, even to evoke something previous to the work, because it is only by recalling the original that the caricaturist can be seen to be exaggerating. In this sense, the caricaturist is the least godlike, most second-hand of all artists. But because the caricaturist is by nature a satirist, and the impulse to satire is denial, he is also the *most* godlike. In his act of creation, the satirist destroys.

He is careful to keep his disquisition simple enough to maintain her interest, but at the same time abstruse enough to guarantee him a beating.

He is drawing the fine isthmus of candle-white flesh above the Tubercle of Pubis. She has loosened her belt and infinitessimally eased her riding trousers down her hips so that he can see it well enough to draw. Three or four hairs of different lengths have strayed from her pubic triangle. He has seen a sufficient number of these hairs, now straying upwards, now straying down, now curling sideways, and now en masse, matted, like a tiny haystack, to reproduce Frau Koch's pubic triangle in its entirety were he of a mind. But he is not of a mind even to imagine it. The three or four stray hairs are more engaging. I am a man with a soul and an intelligence, he tells himself as he draws, I am here in fulfilment of some inscrutable but divine intention, and I will not be here again; yet there is not a part of me that is not at this moment concentrated on a single one of Frau Koch's nether hairs arbitrarily uncovered, a scratchy incidental filament which would assuredly have a sour odour if I could get my nose close enough to its smell, which resembles nothing more beautiful or significant in creation than the torn-off leg of a spider, and of itself and thus disposed fulfils no function worth putting the smallest corner of my imagination to. And yet, precisely for these reasons, and precisely because it grows from the body of a woman who fulfils no function worth putting the smallest corner of my attention to, my self-annihilating absorption in it is bliss beyond the power of dreaming.

She catches the shadow of his satisfaction on his face. 'Why are you smiling, Jew? You are not satirising me, I hope?'

'If I were, I would not be smiling, Frau Koch.'

'I will make it my purpose before I am finished with you, Jew, to drive all satire from your mind.'

'You already have, Frau Koch.'

She sits very still, like a model. Not in deference to his expectations as the artist, but because she does not want him to see anything more of her than his daily allowance. A rigidity which is the nearest she will ever get to understanding the punctilios of his perversion.

His member stirs, and she strikes it.

'And now your face . . .'

He brings his face towards her, an upward arc from below, and she strikes that.

He closes his eyes.

'Open,' she says. 'You cannot work if you cannot see. And you are forbidden to work from memory.'

He likes that idea and wonders if she is getting better. With time he could make the perfect mistress of her. He will say that for the Germans. They learn.

He is half inclined to make a satiric mark on the paper, as an encouragement to her to drive all satire from his mind.

She *is* getting better. She reads what he is thinking. 'Is it Jewish, this satire of yours, Jew?'

'It is, Frau Koch. Satire is written into our natures. Nietzsche believed we invented democracy out of a satiric impulse, as a refusal of aristocrats and heroes.'

She doesn't, of course, know who Nietzsche is. The education of the German people, though advanced, is a long way from being complete.

'So are all Jews satiric?'

'Only the clever ones, Frau Koch.'

'I thought you were all clever.'

'We are, Frau Koch.'

She strikes his face again, with her gloved hand. 'Don't be satiric with me, Jew. I have told you I will remove all satire from your mind. You have said satire is written into your natures. So if I remove the satire from the Jews, there are no Jews, *nicht wahr?*'

Ja wohl, Mendel thinks.

6

Errol had found Zoë in The Library, examining his shelves. If I was to trust her account, he had enquired as to her favourite writers and when she told him Jean-Paul Sartre, Albert Camus, Hannah Arendt and A. A. Milne, he asked her if she had ever seen *Deep Throat*.

'I thought this was intended to be a serious evening,' she told him.

'It is a serious evening. *Deep Throat* is a serious film. It's about a disability.'

She took two paces back from him, thought about quitting the room altogether, then decided to sit down. She needed, she told me, to compose herself.

'Max said you were raising money for some sort of Holocaust Fellowship.'

'We are. Are you interested in the Holocaust?'

Zoë detected insult in that. We were a phobic, perceptually oversensitive, paranoiac couple. Or at least we were when we went out in each other's company. If I didn't detect an insult on my own account, Zoë detected it for me. And vice versa. But on this occasion Zoë had done all the detecting necessary for herself.

'Why shouldn't I be interested in the Holocaust?' she asked. Meaning – but it was obvious what she was meaning.

'No reason. I am pleased you are. It is important that you should be.' With which he opened a cupboard in his bookcases, brought out a bundle of what turned out to be pornographic magazines and films, and tossed them to her on the sofa. 'Holocaust material,' he said. 'You choose.'

'So now,' she told me when I found her, 'I say the same to you. "You choose."'

I made an automatic move in the direction of Errol's 'material'.

'Don't be a fucking moron, Max. What you're choosing is whether we stay or go.'

It was one of those moments. Even at the time it felt like one of those moments. Though of course, as with all moments that are moments, the true consequences are not fully revealed until long afterwards. There it was, anyway. Maxie's Choice. Did we go or did we stay?

It should have been cut and dried. We should have gone. I knew what Zoë thought. *Get us the hell out of here, Max.* The issue waiting to be decided wasn't what we should or shouldn't do, what hung in the moral balance was me.

That I 'chose' unwisely, I put down to several factors. I was tired, and didn't immediately feel like driving home. Errol and Melanie Tobias were my friends, and I didn't see how we could walk out on them just like that. What is more, if Errol had intended to treat my wife insultingly, the right thing was to get him to apologise, not to cut and run. In later conversations, Zoë would have none of these. 'The night held out unholy promise,' she insisted, 'that was why you chose to stay. You chose to stay because you couldn't bear what you would miss out on if we went.' To which my reply never wavered. 'It wasn't the night that held out unholy promise, Zoë, it was you.'

The bare facts were these. Errol had thrown a bundle of porno on the couch for her to look at. There was without doubt sexual provocation in that, though he was not to know that Zoë believed a Jew had only to look at her to see a whore. Upset or not, Zoë could have got up and walked into another room, said not a word about it to me, and that would have been the end of it. For her to have turned it into a melodrama of decision for me – '*Your choice, Max*' – merely proves that she had made herself imaginatively complicit in a narrative which began in porn and ended in her becoming the whore she believed Errol and I took her for. Her fault then, I maintained, if I failed to make the right choice – her fault for enticing me into making the wrong one.

But I accept that even when the charge is enticement, the enticed party, like the insulted shikseh, is free to get up and walk into another room. I could have driven us both home, *should* have driven us both home, however much unholy promise Zoë's frightened eyes held out to me.

It happened, anyway, as Zoë, without a word, had warned me that it would. I am not going to relate it in any detail. One can do justice to degradation in bare outlines. Kalooki'd-out at midnight, the party broke up. Only Zoë and I remained. Errol poured us brandies and turned down the lights. Zoë, never so much as blinking in my direction, did what she had earlier and insultingly been bid to do, selecting *Ilsa: She-Wolf of the SS* as most appropriate to the occasion – unsparing depiction of the Third Reich, in whatever form, being as requisite to her view of history as it was to ours. We watched the flickering screen, roused by the silent act of watching rather than by what we watched. The She-Wolf was the disappointment all heroines of pornography turn out to be when they walk out of your imaginations. Not only was she without interesting views on the Jewish question, she didn't remotely look the part, her sloppy-titted blowsiness bearing more resemblance to the charitable sucklers who had just left us than the louche and lazy-eyed Ilse Koch whose acts of barbarism had scorched the gardens and backyards of Crumpsall all those years ago. I would have said as much to Errol had the opportunity arisen. I would have complained, not least, that there seemed to be no Yiddlers among those whose private parts the She-Wolf was intent on getting rid of. 'So what gives here, Errol? More revisionism? No Jews among the howling castrati?' But criticism of the film was moving along a different groove. Zoë's doing. She had begun by snorting her derision. 'Don't tell me this crap turns you on,' she asked, of me and Errol both. 'Shut up, Zoë,' I told her, not because it did turn me on but because I was trying to work out why it didn't. 'Sit near me,' Errol said, 'if he won't talk to you.' 'You should be ashamed, the pair of you,' Zoë said, 'I'd be weeping if I wasn't laughing.' But she still went over to the couch on which Errol was sprawled, to punish me, I calculated, for being turned on (which I wasn't), for not weeping (which in some part of me I was), for not choosing the option of taking her home (which I wished I had) and for being a Jew (which I couldn't help). That there was no logic in her decision to punish one Jew with another there seemed no point in my arguing. Besides, no sooner did Zoë move to Errol's corner of the room than Melanie moved to mine. What Melanie then made happen was interesting to me only in so far as it might have been a mirror image of what Zoë was making happen. I will say no more. I kept my eyes on the screen until there was no torture left for Ilsa to inflict and no character left living for her to inflict it on. The camp was set alight, Ilsa got hers, the credits rolled and that was the Holocaust that was. After which we turned on the lights, rearranged our clothing (unless I imagined that), thanked our hosts and drove home in bitter silence.

So it was Goodbye, Bollocky Bill.

Not in one bite. I find it hard to remember now how we managed to remain married for so many years in spite of that kalooki night. By not referring to it, partly. By neither overtly charging the other with impropriety. But my failure to be the man I'd promised her I'd be was always with us. And we both knew she would finally have to pay me back for that by leaving me.

I hadn't done what I'd said I'd do. I hadn't broken the chain of disparagement. I hadn't hushed the crashing in her head. I hadn't become the soil in which her genius for genius could flower. I'd stayed Jewish.

She was so distressed when she shook my hand the final time she grew diaphanous. I could see into her nervous system. The *Daily Express* had a 1930s glass-walled factory in Manchester where you could stand in the street and watch the papers coming off the presses. My father, a transparency fanatic, used to drive us into town to look. Zoë reminded me of that building. In extremis she showed you her workings.

I had done a cartoon of her in that condition for one of her birthdays. The Transparent Woman. She hadn't been amused. 'I can't see why the joke entertains you,' she said, 'you being so hidden yourself.'

'I'm not hidden,' I protested. 'I show you everything.'

'No, you don't. You are a devious little prick. You show me nothing that you haven't calculated on showing me. You are entirely hidden. You all are. You have to be. You can't afford to let us see what you are thinking. That's my definition of a Jew. A person who won't ever let you know what he thinks of you, because if you found out you would leave him. That's how terrible the thing he's thinking about you is.'

And was she right? Did I keep a monstrous idea of her somewhere about my person?

Put it this way: I should have driven her home.

As for her transparency, well, apparently I had that wrong too. 'Most of what you think you saw in me you didn't,' she told me just before she left. 'Except of course for the blow job.'

I didn't rise. 'Goodbye, Zoë,' I said.

'The blow job you thought you saw me giving your vile friend whatever-his-fucking-name-was, in that gross palais de drek in Borehamrigid . . .'

'Leave it, Zoë. Just go.'

'Well, you were right.' She gave one of her tinkling little laugh-less laughs. 'I did. I can even describe his prick to you. Slender and sulphurous. And scaly, like a serpent's tail.'

I shook my head, not wanting any of her words to lodge.

'Just thought you'd be pleased to know that,' she said.

And was gone.

THIRTEEN

1

'So who was living here?' Manny asked in a rare outburst of curiosity. As he'd insisted he needed no more than a couple of hangers for his things – 'Three, at most' – I hadn't thought it necessary to clear out the wardrobe.

'An ex-wife. She left a few dresses and I haven't had the heart to get rid of them.' A reward for his rare outburst of curiosity: a rare outburst of candour.

'When did she leave?'

'Seven, eight, nine years ago.'

'And what number wife was she?'

'Two.'

'Two out of how many?'

'Three.' I said it sheepishly. Don't ask me why.

'And didn't the third object to these?'

'To the clothing of the second? No. She never came in here. We weren't married long enough for her to need the refuge of a granny flat. Though long enough for me to wish she'd moved into it.'

Manny ran the tips of his fingers through his omelette hair and made a clicking sound with his tongue which I took to be an act of judgement.

'There won't be any more,' I said.

'You don't have to apologise to me,' he said.

Didn't I?

I believed I did. Or if not apologise, at least be careful. You don't go around advertising the tumult of your marital life to someone who has had no marital life, tumultuous or otherwise. I had behaved badly enough all those years before, flashing him

Märike on the library steps. And that was when he was still in with a chance – on paper, if nowhere else – of finding love and happiness. Now that we could definitely say goodbye to any such thing, it behoved me to proceed with even greater circumspection.

In which case I should probably have thought twice before offering him the flat, or failing that removed the last of Zoë's clothes from the wardrobe. But since I hadn't, I owed it to both of us to question my motivation. It couldn't be, could it, that I was somewhere *still* wanting to exult sexually over Manny?

Ask me what I could possibly have found to exult about and you have me. But what if that precisely was the monkish function I had allotted Manny from the start – he was the measure compared to which my life was *all* exultation?

A thought occurred to me. Was that the function Asher had allotted him as well? Did Asher prance before his brother?

'Who was she then?'

He startled me. I was showing him round the kitchen, thinking my thoughts, wondering if he looked at the world as the world looked at him, or whether by his own lights he didn't remotely suffer in the comparison with me or Asher as I feared – as I, perhaps, had no *right* to fear – because he attached small value to acts of love and desperation. Not everyone was a lover. Not everyone was a husband. Some people – I had constantly to remind myself of this – lived an uncompanioned life because they wanted to.

'Zoë?' I paused. Here we were again. How could I not upset him with Zoë? What version of Zoë was there that wouldn't be unhinging to a man who'd spent his life in detention? 'A woman driven to distraction by Jews,' I decided to say.

He was counting the knives in the cutlery drawer, as though fearing I would charge him with their theft when he left. 'What did we do to her?'

'We made her feel disgusted with herself.'

'For not being Jewish?'

'You have it in one, Manny.'

'It's no more than they do to us.'

'I agree, it's no more than they do to us. But that doesn't make it any better. Indeed it makes it worse, since we know what it's like.'

He fell quiet, starting on the forks. 'That argument has got us into a lot of trouble in the past,' he said.

'And got me into a lot of trouble with Zoë,' I agreed. 'She thought it was another example of Jewish ethical haughtiness. All that Light Unto Other Fucking Nations Bollocks was how she alluded to it.'

'But she married you.'

'Yes. She hoped I might change the way she felt.'

'And you didn't?'

'Oh, I did. I made her hate Jews even more virulently than she had before.'

He was still not looking at me, still counting and sorting cutlery. 'How did you do that?'

'Long story,' I said. 'Look, would you stop with the knives and forks.'

He jumped, startled. Deprived of anything to absorb his attention, he was reduced to facing me. And no sooner did so than he appeared to find me, or something I stood in the way of, interesting. I had the feeling that he was trying to look behind or beyond me. What had I said, I wondered, that he wanted to verify?

'Why do we do it?' he asked.

'Why do we do what, Manny?'

He was still deciding, still verifying. I felt he was interviewing me in some way, testing my worthiness.

'Why do we make it so hard for them?'

'You mean our Christian brothers and sisters?'

'Everybody. Everybody who isn't us.'

I shrugged. What did I know other than that I was growing uncomfortable with this 'we' and 'us' business. What had Manny done to our Christian brothers and sisters? Manny's bag was killing Jews, not Gentiles.

Then I realised that if I shut my mouth and just stared into the vast blue incoherence of his eyes and let him talk, he would tell me at last what I had been employed to hear.

2

Dorothy.

From Zoë, don't ask me how, Manny had got to Dorothy.

From shikseh to shikseh was the overarching logic, of course – it was the individual moves I hadn't followed. But here we were, however we had got to her, at Dorothy.

Dorothy and Asher met again. That much Manny had already told me. Not an arranged meeting, an accident. A happy fortuity, allowing that a happy fortuity for one (or two) people can be a catastrophe for others. A chance happening, anyway. Asher shuffling along, hollow of lung, cavernous of cheek, a ruined man, a holy tramp with a broken heart – a hero of the affections to me, even if he had capitulated to sectarianism – when suddenly, coming in the opposite direction, still beautiful, swinging her hair, but with little grey pinpricks of sadness in her alpine eyes, Dorothy!

KERPOW!!

What I didn't know was that the happy fortuity had taken place in Israel. Crumpsall was where I'd pictured it, and even Crumpsall, in these circumstances, was not lacking any of the romantic associations necessary to send both their hearts skidding from their moorings. Just thinking of their meeting after so many years – ten, twelve, was it? – just imagining that first astonished convergence of their eyebeams, was enough to affect my breathing, however blank in actuality the streets. But Israel! The place where miracles happened. The place where, taking the long view – God's covenant with the Jews, etc – all Dorothy's and Asher's troubles started, and yet where, as the plastic surgeon who wouldn't work on my nose insisted, the reconciliation of every warring people would at last, in readiness for the final trumpet, be effected. If Asher and Dorothy were to be given a second chance of happiness before the world ended, Israel surely was the land to give it to them in.

Asher, it seemed, had been living in Israel for several years. This was why, after he had parted from Dorothy, no one outside his family had seen or heard of him. As part of his continuing convalescence – because running around Lymm in a vest and gym shorts was not mending his spirits – they had packed him off to Israel. For generations of wealthy Gentiles wanting to extricate their heiress daughters from the influence of penniless ne'er-do-wells, some of whom would doubtless have been Jews (for yes, there were, there *are* such), the Grand Tour always did the trick: a visit to the Paris opera, the statuary of Florence, a gondola ride in Venice, the ruins and fountains of Rome, and latterly a finishing school in Switzerland, or a sojourn at the court of Herr Hitler. A change of scenery and language, it was believed, a variety of diet, would change and varify their minds. Imagine, for example, what would have happened to any anglo-Yiddler romance the Mitford sisters might have been enjoying in London once they'd strolled out across the Wilhelmplatz to lunch on pig's knuckle with the Führer. Kaput. All forgotten, you can be sure, all wiped from the memory in one mesmeric smile. Jewish families with a son or daughter to de-Christianise, especially Jewish families with no money, had to make do with Israel. That there was danger associated with this cure never seemed to worry those who resorted to it. As a yeshiva boy, Asher was exempt from conscription, but he volunteered for the Israeli army despite that, only his lungs saving him from combat. He volunteered again at the beginning of the Six Day War, but the conflict was over before

they could check his chest a second time. Poor Asher. I saw something Byronic in it myself. Very likely he wanted to be killed in
a cause unrelated to his sorrow. But whether he did or he didn't,
one thing was certain – however hard his parents would have
taken his death in a desert or at a border crossing, better that, a
thousand times, than death by intermarriage. Irrational in the
extreme, but then those Gentile heiresses had likewise to take their
chances with pirates on the high seas or malaria in Rome. It is
not uncommon for parents of all faiths to prefer their offspring
dead than wed.

Lonely and directionless, unable to martyr himself in the
Zionist cause and unable to forget Dorothy – unable to forget
how he *felt* when he'd been with Dorothy, that was the thing;
unable to reconcile himself to feeling any other way – Asher
began to turn peculiar, growing his hair, wearing flowing robes,
and making a nuisance of himself at the yeshiva where he set
himself to doubt every tenet of the Jewish faith, including God.
There being nothing that teachers at a yeshiva love more than to
argue a Jewish boy out of his erroneousness, he found himself
the centre of attention. When he challenged them to prove
Hashem's existence they cleared their throats and started. Time
was no consideration. If it took them seven times seven years to
prove to Asher that Hashem existed, who worried? Who worried
if it took them another seven times that? Proving that Hashem
existed was what yeshivas were for. Dressed in a long white gown,
with his hair down to his waist, and convinced of the importance
of his views – so attentive were his teachers to his arguments –
Asher began to wander round Jersualem, for all the world another
Jesus Christ, or maybe even the old Jesus Christ come back to
have a second crack at redeeming mankind.

It was then, word having got back to the Washinskys that their
son was passing himself off as the Messiah, and, worse, was not
eating enough, that they sent Manny over to see what was amiss.

Their action might have been concealing another motive. It's not impossible they felt that Manny too would benefit from a change of air. Get out from under the stone he chose to live beneath. Feel a bit of sun on his skin. Who knows, find himself an Israeli wife.

Then again, that could simply have been my interpretation of what he needed.

It wasn't kind of me to have looked so astonished at the idea of Manny travelling to Israel, but there was no hiding it – in all the years I hadn't seen him prior to the gassing of his parents I had kept him safely, like a spider in the corner of my imagination, suspended between Crumpsall and Gateshead. Indeed, that was how I understood the gassing of his parents. He was deranged with the Orthodox uneventfulness – ritual apart – to which his life had been reduced. If it now turned out that he had been a gadabout, a citizen of the world with his own passport and airline tickets tumbling from his pockets – well, I was pleased for him, but he had more to answer for.

The wonderful thing about having the Messiah for a brother, and for Jersualem being his address, is that you walk into him the minute you get off the plane. There is the Temple Mount, there is the Western Wall, there are the observant Jews winding themselves into their cat's-cradle phylacteries, and there is Asher!

Manny hadn't seen his brother for many years. They fell into each other's arms and wept. They were not alone. The Western Wall is a weepy place. Here, with emotion which can be too much to bear, Jews celebrate their unimaginable return. And here the two brothers sobbed over their unimaginable encounter. When they had last talked to each other the Wall was in the hands of the Jordanians. And Jews, as is sometimes forgotten, were not allowed to worship at it. Who could have imagined then, in Crumpsall, that the ancient Jewish hope, 'Next year in Jerusalem' – for so long more a velleity than a hope, the feeblest and most unanticipated of anticipations – would be realised in their lifetime and that they would be able to stand here, under the watchful eye of Israeli soldiers, but otherwise unimpeded, together? Crumpsall – was there such a place as Crumpsall? Were there even such people as their parents?

Manny felt the sun on his neck, smelled his brother's perspiration in his hair, and believed he would never leave.

Asher made up a bed for him in a room no bigger than a hermit's cell in a building so ancient that Manny believed it was only prayer that held it together. He slept for two whole days, exhausted not so much by the journey as the preparations for the journey, the instructions with which his parents had charged him (and which he had now forgotten), and by the white light which had stung his eyes from the moment he had walked off the plane. On the third day Asher shook him awake. 'Time to see where you are,' he said. 'Time to see your country.'

It seemed to trouble Manny that he could not decide what colour Jerusalem was. Was it yellow, gold, bronze, or just luminous – no colour in nature at all, because it was set apart from nature, exquisite in its separation, like the incontrovertible expression of God's will? If you tried to imagine the colour of Elohim's countenance when it shone upon you – what the Jews called the Shechina, the divine refulgence – this was the colour. He also could not decide whether Jerusalem was beautiful or a rubbish tip. Everywhere you looked, stones. Great hewn boulders that might once have been the walls of the Temple, but might just as easily have been the stones rejected at the time of the Temple's construction. Discarded and left to lie where they fell for the next two thousand years. But each fragment with something to tell you. The whole city was like a whispering gallery, every atom of every stone clamouring for your attention. It made some people ill, Asher told him. It made them run from the city with their hands over their ears. But Manny feasted on the stories. He might as well have been deaf for all Crumpsall ever said to him, but he listened to Jerusalem with the attention of a long-lost friend, gorging on gossip.

'You're getting hooked,' Asher told him. 'Let's take a bus.'

From the windows, Asher pointed out the sites of learning and devotion, triumph and resistance, they both knew from the Torah. Manny sat open-mouthed as everything he had ever read about flew by. He was astounded by the variety of Israel's geography, as though the Almighty had put the best examples of his work in this tiny wedge of land he'd reserved for the people whose seriousness and devotion to study pleased him above all others. One minute they were in the mountains, heading for Safed where the ceilings of all the synagogues were bluer than the clouds, the next they were peering into the sink of the planet, the lowest point on earth, where the very light was crystalline with salt. Asher's preference was for the silence of the desert; Manny, to his own surprise, loved the lakes and seaside – the sight of Jews frolicking in their own water as unselfconscious as batesemeh at Morecambe Bay so astonishing him that he would stand there for hours at a time, on the beach or by the water's edge, fully dressed, with his hands in his pockets, shaking his head. Jews running, Jews swimming, Jews fishing, Jews eating what did not to Manny look or taste like Jewish food at all. 'That's because you're used to eating Polish slop,' Asher told him. 'This is *real* Jewish food. It's got the warmth of the Mediterranean in it. Enjoy!'

At first, Manny had been frightened by the Israeli soldiers who looked like Arabs and comported themselves like warriors, themselves afraid of no one; but he grew used to the blackness of their skin – blacker even than Asher's – and the fierceness of their eyes and wished at last that he had not been born the colour and the constitution of cream cheese. If he stayed, would he at last look like them?

He had been sent to see how Asher was, perhaps to persuade him to return to Crumpsall, to save him if he needed saving, but within a couple of weeks of being in Israel Manny believed it was he who had been saved.

Once, when he was sitting by Lake Galilee eating falafel and drinking kosher beer with his brother, he noticed that his legs were extended in front of him. For a moment he wasn't quite sure he recognised them. If those were *his* legs – and whose else could they have been? – then what were they doing there? Manny always sat with his legs tucked under his chair, his trunk tilted forward, no part of him allowed to wander too far from his control. If he wasn't mistaken, what he was doing now, in Tiberias, in the shadow of the Golan, in the sunshine, in his brother's company, was relaxing. Many more weeks of this and he too would be growing his hair long, wearing flowing robes, and – why not? – healing lunatics and walking upon water.

Many more weeks and he might be able to leave Asher's room without trying every light switch a dozen times, for fear that he would leave on a lamp which would burn down all Jerusalem.

This is not to say he was not concerned for Asher's mental health. Even when he seemed most to be enjoying showing Manny their brave new world, throwing himself into talk and explication, Asher was somewhere else: preoccupied, no matter how attentive he was to his brother's curiosity; gaunt, no matter how well they feasted; forlorn, no matter how much they laughed. One warm Tiberias afternoon, as they were walking round the tomb of Maimonides (nicknamed The Rambam after his initials, Rabbi Moses Ben-Maimon), Asher brought up Dorothy, until then a subject strictly not alluded to between them. They were discussing, at Manny's instigation, The Rambam's famous demonstration of the Creator's incorporeality and singleness, his freedom from external influence, his dissimilarity from any other being or concept. If Asher *had* become a sort of Christ figure who challenged his teachers to prove the existence of Hashem, where, Manny wondered, did he stand on at least the first two of those four divine attributes? But it was not Jesus or Hashem who preyed on Asher's mind. 'That expresses exactly how I feel about Dorothy,' he explained. 'There is no one else like her. There *can* be no one else like her. She bears no resemblance to any other being or concept. She is indivisible in that I do not diminish her in my mind by comparing her with other women, and she is incorporeal in that I do not touch or even see her, though I imagine that I see her at least twice every day. So if it is right that we should worship no other God because of His singleness, then it must be right that I should love no woman other than Dorothy because of hers. And don't tell me that immoderate love for anyone who is not God is idolatrous. I know it is idolatrous.'

Manny was not shocked by this. At one level his brother's inconsolability pained and angered him. Unforgivable, he still found his parents' brutal interference in Asher's happiness. At another level he was relieved that his brother had not, after all, become an unbeliever or a Christian mystic.

The Rambam, in his measured way, had written against intermarriage, but not, Asher argued with fervour, because he believed, as the anti-Semites charge the Jews with believing, that Jews were too sacred to be contaminated by union with anybody else. What the goyim never seemed to understand, Asher explained, as though he had forgotten that his brother had been educated into these things too, was that separation was a condition of holiness, not haughtiness. To give yourself to God, which is the same as giving yourself to seriousness of mind, you must sever your connection with the frivolous and worldly. That was the meaning of God's half-promise, half-injunction, that his 'people shall dwell alone, and shall not being reckoned among the nations'. They were to dwell alone, not because they were superior, but because aloneness was the fate for which they were best fitted. In his *Guide for the Perplexed*, Maimonides never once argued that the Jews were special by virtue of being 'Chosen'. His interpretation of the chapters of Deuteronomy that forbade marriage to the daughters of the Hittites and the Girgashites, the Amorites and the Canaanites, the Perizzites and the Hivites and the Jebusites, turned upon God's jealousy. The reason for not lusting after these women was clear: 'For they will turn away thy son from following me, that they may serve other gods.' 'The ridiculous part of it being,' Asher said, 'that Dorothy never once tried to turn me away from Hashem, or from anything else Jewish, come to that. She did not want me to serve other Gods. She wanted to serve mine. And it was I who closed the door on that.'

And yet The Rambam had spoken beautifully of Moses's Torah being for all humanity, and not just the Jews. And went so far as to admonish Jews to love the convert – 'for a convert is a child of Abraham, and whoever maligns him commits a great sin.'

'Not,' Asher went on, 'that we ever gave her a chance to convert.'

Perverse though it might have been to feel this, given his brother's bitterness and distraction, Manny believed he had never before been as happy as he was that afternoon, talking to Asher of holy things among the torn books and sun-bleached dereliction of The Rambam's grave. Several times their conversation was halted by a pilgrim, come to read Maimonides to Maimonides and pray over his thousand-year-old remains. One of them, a pale young man who wore his yarmulke like a tonsure, and actually sang his respects to The Rambam, fluting them like a boy soprano, reminded Manny of himself, that is to say of himself as he could be were he to stay with Asher in Israel and forget that Crumpsall ever existed. Perhaps the part of Asher that craved Dorothy never would be whole again, but these were precious weeks to both the brothers, Manny was convinced, and he imagined them as David and Jonathan, loving each other as they loved their own souls.

And then, KERPOW! Dorothy!

3

Are women as sentimental as men? Do they, too, when they lose the person they love, accept The Rambam's arguments for the indivisibility and incomparableness of the object of their devotion?

The more beloved, like Hashem himself, for never being seen? For dissolving at last from corporeality to idea?

Manny was not the one to tell me. But to generalise from my own experience, the answer is no, they do not. Chloë and Zoë will never have missed me as I have missed them. Of that I am certain. There might be reason for it in my nature. I accept that I might well be an eminently unmissable man. Or it is possible that women are simply less whimsical and self-hurting in their affections, and prefer to love what they can see and touch.

In other words, women are Christians, men are Jews.

In which case we marry out every time we marry.

However you understand it, I deduced from what Manny *was* able to tell me that Dorothy had kept a corner of her heart forever shrouded in sadness for Asher, a little shrine to his memory which from time to time she tended with a sigh, but otherwise did not repine as he did, did not think of herself as a scar that would never heal. If she had not married, that was not because she could not bear to. Asher was a road she had not taken, that was all. A missed opportunity, an opportunity immeasurably important to her, but not the only opportunity that would ever come her way. She had entered the teaching profession, as she had always intended to, and was succeeding well enough at that. Head of modern languages at Bishops Blackburn, the only woman on the staff – imagine! At the same time she was studying for a PhD on the Elimination of the Blood Sacrifice in Judaism, the degree, were she to get it, to be awarded by the extra-mural studies department of the Hebrew University in Jerusalem. In relation to which she had flown out to Israel not more than a week after Manny.

When Shabettai Zvi proclaimed himself the Messiah he circled the walls of Jersusalem twelve times. Dorothy, who was a student of Jewish history, might well have been reminded of this incident when she noted for the second time the man in the long beard and the white robes pass her where she was taking

378

photographs at Damascus Gate. She would not at first have registered that Asher was not alone. Though they had grown close, the brothers still kept their physical distance from each other. And once Asher had pointed something out to Manny he left him to form his own thoughts, not least because he wanted to be alone with his. Asher wasn't the only Jesus lookalike in Jersualem. The city swarmed with them. But to Dorothy's eye he did it better than the rest. His sadness was what struck her. Where the other messiahs were busy garnering attention and looked as though they might try to sell you jewellery if you caught their eye, this one had the authentic disappointed air of a messiah who had been rejected by his people and forsaken by his God. *Eli, Eli, lama sabachthani?* If Jesus were to come again among us, having failed to get an answer to that question, this surely was how he would look.

Did she see that it was Asher, or did Asher see that it was her? Who got there first?

Manny was not sure. In the confusion he even wondered if he had been the one who did the recognising and was recognised, but he wouldn't swear to that. It simply happened, that was all he could tell me. One minute he and Asher were walking along, staring up at masonry and turrets, not talking, barely even aware of each other, the next – as though in a dream, or as though they had wakened from a dream and were back in Crumpsall where they belonged, the Crumpsall they had never really left – there was Dorothy!

He thought she was the first to speak. 'Oh!' he thought she said. 'Oh!' as though she had been caught out in a wrongdoing. Then she covered her mouth with her hands.

Asher too behaved guiltily, raking his hair with his fingers and breaking out into a sweat. 'Not possible,' he said. 'This isn't possible.'

'What are *you* doing here?' Dorothy asked, as though *they* were the surprise, as though it was the most normal thing on earth that *she* should be in the Holy Land, out taking photographs of Old Jerusalem.

'I live here.'

'How long have you lived here?'

'However long it is since I last saw you. A hundred thousand years.'

An expression crossed her face which Manny took great pains to describe, presumably because he believed it partially explained his subsequent behaviour. It was like a cloud darkening her eyes, not with anger but with pleading. She seemed to close her vision down. She compressed her lips, so tightly that grooves appeared in her skin on either side of her mouth, etches of age and suffering. Had she begged Asher to leave her alone, to pass by and pretend they hadn't met, that they didn't know each other after all, that they were mistaken in their recognition, she could not have pleaded more eloquently. It was her mouth that upset Manny most. The sad compression and yet at the same time the moistness of her lips. The resolution contending with the longing – everything she had dreaded but also everything which in foolish hours she had hoped for descending on her without a moment's warning. Manny had no experience of romantic love. It's likely he had never even read a love story. Love of God he knew about, but love of God marks the face differently. So he had never seen sorrow in the full flower of its voluptuousness. Had Asher forgotten all about her, fallen out of love with her over time, he surely would have succumbed to all his old feelings for her again. But Asher had not fallen out of love with her. Imagine, then, Manny urged me, imagine then the excitement in his heart, seeing her like this – seeing *her* like this! – palpitating with regret for what Asher had himself regretted every day for a hundred thousand years.

Because they couldn't stand there like this for another eternity, she silently begging him to go away, he white and trembling, they finally proceeded – Manny's word: *proceeded* – into each other's arms.

Manny stood about for a few minutes, not knowing what to do, then resolved to go back to his brother's hermit cell, collect his belongings and make enquiries about flights home.

4

The fires of romantic love. So fierce they even singed poor love-forgotten Manny.

But then it's foolish to suppose anyone escapes, no matter how unromantically disposed they appear to be. I should have guessed – we all should have guessed – that when Tsedraiter Ike began to absent himself to visit the houses of the dead, he was on a different errand altogether. By the time my father died, Tsedraiter Ike was disappearing to sit shiva with virtual strangers three or four times a week. It ought to have been obvious to us that there weren't enough Jews dying at that rate, not in Crumpsall anyway. It's true that once Mick Kalooki began laying siege to Shani's affections Tsedraiter Ike had reason to leave the house, but even when they moved out into a love nest of their own he continued with his errands of mercy, taking round chicken soup in plastic containers, or bagels filled with chopped liver and wrapped in greaseproof paper, to families too ravaged by bereavement to make their own food.

In fact everything went to the same person. Dolly Balshemennik. For all those years Tsedraiter Ike had told us he was nipping out to comfort mourners he was actually going to comfort Dolly Balshemennik. Hence the best coat and the homburg. Hence the vigorous brushing to which he subjected his single tooth. Dolly Balshemennik. He would not of course have been able to pronounce more than about two vowels of her name. Maybe that was his excuse. It was easier to say he was sitting shiva for the umpteenth time that week than to say he was visiting Dolly Balshemennik.

Dolly Balshemennik – I'll say the name for him. She came to

his funeral. A twittering little woman with broken veins, almost no hair, and permanent tear stains on her cheeks. She lived round the corner to us. Just two streets away. Her being so close a neighbour amazed us even more than her being Tsedraiter Ike's mistress. Two streets away! We couldn't get over that. Had we discovered he'd been catching the early-morning flight to Novoropissik three times a week and flying back in time for supper, we would not have marvelled at his duplicity anything like so much. Two streets away! How do you like it!

There were other things to marvel at in this affair. Dolly Balshemennik had a husband. Sydney Balshemennik. He too came to the funeral. In a wheelchair which Dolly Balshemennik pushed. In a manner of speaking Tsedraiter Ike had after all been visiting a house of the dead. Sydney Balshemennik could no longer be counted among the living. Nothing of him remained in mind or body. More years ago than anyone could remember he had suffered a serious stroke – not the frivolous Selick Washinsky 'vay iz mir my son has run off with a shikseh' sort of stroke – the Jewish double-stroke in which one seizure cancels out another – but the full neurological catastrophe, leaving him incapable of doing anything but smile. So much did he appear to enjoy being tended first by his wife, and later by Tsedraiter Ike, that he saw no reason to die any more than he already had. He smiled when Tsedraiter Ike arrived and he smiled when Tsedraiter Ike left and that was the sum total of his interference in their union.

I watched him at the graveside, smiling.

Back at the shiva house his wife fed him kichels as though he were a slot machine. It had been my father's theory that it was the kichels – those rock-hard little biscuits which Jews like to serve on these occasions with whisky or syrupy sweet red wine – that explained the condition of Tsedraiter Ike's mouth. One of his very last jokes at Tsedraiter Ike's expense – 'If you went to fewer shiva houses, Ike, you'd have more teeth.'

Teeth or no teeth, he would be sorely missed by Dolly

Balshemennik who had already wept more than her own body weight in tears, and was weeping copiously still. When she had stuffed what she judged to be a sufficient number of kichels into Sydney Balshemennik's slot, she held up a little glass of syrupy sweet red wine for him to sip, not looking to see whether he was spilling it or not.

'Your uncle was a saint,' she told me.

'He was always very good to me,' I said.

'Good to you! Max, he never stopped talking about you. He lived for you!' She had what my father used to call 'the shtetl voice', ancient and quavering, full of hurried conspiratorial sorrow, cracked like a rusted bell tolling one more lamentation before the Cossacks rode in. How did she come by that voice? Dolly Balshemennik was born in Crumpsall. By her own admission she had never been near a shtetl in her life. So by what means did the shtetl live on in her larynx? Or in the vocal cords of those thousands of Jews who had never ventured more than a short train ride out of Middlesex or Brooklyn? My theory was that wherever we had been survived in our voices. Just a shame, as my father believed, that we had been to such shitty places.

'Uncle Ike and I were very close when I was growing up,' I said.

'Close wasn't the word he used. He loved you. You were like a son to him. Such pride he took in you, Max.'

I inclined my head. I was one of the principal mourners so it would not have been suitable for me to laugh. Pride! Ha! He'd hated everything I'd done since I left home. Every idea I'd had. Every woman I'd married. Every mark I'd made on paper.

But then so had I.

She saw what I was thinking and laid a trembling hand on my arm. Her whole body had begun to shake. I took the glass from her other hand. It wasn't kind on Sydney Balshemennik, however much he smiled, to have him following it about vainly with his lips.

'You'd be wrong, you know,' she said, 'to think he wasn't proud. He didn't just have all your books, he kept all your cartoons. In cellophane! Such cartoons! Where did you learn to draw like that? A Jewish boy. We have books filled with them. Like wedding albums. Come round and look at them. He always hoped you would. He can come round and look at them, can't he, Sydney?'

Was she telling the truth? I could think of no reason why she should be lying. But in that case why had Tsedraiter Ike not only kept his opinion of my work from me, but actually persuaded me that he thought the opposite? A *nestbeschmutzer*, he had called me. 'I simply ask you to consider,' he had written 'who this is likely to help. Us, or them?' My father, of course, had he lived to see me earning, would have done the same. 'Why have you got such a chip on your shoulder?' I hear him saying. 'What have the goyim ever done to you?' Pushed, he might have told me he didn't mind so much the big tocheses.

Why was this? Was it generational? Could men that age not own up to a bit of simple pride or once in a while dole out a bit of simple praise? Or was it *Jewish* men of *any* age? 'You're such a withholding fucker,' Zoë used to say to me. 'Getting a kind or encouraging word out of you is like getting blood out of a stone, you tight-arsed fucking Jewish bastard.'

Chloë the same. 'What a lovely day,' her mother would announce, when I perchance wound open the roof of our Völökswägen during a spin through the Cheshire countryside. 'Wouldn't you say it is a lovely day, Max, or do you not feel the sun the way we do?'

'No point asking him, Mummy,' Chloë would remind her. 'He's too brainy to waste his praise on a day. Unless it's the anniversary of a day on which a few thousand of his people's enemies were slaughtered.'

'It's our calling,' I told them both. 'We are put on this earth to be hard to please. We are the high priests of refusal. Only God gets our hosannas.'

And now here I was, servant of the holy flame, hierophant of the sacred fucking mysteries, ready to shed a bucketload of sublunary tears because Tsedraiter Ike, someone whose worth as a human being, let alone a critic of the grotesque arts, I had discounted utterly for forty years, had kept a corner of his heart soft for me after all.

My wives were right. The severity of my morality, like the sternness of my aesthetic, applied only to other people. I won't accept that meant only to Gentiles, except in so far as a substantial number of those other people were of necessity Gentiles, because it was Gentile company I sought out. But certainly I operated two standards. One for them, one for me. And to me I was a pussy cat.

But then someone had to be.

So I got my desserts. What happened next flowed directly from my sentimentality towards myself.

I reasoned that I owed it to Dolly, while I was up in Manchester for the funeral, and she lived only two streets away, to pop along and share another kichel with her and Mr Balshemennik. She had loved my uncle and I wanted to thank her for it. And if she needed to talk about him, it was the least I could do to listen. But my true motive was to verify her story about Tsedraiter Ike collecting my cartoons. If he had proudly amassed album upon album of my work, I wanted to see them. I wanted to bathe briefly in his devotion. It wouldn't be like finding your oeuvre in the Library of Congress, but you take what commemorations are on offer.

Visiting Dolly Balshemennik solved the mystery, if nothing else, of why she had a shtetl voice. She had a shtetl voice because she lived in a shtetl. Not the street – the street was only ordinarily ghettoised Crumpsall – but the house was authentic Novoropissik. Barely light enough to see your own hand by, the carpets still smelling of Noah's flood, cats with the droopy melancholy eyes of Russians, a sideboard, missing only a samovar, displaying photographs of long-gone relatives in Caucasian dirndls and skullcaps that looked like fezes from Tashkent, and a sound of something, a little like crickets, which I thought might have been Sydney Balshemennik's heart, but that turned out to be the wheezing of an ancient grandfather clock. No wonder Tsedraiter Ike loved it here. I raised the matter of Barnacle Bill from over the sea, but she did not know what I was talking about. Never heard him sing it. Not once in her presence. But then he wasn't from over the sea when he was here. He was back home.

Thrilling. The hairs rose on the back of my neck at the thought of it. Home is the sailor, home from the sea.

Dolly Balshemennik had a granddaughter who happened to be visiting her when Tsedraiter Ike passed away and who, out of motives no less altruistic than mine, also decided to stay a little longer. A rather beautiful woman if you were able not to see her resemblance to her grandmother. Though I have to say that on someone her age, and framed by a storm cloud of charcoal hair, that tear-stained shtetl look was mightily appealing. She recalled the thousands of photographs I'd seen of Jewish women being rounded up and bundled on to the Jew Jew train to Auschwitz and all stations east. More particularly, in the hoodedness of her eyes, she reminded me of Malvina Schalkova, the Prague-born artist posthumously famous for the sketches and watercolours she made in Theresienstadt, and whose self-portrait, mirroring an infinity of sorrow, I first became familiar with when I visited Theresienstadt with Zoë. In other moods, when something more fiercely animal took possession of her temper, she resembled Gela Seksztajn, the Warsaw Ghetto artist who perished in Treblinka in 1942, aged thirty-five. 'I have been condemned to death,' Gela Seksztajn had written in a diary later found buried with her paintings in the Ringelblum Archives in the Warsaw Ghetto, 'Adieu my dear friends and companions. Adieu Jewish people! Don't allow such a catastrophe ever to happen again.' Words you need, strictly speaking, to read with her blazing self-portrait — if you can only bear to look at it – before you. The burning sarcasm of the eyes, the fleshly hunger of the mouth, adding not poignancy but rage to a farewell we have grown to think of as conventional. 'Never again' – but the exhortation bitter and ireful this time. All this, and more, I saw in Dolly Balshemennik's granddaughter.

And then there was her name. Alÿs.

'As in Wonderland,' I said when she first told me.

'No, not Alice, Alÿs.' She spelled it out for me in air writing, puncturing space with two fingers where the umlaut went.

'With an umlaut! Is it a German name?'

'Celtic.'

Celtic, with an umlaut, and eyes like Malvina Schalkova's! Was this Tsedraiter Ike's parting present to me, from the grave – the nice Jewish girl he had always wanted me to have . . . Alÿs Balshemennik? From Crumpsall Park?

Alÿs Balshemennik. My *Schicksal* – meaning fate or destiny – only this one wasn't a shikseh.

My third wife, going purely numerically . . .

My first wife, counting by Jewish law . . .

5

And the wife on whom I wish I had never have clapped eyes.

Neat, eh? After going fifteen bruising rounds with those Nazi super-yekeltes Zoë and Chloë, after soaking up the best of their punches and not once throwing in the towel or having to retire with a nosebleed, I go down in the first to a scholarly Crumpsall Jewgirl with a Holocaust face and don't get up again.

Couldn't be neater.

But you have to be on your guard against neatness in my business. One of the great misconceptions about cartoonists is that they are unruly. In fact we are a profession methodical to the point of pathology. We tidy up. We order. We regulate our hours and confine our creations in little boxes.

'The style I developed for *Mad*,' Harvey Kurtzman once said, 'was necessarily thoughtful under a rowdy surface.'

The remark had stayed in my mind because 'rowdy' was such a surprising and yet apt word for the activity we shared. We weren't transgressive, we were merely rowdy. And even then we were only *apparently* rowdy. The mistake was to confuse rowdy surface with rowdy substance.

You hold your pencil loose, you let the moment take possession of your arm, your line accepts no limitation and does obeisance to no one and to nothing, but you know the little box is always waiting. At first, you are lured by the sprawl of what Alÿs taught me to call 'sequential art' – or the graphic novel, as laymen describe it – into believing you've found a freer form. No more the confinement of the panel. Things spill and bleed. Words riot, pictures fall off the page, neither time nor order is obeyed. An illusion, all of it. In the end the tyranny of the box asserts itself one way or another, circumscribing speech, restricting character, determining action according to the complexion of your prejudices. Despite our seeming subversiveness, we are no more unconfined, and no more want to be unconfined, than the most strait-laced teller of morality tales.

So I must be careful, when I come to describe my life with Alÿs, not to box it around with over-ordered moral ironies. It makes a neat cartoon, the man who was so hooked on Gentile she-wolves he couldn't do it with a Jewess. Or the man who was so convinced of the sanctity of Jewish women he could only get it up with shiksehs.

Neat, but wrong. We had no sexual difficulties. I did not close my eyes when I bent over her and see my mother. Nor did I wish I could open them again and see Chloë. We functioned fine. She went soft, like summer fruit, and I gathered her in. It wasn't the case, either, that I had grown so used to strife that I missed it when it was not forthcoming. You can find other things to fall out over even when you don't have the Resurrection as a stumbling block between you. No, if my marriage to Alÿs was different to my other marriages (Alÿs herself had not previously been married, so had no such distinctions to make), it was different only in this regard: I couldn't take the gloomy consciousness of history I'd married her for.

She was depressed every day. We have a word for it. Dershlogn. Dershlogn is better than depressed. With depressed you have a chance of coming round. With depressed it's not necessarily all your fault. Dershlogn is dispirited by nature. Dershlogn implies a deficiency of vital juices. At first I took her to be depressed for me. She knew my work – knew *of* my work would be nearer the mark – and not only, I was flattered to learn at the time, from the albums of it gathering dust in her grandmother's house. She taught popular culture at an art college in West London, one of her specialisms being the fantasy comic, a genre to which I could not strictly be said to have made anything but the most marginal contribution, but marginalia were also her specialism, so I figured as a sort of footnote at the far reaches of a discipline that was not much more than a footnote itself. In her view I had not reconciled the artistic impulses at war within me – half wanting to be a prophet of the Jewish people (which was fantastical in itself), and half wanting to stick it up them (which again was fantastical given my belief that enough people had stuck it up them already). This is what I mean when I say I thought I was the cause of her depression. Until I could make sense of these antinomies, as she called them, she didn't see how my work would make the journey from what was tangential to what was central – a not entirely consistent argument since the tangential was precisely what she taught ('Centrality is a masculinist concept,' she told me once), but it seemed that you could be too tangential even for someone who believed in it, and for this reason she was depressed for me.

It was Alÿs who got me to change my style. I don't mean as a man, I mean as a cartoonist. But you could argue that the one wasn't possible without the other. Maybe that was why, contemporaneous

389

with her changing my style as a cartoonist, she moved in with me.

She moved in soundlessly, the way a mouse moves in. This was partly to be explained by her decision to keep her own place in W6, a stone's throw from her college. She didn't – not all at once, anyway – have to bring in everything she owned. But I am not simply talking objects. She barely brought herself in. It is meant to be traumatic, suddenly ceding space to a new person. Your furniture is rearranged. Your favourite pictures get taken down. Photographs which are dear to you go missing. Even if your bed stays where it was, its contours change. None of this happened with Alÿs. Apart from my mind, she left everything as she found it. Shoes belonging to previous wives which I'd omitted to throw out or send on, knick-knacks whose value was obviously romantico-sentimental, even sketches of Chloë, brought out again post-Zoë, done in the manner of the old masters with a few lewd transliterations of my own thrown in – none of these things, assuming that she noticed them, did she appear to be disconcerted by. And it wasn't as though she meant to eclipse them by the vitality of her presence. She just dwelt among them, like a visitor, someone in transit, a person passing through.

In flat shoes.

Her shoes should not have mattered to me, but I had grown up among stiletto'd women and both my wives had strode into my life, and then clip-clopped out of it again, on high heels. The heels themselves were not the issue. Had Alÿs simply favoured shoes that were flat I would eventually have accommodated myself to them. But all I ever saw her in were sandals. Cheap, round-toed buckled sandals of the sort monks and little girls and ideologues wear.

I offered to take the car and pick up the rest of her things – meaning her high heels – from W6. But she kept no high heels in W6. Didn't own any. Had never owned any.

Nor, even when sitting in an armchair with her feet tucked

under her, earnestly watching soaps on television (soaps being another of her specialisms), did she take her sandals off. Tightly buckled was how she liked them – for all occasions. Tightly buckled so that when the call came for her release, she was ready.

'It's not as though I am imprisoning you here, is it?' I remember saying to her once.

She shook her head. She was working at a coffee table, though I had freed a desk for her, and offered to buy her a new one of her own if she preferred. She angled her face to me, her eyelids droopy, her mouth tragic. 'If it fell to human beings to be happy,' she said, 'I'd be happy. But I am content enough, living in my head.'

An old ghetto trick. You shut down all the ingresses to fear and go on with what you're doing.

Another time I told her she reminded me of a refugee. 'You look as though you are waiting for a country to let you in,' I said.

A decent answer to that would have been *My darling, you are my country*. But such effusiveness was beyond her. At least with me.

Instead, she closed her eyes, as though the better to hear when her name was called.

Dershlogn.

I have said we had no sexual difficulties and I stick by that. But every once in a while she did start from me during love-making, actually make to shield her face as if she expected me to hit her. I had told her that my father had been a boxer, so it's possible she feared boxing was in my genes; but I had never made any movement towards her even remotely suggestive of violence. As a lover I was gentle, possibly even apologetic, to a fault. Could she have *wanted* me to hit her?

'Am I being too rough with you?' I asked, the first time I felt her pull away.

'You are being just right,' she said.

'Am I being too exquisitely tender?' I asked the second time –

meaning, 'You wouldn't like it *à la façon du* shaygets, would you?'
Just in case.

'I am happy,' she said.

Happy! I had seen happier faces in photographs of the . . . But
to have said that would have been to play into her hands.

Why wasn't she animated by her work? Fantasy comics, for
Christ's sake! Cyborgs, Angel Gangs, Mutants, Swamp Things,
Dark Knights, Watchmen, Hellblazers, Sandmen – wouldn't you
have thought, since she'd elected to be their champion, that a bit
of their pizzazz might have rubbed off on her? Planets collided,
the marshes of the universe yielded up their terrible secrets, crazed
scientists reversed the very logic of nature, and Alÿs
Balshemennik couldn't so much as raise a smile. Wasn't the point
of zooming out into the furthest stretches of the human imagination a certain payoff in vitality? It's meant to turn your mind,
isn't it? There should be fireballs exploding in your eyes. FUN
FUN FUN at the Hellfire Club, only Alÿs Balshemennik is
staying home with her sandalled toes tucked beneath her, slumped
in a depression. If this was what the margins had to offer, wouldn't
she have had a HELLUVA LOT more FUN FUN FUN at the
masculinist, patriarchal, Abrahamic centre?

Unless this was precisely the reason she'd been brought so low
– the spider at the centre of the centre, the spider *imagining* he
was at the centre of the centre, otherwise known as me.
Arachnidman.

I had no choice, since it was almost certainly my fault, but to
marry her. If I married her she would not feel a stranger in my
house. If I married her I would not go to sleep worrying whether
or not she would be there in the morning. If she agreed to marry
me, that would prove she believed in a future. Not just our future,
but *any* future. The bells would ring, the gates to all the camps
and ghettos of Eastern Europe would fly open, and the Americans
would be there with Hershey bars.

And she didn't turn me down. Yes, she would marry me, but

wished, if that was all right with me, to postpone any decision as to when.

I had the feeling she thought there was more work to be done on me before she could become my wife.

Apart from my mind. She left everything as she found it, apart from my mind.

I came home from shopping one morning – Alÿs never shopped – to find her sitting on the edge of the sofa in tears. She had been looking through a portfolio of unfinished work I had left with her to see if she thought I was heading in the right direction. Caricatures of famous Jews who were either damned in being too Jewish, or damned in being not Jewish enough. Wildly funny stuff, in my view – wildly funny not least about the state of mind of the caricaturist – but too angry or too bilious to know quite what to do with. (The title *No Bloody Wonder* came much later, as a riposte to the mess she had made of me.) She was wearing her inevitable caftan, some sort of Mexican cape with feathers and mirrors sewn into it, a robe designed for dancing and laughing in, but which, on Alÿs, became funereal, a covering one might wear for the Day of the Dead. Her sandals looked buckled tighter than ever.

'So upsetting,' she said.

'Me doing the shopping? Well, there's nothing to stop you doing it with me.'

'You are so hurt,' she said, tapping the portfolio in her agitation. 'I didn't know you were so hurt.'

I was taken aback. 'Well, they are certainly meant *to* hurt,' I said. 'I grant you that.'

'You are fooling yourself. The only person these are meant to hurt is you. You can't go on like this. You will destroy yourself.'

Out, I should have said. *Get the fuck out of here, you fucking ghoul!*

But ours was not a swearing relationship. And then, what if

393

she were right? Not about my destroying myself – that was melodrama. But the implication of her words was that the prisoner in this house was me, not her; and that I was imprisoned in some fatal solipsistic engagement, my rage not finding an outlet, never mind an audience. I knew enough about the frustrations that beset cartoonists, especially Jewish cartoonists, not to suppose I could be a cheerful exception to the rule. The plight of Bernard Krigstein had been before me since I was a teenager. You pursue the Nazi of your nightmares until he falls under the wheels of a subway train, and then how happy are you? Where do you find your victory? As a cartoonist, Krigstein believed nobody recognised how good he was. As a serious painter, he believed nobody recognised how good he was. Would another dead Nazi have given him the recognition, or even just the satisfaction, he craved? Should he have gone out looking? Should he have gone out combing the subways for more enemies of the Jewish people, that's assuming enemies of the Jewish people were truly at the heart of what was amiss with him? That way madness lay. Maybe all ways madness lay. Perhaps Alÿs was on to something. Besides, she was in a privileged position. She taught popular culture. She knew what sold. She knew what the goyim in their fucking millions bought. And they sure as hell weren't buying me.

And thus began my re-education.

She read to me, no doubt as she read to her students on the first day of term, the cartoonist Robert Crumb's description of his methodology or provenance or procedure, call it what you will – '"Doodles, scribbles, worthless foolishness, playful notions, silliness, aimless meanderings" – how much of that do you recognise, Max?'

'Me? None of it.'

'You never doodle?'

'Never. If I'm drawing I'm drawing.'

'And worthless foolishness?'

'Well, that's a verdict others may pass on me, and have, but as a description of my own endeavours to myself I do not recognise it, no.'

'Aimless meanderings?'

'I cannot conceive of such.'

'And why do you think that is, Max?'

'Because I'm Jewish and Jews understand art to be expressly against the wishes – no, the commandments – of Elohim. Therefore when they do it they do it solemnly and in the expectation that the fabric of the planet will be rent in two. You want to see galactic meltdown? Take a look at what's going on in the firmament after a Jewish boy has dared to make a likeness.'

'So why are you a cartoonist?'

'It doesn't say anywhere, Alÿs, what sort of likeness is forbidden. Oil painting, sculpture, caricature – they're all serious infractions to Him. And they're all serious infractions to Me.'

'You're in the wrong branch of the wrong business. You probably always have been. Don't doodle if doodling's not what you care to do.'

'I don't doodle.'

'Exactly. You don't doodle. So do what you do do.'

'It's a little late in the day for me to turn my hand to landscapes. And I won't be making video installations.'

And that was when she introduced me to the graphic novel.

'*Five Thousand Years of Bitterness* not graphic enough for you?' I wondered.

'No narrative.'

'Alÿs, it's the narrative of my soul.'

'Exactly. No narrative that anyone wishes to accompany you on. Your soul's old hat, Max. Your soul's had it. That particular aspect of your soul has, anyway. It went out with the Ark.'

'It began with the Ark.'

She took my head between her hands and looked into my eyes.

Not easy for Alÿs to look at me or anyone, so heavy were her eyelids.

'Some time in your life you jumped off the train that every-body else was travelling on, Max. It was your own decision. You can make the decision to jump back on again.'

The train. Jew Jew, Jew Jew.

6

So jump back on I did.

The Wonderment Express.

Boo hoo, boo hoo! Boo hoo, boo hoo!

And for four or five years, the years before we married, I let it take me – take us, to be exact – where it was taking everybody. Africa, Cambodia, Croatia, Chernobyl, East Timor, you name them, though in plain truth they name themselves – the heart-lands of our bad conscience. I'm not saying we always went there in person. In fact we almost never went there in person. But our sympathies took flight, and what we didn't see with our own eyes Alÿs could always find a research assistant to see for us. The stories Alÿs attended to herself. Linear narratives of bad faith and lost illusions a child could have written. But then a child was meant to have written them. She was quick to seize an important truth, my Alÿs. Never again, not in our time, anyway, would a man's voice – or a man's hand, come to that – be acceptable. If you wanted to be heard or noticed, if you didn't want to scratch at the margins of the margins, you changed your gender or you changed your age. From here on in the man would be allowable only in the boy. I stopped drawing and began to shmeer instead. Life as a child saw it, or as the age chose to believe a child saw it, all pastel wash and finger painting, any vibrancy or discord (and all blacker-than-hell jokes) whited out with Turpenoid. In a trice I was no longer Maxie Glickman but Thomas Christiansen, graphic novelist with heart. Co-author of *Boy of Bhopal*.

Followed by *Boy of the Balkans*. Boy books begging to be loved.

They sold reasonably well. Not sensationally. We were probably too sour, Alÿs and I, to boy it as convincingly as was required. But they sold well enough to disgust me with the people who were fool enough to buy them. I knew how fatuous they were. *I* did them for a quiet life and to make a woman who was depressed for me, a little less so. But what was *their* excuse?

Having, as she believed, got me back on course, she agreed to marry me. We made no provision for a honeymoon. Her decision. We would melt somewhere appropriate when the occasion was right. We would deliquesce into history like my watery paintings.

Neither getting me back on course nor agreeing to be my wife did anything for her spirits. She still began each day with her sandals buckled, so she would be ready when they came to bundle her away, either to the ovens or to freedom.

Wife of Sorrows, I called her.

About six months into our marriage she proposed a honeymoon. Work-related. I dreaded the worst. Ten days in the Congo? A fortnight in Chechnya? I wasn't even warm. Palestine.

'I beg yours?'

'Palestine.'

'You mean Israel.'

'I mean Palestine.'

Now I think back to our time together I cannot recall a single Israel-related conversation. It might have been that we both knew to keep away from each other's views on the subject. Or we might just have been lucky. On our watch, Israel simply didn't come up.

When I say 'views on the subject' I do not mean to imply that I had any. My father believed that Jews bore a special responsibility not to be special, so he hated Israel for existing, then hated it for not existing well. Less bothered by such contrarieties, my mother threw the occasional charity kalooki night for our beleaguered Israeli cousins, the proceeds from which would not have bought a stamp to send what she had raised. I enjoyed a sleepy repose somewhere between their positions. But that did not mean I was prepared to put up with any moralising from the goyim. To the goyim I had one thing and one thing only I wanted to say: You threw us out, you won't now dictate to us where we can go. A Chinaman might be entitled to express an opinion, but a Christian of French or German or even English descent, no sir. Not when the mess, if you go back far enough – and I go back far enough – is all your doing.

Alÿs, I accept, was not a goy. Nor had she, in all fairness, as yet expressed an opinion. Except that calling it Palestine expressed all the opinions it was necessary to express. I saw what was coming. *Boy of Bethlehem*. Maybe worse. Maybe *Girl of Gaza*.

I asked her if getting me on to the train was always the beginning of a process, in her mind, that would climax in her dropping me square in the middle of the shit that was the Occupied Territories. She denied any such intention vehemently. She had been thinking of me. Of the state I was in. Of my work which was bogged down in repetition, contradiction and pointless irony. Nothing else had motivated her, nothing! How dared I impute so base a motive to her! How dared I!!

But what *was* so base about her wanting me to go to Palestine, unless she meant by it that I should shmeer some paint around while I was there and rub it in the faces of my people? 'The fact is, Alÿs,' I told her, 'your outrage proves my fears. You want to de-Jew me. It's not enough you took the man. Now it's the Jew you're after . . . what's fucking left of it!'

She hung her head. Not in shame, in rage. It occurred to me that if she did look up it might be preparatory to an act of murder. I had said enough to *be* murdered, I accepted that. When you accuse someone of taking away what is essential to your life, you are asking for them to take the life itself. Why not finish it? Why not do what you stand accused of?

The strange thing was that she could not, at this moment, have looked more archetypally Jewish herself. In her fury, Judith the beheader. In her rectitude, Deborah the judge. In her sorrow, Naomi. In her fidelity to me – oh yes, in her outraged loyalty – Rachel. In her presentiment of grief – why not say it? – that best of all Jewish mothers, the Virgin Mary herself. And this before we'd started on the martyrs of the diaspora – from the wise and fertile wives who'd kept the flame alive throughout the persecutions of the Middle Ages to those heroines of my own profession, the Malvina Schalkovas and Gela Seksztajns who didn't make it to their middle years. It was no wonder she couldn't lift her head, considering the amount of retroactive narrative it contained.

I hated her. All at once I realised how much and for how long I had hated her without knowing it.

The fucking lugubrious Jewess she was! Ghetto-laden, Holocaust-ridden, God-benighted, guilt-strewn, and now by that latest twist of morbid Jewish ingenuity, Jew-revolted.

The sandals told their own story. Why hadn't I been listening to what my eyes told me? There is only ever one reason an adult person wears a sandal when it isn't summer and they are not winkle-picking on the beach, and that is because they wish to throw their lot in with simplicity. A sandal is a symbol of poverty and, by extension, of oppression. You wear it to affirm that what is good is simple, and what is simple must be true. No doubt there were Jewish settlers who wore sandals too, as an assertion of the simple continuity they enjoyed with Abraham and Sarah. Alÿs had pulled off something spectacular. She wore her sandals Jewishly, in the name of our common ancestors, but also anti-Jewishly in the name of those she believed we had dispossessed.

Not satisfied with being ashamed of all the shame we felt, now we had to be ashamed of not being ashamed enough. You can see why the goyim resorted to the gas chambers. They wanted us to leave their heads alone. But here we still were, still ratcheting up our consciences. Jews refining their Jewishness in the act of refusing to be Jewish.

Or at least here Alÿs Glickman, née Balshemennik, still was. She made my head spin, never mind the poor goyims'. I needed to be wearing sandals myself. I needed my own simplicities back. I needed to be working in vibrant colours again, doing overt violence on the page.

We didn't speak that night. I fully expected her to be gone in the morning. But there she lay, flattened in the bed as though history had rolled over her again while she slept. I left the house, staying out all day, giving her the chance to gather together her things which in truth she could have squeezed into a matchbox. Thirty seconds were all it would have taken her to pack and go. But I gave her a day. Not for a moment did I suppose she would be there when I returned. But she was back at her workstation, bent over the coffee table reading fantasy comics without a zap or flicker of emotion, not making a nuisance of herself, not incommoding me by the disturbance of a single atom.

'If it's your intention to murder me by depressive propinquity, you're succeeding,' I told her.

She didn't raise her eyes. 'It isn't *my* intention to murder anyone,' she said.

The liar!

Why did she stay? That is a question I am still unable to answer. To make me miserable is too obvious. To make herself miserable is more likely. Being miserable, after all, was the thing she did best. No doubt the true answer was to be found in her grandfather, Sydney Balshemennik, who also stayed on long after any decent man would have hopped it. But other than a smile, you couldn't get anything out of him.

As for why I didn't ask her to leave, I was too much the Jewish husband. Gentile men analize their wives then toss them from the top of twenty-storey buildings. Jewish men do not. Jewish men put up with whatever it pleases God to visit on them.

Nor did I suggest she move into Zoë's old space. Good taste, partly. You don't have a stream of wives passing through the same granny flat. And maybe I believed she was a punishment I deserved.

We continued in this vein for the best part of a year. Like two panes of glass in the same door, each trembling to the identical vibration. You can hear glass strained to the limits of its endurance. It seemed just a matter of time. The minute one pane shattered, the other would.

Then one morning, hallelujah, she was gone. No corpse of the Jewish nation steamrollered by my side. No silent reproaches, two thousand years in the rehearsing. No little feet padding in little round-toed sandals. Not a trace of her. Not a single hair to say she had ever been here. Only the books we had done together left, slender spines up, supported by a teapot and a biscuit jar, on the coffee table that had been her desk. Bitter evidence of her wasted years in my company? Proof of the benignity of her intentions all along? Or a reminder of what I would miss without her? The chance she gave me to be a different artist, to be a different man. The chance I blew.

My first impulse was to send them flying. Fuck you, Alÿs. But I was proud of having done no violence, real or symbolic, to her so far, and wanted it to stay that way.

I could smell her absence. It was like spring. I threw open all the windows and inhaled. Ah, yes! Ah, yes, yes, yes!

Then I realised I knew what it was to be a Nazi.

FOURTEEN

1

Asher was on fire.

Those were not Manny's words, but I didn't need Manny to tell me how Asher felt.

On fire. Desire piled upon desire piled upon desire, because desire rekindled and reconfirmed exceeds itself at a rate which is beyond the seemingly straightforward mathematics of reunion. Desire, too, re-enacted in a climate which suited desire better. He couldn't stop touching her and wherever he touched her her skin sizzled. Cold was how he remembered her. Cold with the chill of Crumpsall in her veins. It had been part of their lovers' ritual – having to go back for a cardigan for her, or a coat even in the middle of summer, and his arm always around her shoulder. His job had been to warm her through. One reason why they'd loved each other's flesh – the disparity in their temperatures. Now, hot of her own accord, she was a novel sensation for them both. They imagined how their night would be – assuming, always assuming there would be a night – their kisses viscous, their limbs moist and indistinguishable.

On fire, but not only because the sun coming off the Jerusalem stone was fiery. He was on fire with agitation.

'Just a minute, don't say anything, I need to know how long you're here, where you're going, what your plans are, who you're here with.'

Who you're here with. On fire with not knowing, and on fire with needing to know in an instant what it would take an age to unravel.

She laughed.

On fire with the sound of her. The look of her. Her throat.

On fire with what was familiar, on fire with what was new.

Which was the more exciting – what he recognised or what came as a shock? Difficult choices. A new woman or the previous woman come back? Or was the way to think of it that the previous woman had been returned to him renewed?

On fire with the strange infidelity of holding an ex-lover in your arms.

Except that she wasn't an ex-lover. He had never replaced her. And never thought of her as belonging to a time that was dead. She was his lover, had remained his lover, continued to be his lover in the present, even though he wasn't seeing her and hadn't seen her for so many years that they could have had a son and bar mitzvah'd him in the time.

She the same. How he felt, she felt. She had never stopped loving him.

But there was a subtle difference in how they each received this news. It saddened her and filled her with a sense of wasted years. Whereas Asher was exhilarated by the words. Better than fame, better than being fought over by a thousand women, better than coming back from the dead to find the whole world made distraught by your passing – to be told that you have been held in a single heart, thought about and thought about, missed, longed for, pictured and bodied forth day after day, month after month, year after year, and for all your failings heroised.

'You have come back to me,' Dorothy said when they lay side by side, without blankets, in her Moorish hotel room with its clattering air conditioning. She had discovered she could buy English roses in Jerusalem and liked to fill the room with them. Would he remember that she had talked to him about roses when they visited gardens together, gardens being the best places, he had joked, to avoid being seen by Jews? And the best places to smell flowers, she had replied. Would he smell the roses, and would the smell remind him? She had waited to be sure of him. Waited to hear what he had to say. Waited to find out whether he had married or intended to marry another woman, never mind his protestations of fidelity. Waited to see whether his effect on her would be as it had always been, to say nothing, of course, of her effect on him. But now she was satisfied. 'My hero has returned.'

The return of the hero. He was on fire, as any man would have been on fire, with that. You could see the flames from Jericho.

He had, he would have been the first to admit it, done nothing heroic. Quite the opposite. He had taken fright and run away. But hero was a manner of speaking. When the man returns it is always as a hero. A good woman understands this. A man must live on as an idea, in his mother, in his wife, in his children, in his mistresses. This is why he leaves them. So that he will persist as a glowing abstraction for them, before he returns – *if* he returns – to make that abstraction flesh again. That's the fantasy, anyway. I have it myself, in relation to Chloë, Zoë, even Alÿs. I need to know that they are thinking – if not longingly, at least exceptionally – of me. As a man it is where I exist. Not in the flesh, as a woman exists: in her children, in the home she makes, in the palpable achievements of her devotion. A man is more spiritual. A man lives in the sentimental apprehension of him that women carry around. And when a woman divulges this sentimental homunculus to the man of whom it is an ideation, his happiness can barely contain itself. Asher's spilled over like lava, happiness enough to engulf all Jerusalem. And because Dorothy was as intelligent as she was devoted, because she was in no hurry to deliver herself of her stored-up reproaches on their first night back together – a night she had perfumed with English roses – she didn't begrudge him his childish vanity.

'There is only one thing,' she said.

He was stretched out on her bed in the attitude of a god. Not Elohim. Any god but Elohim. A tracery of perspiration made the hairs on his chest glisten. It was as though dew had fallen on him, she thought.

'Anything,' he said. 'Just ask.'

She made a pincer of her nails and plucked at one of his chest hairs, turned grey in the time they'd been apart.

'Leave me again and I will kill you.'

2

Back in Crumpsall, Manny barely had time to dump his bags in his room before the interrogations began. How come he had returned so suddenly when he had talked of staying on at least another month? Was he ill? Was Asher ill? Had they fallen out? Manny had written that he and Asher had never been so close – what then had occurred to make them not so close?

'I did my best,' Manny told me, 'to be non-committal.'

I did *my* best not to laugh. Manny non-committal was impossible to conceive. Even now, so many years later, he could not conceal the agitation which having to lie for Asher caused him. He was jiggling both his knees. Much more of it and my window panes would start to shatter. It was like having Alÿs back in my life.

I put my hand out to stop him. 'How long were you able to be non-committal for?'

'About a minute.'

I was relieved. I didn't want to be the only one who saw the funny side of this – Manny arrived back from Israel the colour of falafel, with the shock of walking into Dorothy still starting in his eyes, pretending that his last days in Jerusalem had been like absolutely any old person's last days in absolutely any old place.

The surprising thing was, considering the terrible job of concealment he had obviously made, how long it took the Washinskys to come even close to the truth. Illness remained their first suspicion. Asher's lungs had succumbed to something. Asher had been shot. Asher had been blown up. Their guilt talking, no doubt; suddenly imaging the dangers they had cheerfully exposed him to rather than let the fire-yekelte and her daughter have him.

'If you're preparing us for the worst, we would rather you didn't,' Mrs Washinsky said. 'Just tell us what you must tell us.'

Whereupon, in recollection as no doubt at the time, Manny's knees began to jig again.

They got to *a* girl before they got to *the* girl. *The* girl might not have left their consciousness entirely, but she had happened long ago. Asher had been in Israel for years, and they could not have conceived circumstances in which Dorothy would have taken herself there. There were plenty more Jewish boys left in Crumpsall if her heart was still set on one of those. As for what objection there could be to a girl Asher had met in Israel, they were hard pressed to imagine any, short of her being a Bedouin.

'Is she an Arab, Manny?'

'Why do you think there's got to be a "she"?'

'We know our son. There's always a "she".'

'There isn't a "she" and she isn't an Arab.'

'So what is she?'

'I came home because it was too hot there. And I didn't want to go on being a burden to Asher.'

'He's your brother. How can you be a burden to your brother?'

'I know he's my brother. That's why I didn't want to be a burden to him.'

'You didn't want to go on being a burden to Asher when he was doing what? You didn't want to be a burden to him and whom?'

'Look – I'm telling you the truth. Go there yourself if you don't believe me.'

So they did.

'Did you warn him?'

'Did I warn him what?'

'Did you warn him they were coming?'

He began pulling at his fingers and whistling. Usually the sign that I had pushed him further than he could bear to go.

I made tea and served him ginger cake, which he liked. It was becoming routine. Breakfast of granola and honey, or a no less sticky lunch of Nutella and banana pancake, both in the vicinity of the British Museum which I guessed he favoured in the hope of running into the Azams again – his only friends in London, not counting me, the only people he had ever talked to – followed by tea with ginger cake back at my place, and then, if I wasn't careful, an evening in front of the television together. It was not unlike being married. Wife Number Four – Emanuel Eli Washinsky, except that he was unsuitable by virtue of having no diaeresis.

'No,' he said, after a mouthful or two of tea. 'No I didn't warn him. I thought that would have been taking sides.'

'But weren't you taking sides when you got home and told your parents there was nothing wrong?'

He thought about it, looking for the answer on the ceiling. 'No. That was different. That was me refusing to be used as a messenger boy by them.'

'You weren't being a sort of messenger boy for Asher? A messenger boy whose message was to stay shtum?'

'Yes. I know. They all wanted something from me. They always had.'

It was the first intimation I had that he'd been at all put out by the great Jerusalem reunion. Stupid of me. Stupidly romantic to suppose that all the world loves a lover. All the world loves a lover when it's got a bit of love going for itself.

Stupid of me, as I explained to Francine Bryson-Smith over a snatched tea at Patisserie Valerie in Old Compton Street, not to have realised that however delighted he was for his brother, Manny was bound to be a wee bit jealous as well.

'Jealous because he didn't have a little shikseh of his own?'

(*Ways of Saying Shikseh When You're Not Jewish*, Vol. II.)

I put lines around my eyes, where a smile is meant to form. 'Well, that too, but I was thinking jealous because he'd been spending a lot of time with his brother when Dorothy turned up out of the blue. They'd discovered each other. Time had ironed out their age difference and opportunity had made them friends. Think of it – travelling around Israel together, talking theology, looking at the sea, eating kebabs in the sunshine. For Manny, who had never seen sun before, it was like the beginning of a new life. And then at a stroke, it was gone. Dorothy arrived and his brother dropped him. Cruel, but that's the way of it. When love calls, you jump. And poor Manny was back on his own again.'

'So why didn't he gas his brother, do you think?'

'I'll need to think about that,' I said, leaving her to pay the bill.

3

They got there and found everything as they would have wanted it. Asher living on his own, no longer acting the Messiah, no longer with his hair down to his toches, not shot, not blown up, not coughing blood, and best of all not living with a Bedouin.

They had come to take him home, but now they were not so sure. He gave them the tour he gave Manny. Down to the Red Sea, up to the Dead Sea, there the mountains, there the rivers, here there and everywhere the manifest word of God. Had they been able to afford it they'd have stayed. 'Left me in Crumpsall,' Manny said without any smile lines round his eyes, 'and started a little fur business in Netanya.'

Anyone watching the three of them together would have been touched by the spectacle. A loving Jewish son, purple as the seeds of a pomegranate, leading around parents whose every gesture exuded love for him. Too late for them, in all reality, the Israel he was showing them, just as it had been too late for Moses, but they could at least stand on a mountaintop with their boy between them and look out. As far as the eye could see, the Jewish future, covenanted thousands of years ago but now at last, thanks to men like Asher, on the point of being realised.

What you would not have been able to tell just from looking at the three of them together was that the son had thoughts only for the woman he loved, the fire-yekelte's daughter who, at this very moment, was setting up home for the two of them in a Land no less Promised – Higher Blackley.

Was that a cruel deception on Asher's part, or was it a kindness?

'I was being considerate,' was how Asher explained it to Manny when he got home. 'I didn't want to spoil their holiday,'

'Dad says you would have shown more consideration had you given them poison to drink,' Manny told him.

'Dad would. Dad has a taste for overstatement. He's a typical diaspora Jew – he thinks the Jewish world is always on the point of coming to an end. That's what I like about Israel – because they live in a real and not an imaginary Jewish world they don't spend every hour thinking it's going to disappear.'

'That's because they have an army to see it doesn't,' Manny reminded him.

Asher laughed. He was laughing again. Aflame and festive. 'I could do with an army myself,' he said.

'An army won't help. What you need is a team of doctors. Dad's going round clutching his heart again.'

'He's bluffing. Don't worry about it. He'll get over it. They'll both get over it this time. They're used to me not being here. If they don't want to see me they can pretend I'm back in Israel.'

'With a German?'

'The world has changed. You'll see.'

Asher had told them the truth on the plane back. Just before they landed at Manchester Airport. He hadn't wanted to spoil the flight for them either. And just possibly he wanted them both to be confined in seat belts when he told them.

He genuinely believed what he had said. So much time had gone by, everyone was so many years older, the arguments had been gone through so often they were threadbare by now, not even arguments, just rags of prejudice and dogma, and Dorothy had become proficient in Hebrew, was doing a PhD that had been ratified by the Hebrew University of Jerusalem, knew more about Jewish history than they did, for God's sake – surely, in the face of all this, what remained of his parents' objections would melt away.

Manny thought otherwise. Manny had not been out of the country, breathing in other ideas. Being Jewish might have looked different to Asher in Jerusalem, but in Crumpsall it was still the same, maybe even worse. In Israel, as Manny had seen with his own eyes, Jews got a bit of air around themselves. In Crumpsall, excepting those who had opted out of being Jewish altogether, they had begun to return to the bad old ways of the shtetl, retreating behind the defences of an ancient faith, living and breathing it as they'd done in Novoropissik, as though the practice of their religion was the only activity open to them. That or kalooki.

'And today Crumpsall even looks like Novoropissik,' I said, putting in my twopenneth. 'Whenever I go back I expect to see chickens running down the streets. Even my mother's got the old religion now. Once upon a time the only night she didn't play cards was Yom Kippur. Now she won't play on Shevuos, she won't play on Purim, she won't even play on Lag B'Omer. Ask her what any of these festivals are about and she'll admit she doesn't have a clue, she just thinks it's inappropriate to play kalooki while they're happening.'

Manny sailed his vacant blue eyes in my direction. 'You're lucky your family played cards. I never saw a pack of cards. We played with dreidels on Chanukah, that was all. My father used to say that the letters on the four sides of the dreidel – that's a spinning top—'

'I know what a dreidel is, Manny.'

'My father used to say the letters contained the whole history of the Jewish people. Nes, Gadol, Haya, Sham – spelling out "A Great Miracle Happened There"– but also standing for the four kingdoms to which we'd been dispersed: Babylon, Persia, Greece and Rome.'

'What about Crumpsall?'

He wasn't listening. 'Everything was the history of the Jewish people. Even when I came out to play with you it was the history of the Jewish people, and you weren't even Jewish.'

'What do you mean I wasn't even Jewish? Do you think we didn't play with dreidels too?'

'In the eyes of my family you weren't Jewish. Not properly Jewish.'

'But Jewish enough for the vile Shrager to try and make a shiddach between Shani and your brother?'

'And you don't think my parents would have objected to that too? Maybe not as much, it's true. There's not Jewish and not Jewish . . .'

'And poor old half-Kraut Dorothy remained as not-Jewish as it was possible for a not-Jew to be? Did it really change nothing that she'd made a success of her life? Weren't they impressed that she had become a student of Hebrew? Was she still out of the question, even though she had become an authority on the elimination of the blood sacrifice in Judaism?'

'Out of the question. Just as out of the question as she had ever been. More. Because this time Asher had spent all those years in Israel – they'd given him that chance – and if he couldn't find himself an acceptable wife there, he was either doing this to spite them or Dorothy had some power over him. As far as they were concerned her Hebrew studies might just as well have been black magic. She had bewitched him. They went crazy. They knew there was no point their reasoning with him this time. They knew he would close his ears to them. So they called in rabbis and begged Asher to talk to them, but he wouldn't. They appealed to the social services. They wrote to a hypnotist. They tried to find a way of sending Asher back to Israel and getting her passport stopped. What right did she have to be in Israel anyway? When that failed, they made moves to get Asher committed. I think they even hired a private detective . . .'

He was going too fast for me. 'They made moves to get Asher *committed*? What do you mean they made moves? They took him to a lunatic asylum?'

'Not directly. They couldn't get that far. But they talked to doctors and psychologists.'

'And did the doctors explain that falling in love with a shikseh isn't certifiable?' I wanted to adduce my own history with shiksehs as proof of that, but then again . . .

'Well, Shrager was dead by then, otherwise they might have got their way. But the others weren't very helpful, no. Unless Asher was prepared to go along of his own free will and discuss his problems, there was nothing they could do.'

'And what about the private detective? What was he for?'

'What private detectives are always for. To investigate Dorothy's private life. To find things out about her that would bring Asher to his senses. To prove to him she had been sleeping with other men. Do you know, I believe that if my father could have been convinced it would do any good, he would have slept with Dorothy himself and shown Asher the photographs.'

Gorges rise less often in life than they do in comics and fiction. But my gorge rose at this. Rose like a monster from the deep. I could taste it in my mouth. I still can.

'And what would your mother have said?'

'Had it worked, "Well done, Selick."'

'And had it failed?'

'"Thank you for trying."'

No wonder he killed them. I'd have killed them had they been mine.

And yet you had to admire it in a way. Nothing was of no

consequence, everything was epic, no act of wrongdoing was ever less than an abomination, each event still bore upon the future well-being of the race. It was as though we were back in Genesis, among the sons of Noah and the daughters of Lot, all that breeding and begetting and lying with those you had no business lying with. And then, because there was no other way you could answer like with like, all that slaying.

4

A few weeks after Shani got engaged to Mick Kalooki, she rang me at art college. The secretary who took the call and came to collect me from my class couldn't decide whether to be cross or comforting. Students were not rung at college unless something very serious had happened. She closed her office door on me, so that I should have privacy, and touched my arm before she left.

'There is nothing wrong,' Shani told me at once, though of course there was. But at least no one had died. Not yet, anyway. She was highly agitated and had trouble breathing. Mick believed he was being followed. Couldn't prove it, couldn't identify anybody, couldn't even, with his hand on his heart, say that he *knew* he was being followed or be any more definite about why he thought he was being followed. Just a feeling. Hairs on the back of the neck, a trembling about the heart – that sort of feeling. And he wasn't a man to give into either fear or fancy.

Though I couldn't see what I could do that the police couldn't, I volunteered to catch the train to Crumpsall right away. But that wasn't what Shani wanted. What Shani wanted was for me to contact Errol Tobias.

'You think Errol's following Mick? Why would Errol follow Mick? He doesn't even know Mick, does he? He's living in London now, anyway.'

'I'm not saying we think it's Errol. But Errol might know some-thing about it.'

413

'Why?'.

'Because Errol's mother once warned Mick that if he didn't close his business she would burn it down.'

'Christ! The Crumpsall Park Hairdressing Wars.'

'Don't make jokes, Max. It's serious. The Tobiases are very ugly people.'

'I know that. But they haven't so far attacked Mick's business, have they?'

'This might be their way of warning him.'

'So what do you want me to say to Errol?'

'Just tell him our suspicions. If they think we know it's them, they might stop.'

'Wouldn't it be easier for Mick to open a business somewhere else? Otherwise they might stop just tailing him and go straight ahead with the paraffin.'

'You can't be bullied like that, Max. What would Dad have done?'

'Gone round and punched Mrs Tobias in the face. Why doesn't Mick try that?'

'Just speak to Errol for me.'

Easier said than done. I had seen what violence Errol was capable of. He had never come close to threatening me, but who was to say how he would feel were I to accuse him or his family of fingering Shani's Mick. He was highly sentimental about his mother and father, as evil bastards always are. Merely to intimate a suspicion could be enough to send him on a spree of arson that would see not just Mick's shop but my mother's house and maybe even my college razed to the ground.

Two days later, Shani rang again. This time catching me in my digs. 'Have you talked to Errol Tobias yet?' she asked me.

'I haven't been able to contact him,' I lied.

'OK,' she said. 'Don't. Just come straight up here instead.'

'What's happened?'

'Just come. No one's been hurt. Not yet anyway. But they might be if you don't get here quick.'

Tsedraiter Ike.

Mick Kalooki hadn't been imagining things. He *was* being followed. But it wasn't a Tobias or a Tobias henchman who was following him. It was Tsedraiter Ike.

He was cowering in his room when I arrived. My job was to try to coax him out. Or at least get him to take some food. For her part Shani didn't care whether the mamzer starved himself to death, but my mother couldn't allow her own brother, or whatever his relation was to her, to die under her roof.

My other job was to stand in witness. 'I want you to hear this,' Shani said. As though I were my uncle's keeper, or as though I in some way seconded, if not his repulsive behaviour, then his repulsive beliefs. An imputation that went all the way back to my having said Jew Jew, Jew Jew, Jew Jew, that day my mother was bringing me back from New Brighton.

From the other side of his bedroom door, Tsedraiter Ike denied that he had been following Mick Kalooki. What he had in fact been doing was waiting for an opportunity.

'Ask him to do what,' Shani said. 'Ask him to tell you what he was waiting for an opportunity *for*.'

I didn't need to ask. What Tsedraiter Ike was waiting for was the opportunity to tell Mick Kalooki, in a dark and secluded place – as though that was going to make a difference – that we didn't want a shaygets in the family, thank you very much, even one who knew a kreplach from a k'nish.

I only had it half right. 'Tell him,' Shani shouted, 'tell him what else you did.'

There was silence for a while. Though whether it was angry or abashed silence I couldn't be sure. For a moment I even wondered whether I could detect a sound like sobbing. But it might just as easily have been 'It's only me from over the sea, said Barnacle Bill the sailor'. Then at last, defiantly, what Shani wanted me to hear. 'I offered to make it right with him,' he said.

I stared at Shani. 'Make it right with him?'

'Money. By making it right with him he means money. Five thousand pounds. He offered Mick five thousand pounds, cash, to skedaddle.'

My mouth fell open. I didn't live in a world where people tailed people in the dead of night, and then offered them dough to beat it out of town. I'd read a million comic books where such things happened, but I wasn't living in a comic book and this was my uncle, Tsedraiter Ike not Ming the Merciless or Pruneface. I can't pretend that along with everything else I felt, I didn't also feel impressed. That took some doing! Yes, it was obscene, of course it was obscene, and it made a nonsense of the moral high ground in whose name Tsedraiter Ike believed that he was acting, to offer a bribe, to put money on the table in the sacred name of Elohim. But by Christ it took some chutzpah!

And then there was the size of the bribe itself. Five thousand pounds! Where the fuck had Tsedraiter Ike found five thousand pounds?

'Give it me,' I said. 'I'll skedaddle.'

Shani grabbed my arm. 'Don't make a joke of it, Max. Don't let him think there's a funny side. There is no funny side. He offered Mick five thousand pounds to leave me. Apart from anything else, do you not see how insulting of him that was, to suppose there would be any amount of money in the world that Mick would be prepared to leave me for? How insulting to me, and how insulting to Mick? And what does it tell you about his feelings for me, his only niece, that he would go to such lengths as actually to spend money to make me unhappy?'

From behind his door Tsedraiter Ike was insisting that Shani's happiness was all he cared about. Didn't she see? It was precisely to spare her unhappiness that he had done what he had done.

'Fuck you,' Shani shouted at him, which was the only time the F-word – in my hearing anyway – had fallen from her lips.

Which Tsedraiter Ike was just smart enough not to adduce as

evidence that the shiksefying of his niece had already begun.

That evening, as a peace-offering to Tsedraiter Ike, Mick Kalooki cooked a kosher chicken with tsimmes and latkes – the first kosher dinner ever cooked on my mother's stove. In his naivety, Mick believed friendship with Tsedraiter Ike was still possible if only Tsedraiter Ike would sit down and shmooze with him. Despite the smells, which must have reminded Tsedraiter Ike of Shabbes nights in Novoropissik, and would have been too much for a man of less obdurate principle, he refused to budge from his room.

'What's your view?' Mick asked me. 'How can such a God-fearing man be acting in this way. Didn't Ruth say to Naomi, thy people shall be my people, and thy God shall be my God, and wasn't she, though a Moabite, the progenitor of David, King of the Jews? If your Uncle Isaac wasn't a knowledgeable Jewish man, I'd say he was ignorant of Jewish history. But that cannot be, Max, can it? I'd even go so far as to say his attitude to me was racist, but that cannot be either, am I right?'

Sweet. He was a sweet man, Mick Kalooki. He went on to be a good husband to Shani and a good father to their five children, the sons among whom were circumcised in the proper manner, though not without some misgivings on the part of Shani herself. Thirty years later she would have found it hard to meet a Gentile with such a benign attitude to Jews. A Jew can't be a racist? Don't make me laugh!

But even for his times he was naive. 'A Jew is as likely to be a racist as the next man,' I told him. 'Not because of what has or hasn't happened to him, or what he has or hasn't been taught, but because he is a person with a personal psychology. And no God, however kind or cruel, can save you from your psychology.'

I was hot on psychology that year. It was a liberal studies option at art college, one that Chloë was taking, and I wanted to be close to her. Why I wanted to be close to Chloë, who in those days either ignored me or confused me with some other Israelite, was itself a question I thought doing the psychology option might

417

help me answer. Masochism, as far as I could tell from the little reading I had done – masochism was the key to everything. I tried putting it to Mick Kalooki that masochism was the engine that drove Tsedraiter Ike as well. Not racism but – to employ the language proper to the discipline – *Masochismus*.

The way to look at it was this:

What was the proven consequence of any positive assertion by a Jew of his own sense of worth – whether as a man of moral excellence, prestige, or intellectual superiority? Hostility. If any single lesson has been learned by the Jew it is that his apparent arrogance or conceit will land him in deep trouble. Why then does he persist? There can be only one answer to that. He persists because appearing arrogant serves the psychic function of satisfying an unconscious masochistic need to be landed in deep trouble. Tsedraiter Ike's offer of money to Shani's Mick was an assertion of religious and moral superiority. Not only was Mick not fit to be Shani's husband, Tsedraiter Ike's behaviour declared, his unfitness would be demonstrated by his acceptance of filthy lucre (never mind, for the moment, that he refused it). But by acting as he had, and who was to say not in full awareness of Mick's steadfast unwillingness to be corrupted, however large the sum, Tsedraiter Ike had drawn down, and at some level anticipated, a greater obloquy upon himself. Behold, yet again, the Jew laid low. 'And there he is, even as we speak, whimpering in his room.'

'That's total shit,' Shani said. 'Are you telling me that every time a Jewish parent objects to his child marrying out, what he actually wants is someone to kick him?'

'In the toches,' Mick added.

'No. What he actually wants is his child not to marry out. But what he wants and what he is seeking might not be the same thing. Though it might also be the case that the kicking, if and when it comes, will ultimately harden his conviction that he is a thing apart, a victim of a brutal Jew-hating world, which he is therefore right to save his child from if he can.'

418

'Total shit,' Shani repeated.

Throughout all this my mother regarded me with a prune-like expression. She didn't like fancy explanations. You won at kalooki if you had a good knowledge of the deck and could anticipate what the other players were thinking. You worked on the straightforward assumption that they wanted to win. If you had to take on board the possibility that what they really wanted was to lose – well, frankly you wouldn't know where you were.

But she wasn't going to say anything that might add fuel to the fire. She had grown to love Mick Kalooki. And her brother was her brother. She got up from the table, loped her long Ethiopian stride across the room, sat in an armchair and crossed her legs. When you saw my mother's ankles you wanted to cry. They were the best argument for Judaism – its golden allure, its sensuality and its fragility – I had ever encountered. Why, then, I was otherwise attracted; why, when I had grown up with this rich aroma of spiced indolence around me I let my nose lead me in the direction of flesh that was by comparison odourless and colourless, I was not at that time – not having yet done 'Introduction to Psychology II' – in a position to understand.

As for Tsedraiter Ike, he came out of his room at last and resumed his visits to the houses of the Jewish dead. He never addressed a word to Mick Kalooki again. Nor did Shani – against all Mick Kalooki's attempts at conciliation – address another word to him. When Ike died, Mick attended his funeral, hung his head and even shed a tear. Shani stayed at home.

5

I never liked the expression 'stiff-necked', but yes, as I conceded to Chloë's mother in the course of what I now realise had been planned as a goodbye and good-riddance tea, we were an implacable people. 'I doubt we are that by nature,' I told her. 'Nobody is anything by nature, Helène, unless we make an exception of your Judaeophobia. But by bitter experience. Kill or be killed.'

'Bit OTT, your soon to be ex-hubby, Chlo,' she'd said, taking a scone from my plate and wiping it on the sleeve of her blouse, while I sweated to think of a county that had 'fuck you' in it.

But yes. We were, by bitter experience, an implacable people. And we had with reason come to believe that it was only by being implacable that we had survived. True, some of us had had a go at being lenitive. Behold, we are an accommodating bunch. But the last time we had a serious go at that was in Germany. The Haskalah, as we called it. The Enlightenment. Our love affair with the Kraut. And you don't go making that kind of mistake twice.

I wanted to do my best imaginatively by Channa and Selick Washinsky, anyway. As I wanted to do my best by Manny. A moral balancing act of some complication, I accept. Of course you want to have your son sectioned when he falls in love for the second time with the same shikseh. And of course you, Manny, know that for wanting him sectioned they no longer deserve to be among the living.

It was partly to simplify my own feelings that I said to him later that same afternoon, after we too had broken off for tea, 'Christ, Manny, did it never occur to them just to go out and buy a gun and have done with it?'

He had been pulling at his fingers throughout our conversation, cracking them one by one, pulling at them as though he meant systematically to take his hands apart. 'No,' he said, after taking his time to think about it, not looking in my direction, not looking anywhere, 'I don't think so. But it occurred to *me*.'

I laughed. 'I don't see you with a gun, Manny.'

'Why not?'

'I just don't see it. You don't go together. You and guns? Forgive me – it's too incongruous.'

'You think I wouldn't know how to use one?'

'I can't see it in your hand. I can't picture it. If I imagine a gun in your hand it falls out. I mean that as a compliment.'

'So why are you laughing?'

'To express solidarity with your humanity. I can't picture a gun in my hand either. We were brought up to carry books, not guns,'

'That's not what they say in Israel.'

'Israel's different. You don't laugh in Israel.'

'You wouldn't laugh here if I was pointing a gun at you.'

'I don't know about that, Manny. Maybe I would.'

'I bet you wouldn't.'

'I couldn't take your money.'

'Do you want to try?'

I laughed again, though not as easily as I had the first time. 'No,' I said, 'I very much don't want to try.'

The problem with Bernie Krigstein was that he didn't have much of a sense of fun. In the end there are only two sorts of Jews, and I don't mean those who went through the Holocaust and those who only thought they did. I mean Jews who see the funny side of things and those who don't. The mistake is to suppose that those who see the funny side of things become cartoonists, and those who don't go into law. It's often the other way round. Krigstein made history with his comic-book story 'Master Race' because it wasn't comic. Not a line of it that wasn't sombre. 'Krigstein didn't understand the humor,' said Harvey Kurtzman, who employed him for a while on *Mad*. By 'the humor', he meant pretty well the humour of anything he was given to illustrate. 'He did funny grimness,' Kurtzman went on. 'Grimness in slapstick.' Not that there's anything you can call slapstick in 'Master Race'. But then you could argue that commandants of death camps don't as a rule give rise to slapstick much.

I don't know. I never knew. It could have been the house I grew up in – my father's punchy scepticism, my mother's death-defying kalooki nights, or just the physical and psychological ludicrousness of Tsedraiter Ike – but for me nothing was so dreadful that I couldn't see its essential drollery. This could explain why drawing Superman was ultimately beyond me. In my hands Superman's X-ray vision would only have revealed the absurdity at the heart of things. And that included Manny. Here he was, implying he had it in him to be a hit man, and I was supposed to take him seriously. It was so preposterous that I momentarily forgot he *was* a hit man, a man accused and convicted of the murder of his mother and father.

Guns were the problem. For me guns belonged to an inconceivable universe. Not only could I never have pulled a gun myself, I couldn't draw one. I could no more credit a gun with presence than I could the bulge in Tom of Finland's pants. As for whether Manny had ever owned, or, as he seemed to want to menace me into believing, *still* owned a gun, I didn't know what I thought. But the idea was gathering that I ought to be thinking something.

It's a form of disrespect, of course, I acknowledge that, not being able to grant a person the dignity of taking him entirely seriously. But that comes with the territory. Don't expect respect from a cartoonist.

Historically, the laugh was on the sort of man I was. Without any doubt I would have been among those who pooh-poohed the idea that Nazism in 1930s Germany posed any personal danger to me. Housed snugly in the Berlin suburbs, penning Grosz-like satires on pig-faced *bürgerlich* nationalism in the daytime, and slipping out at night to perform cunnilingus on Zoë under a table at Der blaue Engel, I would have hung on until the final hour and beyond, convinced that violence was a joke at heart, that no one beyond the occasional ruffian felt any differently about guns than I did. Even on the Jew Jew train I cannot imagine myself ever really believing that the guns were made of anything but cardboard or that they were taking us anywhere but to the seaside.

This is the price you pay for enlightenment. To be enlightened means to assume the enlightenment of others.

Given which serious miscalculation, I ought by this time to have evolved a world view more adequate to the facts. As Manny, to do him credit, most definitely had. Little by little I was growing to envy him. It behoved a man living in the twenty-first century, as it behoved the dramatis personae of Genesis, to be acquainted with abomination. The laughter I gave vent to when he pulled his metaphorical gun on me was misplaced and false. It masked incompetence and dissatisfaction with myself. Face to face with my old farshimelt friend, a person who on paper had lived no life to speak of, I felt the incomplete one. I hadn't killed my parents. I hadn't held a gun. I couldn't even draw a gun. If anyone hadn't lived a life, I hadn't.

6

Chloë came at me with a knife once. I ran into the bathroom, said 'God fucking help me!' into the mirror, and began to cry.

'I can smell your fear,' she triumphed. 'It's leaking out from under the door.'

'I'm not afraid for myself,' I answered, 'I'm afraid for you.'

'Well, you shouldn't be. It's not me I'm going to kill.'

She kept me in there for two hours, then swore on her mother's life that it was all right for me to come out.

What I hadn't realised was that she'd nipped out of the house in that time. While I was straining my ear to gauge the danger-ousness of her silence, she'd been down to the chemist to purchase a bottle of antibacterial skin-wash.

Swearing on her mother's life always brought a sort of peace between us. If she was lying and meant to knife me the minute I emerged, there was at least the consolation that her mother might die for it.

'There,' she said, when I did at last venture out, 'use this.'

'What is it?'

'It's to take away the smell of fear.'

I thought it was a joke. Forgetting that Chloë didn't make jokes.

'You've got a surprise coming if you think I'll be using that,' I told her.

Whereupon she came at me with the knife again.

For the duration of what was left of our marriage, I used the skin-wash twice a day.

I wasn't lying when I said I was afraid for her. A woman wielding a knife as though she means to use it is a fearful spectacle. More fearful than a man wielding a knife because the woman with the knife appears to be parted more extremely from her nature. But of course I was afraid for myself as well. Not only afraid of being mortally wounded, but afraid that the ordinary condition of my life – a life of jokes, Jews, bitterness and whys – could so easily be disrupted and made to count for nothing. A knife raised in anger made life morally not worth living, whether the blade touched you or not. A gun the same.

And the antibacterial skin-wash couldn't help with that.

7

The moment I got the opportunity I asked Manny what he would have done with a gun had he bought one.

'Shot someone,' he said.

'Who?'

'Who do you think?'

For some reason an event unrelated to any we'd been discussing flashed into my mind.

'Errol,' I said.

'Errol? Who's Errol?'

'Errol Tobias. The meshuggener from our street who used to bully you.'

'I don't remember him.'

Was he lying? I had no idea. Was he lying about the gun, come to that? Again, I had no idea.

But I could see that it illuminated Manny's face to learn that I could imagine more people for him to shoot than he had imagined for himself. He would have liked it, I thought, had I gone on guessing. H-horst S-ssschumann, then? Klaus Endruweit? The judge who pronounced sentence on you? Shitworth Whitworth? The people who made you eat your own faeces from the metal pot? David Irving? Me?

Rather than embark on what might have turned out to be another list of the enemies of the Jewish people, I tried him with a teaser of my own.

'Why, Manny?'

'Why didn't I shoot anyone?'

'Well, that too. But I meant why did you want to.'

His reply surprised me not only by its promptness, but by its vehemence.

'It couldn't go on for ever,' he said. 'In the end someone has to sort things out.'

'With a gun?'

'With whatever.'

Meaning, I supposed, the gas taps. But in that case, why all the gun talk?

'So are you saying you *did* get a gun?' I asked him.

He suddenly turned impatient on me. It was always the same. You asked him one innocuous little sentence – *So did you get a gun or didn't you?* – and he was off.

'I'm going to bed,' he said

An hour later he popped his head round the door. In his dismal green-and-grey-check 1950s pyjamas, he looked disembodied. Though they would have fitted an average-size schoolboy, his pyjamas hung off him. A magician might tap them with his wand and hey presto – they would fall to the floor, and nobody would be inside!

He coughed, wanting my attention.

'Each man kills the thing he loves,' he said, when I looked up.

'The coward does it with a kiss. The brave man with a sword. But sometimes the coward does it with a sword as well.'

With which he wished me goodnight and retired a second time.

So what the fuck did any of that signify?

I found it hard to sleep. Unlike me. Even with Alÿs lying beside me like the ghost of pogroms past I had always managed to sleep. To my astonishment and self-disgust I had slept soundly the night my father died. But there was no sleeping through Manny's riddles, of which the coward and his sword were, to tell the truth, by no means the most perplexing. What about his 'sorting things out' with a gun? What about his daring me to a face up to him with a gun? Was that metaphorical or did he actually have one in his posession, here, in my house, hidden in his suitcase or under Zoë's old mattress?

Present fears aside, nothing he had said to me made any sense. Whatever sorting out had needed doing he had done. He had sealed the door with a sheet – easy because there were sheets piled everywhere in the Washinsky house – turned on the gas tap, and that, ladies and gentlemen of the jury, was the obstacle to his brother's union, sorted. What need of any gun? Unless, to be on the safe side, or as an act of kindness to them, he had shot them first. But I recalled no talk of bullets, and presumably the police, though inexperienced in the crime of double Jewish patricide in Crumpsall Park, would have noticed had any been discharged.

Since my mother kept bohemian hours, playing cards until very late, or sitting up listening to talkback radio half the night, and never minded whatever time I called, I thought I'd ring and ask what she remembered.

'You kalooki-ing or not?' I enquired.

'Just finished.'

'Did you win?'

'The game won.'

'Listen, Ma, did you ever hear anything about Manny Washinsky's parents being shot?'

My mother was elderly now. This was cruel of me. 'I remember something,' she said. 'Weren't they killed in a road accident? Or was that their boy?'

I hadn't told her I had made contact with Manny again, let alone that he had become my lodger. It all felt too complicated to explain. And I feared – I can't explain why – that it might upset her. But she was evidently past upset on the Washinskys' account.

'Fine,' I said, 'I won't bother you any more.'

'Why do want to know? You aren't going to put them in a cartoon?'

'Ma, why would I do that?'

'You tell me. Why would you put me or your sister in a cartoon?'

'I have never put you or my sister in a cartoon.'

'That's not true. You used to get Shani to pose for you in boots,'

How did she remember that? 'I wasn't drawing Shani, I was drawing the boots.'

'Yes, so that you could put her in a camp. I never understood what all that was about, Maxie. Concentration camps?'

'I never put Shani in a camp. I drew the boots, that was it.'

'And you put the boots in the camp. It's the same thing. They were Shani's boots.'

'Ma, it's what you do if you draw. You draw from life.'

'Life I wouldn't have minded. What you were drawing, Maxie, was death. Camps, camps, camps – where did you get all that stuff from? The only camp you ever went to was Butlin's.'

I rang off, making my usual promise to go up and see her soon. Had I been any kind of son I'd have kidnapped her from Crumpsall and brought her down to live with me in Belsize Park, where Jews were not pretending they were back in Poland. Me, my mother, Manny – it would have made a nice household, all that was left of the Crumpsall that had been.

But then again, not if Manny was keeping a gun on the premises.

Unable to sleep, I made myself some tea and paced the floor. *Someone has to sort things out*. If that didn't mean what I had originally thought it meant, what did it mean?

An idea came to me, shocking at first, but plausible the more I thought about it.

Dorothy.

The cleanest, that's to say the most effective way to have sorted things out was to have got rid of Dorothy.

Five thousand smackers would have been the cleanest way to do it, but she would surely have said no to that, just as Mick Kalooki had, and anyway, where was Manny going to lay his hands on that sort of money?

Why, after getting rid of Dorothy, Manny would have needed to get rid of his parents as well was a stage too far in my reasoning. But blaming them for making a murderer of him was certainly one motive. As was sparing them from discovering what he'd done. You can kill out of love as well as hate, as he had just reminded me.

But I was running ahead of my own thoughts. Dorothy shot and killed, or Dorothy shot and wounded, or Dorothy shot and missed, was substanceless imagining. Enough – terrible enough – just to imagine Manny *wanting* Dorothy to be shot. The Eleventh Commandment: you don't go round killing people in your head. Least of all when the worst thing they've done to you is to fall in love with your brother. You should love those, should you not, who love those to whom you are devoted? You should be bound by the concurrence of your affections. As Shani believed Tsedraiter Ike should have been bound to Mick.

Then again, let Dorothy's virtues plead angel-tongued against her taking off, she had wreaked havoc on the Washinskys. Twice, and twice is more than twice as bad as once. Selick Washinsky might make a better job of dying this time round. Asher too might not survive it all again. True, Manny had looked with a brother's love into Asher's heart and imagined it as an empty bed which now, miraculously, was warm. But what if this rerun of old happiness merely presaged a rerun of old sorrows? She had made a ghost of Asher before; who was to say she would not make a ghost of him again.

It should have been over. Tragically over, but over. Manny had been on her side the first time. But her second coming changed the distribution of right and wrong.

And then there was himself to consider. Were his feelings of no account? Dorothy had stepped in between him and his brother – unceremoniously elbowing him aside – palpitating with the greed of life, just as Manny was thinking that his own life, at last, was brimming over with happiness.

Kill or be killed.

I'd have tackled him with this the next day had he allowed me. But he must have known something along these lines was in the offing. He spent the day in bed, whatever he knew. Only coming out to make himself a honey and banana sandwich when he thought I wasn't around.

He spent the next day in bed as well. And the next.

This might have been pure fancy, but it was as though he had turned himself in for a crime for which he had until now escaped punishment, appointing me to be his warder.

It felt quiet and oddly comforting in the house. I half wanted to go round at night, checking the cells, whistling, and jingling my keys.

FIFTEEN

I dunno . . . Maybe EVERYONE has to feel guilty.
EVERYONE! FOREVER!

Art Spiegelman, *Maus*

1

On the evening of the third day, Francine rang. How was our yeshiva boy, she wanted to know. I tried my new theory out on her – not that of my house having become a prison, but Manny pointing a gun at Dorothy.

She was excited by the gun element. 'A gun's good,' she said. 'We like guns.'

'Except,' I said, going off my own theory the minute I voiced it, 'I think it's all baloney.'

'Why do you think it's all baloney?'

'Well, for a start because there's no reason to believe he shot anybody, except in his own head.'

Shooting people in his own head she was less excited by. 'Not quite so televisual,' she told me. 'And besides, I rather liked where we were going last time. Manny sweet on the girl.'

'Manny? Sweet? Manny doesn't do sweet.'

'Every man does sweet, Max. Even weird ones with payess.'

Payess. Hebrew for sidelocks. How did she know payess?

(*Ways of Saying Payess When You're Not Jewish*, Vol. III.)

'Run it by me, Francine,' I said.

'Manny sweet on girl, Manny jealous of his brother, Manny thinking of killing his brother, Manny then sparing his brother out of love for the girl, and killing his parents instead . . .'

'Because he blamed them for putting him in payess and making him unlovable?'

'Well, that as well, certainly, but more I think because he wanted to make a statement about Jewish attitudes to Gentiles. He killed his parents because he could not forgive the things they had said about the girl. He was killing his religion. We can run on that. It's only a shame – from the point of view of narrative I mean – that he didn't then turn the gun on himself. That would have been perfect.'

'Not gun, gas taps.'

'Yes, gas taps, more perfect still.'

But if we were going in that direction, I had another thought. Asher, in despair of ever getting his parents to accept Dorothy, realising that they will never leave him alone so long as he is with her, and discovering, what is more, that they have tried to get him certified as a lunatic, turns the gas taps on them. Manny, out of love for the girl, takes the rap. 'I accept that you love him and will never love me, so be it, and rather than see you suffer another moment's unhappiness I will rot away my life in prison, adieu, my lovely, my golden faigeleh, be happy with my brother, this is a far far better thing, blah blah.' Several years later, when Manny learns that Asher has turned into a love rat, cheating on Dorothy with any woman he can lay his hands on, he thinks of having him rubbed out. No – better still – Dorothy, who warned Asher she would kill him if he ever left her again, goes to Manny and asks him to arrange to have Asher rubbed out. Manny says he'll see what he can do. The gun wasn't literally in Manny's hands. He put a contract out. Not hard to do when you're inside. Whisper, whisper, bar of chocolate, maybe a blow job, and it's as good as done. Only at the last minute he relented. He couldn't make Dorothy husbandless – nor could he make her a murderer in the eyes of God – no matter what sort of mamzer the husband had turned out to be.

A longer silence than usual from Francine. Then, 'Are you taking the piss, Max?'

Who are you, Maxie Glickman? What's your game?

'I don't see,' I said, 'that my narrative is any more far-fetched than yours. Except maybe for the blow job.'

'OK, so do we *know* that Asher was a love rat?'

'We don't know anything. Manny glides away from any discussion of Asher and Dorothy as they are now, *if* they are now, or even as they were when he was put away. I think they stopped for him when his parents stopped. It's them we should ask.'

'Easier said than done. First find them.'

'Isn't that Christopher Christmas's job?'

'I'll speak to him. But in the meantime, Max, can we get the Jewish angle back?'

'This isn't about religion, Francine. I'm coming round to your way of thinking – it's about love. I'm even wondering if we shouldn't make them all Gentiles so as not to get sidetracked.'

'Trust me, Max,' she said, 'it's about religion.'

2

There's a simple rule about temper: if you can't lose it with one person you lose it with another.

In the brief but bruising time I was married to Alÿs – I accept it was brief and bruising for her too – I behaved abominably to my mother. 'If this is what you're like married to a nice Jewish girl,' she said towards the end of one of my more vitriolic Crumpsall visits, in the course of which I'd attacked everything she did and everyone she knew, 'I can't wait for you to be divorced and going out with a shikseh again.'

'Amen to that,' I said. 'And Alÿs isn't a nice Jewish girl. There are no nice Jewish girls. The first Jewish girl I ever touched gave me crabs—'

'Max!'

'Well, it's the truth. And this one wants me to become a

Palestinian. They're either lewd or they're self-righteous. Or they live in the mikveh. Or they play kalooki.'

'Well, that's a variety for you to choose from.'

'But none of them are nice. I've never met a nice Jewish girl.'

'What about your sister? Isn't Shani a nice Jewish girl?'

'Yes but she's my sister, and she plays kalooki.'

'Will you shut up about kalooki!'

'I can't. Why, if you must play cards, don't you at least play bridge? Or poker even. Why don't you go to the theatre? This house used to be full of intellectuals. They talked Marx in the garden, Ma. Where are they now?'

'Dead, Max.'

'So find some more.'

'There are no more. They don't make Jews like that any more. And anyway, they came for your father, not me.'

'That isn't true. They came every bit as much for you. I remember how their faces lit up when they saw you.'

'You can hardly call that intellectual.'

'Yes, you can. Since they weren't, I assume, all having affairs with you, they were in love with the idea of you. And you have to be an intellectual to be in love with the idea of beauty.'

'Thank you, Max. But I was young then. I'm sorry that I haven't been able to stay young for you for ever.'

'Ma, it's not just about being young. You used to dance in the living room with trade unionists. And when you weren't dancing you were arguing. Now you watch soap operas on television and go to see *Phantom of the Opera* with your girlfriends.'

'Twice!'

'Exactly.'

'What's wrong with *Phantom of the Opera*?'

'Everything. But the main thing wrong with it is that it's not Jewish. It's goyisher. You should have some pride.'

'So what are we supposed to do? Watch *Fiddler on the Roof* every night?'

433

'I don't mean that.'

'You marry shiksehs and I watch *Fiddler on the Roof* to make it right! Here's an idea – why don't you stop marrying shiksehs and let me enjoy *Phantom of the Opera*?'

'Because I lose my temper when I'm not married to a shikseh.'

'You're not exactly happy when you're with them, Max.'

'I know. But at least my unhappiness isn't Jew-centred. I can be unhappy and not think it's the fault of our religion. I don't have to be disappointed by another Jew. What's happened to us, Ma? Why are all the Jews up here either make-believe goyim or Hassidim in fancy dress? In hiding, or not in hiding enough. Where did our Jewish seriousness go?'

'The Hassidim you are so rude about are serious. How can you say they aren't? They wouldn't think you were much of a serious Jew.'

'Because I'm a cartoonist?'

'Because you're not a serious Jew. What do you do that is Jewish?'

'What do I do that is Jewish? That's a laugh. What do I do that isn't Jewish? And everything I do is more Jewish than anything they do. They're a sect. They're two centuries old, tip-top. And they're as flaky as Mormons. I'm the real thing, Ma. I go back to the Old Testament. I'm what a Jew is supposed to be. I don't forgive. I separate things. I argue with the Almighty. He likes that. He likes what I do more than he likes their blind obedi-ence or all that ecstatic dancing they go in for. Every time anyone danced in the seeing of the Lord in the good old days He sent down thunderbolts to burn them up. He'd have Hassids for break-fast if He were still around. They're not serious. They're hysterics. Serious was what happened in our garden.'

'Don't upset me.'

But I needed to upset her.

'I want my dad back, Ma.'

'So do I, Max.'

* * *

434

And in the same way, for the very reason that I couldn't tell Francine what I thought of her – not least because I didn't *know* what I thought of her – I took it out on Manny.

'Look, I enjoy having you here,' I told him, when he finally surfaced for breakfast. He hadn't bothered to change out of his neurovegetative pyjamas. His curiously unlined face was crumpled from sleep. He looked like a boy who had gone to bed forty years ago, and woken up an old man.

But not old enough to respond gracefully. No *Thank you very much, I am enjoying being here myself*. No shy smile of gratitude if words were beyond him. But then what the hell! – he never did have manners.

'You can stay for ever if you like,' I went on. 'To my surprise I find your company soothing. But come on, Manny. You know perfectly well what the gesheft is here. You agreed to it. Yes, you said, yes you'd talk to me. And all I get, when I get anything, when you haven't gone into hiding for a week, is Horst Schumann, Oscar fucking Wilde, guns, swords, you shooting Dorothy—'

'Who said anything about shooting Dorothy?'

'You asked me to guess who you might have fancied pointing your little gun at. So that's my guess. Dorothy. Or that *was* my guess. Today I don't think you fancied pointing a gun at anybody.'

'Why would I have wanted to s-ssschoot Dorothy?'

He was growing agitated, banging the tips of his fingers together.

'I've just told you, that isn't any longer what I think. You were winding me up. I let myself be wound. OK?'

'But you let yourself think I wanted to kill Dorothy?'

'Manny, for God's sake – I did, I do, I will, think anything. I am not proof against thoughts. Particularly when another person's prompting them as you were. Don't make anything of this.'

I passed him the toast. Peace.

He took two slices and cut them into narrow segments, like the

435

soldiers children dip into their eggs. Then he stared down at what he'd done. Two hands, of five fingers each.

'Why, of all people, did you choose Dorothy? I was Dorothy's friend. If you want to know, I liked her more than Asher.'

Did he mean he liked her more than Asher liked her, or he liked her more than he liked Asher? You don't ask. You don't quibble over syntax when someone's making human hands out of toast. But it did matter, what he meant. It made a difference.

'That's interesting,' I said. Thinking as I said it that poor old Francine had employed the wrong person for this job. She was right – I did come at everything backwards.

'I'm flattered by your interest. But I want you to explain your thinking to me. You explain what you think Dorothy had ever done to me that I should want to harm her.'

Fucked your life, was the answer I wanted to give. But what I chose to say was, 'Caused everyone great pain. Caused you misery.'

'How had she caused me misery?'

'It caused you immense misery to see everyone so distressed the first time. You told me that. You told me you were having fits. I can easily understand that when she appeared from nowhere, starting the whole thing over, just as you and Asher were getting on well . . . Christ, Manny, you said yourself you felt as though your life had just begun . . . I can easily understand why that would have upset you.'

'*Upset* me?' More out of distress than anger, it seemed to me, he pushed his toast away from him. A couple of pieces fell to the floor. My job to retrieve them, I thought. And maybe my job to stay down there, scrabbling about under the table, while he calmed himself.

'S-sscch-sssch-shit!' he said, rising from his chair. It was the first time he had ever got the word out. The first time I had ever heard him swear.

A great desolation swept over me. Now that he had sworn, the world was a sadder, meaner place. We'd been happy so long as Manny kept the s-shit inside him. We hadn't known it, but we were.

'I'm sorry,' I said.

He went over to the sink and turned the tap on, holding his hands under the water. Not washing, just letting them get wet. 'Sorry. That's all right then, is it? You're sorry.'

'No, it isn't all right if you don't feel it is. But I'm still sorry.'

He was, I thought, resolutely showing me his back, not just hiding himself from me but denying me his face, excluding me from human commerce. Was that what prisoners did? I wondered. Was that how, in a confined space, you withdrew the consolation of humanity?

From behind he resembled a crippled child, twisted and shrunken, the head, on its optimistic question-mark neck, still a little boy's; but inside the dressing gown his bones were disintegrating. Shake the dressing gown and he'd fall out of it in bits.

I could tell from the movement of his neck that he was saying something, emptying words into the sink.

'I can't hear you,' I said. 'If you want to speak to me, you'll have to turn the water off.'

He swung round and bared his little teeth at me. Had he been holding a gun . . .

'You don't kill people,' he said, 'because they "upset" you.'

It was now or never. 'So why *do* you kill people?' I said at long, long last.

3

I knew the official version by heart. On his belated arrest in 1961, the Austrian-born euthanasiast and flautist Georg Renno, deputy director of the SS gassing institution at Hartheim, declared that 'Turning the tap on was no big deal'. According to Manny's lawyers, it was in order to verify this claim that Manny had turned

437

the tap on while his parents were asleep. Renno was wrong, he said in his statement. Turning the tap on *was* a big deal.

I wondered if, over breakfast – over what was left of breakfast – Manny was going to tell me what he'd told his lawyers.

But it was hard to get him off the subject of Dorothy. I cannot reproduce the fits and starts of what he said. Now returning to the table to discuss it all equably, as though he hadn't thrown his toast on the floor, hadn't turned his back on me, hadn't bared his teeth, for all the world as though we were discussing nothing more important to him than an item in the morning's newspapers; then rising from his chair again in what I feared could be the beginning of a fit, going over to the sink, turning on the water as though he needed not to hear himself, shouting into the water and rinsing away his words. But the gist of it was that he saw Dorothy as an opportunity not just for Asher, but for his family, for his father and his mother, and for himself. She was their second chance. In Dorothy something else had happened that wasn't the same old story. She was a release for them. Nothing to do with forgiveness. Nothing to do with making peace with Germans. It wasn't even about her, it was about them. Whatever the rights and wrongs of refusing her the first time, they should, for their own sakes, have accepted her a second. He could see the argument going on for ever. Again and again, round and around, for another two thousand years and another two thousand years after that. Dorothy gave them a way of breaking the chain. Accept Dorothy and it was as good, after all that darkness, as accepting light. He made her sound like a new religion.

I nodded. But my offering to know what he meant made him furious.

'Why are you doing that?' His voice almost became a bark. 'Do you think I am saying this in order for you to agree with me? This was my truth, not anybody else's. I don't invite you to s-ssshare my truth.'

I was careful not to nod my head at that.

But he could see inside my head anyway. Although he didn't look at me I could feel him burrowing away in there, turning his X-ray vision on me. Banality – that was what he saw. *And then you snapped, Manny. And then you felt you could take it no longer. Someone had to make a change, so you did. Quick, before someone else attempted something even worse. Quick, before you had a fit. Unless it was in a fit that you did it. Boom! Hiss!* Whatever noise the instruments of murder make.

Banalities.

So I was prepared for him to be at least more original. And he didn't let me down.

'I didn't kill my parents,' he said, seemingly inconsequentially, and yet very precisely too, as much as to suggest that he had all along been coming to this point, organising his answer not just to the question I had put to him minutes before, but to every question raised by our meeting up again in the first place, if only I'd been patient – 'I didn't kill my parents, I simply stopped protecting them.'

The kitchen, I thought, turned very cold.

I wanted to nod, but yet again I did not dare. I also had the feeling that it was important to him that I should be bemused by this; that he needed us to be a long way apart, of no moral or experiential likeness to each other whatsoever.

Ever since he was a child, he went on, he had believed his parents' safety to be dependent on him and him alone. He could not remember when he hadn't thought the only thing that stood between them and catastrophe was him. There were dangers all round, and it had been his responsibility to avert them for everybody. He was the reason the house did not burn down or flood. He was the reason they were not burgled and killed in their beds. If his father were to escape being put up against a wall and shot, he, Manny, had to watch over him. He knew what they did to Jewish women. What was to stop them doing it again? There was no indignity or degradation or disaster he did not imagine

439

befalling them. He foresaw everything. Foresaw it photographic-ally, pictured them in a picture book, though not the sort of picture books I made. I could laugh all I liked (I hardly need to point out that I was not laughing), but whatever had happened once could happen again. There was even a sense, though he didn't expect me to understand this either, in which everything that had happened *had* happened again, and *was* happening, and happening to them, despite all his efforts to keep them safe. Asher was no use. Asher was incapable of looking out for anybody. Asher, in fact, was just another of his obligations. If Asher did not fall under a bus or forget to wake up in the morning, if Asher wasn't found hanging from a tree in the forest with his genitals cut off, that was only because he, Manny, stood guard to see it didn't happen. He kept them alive, every member of his family, by sheer effort of his will. And kept himself alive for them like-wise, because – he didn't expect me to understand this – these too were among the horrors he imagined on their behalf: his own death, their horror at finding him with all his bones broken at the bottom of the stairs, or drowned in the bath, the grief they would feel, the shock which would itself be enough to kill them, so that he couldn't take a step without being conscious of his own safety and how much he owed them that, how important it was that he stayed alive for them, that he spared them the anguish of his death . . .

'I protected and protected and protected them, and then one day' – I thought he was going to snap his fingers to show how little effort it had cost him to come to his decision, how sudden and serene that 'one day' was – 'I didn't want to protect them any longer.'

The calm that came off him, like the sudden cold in the kitchen, was preternatural. I had not before been privy to an explanation of a murder. I had no idea what happened next. Would he faint clean away? Would he turn to ashes while I looked at him? Or was it up to me to return him to humanity, to enfold him in my arms and keep him there for however long, however many hours or days or years, it took? The language of professional carers: *And who was watching over you, Manny?*

But that was not a language, fortunately or unfortunately, over which I possessed the slightest mastery. *Who was looking after you, Manny? Who is looking after you now, Manny?* Sorry, couldn't do it. Not within my compass. Didn't know how and to be truthful didn't want to. Too emotionally fastidious. The only voice I trusted in myself, face to face with Jews – different with my Gentile wives, but then everything was different with my Gentile wives – was Yahweh's, the voice of the unforgiving mountain god. Between ourselves – *unserer* – there were no pardons granted. Between me and the others – *anderer* – every sort of moral laxity was allowed a voice. But maybe that was because between me and *anderer* nothing counted. That was how *they* understood it, anyway. 'You don't see me,' Zoë told me once. 'I might as well be a ghost. You should be married to a Jew. You only really notice Jews.' 'But I love you,' I told her. 'I believe you,' she replied, 'but what's that worth when you don't value love?'

No arms around Manny, anyway. In the eerie cold, only exegetical austerity, yeshiva boy to yeshiva boy. Something did not yet add up. In the logic of events, inaction and action had been elided. 'But actually turning on the tap, Manny . . . Actually bending to the task of doing that, turning on the fucking tap for Christ's sake . . . If that was not an action in itself, but was merely desisting from an action, then you might as well be telling me it was no big deal . . .'

'You think I have been saying it was no big deal? Then you haven't listened to a word I've said.'

And that was it. Spell broken.

He did not lose his temper a second time. He merely, as it were, washed his hands of me. If I wasn't up to receiving his confidences, I wasn't. No more to say. There was an air of bruised fatality about him. A man too accustomed to being misunderstood or misconstrued, or simply not listened to, to make a fuss of any new instance of incomprehension.

'I think I'll go out now,' he said.

'Go out where?' So far he had never left the house without me. We hadn't discussed it, but I had taken that to mean he was frightened to be out in London on his own. It touched me rather. He was my charge. I was responsible for him. So ought I to be *allowing* him out? 'I'll come with you,' I suggested.

He shook his head. 'I want to walk.'

Walk? Since when did Manny walk? Zikh arumdreying was what Manny did, going around in purposeless circles, but walking . . .

'Where will you walk?'

'I'll find somewhere.'

'Do you want a map? I'll lend you an *A to Z*.'

'No.'

'Do you have money?'

'I'm not your child,' he said.

'And I have no desire to be your parent,' I replied. A remark which in retrospect I realise could have been misconstrued.

I left him to it anyway, taking the papers to my bedroom. There were things I needed to think about. I gave it about an hour, then went back to the kitchen, fully expecting to see him there, staring at his toast. But he was gone. He was gone from Zoë's old room too. Something about the way he'd left it, something about the half-made bed and the empty bedside table, something suggestive of a final evacuation, made me look for his cardboard suitcase. I admit to being disappointed to discover it was still there.

But since it was, I had no choice but to go through it. He had not emptied his clothes into any of the drawers I had made available to him. Nor had he made use of the wardrobe. There they still were, the few shirts and pairs of trousers he'd come away with. Folded neatly, something he must have learned in prison, because the Washinskys had not been folders. I had never seen clothes so uninvested either with the promise or the memory of life. It wasn't so much that they were cheap clothes – though they were that, cheap and drab and thin – as that they gave no idea of the person to whom they belonged, why he owned them, according to what principle he had chosen them. Institution clothes were what they looked, to be worn in a place of incarceration. Clothes without expectancy or anticipation. Clothes which might as well have been the cerements of a corpse.

No gun, however. Assuming I'd have known a gun when I saw one, no gun in his case, and no gun under Zoë's mattress either. Nor anywhere else I searched. Just childish bravado, then, his gun talk.

Unless he had taken it out with him.

4

After two hours persuading myself I didn't care where the meshuggener had got to, I thought I had better go and look for him. Manny's well-being in the big city apart, I believed I had a duty of care to the community: it is irresponsible to let a possibly armed homicidal maniac – a person who thinks of murder simply as a cessation of responsibility – out of your sight.

If he was going to be anywhere, he was going to be in the vicinity of the British Museum. There was no other part of London he knew. And he could hardly be said to know that well. Occasionally, when I dropped into the Comic Shop, he would do some second-hand book browsing, but never more than half a block from me. When the sun shone it was understood that if I lost him I would find him again in the courtyard of the British Museum, on a concrete slab if he could grab one, or on the steps, or just standing against the railings looking at the sky. The cafés which he liked he only ever visited with me. A matter of saving money, partly, since I told him we were on expenses and that if I paid I could always claim the money back from Lipsync, but I suspected diffidence also played a part. It was my guess he would not have known how to ask for the chicken-avocado ciabatta I ordered for us when I was feeling stern, or the Nutella and banana pancake I ordered for him when I was feeling indulgent, because he didn't know what either dish was called.

I tried all the cafés, though, when neither the bookshops nor the courtyard yielded him, going back to each of them three or four times in case he'd shuffled into the one while I was looking in the other. But he wasn't to be found. And there wasn't anyone I could ask. Everyone was here for the day only, and would not have remembered him anyway even had they seen him half an hour before. You don't notice an invisible man.

My own preference, when I was in the area, was for a coffee and a biscuit inside the museum itself, under Norman Foster's glass roof. I liked seeing the sky while listening to the babble of human voices, a noisy sky appealing to me far more than a silent one. Anthropocentric, one of my art teachers had called me. No eye for what wasn't human. The Jewish failing. Laws, ethics, *Spitzfindigkeit* (or kopdreying, to employ the sweeter cartoonery of Yiddish), which means exactly what it sounds: twisting the mind in increasingly over-subtle acts of exegesis – and let nature go hang. Laws, ethics, *Spitzfindigkeit*, and now Manny. In one sense I was freer of him than I'd been in weeks. He had filled me in. I could stop imagining that if I kept asking I would discover he was innocent of any crime. No, Asher had not done it; Dorothy had not done it; Dorothy's father – out of motives of fatherly concern and recrudescence of Teutonic loathing – had not done it; Errol Tobias – as an expression of unfocused malignity – had not done it; Shitworth Whitworth – out of whatever hatred governs geography teachers – had not done it; some passing anti-Semite – giving vent to passing anti-Semitism – had not done it; the Washinsksys themselves – sick of the strife and the shame – they had not done it to each other; and nor – as an act of the imagination, hating so virulently the idea of Jew which the

Washinskys put into the world that I turned the tap on psycho-kinetically — nor had I. Manny had done it. Which should have been all right, but wasn't.

I couldn't let him alone. In some way I could not explain or give any reason for, I wanted to call him to my account. The State had completed its business with him. For all I knew God had completed His business with him. Now I needed us to settle our affairs. But what on earth did Manny have to answer to me for?

I drank more coffee, wondering what I would do if I didn't find him, then saw him, much as if he'd been there all along and I hadn't known how to look, sitting at a strange angle, half on, half off a swivel stool, at a table with a group of six or seven children, Asians or Arabs or Israelis. I wasn't sure, from the distance between us, whether the Azams were among them. Assuming that they didn't visit the British Museum every day, it was hardly a reasonable expectation that they should have been. Unless Manny had been in secret communication with them, which was surely impossible. But he looked at home with them, whoever they were, examining with minute interest what they'd bought from the museum shop, joining them in winding thongs around his wrists, opening books as they did, in that violent way of children, as though they meant to throw away the page now that they had finished with it. And they, in turn, appeared to be enchanted with him, light flashing from the fishpools of their Heshbon eyes when he played the fool, laughing like the children of gods when he pretended to a panic because he could not free his finger from a Chinese finger-trap in which one of them had trapped him. That's if he was pretending.

Nutters get on with children, I had observed that before. Maybe their size is right. Maybe they don't notice the nuttiness. I won't go down the route of claiming that they share visionary qualities. They looked as at ease with him as they were with one another, anyway. So much so that I found myself wondering whether he had a paternal gift which, tragically, he had never found the opportunity to exercise. He was up against uncommonly good opposition. At every other table a father was demonstrating the art of modern parenting: holding his child to his chest so he could plug in to the soothing beating of Daddy's heart, kneeling to point out a detail of architecture or sculpture – 'You see that statue, there, of a man on a horse' – showing infinite patience in the face of a display of blank unreasonableness for which a father of my father's generation would have sent us to our rooms without dinner. Finished, all that. No more patriarchs. The boy-father of today, mindful of every psychological scar in the catalogue, strews rose petals before his offspring's baby feet. Which doesn't augur well for circumcision. Or any other of the Primal Father's cruel exactions, come to that. We are falling out of moral fashion. Once upon a time, confusing circumcision with castration, the Gentiles saw us as an effeminised people. They even believed we menstruated. The men, I mean. So degenerate were we, we bled like women. Hence our unquenchable thirst for Gentile babies' blood: we had to replenish our own exhausted stocks. Chloë – speaking of my having been effeminised – took me to see an S&M all-leather *Salomé* in Hamburg once, partly for the satisfaction of drawing my attention to the dramatis personae – Jew One, Jew Two, Jew Three, Jew Four, Jew Five. 'You're all essentially so alike,' she said, 'I think calling you by numbers is as satisfactory a system as any. From now on I'll know you as Jew Thirteen.' But chiefly she wanted me to hear what peevish, caterwauling eunuchs Richard Strauss had made us. The squeaking Jew, without a sinew in his body.

Now, at the beginning of the twenty-first century, we were too harsh.

Watching Manny with the children, you might have picked him for our saviour. Thanks to Manny, unselfconsciously engrossed with kids, as restless and awkward at the table as they were, without any pretence to Old Testament authority – Manny shy, Manny gentle, Manny wriggling about – we had a future. I caught myself smiling watching him, as though he were a child of mine. I had sent him out to play – *Go on, swap comics with them* – and he had found himself some little friends. I won't pretend I wasn't even upset by the sight, as though I knew I would eventually have to let him go. It was only when I saw him reach along to touch the hair of the boy sitting next door but one to him – so it wasn't anybody's hair; it was specifically *this* child's hair he wanted to touch, hair as gleaming dark as damson jam – that I took fright. The man had spent half his life behind bars, his mind impaired by abnormality. Of what he had done or become in prison, of how he had solaced himself, or imagined solacing himself, I knew nothing. It wasn't completely out of the question that he had a gun on him. And I was smiling benevolently on the easy way he had with children. Had I taken leave of my senses?

Out of the question to go over and haul him out. And I certainly wasn't going to call someone in British Museum uniform and tell him my suspicions. If he needed watching, I would watch him. He wouldn't be there all day. Children don't have long attention spans. Neither did he. It wouldn't be hard for me to sit him out, and so little notice did he pay his surroundings, so uninterested was he in anyone but his coal-eyed Lilliputian company, that there was no danger he would see me, or guess my purpose, however intense my scrutiny.

The party stayed together another half an hour. In that time I did not see Manny do anything untoward, unless the simply being with them was untoward enough. He did not again touch anyone's hair. And even that touch, as I replayed my memory of it, was the merest brush; however deliberate, as innocent as we can these days allow any touching by an adult of a child to be. A man might put his palm up against a slab of stone or run a piece of material between his fingers and be suspected of more devious intention. When they got up to leave, Manny with them, I followed at a distance. I watched them walk down the steps into the sunlight, and then disperse, callously in the way of children, barely pausing to say goodbye to him, one group skipping off purposefully through the main gate, the other apparently going in search of someone they were expecting – a parent, a teacher, another friend. Manny stood in the courtyard and looked at the sky. He had not exchanged anything you could call a familiarity with a single one of them. He had not even shaken their hands. Just a brief unanswered wave, and then the sky.

I couldn't see his face. But from the tilt of his head I wondered if he was yammering. You can always tell, even from behind, when a person is grieving. There is some ravage in the posture. And something in the air about them that tells you that your being there, observing or not observing, is a profanity.

I didn't call his name. Nor did I follow him. He had got here on his own. He could get back. I was not his keeper.

I stayed out late, sitting in cafés, sketching. Nothing malicious. Where I didn't see anything I liked, I didn't draw it. When I returned I found a little package waiting for me in a British Museum plastic bag. It contained a tie. A silk British Museum tie illustrated with a scene from the *Egyptian Book of the Dead*. An elegant little card, explanatory of the scene, came with the tie. Ani and his wife Tutu watch as Ani's heart is weighed in the balance against an ostrich feather representative of Maat, goddess of truth and justice. Anubis, the canine god of the dead, affirms the accuracy of the scales. Ammut, the obscene waste-disposer of the netherworld, part crocodile, part lion, part hippopotamus, stands ready to devour any heart made heavy by sin.

There was no message with the package. But then what was there to say?

When I looked into Manny's room this time I was certain his cardboard case would be gone. And it was.

Before going to bed I put the tie around my neck. It fell nicely, Ammut the heart-gobbler pushing his snout into my chest. So, had I sinned? Egregiously, if promiscuous suspicion is to be

448

called a sin. For the first time I understood what was meant by a statute of limitation. You pay your debt and that's enough. But I had weighed down Manny with more crimes than hell had room for, imagining him capable of everything except competence, so that in the end I didn't know whether to take him seriously or lightly, as a monster or a buffoon, or ultimately as both. And, much as with his father when we played street cricket, trying to hit an 'eight' through the window of the dark little room where he sewed himself blind, for no other reason than that he was a Jew of the wrong sort. Suspecting Manny of wishing harm to Dorothy – merely wishing it, no more than that, merely *thinking about* it – wasn't the last straw. The last straw was not allowing him, the author of his doom, his own version of events. '*But turning on the tap, Manny . . .*' What right did I have to insist on the appropriate language to describe a murder, or to demand a proper acknowledgement of guilt, I who sought to contain the world in the panel box of a cartoon and burst into tears the minute a woman in high heels came running at me with a knife?

But even that did not mark the extent to which my waste-disposal jaws had opened. Did he know that I had decided nothing was beyond him? That I piled abomination upon abomination on him until, in my mind, not even a child was safe in his company?

Did he know I'd been watching him at the British Museum? Did the tie imply a commentary on that offence as well? It was possible. But even if Manny hadn't caught me spying on him, Ammut had.

And now, part crocodile, part lion, part hippopotamus, he was waiting to devour me.

5

I didn't answer my phone for the next three weeks. I cancelled all social engagements. In another time and in another place I would have wandered into the wilderness. For my heart was withered like the grass.

449

You can, all on your ownio, even without the help of a Chloë or a Zoë, come to dislike your own mind. 'Whoso privily slandereth his neighbour, him I will cut off.' Sometimes, when you've steeped your neighbour in slander as high as the offended heavens, you need to cut yourself off.

I took long walks, kicking stones and shaking my head where no one could see me. Had I encountered anyone I knew I would have hidden or pretended to be someone else. *Max Glickman? You've got the wrong person. Never heard of Max Glickman.*

Every three or four days I played back my telephone messages, just in case. A number were from Francine Bryson-Smith, growing bothered that she couldn't raise me. I detected a note of false concern, as though she expected me to believe that she feared Manny might have gassed me. 'Everything all right, there? If you're in, will you pick up? Mmmm. OK.'

It interested me to note that her beauty was no longer audible to me. Was that because she wasn't speaking live? Did her beauty need an interlocutor in the same way as all beauty is said to need a beholder? I liked the idea that the beauty I normally heard when she spoke directly to me on the phone was an effect we cooked up together, a conspiracy of two. Did that mean I could make her vanish altogether in the end, just by never picking up? I'm not saying I wanted her to be gone. But it was her fault that I had ashes in my mouth, and that I did not want to see my own face in the mirror; had she not come to me out of the blue to put some flesh on her little project, I could have left Manny where I'd safely stowed him all those years before, not to be thought about, expunged, not to be Jewed up all over again in my unpleasant mind. So let her stew. She could wait till I was good and ready.

Ready, anyway.

Then, sandwiched between her messages, came one from Errol Tobias. He, on the other hand, lost nothing of his characteristic loathsomeness when he left a message. You'd have thought it would be the other way round. If the devil has no shadow or reflection, you'd expect him not to be there on an answering machine either. But he came over undiminished. So maybe it was Francine Bryson-Smith who was the devil. Which, as it happens, was exactly what Errol was ringing me to say.

Errol's message began with a couple of new entries to his *Who Is Jewishly Who*. Did I know that the porn star Traci Lords was actually born Nora Louise Kuzman, and the porn performance artist Annie Sprinkle was Ellen Sternberg? Neither piece of information moved me much. Annie Sprinkle I knew of, and since she looked and behaved Jewish it was no surprise she *was* Jewish. Nor did the false name Sprinkle constitute a Gentilisation proper. It was a joke obscenity, even sounded vaguely like a Jewish joke obscenity, and so didn't count as apostasy. Traci Lords, I was prepared to grant, was different, but as I didn't know who Traci Lords was I couldn't manufacture any anger towards her.

When I rang him back to express these views to him, he trumped me with the phallic prince of 1980s and 1990s porno, Ron Jeremy. Jewish. Born Hyatt. What did I make of that?

'Errol, any fool can see he's Jewish. And what is more, Jeremy as a surname sounds far more Jewish to me than Hyatt does. It even begins with the first two letters of Jew. Sorry, but I don't think we can charge him with anything. Except filth, that is.'

'Whatever you say. You're the filth artist. Which is presumably why you have a soft spot for this Francine bint.'

'*Francine bint*? If you're talking about Francine Bryson-Smith, I don't have a soft spot for her. But how come you know her, anyway?'

'As always, we have a friend in common, Max.'

'Errol, Francine's not my friend.'

'I don't mean her. I mean Kennard Chitty.'

'The nose man?'

'As opposed to . . . ? How many Kennard Chittys are there?'

'Well, I know just the one. But how do you know him?'

'I could ask you the same thing, Max.'

'I haemorrhage from the nostril, Errol. Chitty was my first stop before the otolaryngologist. What's your excuse? You don't need a nose job. You've barely got a nose.'

'It isn't strictly me that has the connection. It's Melanie. She went to see him, just between ourselves, to get her breasts done.'

'Melanie went to Kennard Chitty to get her breasts done! Errol, forgive me, but you can't have bigger breasts than Melanie's.'

'To have them made smaller, shmuck. But that's confidential. You aren't to say anything when you see her—'

'Like where have your tits gone, Melanie—'

'I knew I could count on you.'

'Won't you be desolate?'

'She didn't go through with it. He dissuaded her.'

'He dissuaded me too. And I don't mean from having my breasts reduced. But this is unusual behaviour, wouldn't you say, from a plastic surgeon.'

'His heart's not in it. His heart's in Jesus.'

'I know that. That's why he wouldn't touch my nose. He won't cut into Jews because that would be like cutting into the body of Jesus. Do you think that's why he dissuaded Melanie?'

'Well, if he can see any trace of Jesus in Melanie, good luck to him. But, yes, he gives her a lot of literature. She burns it all when she gets home, but I think she secretly fancies him. No one's offered her the missionary position for years.'

'And you put up with him trying to make a Christian of your wife?'

'Listen, it gets her out of the house. And anyway, you know my motto. Know your enemy. Which is why I'm ringing you. This Francine Bryson-Shmyson whatever the fuck she calls herself. Be careful. No, don't be careful, be gone.'

'Are you telling me she's in cahoots with Kennard Chitty? I have to tell you she hasn't tried to missionarise me yet.'

'Wait a minute, wait a minute. We were at Chitty's last week, having dinner. He buys his wine from me, not that that's relevant. This Francine bird was there. Sexy woman. I can see why you might be interested—'

'Errol—'

'Let me finish. There were a couple of your cartoons on the wall. One Jew saying this or that to another Jew. Signed. Not that they needed to be signed for me to recognise the hand of a master.'

'If you've rung me to discuss my work, Errol—'

'I haven't. You know what I think – half of what you do I love, the other half wouldn't be out of place in Hitler's bedroom. But never mind that. "This is a coincidence," I said, "Maxie Glickman's my best friend. We grew up in the same street. We went to the same school." "You think that's a coincidence?" Francine says. "He's doing work for me this minute." "A cartoon?" "A script." "Maxie writes scripts?" "Well, a treatment anyway." "Subject?" "Confidential at this stage. But it's based on the story of someone Max knew who murdered his parents. You might even remember the case yourself." "Jewish?" "As it happens, yes." As it happens, fuck you, lady. Max, of course I remember that meshuggeneh friend of yours, and what you want to do with him is your affair. What do I care? He got what he deserved. For all I know his poor parents, alevasholam, got what they deserved. But why with this woman? Couldn't you smell it on her? I knew as soon as I saw her. Maybe her name rang a bell. Maybe I'd even seen her picture. And I'm prepared to concede that I was suspicious of the theology of anyone I might find at Kennard Chitty's table even before we got there. But I swear I sniffed it in the room the minute we entered. They say they smell it on us – you know James Joyce's joke: "the fetor judaicus is most perceptible". I say the fetor anti-judaicus is just as perceptible on them. Max, she reeks of it.'

'If you're telling me she's an anti-Semite you're not telling me anything new. Of course she's an anti-Semite. They're all anti-Semites. They can't help it. They drink it in with their mothers' milk. And compared to some of the anti-Semites I've been married to—'

'Max, I'm not talking your ordinary friendly neighbourhood anti-Semite. This one's a Nazi. She's the real thing, Max. She's one of them. I've dug up more stuff on her than you've got years left to read. Do you know what her other current project is, beside you?'

'I seem to recall her mentioning Vanunu.'

'Well, that should have told you something in itself. Who else would want to do Vanunu? But this is better. You know that our civilised allies the Egyptians serialised *The Protocols of the Elders of Zion* for television recently . . . Well, your new friend has been trying to buy the rights to distribute it selectively here and in America. For the public good, needless to say.'

'It's an argument. Someone needs to show us what the Arab world thinks a Jew is.'

'Don't be naive, Max. We know what the Arab world thinks a Jew is. They think a Jew is whatever the Nazi bastards tell them he is. They're just a bit slow catching up with the literature. What I'm saying to you is that you have to look at what she's up to altogether. Put *The Protocols* libel with Vanunu. Put the two of them with what she's getting you to do – the story of a frum Yiddisher boy with his tzitzis hanging out who kills his family. That sound like a portfolio of even-handedness to you? She's a conspiracist, Max, and doesn't even try to hide it. Did you ever take a look at what she's made? A nice nasty little earner about Jews controlling Hollywood, but not so nasty that only the crazies would watch. A docudrama about the Rosenbergs, ditto. A so-called science programme about the Jews who made the bomb. And a film, still to be released, detailing the greater cruelty shown to Jewish prisoners by Jewish Kapos than by the SS. Put them together and what have you got? – Bibbitty Bobbitty Boo. Plus she's a paid-up revisionist, and if she doesn't admit to being a straight-down-the-line Holocaust-denier she spends a hell of a lot of her time fucking with people who do. Remember Zundel? Distributor of *Did Six Million Really Die?*. She visited him in prison in Toronto. I've got a snap of her standing outside the gates holding roses. White fucking roses, Max. I'll email it to you. And I'll email you another one of her shmoozing with Klan members at a hate rally in Mississippi. I'm not joking. And you want to see the way they're looking at her. Even under their fucking hoods you can see they're smitten. Now I'm joking. But in fact I'm not joking.'

'I believe you're not joking,' I said. 'But if what you say is true, how does she think she can get away with it? She's not exactly an invisible person.'

'Who's checking? As long as she isn't found on her knees in a Jewish cemetery with a can of spray paint in her hand, no one cares. So she shmoozes with racists? Big deal. That's not exactly going to make her stand out in this country. The Mitford sisters canoodled with Der Führer in public view, and we still have a soft spot for them. The English like a girl to show a bit of spirit. Had Hitler cut a deal with us, Unity might have been our first lady.'

'She's a programme-maker, Errol. They might like a girl to show a bit of spirit, but that doesn't mean they're going to transmit a hate programme.'

'Don't be a shmuck all your life. She won't be making hate programmes. Would she have come to you for a hate programme? She'll just whittle away, Max. A dig here, a wound there. Undermine, undermine. And the more often she can find a willing Jew like you to do it for her – Jew eat Jew – the cleaner her hands will look. She's lethal, Max. She's lethal because she's white, because she's English, because she's educated, because she's plausible, because she's not frightened, because she fits in, because she's beautiful, because she's got a middle-class voice, because she's got nice tits, and because she's a woman. That's enough to fool a lot of people into believing they're talking to a reasonable, warm-hearted educated human being who wouldn't hurt a fly. Especially the woman bit. It fooled you.'

Did it? Or had I nosed her out as well? Had I nosed her out and not minded? Or even nosed her out and liked it, whatever I smelt?

A queer, weightless sensation of surpriselessness floated through me like lethargy. At the last there are no revelations. Everything has been there at the beginning, always will be there at the beginning, everything you will ever need to know, waiting in the baby fist of time. You prise the fingers open or you don't. Good for Errol. He'd rip the hand off if he had to. I – I was a gentler soul.

'I'm listening,' I said.

'You want more? I've finished. That's it. You can have all I've got on her. I'm not making a word of it up. If you want my advice I'd shtupp her and then get the hell out.'

'We always did things differently, you and me, Errol.'

'What does that mean? You're going to go on working with her?'

'No. But I won't be shtupping her either.'

'Pity,' Errol said. 'I'd hoped you might bring her round to watch a video.'

6

I rang the next day and asked to take her out for lunch. You don't hang about when you know the Nazis are after you. For old times' sake I suggested the rabbit-hutch restaurant in Soho, halfway down the passage a dog wouldn't piss in.

'It's not happening,' I told her.

Hardly a surprise to her. I too had been waiting in the baby fist of time. Not someone she had ever trusted much in the first place, I hadn't contacted her for weeks, hadn't answered her calls, and finally, in a dead voice, had invited her out.

My treat, Francine.

Of course it wasn't happening.

She inclined her head at a folder of papers I'd brought with me. 'Treatment?' she asked. Good joke. You know when someone has got a stash of evidence against you on the table. But she was daring me to deliver. She was brazen, I had to give her that. She looked utterly unworried by anything I meant to say to her or show her.

'People are allowed to hate Jews,' I said.

She fixed me with her green, fascinator's glimmer. Funny, how it helped some women to have bad eyesight.

'Who hates Jews? I don't hate Jews.'

'Some of your best friends . . .'

'Well, you said it.'

'Francine,' I said, 'why did you take my photograph?'

'I am not aware that I ever did take your photograph.'

'In this restaurant. You got a waiter to take a photograph of us together.'

'Ah, that's different. I like to have photographs of people I work with. I'm sentimental like that. Why do you find it sinister?'

It was a hard question to answer. The reason I found it sinister was that I believed that somewhere there was a photographic archive of Francine with Jews, which would one day be brought out and adduced as evidence of how much she liked them. And they her. But I couldn't quite say that without sounding like a megalomaniac.

I tapped the file. 'Photographs can be very damning,' I said.

'They can also be faked.'

'Why would anyone want to fake your photograph?'

'Why would anyone want to do anything? Why would anyone want to do something sinister with the photograph the waiter took of us?'

I tried meeting her gaze. Then asked her, 'Why are you so interested in Jews?'

'I'm not.'

'What was it you wanted me to get from Manny? How did it feel? How did it feel to be a Jew, of all people, turning on the gas taps? Did your fingers tremble? What was it like for a Jew who is enjoined above all things to honour his father and his mother to murder them in their beds? Were you glad? Was it a relief to you? Did you hate them as you did it? I want to ask the same of you, Francine. Does it give you an unholy thrill to imagine the Jew not the victim, but the author of atrocities? Is it the same as accusing Israelis of being Nazis – are you exacting a sort of retrospective justice?'

'You're raving, Max. There are no thrills in this for me, holy or unholy. And honouring his father and his mother isn't what a Jew is enjoined to do above all things. Above all things a Jew is enjoined to have no other God. Not to bow down himself unto them, nor to serve them. Genesis 20.'

'For I, the Lord thy God, am a jealous God. Why are you so interested in Jews, Francine? Are you jealous of our jealous God?'

'Why would I be?'

'Why wouldn't you be? Perhaps you feel excluded from His love.'

'Aren't I meant to be excluded from His love?'

'As a Gentile?'

'As a goy.'

'Ah, it's the goy thing.'

'Ye shall destoy their altars, and break down their images, and cut down their groves – For thou art an holy people unto the Lord. Deuteronomy 7. How do *you* deal with that, Max?'

'As something in a book, Francine. As a founding myth. All religions have them.'

'And he shall deliver their kings into thine hand, and thou shalt destroy their name from under heaven . . . Yes, it's a goy thing.'

She smiled at me, loosing her silvery aura about me like a net. We were in a small restaurant. Had they chosen to, every diner at every table could have been privy to our conversation. It was a necessary gift, given the places she liked to eat, her ability to throw a bubble of confidentiality around herself and the company she kept. Infinitely soothing I had found it in the past, when I was in the mood for it. As though a goddess had stretched down her hand and scooped you away in it to another realm, into another layer of reality even.

This time, though, I didn't want to be anywhere else. I smiled back, without the aura. 'Get a life, Francine,' I said. 'Get another life. Go somewhere where there aren't any Jews. Give yourself a break from us. It isn't healthy to be doing what you're doing. You wallow in us. You seem not to be able to know or get enough of us or our religion. You have more knowledge of us than we have about ourselves. Which of course means that who you know is not in fact who we are. But that aside, how do you explain this infatuation? It resembles the behaviour of a rejected lover, now showing us how little we matter to you, now unable to do anything but dog our footsteps. How did we let you down? What did we promise you that we didn't deliver? Did we unrequite you? Whence the hurt, Francine?'

I was banging my chest for emphasis. Did we hurt you here? *Here?* An action which Francine took to be too demonstrative in this crowded space. 'I would ask you to keep your voice down,' she said. 'This is a favourite restaurant of mine.'

'And mine,' I reminded her.

'And I would ask you not to menace me.'

'Francine, I have not menaced you.'

But I was not able to say that with the force it required without throwing open my arms – another action too demonstrative for this crowded place. Unable to confine our conversation within her silvery net, she was beginning to look around her in alarm.

All at once I realised I didn't want to go on with this. It had been uncouth of me, in breach of the laws governing social intercourse. Your heart did not have an entitlement to speak through your mouth on all occasions. The comedian Tommy Cooper was right in his assessment of what you say when you find yourself sharing a train compartment with Adolf Hitler. *Sssss!* Anything further wants decorum. And Francine Bryson-Smith wasn't Hitler, whether or not she would have taken roses to him in his bunker.

Sssss! Anything more you must deny yourself. That used to be where God came in. Anything more He would take care of for you.

Sssss!

'It's not happening,' I repeated, rising from my seat, remembering to leave sufficient money on the table to clear the bill.

7

Through his lowered head he sees her. The lozenge pattern on her dress, like involuted diamonds, similar to one his mother used to wear, for casual but smart, a shopping, striding dress. He remembers the sound it made when she increased her pace, a soft sucking, like a kiss in reverse, lips coming away from the skin.

TTSSSSSSSSKKK!

He stands behind her in the queue for the ticket machine, then follows her down the escalator. Her hair is grey now. His too, what there is of it. But he is more distressed by hers. Grey hair on a woman measures loss more poignantly than on a man. But on this woman it also measures injustice. She should have died aforetime, when her hair was gold. That she has grey hair means she has got away with it.

BOOO!

He doesn't like the Underground. It upsets him to be dependent on artificial lighting. If the lights fuse it will be as black as unfathomed space down here. And then the rats will come out. The idea of tunnelling upsets him too. In a way he can't explain, it feels contrary to God's will. God made the earth and now man in his ingratitude tunnels underneath it. Underearth is where the dead only belong.

It is always either too busy or too quiet. Tonight it is too quiet. There are only the two of them on the escalator, he nine or ten steps behind her, looking down into the greyness of her hair, imagining that she is descending into hell.

It is hot enough for hell. This is the other reason he never travels on the Underground if he can help it. The stuffiness and the heat. The smell of fuel and smoky rubber in the stations, and on the trains the smell of flesh going quickly off.

She doesn't like it either. He can tell she doesn't like it. She holds herself as though every outside sensation assails and hurts her. Good. He will gladly suffer any inconvenience or perturbation, any anxiety or alarm, in the knowledge that she is suffering them as well. He always wanted there to be a certain harmony of pain between them, and now they have it. She doesn't know they have it, but he does, and that's all that counts. She wouldn't recognise it anyway. She is too stupid to understand the concept. The disappointment to him she always was. Except that debasement is never more refined than when the human cause of it is stupid. Any man can be the slave of a countess. It takes a sort of genius to understand why it's better to be answerable to a scullery maid, skivvy, servant girl, bedmaker, fire-yekelte, dogsbody, *femme de chambre* . . .

SLAVER! DROOL!

Not that there will be any more of that. He is long past that. She too, what she ever understood of it.

There is no one on the platform. Just the two of them. A fat rat crosses the rails.

He sits, she doesn't. She paces. Good. Pacing is good. People who pace have active minds. 'Mind' is too flattering a word for what she has, but however you describe the space between her ears, it is evidently busy with something. Torment, he hopes. Demons, he hopes. Or if none of those, at least that existential nausea to which even the wicked and the stupid are susceptible. Mental disgust with one's fleshly condition. Unless she is of another species altogether – and some would say she is – she will wake every morning wishing that she hadn't. The revulsion that comes with waking – this is what he wishes on her. The horror of being alive. Or *Weltschmerz* as she will know it, only *Weltschmerz* is a touch self-pleasing for what he has in store for her. Too Sorrows of Young Werther-ish. The monsters brought forth by Goya's *Sleep of Reason* are more like it. A sky blackened with birds with human faces, batwinged and jeering.

YIPES!

The train pulls into the station.

JEW JEW! JEW JEW!

Only it isn't that sort of train. Except that every train is that sort of train. Which might be why she comes down here.

She gets into the train. He gets into the train.

She stares out of the window. Where is she? Is she remembering? Is she back *there*?

The train pulls out of the station. He gets up to open a window. Nobody in the compartment but the two of them, and a drunk asleep. ZZZZZZZ! The sound of shikkered shaygets sleeping.

When he returns to his seat she sees him. 'You!' she says.

CHOKE!

He could expose himself to her. He has thought of that a thousand times. Look. Remember? Remember me?

AARGH!

But what would he achieve by exposing himself to her? And what if he exposed himself erect? How would that serve his cause? Still weird after all these years, is that what he wishes her to see? Still fucked in the head?

She clasps her hands together.

GULP!

Should he ask why she hates Jews? Or will she tell him he's raving. *I don't hate Jews. You're raving.*

So what should he say to her? *SSSSS! You are a very bad person. SSSSS!*

The train SCREECHES! to a halt. The doors SSSSSLIDE! open. This is her chance. Run for it.

RUN! as you ran the last time. RUN! as you ran from those who allowed you to run because they didn't know what else to do with you. RUN! from yourself.

She is in front of him again, RUNNING! The lozenge-pattern dress is tight across her back. It is a young mother's dress, not an old lady's. She looks ludicrous in a dress that clings, and then makes a soft sucking sound when it comes away from her thighs. Something more becoming would be more becoming. And a stick. If she had a stick he could attack her with it. An eye for an eye, a stick for a stick.

THWAAAACK!

The platform is deserted. Not even a rat wants to be down here.

'HAVE PITY!' she cries as he pursues her. 'PLEASE!'

You dream that they will beg you to HAVE PITY! You promise that if you ever again meet them and they beg you to HAVE PITY! you will devote the rest of your days to the service of Elohim. Not a lot to ask. Just sit them next to me in a JEW JEW! train, have them beg me to show PITY! and I am yours, O Lord.

He is gaining on her, which isn't difficult, given her age, given her dress, given her fear, when she loses her footing. It is all in slow motion, all happening in high, narrow incontrovertible frames, the wicked falling from the height of their wrongdoing, the good almost static in their icy vengefulness, never to be satisfied, inconsolable.

She falls, frame by frame she goes over, just as another train is coming into the station.

JEW JEW! JEW JEW!

He stands stiller than justice, and watches. The train, the woman, the train, the woman, the train   SPLAAAAT! the train.

And then the faces in the window, each as blank and pitiless as his own.

Thank you, Elohim. Have pity? NO!

'What happened?' people gather from nowhere to ask. 'Ever see her before?'

'No,' he answers, averting a head which is blackened, however the shadows fall on him. 'No, she . . .'

Then as to no one, his back turned, impassive, sepulchral, denied, as the impenetrable dark swallows him – it's the number of shades of darkness he has found that you admire the cartoonist for, that and the elegant chasteness of the overall design – 'She was a perfect stranger.'

SIXTEEN

A painting is finished when the artist says it is finished.

Rembrandt

Yisgadal veyiskadash . . .

For my mother this time. They all leave you. One by one, they all depart. *Yisgadal veyiskadash shemey rabo, Be'olmo di'vero chir'usey.* May His great Name grow exalted and sanctified in the world He created as He willed. Amen.

I had not been expecting it. She had been growing forgetful, but she had lost little of her slender youthfulness, even her ankles still worth stealing a glance at had any of her old admirers been alive. And I had thought that kalooki, if nothing else, would keep her immortal. You live to a riper age, they say, if you stay mentally agile. The more you perplex your mind, the longer it works for you. Kalooki wasn't quantum mechanics but it did engage her in calculations that needed a bit of knotting out. Not just computing what you could do with the cards you held yourself, but what everyone else could be expected to do with theirs. Likelihood theory. What must Ilsa Cohen have in her hand for her to have discarded the jack of spades. How would Gittel Franks respond, knowing Gittel Franks, if you held on to your cards for one round more. The trouble was that Ilsa Cohen, though nominally alive in defiance of her own rogue hand's attempts to do away with her, had lost her mind and was languishing in an old persons' home where at least, Shani told me, the staff continued to paint her fingernails with hearts and diamonds, spades and clubs. And Gittel Franks had collapsed and died while being Shirley Bassey at a karaoke night thrown to celebrate her great-granddaughter's sixteenth birthday. Not all at once, though the shock of realisation was sudden enough, my mother woke up to the fact that they were leaving her. And you can't play kalooki on your own.

They stopped coming and that was the end of it. She barely had what you could call an illness. Her heart failed. It was as simple as that.

Shani rang me and I flew back up. You can't hang around when it comes to Jewish burial. Blink and they've put your mother in the ground. Habdalah. Keep the quick from the dead.

Shani and I hugged for a long time. We weren't hugging siblings but we were on our own now. We said the usual things, that it was good she hadn't suffered, that she went as she would have chosen to go, that she had loved Dad and stayed faithful to him, and how touching it was that she had viewed that – though she could easily have had another nibble, another bite even, at romance – as the one and only important relationship of her life. I began to say I wished her time had not been given over so exclusively to a simple card game; that it was a pity she never went to the theatre or the opera, a tragedy that she didn't read, that she didn't listen to good music, that she didn't welcome abstract thought, that she hadn't, as a Jew, availed herself of Jewish seriousness – but Shani reminded me that that could just as easily have been her life I was describing. 'It's not a sin to be a philistine,' she told me. And I didn't tell her that for a Jew I thought it was.

Mick Kalooki tried hard, for Shani's sake, not to go to pieces. But it wasn't easy. Only in the nick of time was Shani able to stop him ordering a wreath for the coffin in the shape of a deck of cards. He couldn't understand why not. Why shouldn't Leonora be buried surrounded not only by those she loved but in the company, so to speak, of *what* she loved? It was tough, without hurting his feelings as an honorary Jew, trying to explain to him that Jews didn't as a general rule do flowers in a big way at funerals, and never at all on the coffin itself. Flowers at funerals were common and showy. The word MOM made of pink roses was unthinkable to a Jew. POP done with red geraniums the same. Simplicity was the thing. An austere simplicity before the great democracy of death. Start having flowers on your coffins and soon the rich man will be buried in greater pomp than the pauper.

'It's a very beautiful religion,' Mick said. He was unable to keep the tears back.

He loved my mother. But I also knew it upset him to realise there were elements of Judaism he was never going to master. All those hours put into k'nish and kreplach, and still flowers for the dead could floor him.

I lost all control of myself at the cemetery. When it came to the shovelling of soil on to my mother's coffin – a mitzvah for a Jew, a sacred duty of love – I staggered back from the grave and let the shovel fall from my hand. I couldn't throw dirt on her. I couldn't accept her returned to dust. If it had to be, it had to be, but I didn't have to be party to it. Shani took me by the hand, like a mother with her child, and helped me. We held the shovel together, but I was unable to look. Just hearing it was bad enough. Gravel on wood. The end of us.

As I was leaving the cemetery I saw Manny. He was wearing a long black coat and a yarmulke. Had he not been standing at a distance from most of the other mourners, as though he believed he had no real right to be there, he could have been mistaken for the officiating rabbi. A little old rabbi flown in from Novoropissik to do the business as they used to do it in the old country. I went over to him and held out my hand. He wished me 'long life'. I inclined my head. I hoped he was not going to say he envied me not having a mother.

'I'm sorry,' was what did he say. 'I remember your mother. She was a very nice person. My parents always spoke highly of her.'

For the second time that afternoon I wondered if I was going to faint. 'It's nice of you to have come,' I said.

I was surprised to see he was not on his own. A woman who had been standing even more removed from the proceedings

467

than he was, brought herself forward, also to wish me 'long life'. She was not anyone I knew. A woman a little older than me, I estimated, a touch heavy in the torso, with a strong square face and a fiercely vulnerable expression. Pretty still, or maybe pretty, as sometimes happens, only since she'd aged. Some issue of age, over and above the usual ones of regret and apprehension, hung over her. The prettiness spoke of it, the unnaturally piercing blue eyes spoke of it, and the long hair, worn down her back like a girl's, proclaimed it – notwithstanding everything else I had to sorrow over – to a degree I found painful. From the way she positioned herself by Manny I surmised that she was in some caring or even custodial relation to him. Could Manny have been rearrested and reincarcerated? I wondered. Had they let him out, just for the afternoon, on humanitarian grounds, and could this woman have been his nurse or his prison guard? Were they even, for the duration of my mother's funeral, manacled together?

I thanked them both for their attendance and was about to walk away to join Shani and Mick when Manny suddenly said, 'Max, this is Dorothy.'

There are no revelations. Everything you learn, you know already.

I insisted they return with me to the shiva house. I wanted to give them something. Wine sweeter than sweet sherry, and kichels. 'Be careful, you can break your teeth on those,' I told Dorothy. But of course she knew that already.

I stuck Mick Kalooki on to Manny. If there were things about the faith Mick had not got to the bottom of yet, Manny was the one to ask. A crying shame they hadn't been introduced to each other earlier. Dorothy I engineered into a corner, by the cello-shaped cabinet where my father's boxing gloves were still on display, and where my mother kept the glasses and the doilies for kalooki, sitting us both down on those low stools which mourners

468

are meant to occupy for the duration of the shiva. And there I got her to tell me everything I knew.

The house, of course, to which Manny had once invited me and where we'd pitted Rothko against cartoons, the house I'd imagined was a charitable home for Jewish men who'd killed their parents, was of course – of course of course – Dorothy's. I'd fancied it was near to where she had walked Asher to meet her father in the days of their innocence before all their worlds fell in, but I'd got that slightly wrong. It wasn't near her old home. It *was* her old home. And Manny lived there. Not as a lodger, she wanted me to understand, though she wasn't always able to get Manny himself to understand that. But she hoped that I did. Not as a lodger. It was his home too. Had been his home from the day he was released. She had gone personally to collect him. As how could she not? Who else was going to do it?

The question on a day of tears made me want to cry again. Who else? Well, why not Asher?

She looked at me I wasn't sure whether with astonishment at what I didn't appear to know, for someone who appeared to know everything, or to be certain that I was strong enough to hear speak of it now. I made similar enquiries with my eyes of her. *Me?* her expression said. *I'm strong enough for everything.* And I didn't allow my eyes to say in return *Is that why you let your hair grow down your back like a girl's?*

I wasn't strong enough and never will be. I bleed easily. Epistaxis of the imagination. The membranes of the brain dry quickly, then are quick to rupture. Many cartoonists suffer from the same condition. But I was obliged to learn a lesson from my father. You stay on your feet no matter how much blood you lose.

Asher.

The Jew I envied above all others. Marked black like Cain, the way I'd have liked to look. Seeded like a pomegranate with the sorrows and the tribulations of his people, but juicy with the wine

469

of the pomegranate, too, spicy with spikenard and saffron, calamus and cinnamon, his lips like a thread of scarlet.

But he was seeded with a sorrow too many. When the police roused him from his bed (Dorothy beside him) to tell him that his parents had been murdered, he bent double as though a horse had kicked him in the stomach, and bawled blood. His doing. He was marked black like Cain. It was his doing. Yes, his brother had lost his reason, but what had *made* his brother lose his reason?

And the Lord said, What hast thou done? the voice of thy brother's blood crieth unto me from the ground. And now thou art cursed from the earth . . .

Cursed from the earth, Asher knew at once that he would never be able to resume relations with the woman he loved and had wanted, for as long as he could remember, for his wife. Whenever he looked into her face, he would see them. As for his brother, Asher could not even begin to describe the abhorrence he felt. He was bereft of everything, and at his brother's hands. Was that what Manny had wanted – to put an end to everybody's happiness if he could have no happiness of his own? He could not have been so deranged, could he, as to suppose that with his parents dead, Asher would settle down to a carefree life with Dorothy? No one could be so deluded. So it had been an attack on all of them. Manny had gassed them all – his mother and his father, and Asher, and Dorothy, and himself.

Dorothy, after many years to think about it, did not agree with Asher. Yes, she believed, Manny *had* been deluded. She believed he had done it, partly, for her. Out of deluded love for her. Not selfish love. The very opposite of selfish love. And you can't get much more deluded than that. Even at the time, she wanted to tell Asher that. Forgive your poor brother. He did not comprehend what he was doing. He doesn't think as other people think. But Asher had gone again. Gone once, and now gone a second time. Gone not to come back. And she was not able to tell him anything.

'For which abandonment of you, after all he had done to promote your happiness, Manny fantasised about shooting him?'

She was surprised I knew that. 'To this day Manny believes he did in fact shoot his brother, yes,' she said. She had begun to rock a little on her chair. 'So he told you that?'

'Not in so many words. But I wonder why he doesn't also believe he shot you.'

'Because I'm here. Because he can see me. Because I'm not dead.'

Ah.

So we had got to it at last. What I needed to be told but had always known. That Asher was out of it. Lying under a shovelful of dirt, just like my mother.

It seems that he went back to Israel. 'Seems', because Dorothy too had had to piece it all together. Did not stay for the inquest into his parents' death or for their funeral, never looked upon his brother, never spent another hour with Dorothy, never spoke to her or otherwise informed her where he'd gone, never even packed a bag. And in Israel, not many years into Manny's sentence, they shot him. He had thrown in his lot with the fanatics, stood guard at the iron gates of a settlement in Ramallah, with his rifle in one hand and his Bible in another, claiming back what Elohim had promised to his people, where they shot him.

'They being terrorists?'

She hesitated. Was I meant, I wondered, to have said 'freedom fighters', as Alÿs would have demanded? But that wasn't the reason for the hesitation.

'They being, according to Manny,' she said, 'the agents of Manny's will. Which if you take the long view, they were. But terrorists, yes.'

'So that was Manny's gun?'

She didn't quite understand what I meant. But yes, 'Yes, he believed and still believes he pulled the trigger.'

Couldn't quite own to turning on the tap, which he had done,

471

but wanted to have pulled the trigger, which he hadn't. Explain that.

'And you never heard from him?'

'From Asher, no.'

'No communication of any sort?'

'No.'

'Not a single, solitary line?'

'No.'

'We are an implacable people.'

She thought about that, pushing away a stray strand of grey hair from her eye. 'Well, you've been an experience,' she said.

'Have you married again?'

She shook her head. Then she laughed, not as girlishly as she might have. 'Unless you call being with Manny a marriage.'

I smiled back. I knew something about that.

I looked across the room to where he was still being held in conversation by Mick Kalooki. He was fluttering his hands, his lizard tongue licking at something or nothing in the air before him, his head still the shape of a small boy's, his eyes dead. No, I could not call being with Manny a marriage. But then I had funny ideas about what constituted a marriage.

'I am surprised,' I said, 'that you don't curse us all for ruining your life.'

'*My* life?' She seemed astonished I should suggest such a thing. 'My life's just a life. It's your lives that are ruined.'